Dark Summer

Jon Cleary, an Australian whose books are read throughout the world, is the author of many novels including such famous bestsellers as *The Sundowners* and *The High Commissioner*.

Born in 1917, Jon Cleary left school at fifteen to become a commercial artist and film cartoonist – even a laundryman and a bushworker. Then his first novel won second prize in Australia's biggest literary contest and launched him on his successful career.

Seven of his books have been filmed, and his novel *Peter's Pence* was awarded the American Edgar Allan Poe Prize as the best crime novel of 1974.

Jon Cleary's most recent novels have been *The Phoenix Tree*, *The City of Fading Light*, *Dragons at the Party*, *Now and Then*, *Amen*, *Murder Song*, *Pride's Harvest* and *Bleak Spring*. He lives in Sydney and travels the world researching his novels with his wife Joy.

'Mr Cleary is a most expert novelist. His scenes slide noiselessly into gear'   *Times Literary Supplement*

'The man has a noble gift for storytelling and a nice dry humor'   *New York Times*

'Jon Cleary's books all bear the stamp of craftsmanship and quality'   *Sunday Telegraph*

JON CLEARY

DARK SUMMER

HarperCollins*Publishers*

HarperCollins*Publishers*
77–85 Fulham Palace Road,
Hammersmith, London W6 8JB

Special overseas edition 1993
This paperback edition 1993
1 3 5 7 9 8 6 4 2

First published in Great Britain by
HarperCollins*Publishers* 1992

ISBN 0 00 647202 8

Set in Linotron Times

Printed in Great Britain by
HarperCollinsManufacturing Glasgow

for
Shaun Roach
for his considerable help

CHAPTER ONE

I

'Daddy, there's a dead man floating in our pool.'

Malone came awake, dimly conscious of his relief that what he had heard had been only a part of a dream. He had stayed up late, looking, almost against his will, at the latest newsreels on the Gulf war; the images had gone to bed with him, the camera eye in the dream becoming his own eye. Now he felt the hand still on his shoulder, the grip tight, and he opened his eyes to see Maureen standing by the bed in her swimsuit.

'What?' He sat up, feeling Lisa stir beside him.

'There's a dead man in our pool.'

His first thought was for the effect on his middle child: he looked at her for the marks of shock or fear. She was ten years old, a tomboy usually bursting with energy and curiosity; the one of his three children who, he had thought, would never be vulnerable to what life threw at her. But he had been looking at the future: not at now, a hot January Monday morning when she was only ten years old and had got up for nothing more threatening than an early morning swim.

'You all right?' She nodded; and he turned to Lisa, now wide awake. 'Keep her here, darl. Stay with Mum.'

Lisa said, voice still thick with sleep, 'I hope this isn't some stupid joke –'

He shook his head warningly, pushed Maureen into the bed as he got out of it. He could feel the trembling in the thin body and he felt a sudden spasm of anger. Any

7

intrusion that cracked the peace of the life he had built for Lisa and the kids always angered him.

In his pyjama trousers and bare feet he went out to the back of the house, opened the screen door and stepped out into the back garden. It was not a large area, maybe eighty feet by fifty, and a good part of it was taken up by the swimming pool and its fence-enclosed surrounds. He went through the spring-loaded gate, feeling the bricks beneath his feet still warm from yesterday's scorcher, and stood on the side of the pool and looked down at the small, fully clothed man floating face-up in the blue-tinted water. It was Scungy Grime.

Malone picked up the long pole with its skim-net, hooked the net over Grime's head and pulled the body in to the side of the pool. There was no doubt that the little man was dead, but, routinely, he knelt down and felt for a pulse in Grime's neck.

'Hi, Scobie. Going to be another scorcher, looks like – What's that?'

Keith Cayburn was the Malones' next-door neighbour. His house was two-storeyed and from the rear balcony, where he now stood in his pyjamas, he could look down on the Malones' garden.

'A dead man. Keep Gloria inside the house till I get him out of sight.'

'Sure. Holy shit! Can I do anything to help?'

'Maybe later, Keith.' Though how he could help, Malone had no idea. Dead small-time criminals in swimming pools were not common in Randwick, not objects for community action by Neighbourhood Watch.

He left the body in the water for the Physical Evidence team and hoped that Gloria Cayburn, an hysterical type, would not come out on the balcony, despite her husband's pleas, and throw a fit. As he went back into the house to call the police (*call the police? Dammit, I am the police!* But that was the way the system worked), Scungy Grime, in death as in life an incorrigible, drifted away towards the

8

middle of the pool again, the skim-net still over his head like a fly-net, the long pole now caught in the crook of his limp arm.

Malone picked up the phone in the kitchen and rang Randwick police station. He spoke to a young constable, who said 'Holy shit!' and that he would get the local detectives round there right away. Malone hung up, rang Police Centre and got the duty officer in Physical Evidence, who said 'Holy shit!' evidently the religious thought for the day, and told him the team was on its way. Then Malone rang Russ Clements, who, half-asleep but still awake enough to be concerned for the Malone family, said only, 'Lisa and the kids all right? Okay, I'll be there soon's I can.'

Malone hung up the phone and turned round. Claire, in her shortie nightgown, stood in the kitchen doorway, frightened and puzzled. 'Is it true, Dad? Is there a dead man in our pool?'

'It's true. Where's Tom?'

'In with Mum.'

'How's Maureen?'

'Quiet. It's not like her, she's not saying a word.'

'Get dressed, the police will be here soon.' He hoped they would not arrive with sirens blaring, lights flaring; sometimes the theatricals of police work, though necessary, embarrassed him. This section of Randwick, mostly white-collared and comfortable, was a quiet neighbourhood and so far he and Lisa had fitted in. 'And don't go outside, understand?'

'I've never seen a dead person.'

She was fourteen, on the verge of becoming a beautiful woman; sometimes, forgetting the contribution of Lisa, he was amazed he could have sired such a beauty. There was also a matter-of-fact serenity to her that she had inherited from Lisa; or there normally was. But not now. The death of strangers, he knew, though not as shattering as that of loved ones, never left any but the most callous untouched.

'You're not going to start now,' he said, trying to keep his tone gentle. 'Go and get dressed.'

He went into the main bedroom, where Lisa was sitting on the side of the queen-sized bed with her arms round Maureen and Tom. She looked up at him and said accusingly, or so it seemed, 'What's happening?'

'They're all on their way, the local fellers, the Crime Scene team. They'll all be here in minutes. Russ is coming, too.'

'Can I watch, Dad?' Tom was almost eight: the world, and everything in it, even the horrible, was for watching.

'Not this time, Tom. Get dressed.'

Lisa rose to take the two younger children out of the room. As they passed him, Malone pressed Maureen's shoulder. 'I'm sorry, love.'

Both children looked at him, puzzled; but he saw that Lisa understood. 'What for, Daddy? Sorry for what, the dead man?'

'Yes, I guess so.' It would be useless trying to explain his regret at what, through his police work, he had brought into their lives.

There was no time for a shower. Normally, at this time of morning, he would be in the pool; that, too, was out for the time being. He had a quick wash, throwing the cold water into his face as if to convince himself that he should be fully awake; which he was. He put on a short-sleeved shirt, cotton trousers and a pair of canvas shoes and went out to get the newspapers. He had no intention of reading them; it was force of habit. Today was Australia Day, a national holiday, when the natives, a notoriously phlegmatic lot, searched in themselves for a sediment of patriotism. This weekend, with the Gulf war promising to be more than a nine-day horror, with the country's economy up to its crotch in recession and sinking further, the flag-waving would be even more desultory than usual. He glanced at the headlines. Saddam, the medieval thug, was playing dirty: he was flooding the Gulf with oil. President

Bush, always with an eye to the vote, was calling him an environment terrorist. Malone, taking a narrow view, wondered which was worse, oil in the Gulf or a dead man in your kids' swimming pool.

He was about to go back into the house when the two police cars, silent and with no blue and red lights flashing, pulled up at the kerb. Detective Sergeant Wal Dukes got out of the first car.

'I was just knocking off, Scobie, when they told me you had a problem.' He was a big man, a one-time Olympic heavyweight boxer now run a little to fat; he was reliable, but sometimes a bit heavy-handed, as if he thought he still had a few rounds to go in his last bout. 'Crime Scene on their way?'

'Yeah.' Physical Evidence was still called Crime Scene by the older men in the Department: change for change's sake was something they didn't favour. Malone closed the front door. 'Let's go round the side. I want to keep the kids out of this. The bloody place is going to be over-run in a while. Stick to the path, in case there are some shoe prints in that grass strip there.'

They went round to the back of the house, followed by Dukes' junior, a young detective named Lazarus, and the two uniformed men who had come in the second car. Grime was still out in the middle of the pool, the skim-net still over his face, looking for all the world like a drunk who had decided to have a floating sleep.

'He's Normie Grime, Scungy they called him. I've been using him as an informant for the past three months, since he got out of the Bay.'

'What was he in for?'

'Passing dud notes. He was into everything, but he was always just a hanger-on, never big time.'

'What were you using him for?'

'I've been on a homicide, a young Vietnamese was murdered in a back lane in Surry Hills. He was into drugs, the Asian, and I hoped Scungy could give me a lead or two.

Scungy himself, as far as I know, never sold the hard stuff, but he knew everyone who did.'

'Was he coming here to see you?'

Malone looked at him as if he had been accused of corruption. 'Here? Wal, I don't even let *cops* come here! Except Russ Clements.'

'Well, we're here now.' But Dukes said it as gently as he could, though gentleness was not one of his talents. He looked out at the drifting Grime, who had floated close to the far side of the pool and was now staring up through the skim-net at one of the uniformed men as he reached out for the long pole. 'Watch out, Kenny, you're gunna fall in!'

Kenny fell in, with a loud splash and a muffled curse. Dukes turned back to Malone. 'How do we divide this one up? It's in my territory, but he's your property, as it were.'

'I'll hang on to him, Wal, if it's okay with you. If I need any help – ?'

'Sure, all you need.' The uniformed cop, Kenny, had pushed the body to the side of the pool. It was now floating at the feet of the two senior detectives. Dukes looked down at it. 'Fuck 'em!'

'Who?'

'Crims. Why don't they go out into the middle of the Nullabor Plain when they wanna bump each other off?'

Ten minutes later Russ Clements and the Physical Evidence team arrived simultaneously. All at once the back garden was seething with activity, a police production; for the first and last time in this life Scungy Grime was a star. The Cayburn family stood on their balcony, the parents and their two teenage sons, Gloria Cayburn with her hand over her mouth as if stifling a scream; beyond the opposite side fence the Malones' other neighbours, an elderly couple named Bass who normally minded their own business, stood on a ladder, one above the other, like a geriatric trapeze pair about to climb to the high wire. Malone, catching a glimpse of them, waved to them, then looked sourly at Clements.

'You reckon we should charge admission?'

'Take it easy, mate. They're neighbours, for Crissake. You'd rather they turned their backs on you?' But the big, rumpled man knew what was causing the tension in Malone; he had gone into the house as soon as he had arrived and spoken to Lisa and the children. He was the surrogate uncle and he was as anxious as Malone to see that this murder did not throw too long a shadow over this house. 'Let's go inside.'

Then he looked past Malone and suddenly smiled, an expression of abrupt pleasure out of keeping with his sombre mood of a moment ago. 'G'day, Romy. You didn't say you were on call today.'

'They've given all the Old Australians the day off. We've been told we can wave the flag next year.' She was smiling as she said it, there was no sourness. She was the GMO, one of the government medical officers from the Division of Forensic Medicine in the State Department of Health. She was Romy Keller, slim and attractive, dark-haired and dark-eyed, with just a trace of accent, ten years out of Germany and still trying to be an Australian. 'I didn't know this was your place, Inspector. When they called me, they just gave me an address . . . When did it happen?'

'The murder? I don't know. My daughter found him in the pool.'

'Poor child.' She glanced towards the body, which was now lying on the bricks beside the pool, a green plastic sheet thrown over it. 'Anyone looked at the body?'

'Sergeant Dukes gave him a once-over,' said Clements. 'There's no sign of any wound. It could be a heart attack.'

'Then it wouldn't be murder, would it?' She looked at Malone.

He nodded. 'Righto, you're right. I jumped to con-clusions. Maybe it's some sick joke. Some mate of his found him dead and decided to dump him in my pool. I just don't think that's the way it is.'

She sensed the tension in him, gave him no immediate answer, looked once more at the sheet-covered body, then said, 'Okay, we'll take him away and look at him in the morgue. I'd rather do it there than give a show for them.'

She made a sweeping gesture, at the Cayburns, the Basses and at the back fence, where a family whose name Malone didn't know were lined up, all seven of them, on chairs, their faces hung above the palings like pumpkin halves.

'Take him away then,' said Clements. 'You doing anything tonight?'

She glanced at Malone before she answered Clements. 'No. Call me at the morgue.'

'I've never had a girl say that to me before.'

'You haven't lived, Russ.' She smiled at him and Malone and left them.

Malone opened the screen door and ushered Clements into the kitchen ahead of him. 'Is there something on between you and her?'

'Just the last coupla weeks.'

'You kept that pretty quiet.'

'You know what it's like. It gets out you're dating someone connected with the Department and they put out an ASM. There's nothing in it. She's just a good sort.'

'Who's a good sort?' said Lisa, coming into the kitchen. She was dressed in slacks and shirt and her hair was pulled back from her face by a bright blue band. She looked composed enough, but Malone, a sixteen-year veteran of marriage and a policeman to boot, could recognize the signs of tension.

'You are,' said Clements and pressed her arm. Over the years he had gradually fallen in love with Lisa Malone, but neither she nor Malone thought it was anything more than just affection.

'Where are the kids?' said Malone.

'I told them to stay in our bedroom, not to come sticky-beaking out here. At least till they've taken the – the body away.'

'I think it'd be an idea if you took 'em over to your parents' for the day. The Crime Scene lot could be here for a while.'

'I've already rung Mother. We'll go over to Vaucluse after I've made breakfast. Have you eaten, Russ?'

Malone left the two of them in the kitchen and went into the main bedroom at the front of the house. The two girls, dressed in shorts and shirts, were lolling on the bed; Lisa, with her Dutch neatness, had already made it up. Tom, in shorts and T-shirt, was flopped like a rag doll in the armchair in the corner by the window. Occasionally he would raise his head and peer out at the police cars in the street and the small knots of people outside the neighbouring houses. Disappointment clouded his small face: all that excitement going on outside and here he was stuck in the house as if he was sick or something!

'What's happening, Daddy?' Maureen had regained her natural curiosity; she would never allow the world to keep its secrets from her. Of course she would never know even half its secrets; but Malone knew her questioning would never cease. She still had not regained her normal bouncing energy, but at least she no longer seemed frightened. 'Have they taken the corpse away?'

'Not yet. When they take it out, don't hang out the window like a lot of ghouls, okay?'

'What's a ghoul?' said Tom, who had his own curiosity, not about the world but about words.

'Explain it to him,' Malone said to Claire. 'Don't lay it on too thick.'

She gave him her fourteen-year-old-woman-of-the-world look. 'I'm not *stupid*, Inspector. But what was that man doing in our pool anyway?'

'I wish I knew,' said Malone and went out into the

hallway and rang Superintendent Greg Random, commander of the Regional Crime Squad.

'Sorry to ring you at home, Greg, but I've got a problem.'

Random listened to what Malone told him, then said in his slow voice, 'You want to stay on the case? Not to be too obvious, it's a bit close to home.'

'Grime was my pigeon, Greg. I'm not sure it's murder yet, I'm only guessing. But if it is, whoever did him in has got something against me. I'd like to find out who it is.'

Random took his time; silences were part of his personality and character. Then: 'Okay, stay with him. But if this gets any closer to home, I mean if there are any threats against your family, you're off the case, understand? Who's assisting you?'

'Russ Clements is already here.'

'I might've guessed it. Are you two holding hands?'

'Only when my wife isn't looking.'

He hung up and went back out to the kitchen. Lisa had drawn down the blinds on the window that looked out on the swimming pool; Clements and the children were now seated at the kitchen table waiting for her to serve breakfast. The scene looked cosy enough, but there was an alertness to everyone, that stillness of the head and stiffening of the neck of someone listening for a warning cry. Outside the house the Physical Evidence team were keeping their voices to a low murmur, as if this crime was on a new level, committed in an environment that had to be protected.

Dr Keller came to the screen door. 'Inspector Malone? I'm finished here, we're taking him away.'

Malone pushed open the door and went out, aware of Lisa's and the children's eyes following him. 'You find anything on the body?' He kept his voice low. 'Any needle-marks or anything?'

'Not so far.' She moved away back to the pool fence and he followed her, thankful for her discretion. She had a low pleasant voice; she stood close to him, as if sharing an intimacy. Which they were, in a way: the death of Scungy Grime. She was wearing some sort of light perfume, a sweet-smelling GMO; he wondered if she wore it against the pervasion of formaldehyde and other laboratory odours. 'Was he a drug-user?'

'Not as far as I know. You don't use junkies as informers, unless you have to. They're too much of a risk.'

'He could have died of just a heart attack – I shan't know till I get to work on him.' She looked after the green-shrouded body as it was carried past them. Crumbs, thought Malone, we all finish up looking like garbage; the body-bags of war were made by manufacturers of garbage-bags. Suddenly he felt a pang of pity for the dead man.

Wal Dukes and the senior constable in charge of the Physical Evidence team joined them. Constable Murrow was a chunky man in his early thirties with a pale blond moustache and almost white eyebrows; yet his eyes were dark brown. The first impression of his face was that his features were totally unrelated, that he could be the mix of half a dozen fathers. He had the air of a man not quite sure of source or destination, but Malone knew that he was, at least, on top of his job.

'What have *you* got, Wayne?'

'We found some heel impressions around the side of the house. It looks like he was carried in here by one guy.'

'He was small enough,' said Wal Dukes, who was big enough to have carried a couple of men of Grime's size.

Malone looked past him, saw the TV cameraman come round the back corner of the house, camera already whirring. 'No!'

'I'll fix him.' Clements had come out of the screen door, was moving on heavy, deliberate feet towards the cameraman, who was still glued to his eye-piece when he was grabbed by the shoulders from behind and spun round out of sight beyond the corner.

'Jesus!' Malone could feel himself quivering.

Romy Keller and the two policemen looked at him sympathetically; he was surprised that it was the GMO, the outsider, who put her hand on his arm. 'They're always scavenging, you know that. It's part of the business.'

'I'll see there's a guy posted out the front to keep the vultures out,' said Dukes. Relations between the Department and the media were always touchy. The media were fortunate, they were responsible only to toothless tribunals. The police were responsible to public opinion, which has fangs. 'I think it'd be an idea if you moved out for a day or two, Scobie.'

'No!'

Then Malone abruptly simmered down. It was unusual for him to allow his anger to erupt as it had; he was not without anger, but normally he could put a lid on it as soon as it started to bubble. But these were not normal circumstances; not that murder in itself was a normal circumstance. His *home* had been invaded, his family threatened: he did not immediately think in such melodramatic phrases, he was too laconic for that, but his feelings were dramatic enough. Now he had himself under control again, he was mapping out the immediate future.

'No.' His voice was quieter. 'That'd be a point scored for whoever did this.' He gestured at the pool, empty now of Scungy Grime but still surrounded by members of the PE team. 'I'm moving my wife and kids over to the in-laws, but I'll stay here.'

'Have it your way then,' said Dukes. 'I think I'd probably do the same. We can't let the shit get away with it. Sorry, Doc.' He was the old-fashioned sort who didn't swear in front of women, at least women he didn't know.

Romy smiled. 'I think I'd better be going. I'll call you, Inspector, at Homicide as soon as I have something.'

She left them, stopping at the corner of the house to speak to Clements as he came round from evicting the cameraman. Then she was gone, but not before she had put her hand on the big man's arm and left it there a moment, a gesture of intimacy beyond her sympathetic touch towards Malone.

Clements looked at Murrow as he joined the three men. 'Any prints or anything, Wayne?'

'They're trying to get some prints off the pool gate. Did you touch the gate, Inspector?'

Malone nodded. 'I wasn't thinking . . . Whoever dumped him in the pool made sure of the security lock when he was leaving.'

'Nice of him,' said Clements. 'Didn't want some toddler from up the street wandering in and falling in with Scungy.'

'Anything on Scungy?' Malone asked. 'Wallet or anything?'

'Nothing,' said Murrow. 'He's skint. Anyone know where he lived?'

'I do,' said Malone and looked at Clements. 'I'll get changed. You and I can go and have a look at his flat.'

'You haven't had breakfast.'

'I don't feel like it.'

'Tell that to Lisa.' Clements was not only an adopted uncle, he was sometimes an adoptive brother. 'Get something into you. You know she won't let you leave the house till you've eaten.'

'Women!' Dukes and Murrow, both married men, looked at Malone with sour understanding. Then Dukes said, 'I've got men interviewing everyone in your street, in case they saw something, a car or something.'

Malone was grateful that he had not had to go out and confront the neighbours. He valued his privacy and respected theirs. Last week, in the northern suburbs, a small tornado had struck; neighbours had rallied together, help had been generous and welcome. But murder was another storm altogether.

'I'll get things tidied up here, Scobie, then I'll hand the running sheets over to you and Russ. Call on me if there's anything further. Or do you want me to set up a Crime Scene room down at the station?'

'Let's keep it small for the moment. Handle it without too much fuss, Wal. I don't want our street turned into the Mardi Gras.'

Lisa had Malone's breakfast on the table when he went back into the kitchen: apple juice, muesli with sliced mango, toast, honey and coffee. 'I heard those remarks out there. You're right, I wouldn't let you leave the house with an empty belly.'

'Any clues, Daddy?' Maureen had recovered. Given her head, she would have been out in the street giving interviews to the media. Her father had the most interesting job in the world: solving murders was heaps better than making a fortune buying and selling crummy old buildings or being a general fighting a crummy war. 'I heard you say his name. Scungy something. *Scungy* – what a name!'

'What's it mean?' said Tom, adding another word to his catholic vocabulary.

'Creepy,' said Claire, his teacher. 'Sleazy. God, tomorrow it's going to be absolutely stoking at school! First day of term and all everyone will want to talk about is our murder!'

'What's wrong with that?' said Maureen, story already rehearsed.

'*Our* murder?' said Lisa, looking at Malone from the other end of the table. 'If I hear anyone say that again, there'll be another murder. Okay?'

The children suddenly sensed their mother's displeasure; what disturbed them was that it seemed to be directed against their father and not them. Malone himself felt the impact. He chewed on a mouthful of muesli, chewing on the right words too: 'There'll be no more cops here, I promise. They'll get everything cleared up today and that'll be it.'

'I wanted to take pictures.' Tom had been given a camera at Christmas, a present from Lisa's parents who, in Malone's view, always lavished too much on the children. The pool outside had been a present from Jan and Elisabeth Pretorius and when Malone had first dived into it the water had stung him like a bathful of vinegar.

'If he's going to take pictures, I'd like copies of the running sheets,' said Maureen. 'I'll write an essay for Social Studies –'

Malone abruptly got up from the table and as he went out of the kitchen he heard Claire say, 'Shut up, motor-mouth. This is a domestic.'

God, he thought, they've even learned the jargon. What have I done to them? Then he was aware of Lisa behind him in the hallway. He stopped at their bedroom door.

'It's not my fault, y'know.'

'I know that. But whom do I bitch to?' *Whom*: Dutch-born, she had a respect for English grammar that the natives had recently tossed into the waste-basket.

'Did you hear what Claire said? *This is a domestic.* Are you going to beat the hell out of me?'

'I always thought it was the other way round, husbands beating up their wives.' She put her arms round his neck. 'This doesn't mean they'll be looking for you next, does it?'

He went stiff in her embrace. 'Start thinking like that, I *will* beat the hell out of you! Jesus, darl –' Then he relaxed, feeling the stiffness in her; he was only increasing her fear, his denial sounded too forced. 'Putting Scungy in the pool is just some sort of sick joke, that's all. Even his name is a sick joke.'

She was not convinced. She knew that he loved her as deeply as any man could love; but she knew too that a man's passion is rarely as deep, never as consuming as a woman's can be. Scobie would die for her, she knew; she would do the same for him, but gladly. She wasn't sure that men ever died gladly, least of all for love.

She kissed him. 'I want everyone out of the place by tomorrow morning, the Crime Scene tapes taken down, everything gone. I'm coming back to my home first thing tomorrow morning and I want Scungy whatever-his-name-is scrubbed right out, not a trace of him. I love you.'

'I was beginning to wonder.' He grinned, though it was an effort, and returned her kiss.

2

The heat was already building up as Clements drove them into the city, to Woolloomooloo. The morning sun, reflected from the sheer glass walls of one building to the glass walls of another (Malone had begun to suspect that lately architects were turning Sydney into a City of Glass. Some day in the future they would find a singer who could hit an absolute top note, they would amplify it all over the city, all the buildings would shatter and the architects could start in all over again), till it seemed there were dozens of small suns, all striking at the eye. There was no breeze, the flags would hang limp on this Australia Day.

'How did you get Scungy on side?' Clements asked.

'When he came out of Long Bay, Fraud were waiting to send him up on two more charges. I talked 'em out of it and told him he owed me.'

'Did he come up with anything?'

'Nothing I could use. He said he knew Joey Trang, the Vietnamese, but he didn't tell me anything I didn't already know. I saw him last week and he said he was on to something, but he'd let me know when he was sure. He didn't seem to believe what he'd heard.'

'You didn't try to squeeze it out of him?' Then Clements shook his head. 'No, you're too soft, mate. A belt under the ear works wonders, you should try it some time.'

Malone looked at him seriously. 'You really think I'm too soft?'

'I dunno, to tell you the truth.' Clements took the car down the curve at the bottom of Macleay Street and along the waterfront where the navy ships were moored. A large crowd already lined the tall wire fence, most of them there to celebrate the national holiday, a few protesters holding up banners demanding *Peace in the Gulf!* Beyond the ships the waters of the small bay glinted like broken blue glass. 'When did you last clock a villain, give him a real going-over?'

Malone thought a while. 'About ten years ago. But I tell you what – if I find the bastard who tossed Scungy into our pool, I'll beat the shit out of him before I book him.'

'Good. I'll hold your coat. If he's too big and young for you, I'll hold *him*.'

Woolloomooloo is a pocket between two shoulders just east of the city centre. For over a hundred years before Malone was born ships, sealers, traders and passenger liners had docked in the small 'Loo Bay; pubs and brothels had for years put a ceiling on real-estate values. Sailors and prostitutes met in a common market and it was said that even a decent girl, if she slipped and fell on the broken pavements, would earn a quid before she was back on her feet. Gangs used to whet their razors on the local rocks before going up the eastern hill to Darlinghurst and Kings Cross to carve up the competition. For years poverty had hung over the 'Loo like a harbour mist. Across on the western ridge, on the edge of the Domain, one of the city's parks, stands a statue of Henry Lawson, the proletarians' poet. He had once written, 'Sorrow and poverty taught me to sing'; but only drunken bawdy songs had come out of the 'Loo. Lawson, an alcoholic, might have understood and wept for those who sang them.

In recent years there had been efforts to coat the 'Loo with respectability. Old terrace houses had been gentri-fied, crones taken to a beauty parlour; blocks of Housing Commission flats had been built under the lee of the east-ern hill. The merchant sailors no longer came to this part of the port of Sydney and the girls, or their daughters or granddaughters, had moved up the road to William Street or the Cross. Still, there were reminders of poverty: a men's hostel stood in the shadow of the railway viaduct and every night the derelict and homeless stood in line waiting for a bed. They would be the skulls, the *memento mori*, at today's anniversary party.

Scungy Grime had lived in one of the Commission flats. Up the road some winos sat in the gutter in the morning sun, sweating out last night's plonk. When Malone and Clements got out of their car the bleary eyes sharpened for a moment and the red noses lifted like those of pointer dogs waiting to be put down. They hadn't lost their sense of smell of a mug copper.

The two detectives went into the block of flats, found the superintendent and had him let them into Grime's flat. 'He was murdered, you say?'

'No, we didn't say that,' said Malone. 'What made *you* say it?'

'I dunno. I guess I just jumped to conclusions.' He was a fat man whose stained panama hat looked as if it would be a permanent fixture on his head; it had a screwed-on look, Malone thought, like a jar-lid. He was not surprised by his tenant's death; he was a 'Loo resident, born and bred, he was familiar with a dozen ways of dying. 'Someone come looking for him last night, but he'd already gone out –'

'You see who it was?'

'Nah. He was out there on the landing, the light was out – bastards around here are always pinching the globes. I was down the stairs, I just saw him knocking on Normie's door. I sang out there was nobody home, I'd seen Normie go out –'

'Describe the man.'

'I can't.' The fat shoulders shook in a shrug. 'I told you, the light was out, there was only the light from the landing below. He didn't even look down at me, he just went along that hallway outside and disappeared – there's another flight of stairs further along . . . Normie always looked a bit jumpy, you know what I mean? He come home Sat day

24

night and I spoke to him, he didn't see me, and he jumped like I'd jabbed him with a needle or something. I got the idea, talking to him occasionally, he'd made some enemies when he was out at the Bay.'

'You knew he'd been in jail?'

'Oh, sure. You work here long as I have, you get to know everyone's history.' He would make a point of it, it was one of the perks of the job. He went to sit down in Grime's small living room, to take a load off his feet, as he put it, but Clements stood holding open the front door.

'We'll check with you on our way out, Mr Shanagan.'

Shanagan could take a hint; in the 'Loo, if you didn't, you often took something else, like a fist in the face. 'Sure, sure. You know where to find me. Take your time.'

Clements closed the door on him and Malone said, 'We'll talk to him later. He's busting to tell us anything we want to know.'

'You think he knows any more than he's told us?'

'Your guess is as good as mine. I'd say no. He's a bull artist, the sort who'll break their neck to be called as a witness. We'll send one of the young blokes back to talk to him.'

The flat was small. A bedroom, bathroom, living room and kitchen: you could swing a cat in it, but the terrified beast would have been scratching the walls with each swing. It was neat, a place for everything and everything in its place. Including a diary and an address book, one placed neatly on the other; the morbid thought struck Malone that perhaps Grime had laid everything out for them. He had always thought Grime a cheerful little man, one who would have turned a blind eye to the possibility of his own death. But maybe he had been wrong about the little man.

'Nothing's been disturbed,' said Clements, coming back from the bedroom. 'Doesn't look as if he died here. The bed's still made, with the cover on it. He's even got his pyjamas laid out on it!'

'Where do you lay yours out? On the floor?'

Malone looked around. This was a lonely man's home; one could *feel* the loneliness, like a sad current in the air. There was a solitary photo: a young Grime between a couple who could have been his parents. All three were smiling: a happy day long ago. Malone wondered if Grime had remembered when the photo was taken. He turned it over. On the back was a date: 1963, November 22. Not really a happy day, though he doubted that Scungy Grime, even then, would have been upset by the assassination of a President. He had always had a limited view of the world.

'Did you know he worked on the wharves?' Clements held up a card. 'This is a WLU ticket.'

Malone shook his head. 'He told me he was still on the dole. How would he get into the Wharf Labourers Union? He couldn't lift a box of cornflakes.'

'You're living in the past, mate.'

'My old man's past. He worked on the wharves. Yeah, I know it's all mechanized these days, but they still look for muscle.'

'He could've been a tally clerk.'

'If he was, God help the balance of payments. Put a pencil in his hand and he couldn't do anything else but make two and two add up to five. Check with the WLU.'

'What about his family? Did he have any?'

'He had a wife one time, down in Melbourne. He came up here about ten years ago. He had a record down there, the same things he did up here, small-time stuff.'

He was looking through Grime's diary. No full names were mentioned, as if the dead man stood by the old army and criminal code: no names, no pack drill. But occasionally a given name appeared in front of an initial, as if to distinguish that person from someone with the same initials. One name and initial figured twice in the diary, the last entry only two nights ago. *Ring Jack A . . .* 'Where would a 905 number be?'

Clements was a grab-bag of inconsequential information, with a mind like the waste-bin of a computer. He frowned, bit his lower lip, then said, 'Somewhere around Manly. Maybe Harbord, around there.'

'Who do we know named Jack A. who lives in Harbord?' But they both knew and they looked at each other with that cynical surprise that passes for excitement with cops of long experience. 'Jack Aldwych. Why would Scungy be ringing our friend Jack? He told me he'd given up working for Jack even before he went into the Bay.'

'You think Jack had him done in?'

'I hope not.'

He did not want to take on the biggest crim in the country, not if Scungy Grime had been Jack Aldwych's calling card left on the doorstep of the Malone home.

3

He and Clements drove over the Harbour Bridge and out to Harbord, one of the closest of the northern beaches. The main road was clogged with holiday traffic. The northern beaches were supposed to be cleaner than the beaches south of the harbour, the sewage spill apparently knowing where the fortunate northerners swam and obligingly avoiding them. So people came from the south and the west and piddled in the northern waters and everyone cursed the Water Board and the government for not doing their job. The sun blazed down and everyone was slowly dying of sun cancer, but what better way was there to spend a hot summer holiday?

The air-conditioning in Clements' car suddenly stopped working. Clements, patience exhausted as he halted for the fifth time in a traffic jam, reached for the blue light that he wasn't supposed to carry in his private vehicle, put it on the roof and blared his horn. At once two youths jumped out of a stolen car and ran off down a side street and half a dozen other drivers looked guilty, wondering if they had been chased all this way for breaking the speed limit over the Bridge. Clements pulled his Nissan out on to the wrong side of the road and drove down against the oncoming traffic.

'You're going to get us booked for this,' said Malone. 'I'll tell 'em you did it against my express orders.'

'Tell 'em I went mad with the heat. Hello, we've got company.'

Up ahead a motorcycle cop, straddling his bike, was waiting for them directly in their path. Clements pulled up, got out and approached the officer. He was back in less than a minute.

'Righto, what bull did you feed him this time?' said Malone.

'I told him the truth – or anyway, half of it. I said a dead man had been dumped in your pool and we had to get to the chief suspect before he packed up and fled the country. Hang on!'

'You mention Jack Aldwych's name?'

'Who else? It'll make that motorcycle cop's day. Better than picking up mug lairs exceeding the speed limit.'

'You're exceeding it. What if he radios Manly and we get half their strength as back-up?'

'I told him we'd already called Manly.'

Half-truths are weapons police and criminals use against each other; they have learned from the black-belt masters, the lawyers. Malone hoped that the motorcycle cop up ahead, siren now screaming, showed a sense of humour when he learned the full truth.

The motorcycle cop took them out of the main stream of traffic, through side streets, and within five minutes brought them, his siren still screaming, to the front gates of Jack Aldwych's mansion. It was a big two-storeyed house with verandahs right round it on both levels. It had been built at the turn of the century by a circus-owning family and it was said that the ghosts of acrobats still tumbled around the grounds at night and a high-wire spirit had been seen flying across the face of the moon. Ghosts didn't protect Jack Aldwych, just a black-haired minder built like a small elephant.

He stood inside the big iron-barred gates, shaking his head at Malone and Clements. 'Mr Aldwych aint here. No, I dunno I can tell you where he is, he don't like being disturbed.'

Clements said, 'Would he be disturbed if we ran you in?'

'What fucking for?'

'Swearing at an officer. Come on – Blackie Ovens, isn't it? You better tell us where we can find him or we're gunna camp here till he comes home. It'll lower the tone of the neighbourhood. Jack wouldn't like that.'

Ovens pondered, then shrugged. 'Geez, youse guys are hard. Okay, he's out at the Cricket Ground. He's got a private box in the Brewongle Stand.'

'He's a cricket fan?' Malone's voice cracked with surprise.

'Nuts about it. I'll tell him you're coming.' He unhitched a hand-phone from his belt. 'Don't worry, he'll wait for you. He wouldn't leave a cricket match even to see the Police Commissioner bumped off.' He grinned to show he was only joking; the three officers stared back at him. 'Sorry.'

As Malone and Clements got back into the Nissan, the motorcycle cop, already astride his machine, eased in beside them. 'So you were afraid the chief suspect was gunna split overseas? He's out at the *cricket*! Next time you come over this side of the harbour, go through the proper fucking channels!'

He roared off and Clements looked at Malone. 'They're not very polite this side of the harbour, are they?'

'What are you going to do, pull rank on him? Forget it. We asked for it and we got it. Take me out to the Cricket Ground and then go on out to my place and see if they're finished there. Lisa wants everyone out by this evening. Make sure she gets what she wants.'

'Anything else?'

'Rustle up someone and send him down to talk to that caretaker at Scungy's flats. Get him to talk to the other people in Scungy's block.'

'What if he just died of a heart attack or something?'

'I still want the bastard who dumped him in my pool. Maureen was shivering when she came in to tell me she'd found him. What are you doing?'

Clements was getting out of the Nissan. 'I don't run to a car-phone, I've just got the radio connected to Police Centre.'

He went back to the gates, spoke to Blackie Ovens, who handed him his hand-phone. Clements punched a number, waited, then spoke into the mouthpiece. Malone was too far away to hear whom he was calling or what was being said. Then Clements handed the phone back to Ovens and came back to the car.

'I just called Romy Keller. She thinks Scungy was poisoned. It looks as if you're gunna get your murder after all.'

When Clements dropped Malone at the Cricket Ground people were still queuing to get into the ground. Malone flashed his badge at the attendants on the turnstiles into the Brewongle Stand, but his name meant nothing to them. He had played for the State on this ground twenty years ago, but these men would have been only boys then and he had never been big enough to be a boyhood hero. He went up in the lift to the floor where the private boxes were situated, flashed his badge again at the floor attendant, an older man who remembered him, and knocked on the door of the suite marked *Saltbush Investments*. It was opened by a waiter in a white jacket, whose small thin face went whiter than the jacket when he saw Malone.

'Hello, Larry. You do a waiter's course last time you were inside?'

'G'day, Inspector.' Larry Quick gave his con man's smile. 'You wanna see me or Mr Aldwych?'

'The boss. I think he might be expecting me. Didn't he get a phone call?'

'Yeah, but he doesn't always tell me everything.'

Malone followed Quick through the small private lounge and out to the seats on the balcony. Jack Aldwych, tall and heavily built, broad-brimmed white panama on his silver hair, regal in a cannibal chief way, sat there alone.

'Inspector Malone.' His dead wife Shirl, a respectable woman, had taught him to be polite; it was an effort, but occasionally he succeeded. 'I got a message you were on your way. Come to see the match? You must wish you were out there now, eh?'

Malone looked out at the famous ground, a bright green lake surrounded by cliffs of stands speckled, as if with the child's decoration of hundreds and thousands, with the huge crowd's colours. In the middle two Australians, in green and gold, were batting; spread around them, in two shades of blue, were the eleven Englishmen. This was a one-day match, a type of game that hadn't been invented when Malone was playing. Its accelerated pace, the almost desperate chase for runs, the pyjama-like uniforms, the hoopla and exaggerated behaviour of the players, all of it had brought the crowds back to cricket, but Malone was one of the old school. If a team-mate had kissed him when he had taken a wicket, he would have run a stump through the molester.

'No. I was a bowler, Jack. One-day games aren't meant for bowlers, they're for batsmen. You never hear of a groundsman these days preparing a wicket for bowlers – the Cricket Board would have him jailed. All the crowd wants to see is big hitting. It's Happy Hour for the batsmen and bugger-you-Bill for the bowlers. You come here often?'

'Every day there's a match, one-day games, Sheffield

Shield, Test matches. I'm a cricket-lover. Most of the crims you and I know, they all go to the races, the horses or the dogs. But I love cricket. A gentleman's game — or it used to be.' He smiled an old crim's smile, full of wry irony. 'I bought this private box through one of my companies and I come here as a guest of meself and watch in comfort. I tried to become a member here, but they always found a reason why I couldn't make it. It's okay if you're a white-collar crim, but not if you're a blue-collar one like I was. So I pay forty-two thousand bucks a year, but I don't have to sit down there amongst the hoi-polloi, God love 'em, and I can sit here and jerk my thumb at them across there in the Members' Stand. What d'you want?' he said abruptly, turning his head sharply to stare at Malone, who had sat down two seats along from him.

There were no dividing walls between the boxes out here on the balcony, only iron railings. Too much privacy might suggest elitism and that, God knew, was worse than bloody multiculturism. The neighbouring boxes were packed, mostly with men; the few women amongst them were watching Jack Aldwych, having been told who he was; they could hear nothing for the chatter of their own menfolk, who were already well oiled by the free grog of their hosts in the corporation boxes. Still, Malone dropped his voice almost to a murmur: 'Jack, one of your fellers, Scungy Grime, turned up in my swimming pool at home this morning. Dead.'

'Scungy? Poor little bugger.' Aldwych showed no surprise. 'You want something to drink?'

The morning heat struck into the balcony; the ground was slowly turning into a cauldron. Malone had taken off his jacket, but his armpits were marshes of sweat. 'I'd like a light beer, if you've got one.'

Aldwych looked up at Quick, who had appeared in the doorway to the lounge. 'A light beer for Mr Malone . . . Larry's become my handyman. He's lost his nerve. Makes you wanna laugh, a con artist who's lost his nerve. But it's

32

sad, don't you reckon? There aint too many artists left these days in our game.'

'Jack, don't change the subject. What about Scungy? *That's* sad, being dead.'

'Oh, you're right about that. But you're wrong about him being one of my fellers. Scungy wasn't working for me for at least three months before he went in last time. He started talking drugs.'

'Scungy? Thanks, Larry.' Malone took the light beer, slaked his thirst. 'He was talking drugs *before* he went in?'

Aldwych nodded, sipping his own beer. 'Yeah. Why, was he talking to you about them recently?'

Malone hesitated; then decided to give a little information in the hope of some in return. 'I've been using him, Jack, since he got out of the Bay.'

'T'ch, t'ch,' chided Aldwych, watching the game out in the middle. 'Blokes who give information to coppers aint my favourites. Oh, nice shot! You see that?'

'I saw it,' said Malone sourly. Alan Border had clipped the English fast bowler in the air between slips and gully for four. 'He'd never think of risking a shot like that in a real game. If it's any consolation, Scungy never mentioned your name to me.'

'Then why are you here?' Aldwych looked back at Malone.

'I came across your initials and your phone number in a diary he kept.'

'Did he say anything about me in the diary?'

'Jack, I'm not laying all my cards on the table, not yet.'

'There would have been nothing Scungy had on me.' He tipped his panama back. 'I'm retired, Scobie – you mind if I call you Scobie? I'm seventy-five years old, my wife died eight months ago, and I'm tired. I've been a crim for over sixty years, I started when I was fifteen – they could call me the Godfather, if we went in for that sorta stuff out here. But for the last year, when I knew my wife was dying of cancer, I been as clean as a young nun. What could Scungy tell you about me that would interest you? Do you think I killed him?'

Beyond Aldwych, Malone saw a woman in the next box lean forward, ears popping out of her blow-wave like rabbits out of long yellow grass. 'The thought occurred to me when I saw your initials in his diary.'

'Scobie, I don't kill people.' He was a liar, but a good one; honesty shone out of his rheumy blue eyes like a smuggler's beacon. When he was younger he had killed four men, but he had been acquitted of two of the murders and never been charged with the others. In later years he had hired other men to do the killing, as a good general should. 'I'm sorry Scungy is dead, but if he was dealing in shit he deserved what he got. I've done everything else in my time –' He suddenly looked over his shoulder at the eavesdropping woman. 'Am I talking loud enough, madam?'

Malone almost burst out laughing at the look on the woman's face. She reared back, the blow-wave bobbing on her head as if a strong wind had blown through it. She said something to her husband, a man recognized as one of the town's top stockbrokers, but he, a man who knew when to buy and when to sell, was not buying into this. He said something to her, obviously a caution, and went back to watching the cricket, a much safer occupation than trying to pick a fight with a top crim. The woman abruptly got up and went back into the lounge.

Aldwych turned back, winked at Malone and went on as if there had been no interruption. 'I've done the lot, Scobie. Sly grog, SP betting, robbed banks, run whores, you name it, I've done it. You blokes know all that, but you aint been able to put me away in years. One thing I never touched was shit. Shirl, that was my wife, she made me promise never to do that and I never did. Oh shit, Border's gone! We're in trouble now. What's that? Four for fifty after, what, fifteen overs?'

'The bowlers look like they're on top,' said Malone,

licking his lips. The Indians were beating the bejesus out of the 7th Cavalry; or, in this morning's headlines, it was as if the Iraqis had suddenly started to win the Gulf war. 'Good.'

'You didn't say how Scungy was killed.'

All along the balcony people were standing up to stretch their legs while they waited for the incoming batsman. In the boxes immediately on either side of the Aldwych box, men and women had their heads in peculiar positions, as if they had become paralysed, as they tried to catch the conversation in Box 3A; ears were being dislocated and peripheral vision was strained to the point where one could imagine eyeball muscles twanging. One or two of them would cheat or swindle in business, but they could not bear to be caught eavesdropping.

Malone had a quiet voice; he made it even quieter. 'He was poisoned, we think.'

'Poisoned? And you think I might of done it? Or had it done? Inspector, I belong to the old school – you know what I mean.' He put out his forefinger, made a rough imitation of a gun; then he raised the finger to his throat, turned it into a razor. He was smiling all the time, sharing the joke with a cop. Then he looked up behind Malone. 'Oh, hello. You dunno my son, do you, Scobie? Jack Junior, this is Inspector Malone.'

Jack Aldwych Junior was as tall as his father but trimmer. He was about thirty, good-looking in a manufactured way, as if he had been put together by a hairdresser, a cosmetician and a tailor rather than just sired and borne. But his smile was genuine, if everything else about him looked artificial.

'Inspector.' His handshake was firm. He was casually dressed in sports shirt, blazer, slacks and loafers, but he was labelled all over: Dunhill, Ralph Lauren, Gucci. Malone, whom Gucci would have looked at and sent away barefoot, wondered if the Aldwych underwear was labelled. 'Has Dad been up to something he shouldn't have?'

'He's just been telling me he could run for Pope.'

'Jack Junior runs the family companies. The legitimate ones.' Aldwych smiled, a robber baron safe in his keep. He was one of the richest men in the country, but he never figured in any of the business magazines' Rich Lists. Some of the other robber barons who *had* figured in those lists were now bankrupt and disgraced, but Jack Aldwych still had standing with some of the leading banks, though none of them would have wanted to be quoted as saying so. 'This year he's up for president of the Young Presidents.'

'Then he wouldn't have known Scungy Grime?' Malone addressed the question to Jack Senior, but he had one eye on Jack Junior.

'Who's he?' said Jack Junior.

'A small-timer,' said his father. 'He worked for me once upon a time. Who've you got with you today?'

Jack Junior glanced back through the wide window into the inner lounge. 'Her name's Janis Eden, she's a social worker.'

'That's a change. They're usually models or society laya-bouts,' Aldwych told Malone. He had his class distinctions, it came of being a self-made man.

Then the girl, a glass of champagne in her hand, came out on to the balcony. She was no startling beauty, but she had made the most of what looks she had; and some-how she looked less artificially handsome than Jack Junior. She was well dressed, in a casual way, and Malone won-dered if she looked as elegant as this, Monday to Friday, when handing out comfort and advice to the battlers. But perhaps her welfare clients were bankrupt robber barons.

She pushed her thick auburn hair back with her free hand and gave Malone a cool nod when they were intro-duced. Malone knew that a lot of social workers were antagonistic to the police, but he had hoped for a little more sociability on a national holiday and here at the cricket.

'Inspector Malone had a murdered man dumped in his

swimming pool this morning,' Aldwych offered. 'It's no way to start the day.'

'It was this Scungy what's-his-name?' Jack Junior shook his head; not a hair in the thick dark mane moved. The girl's hand moved towards the head, then she seemed to think that might not be appreciated and it landed on his shoulder. 'I'm glad Dad's put all that behind him.'

Malone looked at the girl, wondering if she knew who Jack Junior's dad really was. She read the question in his face: 'Oh, I know all about Mr Aldwych.' She gave the old man a sweet smile. 'Jack didn't tell me about you. I read up on you.'

Aldwych didn't appear to be put out; his reputation had never been a hair-shirt. 'You mean there's a file on me? In Social Services? You got one on me, too, Scobie?'

'Not yet,' said Malone, trying to sound good-humoured and sociable.

Janis Eden looked at him from above the rim of her champagne glass. She had certain studied mannerisms, as if somewhere there was a hidden camera photographing her for a television commercial. They would not go down well at Social Services, but maybe she used them only at weekends.

'How do you police feel when crime lands, more or less, on your doorstep?'

'We don't like it. I hear you're a social worker. What field?'

'Drug rehabilitation. We're kept busy.'

'I'm sure you are.' Malone stood up. The new batsman, Mark Waugh, had just begun his innings by belting three fours off the first three balls he had received. It was time for an old bowler to depart, before the insults started. 'Well, I better be looking busy, too. Sitting here isn't going to tell me who dumped Scungy Grime in my pool.'

Aldwych had been looking at the action out on the field, but he turned his head as Malone stood up. 'Don't you really wish you were out there now?'

'No, Jack. I'm like you, I retired at the right time.'

He left them on that before they saw the lie in his face. He would dearly have liked to be out there on the field, even wearing coloured pyjamas and being belted all over the field by those hated bastards, batsmen. Life then, though it paid peanuts in those days, had been simple, uncomplicated and uncorrupted.

But as he went down in the lift he had the itchy feeling that Jack Aldwych, retired or not, knew more about the last months of Scungy Grime's life than he had told.

4

When Malone had gone Jack Junior saw some acquaintances in one of the private boxes farther along the balcony and said he would go and say hello to them.

'You want to come, Janis? It's a chance for you to meet some of the guys who make the wheels go round in this town.'

'No, thanks,' she said, moving into the seat next to Aldwych Senior and settling herself. 'I'll stay and talk to your father. I think he made more wheels go round than those men along there, no matter who they are. Am I right, Mr Aldwych?' She gave him a full smile.

He nodded to his son. 'You go along there, Jack. Janis and I are gunna get to know each other a little better'

Jack Junior hesitated, like a man who did not trust either one or the other or both of them; then he smiled. 'Don't let her rehabilitate you, Dad.'

When his son had gone, Aldwych said, 'You're not afraid of my reputation, Janis?'

'That's past, Mr Aldwych. You've reformed.'

He shook his big silver head. He had always been too beefy to be strictly handsome, but age had found some bone in his face and now he had the craggy look of a chipped and cracked Roman bust. But he never went to museums, so he never saw the resemblance. 'No, I'm not reformed. Retired. There's a difference.'

He turned his head for a moment as there was a roar from the crowd; one of the Australian batsmen had cracked another boundary. Then he looked back at her, his gaze as impenetrable as smoked glass. It was the look his enemies had seen when their fate hung in the balance.

But she did not seem disturbed by it. 'Well, whatever. The law is no longer chasing you, is it?'

Only his wife Shirl had spoken to him like this; but she had not had the education and poise of this girl. He was not used to dealing with today's generation, especially the female side of it. He had known some tough women in his younger days, Kate Leigh and Tilly Devine had been two of them, but they had been rough and ready, their sense of gender equality based on the razor- and knuckle-men they employed. They had had none of the smooth arrogance of this young woman.

'Would you be going out with Jack Junior if the law was still chasing me?'

'For one thing, I don't think of him as Jack *Junior*. That implies he's not his own person. Have you ever thought of that?' She turned and looked back through the plateglass at Larry Quick and held up her champagne flute.

Aldwych was annoyed at her self-confidence. Women, he thought, had too much independence these days; he was glad he was in the home stretch of his life. Though he was not given to metaphors of the turf: horses and jockeys were as unreliable as women. Women in general, that is: he had never lumped Shirl with the rest of them. 'No, I haven't. His mother christened him, not me. He's done all right.'

Her glass refilled, she turned back to him. She had no interest at all in what was going on out in the middle of the ground; that, too, annoyed him. In his youth she was the sort of girl he would have belted; but Jack Junior would never do that, he was sure. His son, he sometimes thought, was a wimp, too influenced by his mother, who had believed in Christian morals and respect for girls and other hopeless ideas.

'To answer your question, yes, I'd still go out with Jack, whether the law was after you or not. I'm very single-minded, Mr Aldwych. Much like you used to be, I'd guess.'

They were now sitting in the middle seats of the back row on the balcony, several seats distant from the boxes on either side. The inquisitive woman had not reappeared and the men on both sides were more interested in the cricket than in trying to listen to the conversation between the attractive young girl and the old criminal. Old men rarely have interesting conversations with young girls, not unless they're dirty old men, and the young girl looked too composed to be listening to that sort of approach.

'Are you after his money? He's gunna be a rich man some day.'

'Yes, I suppose I am, in a way. I'm in danger of losing my job, the State's cutting back on welfare, and the thought of being poor and out of work doesn't appeal to me.'

'Well, one thing, you're honest.'

'No, I used to be. I've reformed.' She sipped her champagne, her eyes smiling at him above the flute. There was no coquetry to it; it puzzled him at first what it was. Then he recognized it: it was the look of another criminal. or anyway a potential one. He began to worry for Jack Junior, if only for Shirl's sake.

'You've never been poor?' he said.

'No. I come from a family that could afford to send me to a good school and then to university. But my father committed suicide after the stock market crash in eighty-seven and we found he'd left us no money at all. My mother now draws the pension and I have a brother who works as a barman in a pub, the only job he could get with a PhD in archaeology.'

Aldwych wondered why anyone in Australia would want to take a degree in archaeology; but he had never been one for digging up anything, unless it could be used for blackmail. 'So you've set your sights on my son?'

'Yes.'

'Does he know it?'

'He'd be dumb if he didn't. And I don't think he is. Why did you become what you are?'

'You mean a crim or a success?'

Out on the field another Australian wicket had fallen; things were going from bad to worse, the bloody Poms were on top. He hated the English, despite his English name and lineage. His convict great-great-grandfather had spat on England the day they had transported him for assaulting and robbing a gentleman, and the family ever since had carried on the tradition. Three years ago, during the height of the Bicentennial celebrations, Aldwych had applied for membership of the First Fleet Pioneers, a society of the descendants of the first settlers; but he had been rejected. It was permitted to have had a convict as an ancestor, but the stain was supposed to have been washed out in succeeding generations. Criminality was not supposed to be part of the national heritage, though other nationalities were loud in their doubts of that belief.

Janis said, 'I know why you became a success – you were ruthless. Why did you become a criminal? Was it because you had a deprived childhood? That's what I hear a lot from the junkies I counsel.'

He laughed, a sound that still had some volume despite his age; some men in the box on their right turned their heads, wondering if the old crim was laughing at what was happening to Australia out there on the field. You never knew where a crim's loyalties lay.

'I was born what I grew up to be. My mother reckoned I was bad from the day I was weaned. I belted other kids and pinched whatever they had. I went to a State School and hated it and the teachers. I left soon's I turned

41

fourteen and I joined the old Railway Gang with Chow Hayes and Kicker Kelly and other blokes, all of 'em older than me. Then I become a stand-over man for Tilly Devine and her sly-grog racket . . . You want me to go on?'

She was smiling; it was difficult to tell whether she was impressed or disgusted. 'You're really proud of what you were, aren't you?'

'No. I'm not ashamed of it, either. It's a fact and you never get anywhere in life denying facts. That's why this country is in the mess it is right now, the politicians keep denying facts. One thing I never had was conceit. That was what killed more than half the crims I come up against. They thought they were better than me and they weren't. That was a fact they denied.'

'Did conceit kill them or did you?'

He looked at her steadily. 'I thought you said you'd read up on me?'

'I did. It said you were charged with two murders, but were acquitted.'

'Don't you believe in the jury system? Twelve of your peers who judge you innocent or guilty?'

'No,' she said, her own gaze as steady as his. 'I've gone into court with junkies and seen the jury condemn them before they've heard the evidence. We're all full of prejudices, Mr Aldwych.'

He continued to stare at her, then he said, 'You and me are gunna get on all right, Janis. Now let's watch the cricket.'

As he turned away to watch the play out on the field, he wondered if he had retired too soon. This girl had enough conceit, if that was the word, to smother Jack Junior.

CHAPTER TWO

I

Malone caught a cab back to Homicide in Surry Hills. Till three months ago Homicide had been headquartered in the big new complex, the Police Centre, across the road. Lavish in its space, antiseptic in its cleanliness, its attraction had proved too magnetic for the desk generals of Administration and another of the now-too-frequent reorganizations had taken place. Homicide had been moved across the road to the Hat Factory, a one-time commercial building which had indeed been a hat factory. Jokes were made about size 7¼ homicides, but the general feeling was that the working police, as usual, got the backwaters while the Minister and the brass got the harbour views. The sourest joke was that the old Hat Factory could never have made a hat that would have fitted the head of the Police Minister, Gus Dircks.

Clements was waiting for him, followed him into his room. It was no more than an office built into one corner of the main room, the upper half of it glass-walled. The squad room had been given a new coat of yellow-cream paint, the blue-grey carpet was not yet worn, the beige filing cabinets not yet chipped and dented; yet Malone had a feeling that everything was makeshift, that as soon as a further backwater could be found, they would be moved again. All that could be said for it was that it did not have the sleazy look that distinguished most squad rooms he saw in American films or on TV. No Hill Street blues were sung here, not yet.

'How'd you get on?' Clements asked.

'See what you can find out about a social worker, she's in drug rehabilitation, her name's Janis Eden. She's a girl-friend of Jack Aldwych's son. Any word yet from your girlfriend?'

'Lay off. Romy and I are – just friends. No, she hasn't called with anything more. Wayne Murrow phoned in – they got a print or two off the pool gate. They're checking records now. G'day, Peter.'

A man in white overalls, carrying a large plastic waste-bag, had come into the big outer room and moved down towards them, emptying waste-baskets as he passed each desk. Now he stood in the doorway of Malone's office.

'Sergeant.' The man gave a nod, a slight formal bow of recognition. He was in late middle age, thick dark hair streaked with grey, fleshily handsome, sad-eyed yet at the same time arrogant-looking; Malone had seen the type countless times, the immigrant who hadn't managed to achieve his old status, whatever it had been. He had not seen this particular cleaner before. 'May I clean out the basket?'

'Sure. This is Inspector Malone. Peter Keller. He's Dr Keller's father.'

Malone, sitting on the end of his desk, stood up and shook hands with the older man, who hesitated a moment before putting out his own hand. But the grip was strong: having made the decision, he was declaring himself an equal.

'Peter was a cop in Germany,' said Clements.

Malone had picked up his waste-basket, was ferreting through it; once or twice he had carelessly disposed of notes that he had later needed. 'No, nothing in there.' He handed the basket to Keller. 'So you were a cop?'

'Yes, Inspector. I was a sergeant.' He spoke as if rank were everything.

'Did you ever try to join our force?'

'I was too old by the time I came here. There was also the language – my English was not very good then. A pity.

44

I had the experience with criminals.' He emptied Malone's basket into the big bag he carried. 'This is the closest I get now to what I used to be. Excuse me.'

He moved on out of the office, straight-backed and a little flamboyant, making a ritual out of a menial task. Clements waited till he was out of earshot. 'I met Romy through him – she came to pick him up here just after he'd started, about a month ago.'

'He got any politics?'

'You mean is he an ex-Nazi or something? I wouldn't have a clue. Who cares now, anyway? What about this Janis Eden? Do I put her name on the Grime sheet?'

'Not yet. I didn't get anywhere with Jack Aldwych – he tells me he's retired and maybe he is, I've heard the rumour before. But this girl . . . I'd just like to know how a social worker gets to go out with the son of one of the richest men in the country, especially if Dad's a crim like old Jack.'

'Maybe they met in a disco or somewhere? You ever been to one? Some of the top ones, where you can't get in unless you're rich or good-looking, you meet all sorts. She good-looking?'

'Yes. You telling me you've been allowed into these joints? You're not rich and you're not good-looking.'

'I flash my badge at the guy on the door. Also, last time I went I was with Romy, she's good-looking enough to get in anywhere. Mate, this is a democratic town, at least for the young 'uns. You pick the right place and your luck's in, you can meet practically anyone. Is Jack Junior – I've never met him, but I hear that's what he's called – is he the disco type?'

'How would I know? I didn't know you were the type.'

Then his phone rang: it was Romy Keller: 'We haven't opened Mr Grime up yet, Inspector. We're waiting on the AIDS or hepatitis tests – we have to send a blood sample out to Westmead. Things aren't as quick as they used to be, not now we're all so AIDS-conscious . . . I've gone right over the body and all we've found is a needle-mark in the fold under the right buttock. I don't know if it means anything. I suspect he may have died of some sort of poison, but whether it was given orally or by injection, I don't want to commit myself just yet. I don't think we'll have anything definite for you before this evening.'

'Thanks, Doc. There are no signs that Scungy was a drug-user?'

'None. No needle-marks, no sign of any wear on the nasal membranes from cocaine use. We've only made a cursory examination till we get the all-clear on the AIDS and hepatitis tests, but I'd say Mr Grime was clean as far as drug-taking. Is Russ there?'

Malone handed the phone to Clements, got up and moved out of his office. As he went out into the main room Andy Graham and Phil Truach came in. Graham was tall and heavily built and restlessly energetic; one sometimes had to wear dark glasses against the glare of his enthusiasm. Truach, on the other hand, was slim and bony and his enthusiasm, if he had ever had any, had soured into cynicism. They made a good, well-balanced partnership.

'Where've you two been?' Murder doesn't take a holiday, but on public holidays Homicide usually operated with a skeleton staff, with certain members on call.

'We've been down Palmer Street.' Graham took off his jacket, bounced around his desk as if debating whether to do handstands on it. 'You know Sally Kissen, she runs – *ran* a brothel down there. Half the girls in William Street used her place.'

'We got a call from one of the girls an hour ago,' said Truach, who was already seated rock-like in a chair, as if he knew he and Graham were an act and he had to play up the contrast to his partner's restlessness. 'They found Sally dead in bed. Some of the Crime Scene boys are down there still. I gather they'd just come from your place.'

Malone told them about Scungy Grime; then he said,

'For Pete's sake, Andy, sit down!' Graham dropped into a chair, but then couldn't make up his mind whether to cross his legs or shove them straight out in front of him. Malone sat on the edge of the desk, turning his back on Graham. 'How did the Kissen woman die? Shot, stabbed, what?'

'We don't know. The GMO, old Joe Gaynor, couldn't find any wounds or bruises. She took drugs, there were needle-marks on her arms, but it didn't look as if she'd OD'd. It could of been a heart attack, but I don't think so. Doc Gaynor didn't think so, either. He thought she might've been poisoned.'

'Where's the body?'

'It's gone out to Glebe, to the morgue.'

'Righto, give me copies of your sheets. And Andy –' Graham was a speed typist, bashing at his typewriter with his usual energy. 'Keep your typos to a minimum. The last sheet I saw of yours looked like a wallpaper pattern. The same on the computer.'

He went back to his office. Clements was about to hang up, but Malone held up his hand. 'You still talking to the doc? I want to speak to her.'

Clements handed him the phone, but first said goodbye to Romy Keller in a voice full of kisses, a tone that raised Malone's eyebrows. With his hand over the mouthpiece Clements said, 'You don't know my romantic side.'

'Spare me . . . Doc? There's another body on its way out to Glebe. Ask Doc Gaynor if you can have a look at it. The name is Kissen, Sally Kissen, she was a hooker. I think she may have gone the same way as Grime. Oh, take care. She was a drug-user.'

'Then we'll have to do the AIDS and hepatitis tests before I can touch her. I don't think I can give you anything conclusive on either corpse till tomorrow. Can you wait?'

'They're dead, Doc, and I haven't a clue what happened to them. How long have you been a GMO?'

'Three months.'

'You'll learn that here in Homicide we're patient. Even Russ.'

'You don't know him,' she said, but he thought she laughed before she hung up.

Malone sat down again at his desk, picked up Grime's diary. The entries were cryptic; Grime had not been making notes for posterity. Yet, when a man was murdered, posterity had to take over. Most of the entries were the trivia of a person's life: bills to be paid, a doctor's appointment, a change in work shift. Initials sprinkled the small pages: Drink with B.H.; Call J.A. (those same initials again); Ran into K.L. Then, on a date three weeks past, there was a query, the only query amongst all the entries, and it was in capital letters: WHAT IS S.W. DOING UP HERE?

Malone handed the small book to Clements. 'What do you make of that?'

Clements looked at the entry. 'Do we know any S.W.? And what does *up here* mean?'

Malone shrugged. 'If Scungy worked at Darling Harbour or Walsh Bay, maybe they think of Port Botany as *down there*.' Port Botany was about twelve kilometres south of Port Jackson, the official name for Sydney Harbour; in Malone's youth it had been known, as it had been for almost two hundred years, as Botany Bay. Now it had been renamed and was a major container port. 'What upset him so much, the entry's in caps?'

'Let's check with the WLU, see where Scungy worked.'

But the WLU office did not work on national holidays. Clements hung up the phone. 'I'm getting naïve in my old age, expecting seven days a week from a union office.'

Malone grinned; Clements spread his prejudices wide. He stood up, picked up his jacket. 'I'm going home. Detectives shouldn't have to work on holidays, either.'

'What am I supposed to do?'

'Try and trace Scungy's wife, give her the bad news.

Ask Wayne Morrow to send one of his fellers down to Scungy's flat, go through it with a vacuum cleaner. The point is, we can't do much till Crime Scene comes up with something and your friend Doc Keller tells us what killed Scungy.'

'You're spoiling my Australia Day. I was gunna go out and sell flags.'

'Mine was spoiled at seven o'clock this morning when Maureen found Scungy in our pool.'

'Sorry.' For all his rough exterior, his obviousness, Clements was not insensitive. 'You want me to drive you home?'

'I'll get a cab, charge it to petty cash.' He was a tight man with his own money. One of the heroes in his pantheon was J. Paul Getty, the oil billionaire who charged his house-guests for their phone calls. 'If Doc Keller has anything interesting to tell you this evening, ring me at home.'

As soon as he stepped out into the street, his jacket over his arm, the heat hit him, threatening to fry him on the pavement. He squinted in the glare, thinking perhaps he *should* start wearing sunglasses, as Lisa was always insisting he do; then out of the bright yellow furnace appeared a cab, a miracle at this time of day on a holiday. A true-blue Aussie egalitarian, he got into the front seat beside the driver, a young Chinese student.

'You're a cop?' the driver asked warily, eyes slanting sideways at his passenger.

'Do I look like one?'

He was only six months in from Singapore, but already he had the Australian nose. 'It's not so much what you look like . . .'

'You mean we have a smell to us? Relax –' as the cab wavered '– I'm not going to pinch you for insulting an officer. Where do you come from? Singapore? What are the cops like there? Can you smell them, those in plain-clothes?'

The driver was frank, a most un-Chinese habit. 'I was a student, you had to learn to recognize them. Otherwise you finished up as a guest of Mr Lee. At least you police here aren't political.'

'Thank you,' said Malone, but wondered how many of the native students would agree.

Before he got out of the cab he paid the exact fare, sorting out the change in his pocket; tipping was un-Australian, despite the propaganda of immigrant waiters, and in Malone's case it was unheard-of. The Chinese driver, studying for an economics degree, was philosophical. 'You want a discount for cash?'

'Funny bugger. I'll get you deported.'

The cab drove off and Malone stood on the pavement and looked at his home, his castle gift-wrapped by Physical Evidence blue-and-white-checked tapes. Somehow, the tapes were an obscenity, like insulting graffiti; countless times he had stepped over them going into other people's homes and he had not been unaware of how they changed the aspect of a house or an apartment. This, however, was different: it was, as Greg Random had said, too close to home.

A young policeman, in shirt sleeves, put on his cap and came along to Malone from the marked police car standing at the kerb. 'I've been told to stand by, Inspector. Everyone's gone.'

'You know if they had any luck with the neighbours? Anyone see anything?'

'Not as far as I know. The lady next door, Mrs –' he took his notebook from his pocket '– Mrs Cayburn said she heard a car draw up during the night. She doesn't know what time it was, but it was still dark.'

Malone looked up and down the street. This was one of the few streets still left in Randwick that had no apartment blocks; two rows of older, solid houses on their sixty-foot lots faced each other across the roadway. The houses had a respectability about them; they had been built in a time when respectability had a value. Some, like Malone's, had been built at the time of Federation, at the turn of the century; the rest had been built during or just after World War I. Up till now, as far as Malone knew, none of the houses had known murder or wife-beating or scandal; at least none of them had called for blue and white taping to be stretched around them.

'You've got a visitor, sir.' The young officer was obviously a surfie when off-duty; he was all mahogany, in colour and in muscle. On such a day, he should be down amongst the big ones, riding them on his board. Instead, here he was riding herd on a house where all the excitement was finished. 'An old guy, said he was your father.'

'You checked him?' Why did he think that the old guy might be Jack Aldwych? He was becoming edgy again, the Crime Scene tapes were binding too tightly.

'He wasn't much help, sir. Said he'd never had to identify himself before to get into his son's place. I asked him for his driving licence, but he said he didn't drive, why'd he want a licence? Finally, I got him to show me his pension card. He's an obstreperous old coot, isn't he?' He looked cautiously at Malone as he offered the opinion.

Malone grinned and relaxed. 'That's my old man. He hates cops.'

He left the young cop with raised eyebrows and the unspoken question and went into the house. Con Malone was sitting at the kitchen table, a glass of beer in front of him. The old man lived in the past, pottering around in his bigotry and old habits. He had never learned to appreciate beer from a can, he had always drunk it from the bottle or a glass and he wasn't going to risk cutting his lip on a flaming piece of tin and spoiling the taste of the beer with blood.

'Why didn't you ring us?' he demanded as soon as Malone came into the kitchen. 'I had to hear it on the wireless, one of my granddaughters finds a dead man in the swimming pool.'

'I was going to ring you, Dad –' He had no excuse, really. He had been too concerned with the assault on his own feelings and those of Lisa and the kids. 'How's Mum?'

'Out of her flaming mind with worry about the kids. About you and Lisa, too,' he added. But Malone knew his mother: she had never learned to show her love for him, her only child, but she shouted her love for her grand-children like a Catholic Holy Roller. 'Lisa rang her and she's gone out to Vaucluse, to the Pretorius place.'

Malone once again recognized Lisa's talent for diplo-macy. She would have known that Brigid Malone would have resented being left out of the comforting of the chil-dren. Brigid was not a mean-spirited woman, but her time was diminishing and any time lost from her grandchildren was time lost forever.

He went to the screen door, looked out at the pool; the tapes were still in place there. He could be thankful that there was no taped outline of Grime's body: the water was crystal-clear of death.

He turned back into the kitchen, got himself a beer from the fridge, poured it into a glass as a gesture to his father and sat down opposite Con. He looked at the old man, once again seeing the tired wildness in the walnut face and the once-muscular frame; Malone knew that only his mother had kept his father out of jail. Con would never have been a criminal, but the Irish in him had always had a contempt for law and order, especially law and order based on any British model. He had hated authority, police, Masons, any conservative politician, Dagos, reffos; now he hated wogs, Asians and any man with long hair and an earring. He couldn't bring himself to believe that lesbians did what he'd heard they did and he had no doubts that poofters deserved what AIDS did to them. He was, in his own opinion, an average Aussie, one of the real natives, not the bloody Abos. Malone loved him, but could never tell him.

'Dad, what's life like on the wharves now? The bloke

we found out there in the pool, he could've worked as a tally clerk.'

'Tally clerks don't work, they're all bludgers.' His net of prejudices was wide. 'Why'd he finish up in your pool?'

'He was working for me. Someone must have resented that.'

'Working – ? You mean he was an informer, a stoolie? Jesus, aint you got any shame? Using a man to dob in someone else.'

Malone said patiently, 'Dad, we do it all the time. You think the crims go in for a code of ethics?'

'They don't dob in their mates. Not the decent ones.'

'How many decent crims do you know? Don't give me any crap, Dad. I've had a bad morning.'

Con Malone gave his form of apology, which was to change the subject: 'About the wharves? They're nothing like they used to be. They're –' he searched for the right word '– they're antiseptic. Yeah, antiseptic. Compared to what they used to be.'

'How much skulduggery went on?'

'Oh, it was dirty, real dirty. There was no guaranteed work when I first started on the wharves, there was just the call-up each morning. The stevedore boss played favourites. Or you were in sweet with the union boss and he saw you got work or there'd be trouble. There were stand-over blokes who ran things, some for the stevedore firms, some for particular union bosses who didn't want any competition at the elections. There were some decent union men at the top, but they had just as hard a battle as the blokes at the bottom.'

'What about smuggling, pillaging, things like that?'

'Oh, that was on for young and old. I did it meself, pillaging, I mean, not smuggling – I never went in for that, that was big-time and too dangerous. Some of the foremen were tied up in the smuggling racket, they were the blokes on site for the big men, the ones who never came near the waterfront, who had nothing to do with the shipping game.

53

Gangsters, big businessmen, there was even one politician in the racket. Drugs, gold, they had it all wrapped up. You must of known all about that?'

'I'd heard about it – Russ Clements was once on the Pillage Squad. But you never mentioned it.'

'Your mum was protecting you. She knew about it, vaguely, and she laid down the law to me that I was never to talk to you about it. By the time you was old enough to talk to, you'd become a copper. How could I talk to you then?' Con Malone asked what he thought was a reasonable question.

Malone agreed with a grin. 'Sure, how could you? How did you fellers work under a foreman who was in on the smuggling?'

'We turned a blind eye. We had to, or else. Foremen were different in them days, few of 'em were popular, we looked on 'em as the bosses' men. We never drank with them after we'd knocked off work, nothing like that.'

'I want to go down to the wharves tomorrow. You know anyone I can see?'

'Roley Bremner,' Con Malone said without hesitation. 'He's been secretary of the New South Wales branch of the WLU for the last ten years and he's as straight as a die. Him and me worked together when he first started. Tell him I sent you. It's a pity you'll have to mention you're a cop.' But he had the grace to grin.

'I'll try and keep it out of the conversation as long as I can.'

Then the phone rang. Malone picked it up. 'Inspector Malone?'

'Who's this?' He had an experienced cop's built-in defence: never identify yourself till you have to or there is some advantage to it.

'Malone,' said the voice, flat but distinct, 'stay in your own paddock. Don't mess around with something that's none of your business. You've had one warning. This is your second and last.'

At 7.30 Tuesday morning, while Malone was preparing breakfast for himself, Lisa returned home with the children.

'I see they've taken down all the decorations.' The blue and white tapes had been removed last night.

'I was going to bring all the girls down from my class.' Maureen, it seemed, had made a full recovery. 'I phoned 'em yesterday from Grandma's. They were going to bring their cameras.'

'Get ready for school before I get my whip out,' said her mother.

When the children, grumbling, had gone into their bedrooms, Malone looked at Lisa. 'You still cranky?'

'Do you blame me? Well, not *cranky*. But yes, I'm – I'm on edge. Are you any closer to finding out who dumped that man in our pool?'

'No.' He had had a restless night, hearing there in the darkness the flat threatening voice. He had called Lisa last night with the intention of telling her not to bring the children home, but as soon as she had spoken, before he had had time to ask how she was, she had told him she was coming home and there was to be no argument. Her voice had had the same flat adamancy as the stranger's: it had had the added adamancy of a wife's voice.

'There's still a police car parked outside. Do we have to have that?'

He spread some marmalade on a slice of cold toast; he could have been eating chopped grass spread on cardboard, for all the taste he had in his mouth. Then, forcing the words out of his mouth, he told her about the phone call and the threat. 'It's either police protection or you go back to your parents.'

She took her time about replying. 'I'm not going to be driven out of my own home.'

'What about the kids?'

'Darling –' She sat down opposite him, leaned forward. Normally she was one of the coolest, calmest women he had ever met, but when she became intense, there was a passion in her that, he had learned from experience, had to be handled carefully. He was no ladies' man, but he was a sensible husband, which is more difficult. 'Darling, the kids *are* my home. You and them – not the house. That's just the shell. When I married you I wasn't marrying a pig in a poke –'

'Just a pig in plainclothes.' He could have bitten his tongue. Jokes, especially feeble ones, should never be fired on a battlefield as dangerous as a domestic.

'Don't joke!' She slammed the table with her fist.

He reached across and put his hand on her wrist; he could feel the tension quivering in her. 'I'm sorry, darl. That slipped out – I'm as on edge as you are –'

She turned her arm, unclenched her fist and took his hand in hers. 'I know. What I was trying to say was, I knew what I was getting into when I married you. I've worried myself sick a dozen times since then, wondering if you were all right. All I've had to hang on to, my rock, if you like, has been *this* –' She waved her free hand about her, but without taking her gaze from his face. 'This house, the children. I can't explain it, maybe only a woman would understand –'

'No, I understand.' And he did; *this* was his rock, too. 'But if you won't leave here, let the kids go. Your parents won't mind having them –' But he could already imagine what his own mother would feel at not being able to take them into the small, narrow house in Erskineville. It was the house in which he had been born and brought up, but it was dark, permeated with the smells of a hundred or more years of bad cooking, sibilant with the sounds of a cistern that never worked properly. It could not be compared with the large house in Vaucluse with the pool and the lush garden and the three guest bedrooms that were always ready for the children's visits. And there would be the Pretoriuses' two cars, ready to bring the children across to school at Randwick each morning. But even as he posed the sensible alternative, he felt he was losing his independence, that somehow he was failing his kids. 'It'll only be for a few days at the most –'

'Then if it's only going to be for a few days, we'll stay together.' She took away her hand. 'We'll have the police protection.'

He knew there was no use in further argument. 'Righto. But I don't want the kids walking to school. Borrow your mother's car and drive them there. One of the uniformed men can go with you.'

'I've already borrowed it, it's outside.'

He might have known. If she were still at home in Holland, she would inspect the dykes daily, never relying on anyone else's word.

3

As he was backing his Commodore out into the street, Keith Cayburn came out of his front gate and approached him. 'We had a meeting of Neighbourhood Watch last night, Scobie. If there's anything we can do . . .'

Form a circle of wagons around my house . . . 'I think everything's under control, Keith. I'm asking for police surveillance for a few days, it's standard procedure.'

Cayburn looked dubiously at the police car at the kerb. He was a lean, tall man with thinning yellow hair and bright blue eyes, that, though not furtive, had a tendency never to be still; perhaps, Malone sometimes thought, it came from his occupation. He was a high-school principal, who looked upon all teenagers as potential evil-doers and so ran a good, tight school. Decency ran through him like a water-mark, but he had no illusions that it ran unbroken through society at large. He warned his students of the worst, yet he had been shocked by what had happened next door in the Malones'.

'It's a bit unsettling, Scobie. Cops camped on your doorstep.'

'I'm not jumping up and down over it, Keith.'

Cayburn was not tone-deaf: he noted the asperity in Malone's voice. 'Scobie, nobody's blaming *you*. It's just – well, it's not something you expect, is it?'

'No,' said Malone. 'No, I didn't expect it.'

'Well, we'll keep an eye out. That's what Neighbourhood Watch is for, isn't it?'

'That's true.' But he wondered if the neighbours would watch or would turn away when the enemy, whoever they were, made their next move. Keeping an eye out for car thieves or house-breakers was one thing; watching for murderers was something else again. 'Things will be back to normal in a day or two, Keith. How's the new year at school facing up?'

'I'll be under-staffed and over-enrolled. The system's going to the dogs. You think you've got problems in the Police Department?' He went off grumbling.

Malone drove into Homicide, left the Commodore and joined Clements in an unmarked car; they headed for Glebe and the City Morgue. 'You hear anything from Doc Keller?'

'I had dinner with her last night, then she went straight back to the morgue. Doc Gaynor gave her permission to work on his stiff, besides working on Grime.'

'Neither of them have AIDS or hepatitis?'

'No.'

'What's it like, taking out a girl who works amongst stiffs all day?'

Clements grimaced. 'She says one or two of the married ones, if they've been working on a decomposed body, say, their husbands make them take two showers and wash their hair twice before they let 'em get into bed with them. The first night I took Romy out, I took her flowers. She

58

said she'd rather have perfume. That answer your question, Inspector?'

'I wish all witnesses were like you.'

'Up yours.'

The City Morgue was on Parramatta Road, running right through to a rear street. Across the main road from it was the entrance to the playing fields of Sydney University; in his youth Malone had played cricket there against the university team, the closest he had ever come to tertiary education. There were no regrets that he had never made it there, but he was determined that none of his three kids would be denied the opportunity. These days education, not love, made the world go round, even if sometimes in the wrong direction.

They were told Dr Keller was working down in the Murder Room. Both detectives knew its location and they went through the long main room where several assistants, in their long white rubber aprons, were at work on corpses. There were sixteen stainless-steel tables, plus sinks, on either side of the main aisle; between each pair of tables was a hanging scale, such as Malone had seen in the local greengrocer's. Blue-barred insect-killers hung from the ceiling like neon honeycomb and half a dozen air-conditioners whirred softly. A mixture of smells clogged the air: chemicals, blood, decomposing flesh. The staff looked up as Malone and Clements walked down the aisle, one or two of them tossing jokes as they leaned on the cadavers on their tables. Malone, a man with a reasonably strong stomach, kept his gaze above table level.

The Murder Room was at the far end of the main room and set off to one side. It was about twenty foot square, its doors lead-lined, a blue-barred insect-zapper on one wall, an X-ray machine above one of the two tables. On the other table, under a large green-domed lamp, lay Scungy Grime, naked, face down.

Romy Keller, in white gown and rubber apron, looked up as they came in. 'I have nothing definite for you yet.

59

Kissen, the other corpse, is outside in the filing cabinet.'
She didn't smile, so Malone guessed that what had once
been a joke was no longer so. 'She has a puncture under
her right buttock, just as our friend here has.' She lifted
the fold of Grime's waxen buttock; the puncture was
barely visible. 'I'm still guessing, but I'd say they both
died from the same means. Injection by an instantaneous
poison, or as near as dammit to instantaneous.'

'Kissen was a drug-user. She couldn't have OD'd?'

'No. When they OD, you usually find the needle somewhere near the body. More often than not, you find it still
stuck in their flesh.' Then she smiled. 'What am I doing?
Teaching my grandmother to suck eggs? You know all
that. No, Kissen didn't kill herself. In fact, I think she
might have been off the heroin for quite a while. But she
was on coke, pretty heavily, I'd say. There's damage to
the nasal membrane.'

Clements said, 'What's your guess on the poison, then?'

'The toxic lab is working on that now. I'm only haz-
arding a guess, but I think they might come up with
alcuronium chloride. It's a synthetic derivative of curare.
It's a muscle relaxant they use in surgery. Given an overdose, there is neuromuscular blockage, respiratory paraly-
sis and cardiovascular collapse, all pretty instantaneously.
Mr Grime and Mrs Kissen would have felt the stab of the
needle and that would have been just about it if the dose
was large enough.'

'Where could anyone get this whatever-it-is?'

'The commercial name is Alloferin. It could be got from
any hospital dispensary or from the hospital's emergency
clinic. It would have to be stolen, it would never be handed
out without authorization.'

'So a doctor or a medical student or a nurse could have
used it to kill Grime and Kissen? Assuming Alfo – Alloferin? – is what was used?'

'In the case of Mrs Kissen, you can eliminate a nurse,
unless it was a male nurse. Just prior to death there'd been

60

intercourse. We found semen in the vagina. I understand Mrs Kissen was on the game?'

Malone nodded. 'Have you kept the semen trace?'

'Yes, in case you pick up a suspect. We can apply a DNA test. The lab is doing a DNA profile on Kissen now.'

'Are you doing one on Grime?'

'There's no point at this stage, he wasn't sexually assaulted. But if we prove both died from alcuronium chloride poisoning, the odds will shorten that they were both murdered by the same person. Unless there's a corps of curare killers roaming around Sydney.'

'Why wouldn't the killer use a condom? Most of the girls insist on it. Unless he was a regular, someone she trusted.'

'Maybe he was a Catholic,' said Clements.

The two Catholics gave him a look that should have laid him out beside Scungy Grime. Malone said to Romy Keller, 'I'd better get him out of here. The atmosphere is getting to him. How do you stand it, day in, day out?'

'I'm hoping for better things.' She took off her rubber apron and followed them out of the Murder Room. 'I'm studying to become a specialist in obstetrics. Bringing people into the world will be a little more rewarding than taking them out of it. Do you want to look at Mrs Kissen?'

'No, thanks.' Malone had had enough of death this morning; it hung in the air, clogging the mind as well as the nose. 'Let me know as soon as you have something definite on the Alloferin, Doc.'

She nodded, then looked at Clements. 'I'm not working this evening, Russ. Come home for dinner.'

'You cooking?'

She smiled. 'No. And I promise to have two showers and wash my hair before you arrive.'

Malone looked at the crumpled Clements. 'And I promise to run a steam iron over him before he leaves Homicide.'

Outside, the two detectives got into the hot oven of the

police car. Heat lay on the city like a yellow blanket; on the outskirts bushfires raged, the horizon in three directions lost in a yellow-grey haze; the roadway shimmered like hard blue water. In the trees in the university grounds the cicadas sang their brittle chorus; in Malone's ear it, and not the splash of surf or the crack of bat on ball, was always the sound of summer. Clements turned on the air-conditioning, another summer sound but artificial and unimpressive.

'Where do we go? Palmer Street or do we stick to Grime?'

'I want to get him cleared up first, if only for Lisa's sake. She's very cranky about her routine being upset.'

'So would I be, and I don't have any kids.'

He made it sound as if Malone were to blame, though the latter said nothing. Guilt made him dumb.

They drove back into the city and down to the head office of the Wharf Labourers Union near the waterfront. It was housed in one of the few narrow-fronted colonial warehouses, converted to offices, that had managed to survive the development of this part of town. Huge glass monoliths towered on either side of it, reflections of huge debts: For Lease signs were plastered on all façades, like great Band-Aids trying to hold the building together till better times returned. The WLU building sat amongst them looking smug and old-fashioned. Once it had stood right across the road from the wharves; now it peered under an elevated bypass at a car park and, beyond it, a sliver of water that looked narrow enough to hold only a canoe. A union flag hung limp as a dishcloth from a pole on the roof, a banner of other, more militant days.

Roley Bremner recognized them for cops as soon as they appeared in his office doorway, but he forgave them as soon as Malone mentioned he was Con Malone's son. 'Salt of the bloody earth! He was a cantankerous old bastard, even when he was young, but a real good union man. Never let anyone stand over him. I remember him telling me when you become a cop. Never felt so ashamed in his life, he said.'

He was short, only a little more than five foot high and almost as wide; one got the impression that he had been rolled into a ball of muscle and bowled out into life. He had a round head, bald but for fringes of ginger-grey hair along his temples, and his face seemed to be a collection of smaller balls fitted in as cheeks, brows, nose and chin. He had a hoarse gravelly voice and bright blue eyes that looked as if they could see right through any fog that blew up from the harbour.

'Normie Grime? Yeah, I knew him. Not well, but he come up here once or twice to pay his dues while I was here. He's dead? *Murdered?* How? In your swimming pool? You mean, at your *home?* Jesus, that don't bear thinking about!' He sat back in a battered old swivel-chair. The office was small, its walls plastered with posters of old battles, like regimental battle-flags. The whole building creaked with the arthritis of militancy that had outlived its time. A fan, standing on a filing cab, whirred slowly and metallically, like a pacemaker trying to keep the spirit, if not the place, alive. Bremner said, 'In a way I'm not surprised. I mean, Grime being done in.'

Malone and Clements had sat down on chairs as rickety as Bremner's own. 'What do you mean by that?'

'I just didn't expect it to get so drastic so soon.' Bremner seemed to be talking to himself, collecting his thoughts like lottery marbles in the ball of his head. 'I didn't think Grime was connected to it. He never struck me as the political type, not even a good union man. Or was he a crim?'

'Yes.' Malone showed his usual patience. 'Connected to what?'

'Oh, you wouldn't know about it, would you?' Bremner focused his gaze on the two detectives, coming back from his reverie. 'There's a union election coming up next month.'

'You think Grime might've been mixed up in that?'

'If he was, he never give me any hint.'

'How'd he get a ticket to work on the wharves?' Malone knew, from what his father had told him, that a union ticket to work on the wharves was almost an inheritance, handed down from father to son in many cases.

Bremner hesitated a moment; then: 'Word come down from United Unions Hall, we had to find a job for him.'

United Unions Hall was the secular Vatican; its alumnae were spread throughout union and political offices in the State. Con Malone, when he was still working down here, used to bless himself when its name was mentioned. It had led the fight for labour in the past, but its power had waned in recent years. There were, however, still powerful men in State and Federal Labor politics who had learned their skills in the corridors and offices of United Unions Hall.

Malone looked at Clements. 'The little bugger had more clout than I thought.' He looked back at Bremner. 'Had he worked on the wharves before?'

Bremner got up, went out of the room and in a couple of minutes was back with a manila file. 'We got computers, but I don't trust 'em, they're always breaking down. Besides that, outsiders can hack into 'em, you're not careful.' He opened the file, looked at the one page it contained. 'Yeah, here it is. Grime worked on the wharves in Melbourne nineteen seventy-two to nineteen seventy-four.'

So *up here* was Sydney and *down there* was Melbourne, not Port Botany. 'Do the initials S.W. mean anything to you?'

The balls of Bremner's face rolled together, then the eyes lit up; but with alarm, it seemed, not excitement. He sat up, the chair cracking under him like a gunshot. 'That'd be Snow White! His name's Dallas White, but he's known as Snow. He's one of the ex-Melbourne push, he's running against me for secretary. He's spending money like water, Christ knows where he gets it from.'

64

'The Melbourne push? Who are they?'

'They started drifting up this way six or eight months ago. They worked on the Melbourne wharves, they're crims every bloody one of 'em. They've all got records. I done me best to keep 'em outa Sydney, but like with Grime, the word come down from Unions Hall, our Federal headquarters stepped in and I was told to pull my head in.'

He abruptly got up, came round past the two detectives, shut the door and returned to his seat. The small room was suddenly thick with secrets, like long-dormant dust that had been disturbed.

'It's building up to be a re-run of the old days, like it was when your old man worked down here, Scobie. I thought them days were gone forever . . .' He stared into space again for a moment, as if forgetting he was not alone. Then he looked at Malone and Clements again. 'It used to get pretty ugly in them days sometimes, but you knew what you were up against. It was either the Commos or the Groupers, the Catholics, or you were up against the bosses. Now I dunno who I'm up against. This bunch of crims from down south want to take over the waterfront up here, but someone's organizing 'em and we dunno who.'

'Where could we find White?'

The balls rolled into a smile full of cheerful malice. 'I keep tabs on him. He's working on Number 9 wharf. He's there with The Dwarf.'

'A dwarf?'

'Wait till you see him.' Bremner stood up, the chair cracking once more like a gunshot, and held out his hand. 'Don't tell Snow White I sent you. But if you arrest the bastard, lemme know. It'll make my day. Give my regards to your old man. He was a real terror in his day, y'know. Drop a crane hook on a boss or foreman, soon as look at him. Great union man.'

Malone and Clements drove round to Nickson Road. The wharves lined the western side of the roadway; on the eastern side were the hill and cliff-faces that led up to the central business district. There were few major cities in the world where the country's imports were dumped on the doorstep of those expected to pay for them; in the glass castles along the top of the hill executives stared morosely down at their growing debt. Champagne had been drunk in those castles two or three years ago; now they were drinking mineral water. Domestic, of course.

Malone flashed his badge at the gatekeeper on Number 9 wharf and they drove on to the big expanse, like a concrete field, where containers were stacked three storeys high like townhouses in which the builders had forgotten to insert doors and windows. Three large container ships were moored dockside, stretching through to the neighbouring wharves. A giant yellow mobile crane, looking large enough to lift the national debt, loomed over the police car as it came round the corner of a stack of containers. Clements braked sharply, throwing Malone against his seat-belt. Two men abruptly appeared from between the containers: Malone's quick impression was that they had been lurking there like muggers.

'Where the fuck you think you're going?'

Malone got out of the car, waited till the crane inched its way past them, then he showed his badge and introduced himself. 'Where can I find Snow White?'

'You've found him.' He looked middle-aged, but it was a look that might have been with him since he had left school. The brown eyes were old and cunning, the lines in the cheeks like chisel-marks in leather, the mouth a brutal line above the pugnacious jaw. He had dark hair cut short back-and-sides and ears that lay along his head like a faun's, the only soft note about his whole appearance. He was of medium height and bulged with muscle, the result, Malone guessed, of many work-outs in prison yards. 'What's on your mind?'

Malone looked at the huge man beside White. He was about two metres tall and seemed all body and limbs; his tiny head sat on his wide shoulders like an afterthought at birth, something stuck on when the doctor had discovered the newborn infant was incomplete. The small face still had a baby look to it, blank but for a permanent frown of puzzlement between the small blue eyes. Malone guessed that The Dwarf would have a one-track mind: two thoughts at the same time in that small head would only cause a traffic jam. Snow White would do the thinking for them. 'Your name is – ?'

The Dwarf hesitated, as if the question had baffled him, then he said in a surprisingly soft voice, like a girl's, 'I'm Gary Schultz.'

'What's this about?' said White, whose voice was anything but girlish; it had the threat of fists or even worse behind it.

'Did you know a man, a tally clerk, named Normie Grime?'

'No,' said The Dwarf, quick off the mark for once.

White glanced at him, the mouth tightening still further till the thin lips disappeared; then he looked back at Malone. 'Gary's forgotten. Yeah, we knew him. We worked with him once on a job over at Walsh Bay.'

'When did you last see him?'

'I dunno. Before Christmas, maybe, I dunno. What's up with him?'

'He's dead,' said Malone, 'that's what's up with him. Murdered.'

The four men were silent for a moment. Beyond their circle there was the rattle of a chain, a man's shouting, the hum of a fork-lift as it sped past. Heat came up from the concrete in an eye-searing blaze, was reflected off the red metal containers, pressed down from the glaring sky; Malone could feel himself being boiled and shrunken by it, his skin closing up, suffocating him. Between the bow of one ship and the stern of another he caught a glimpse of water, but it looked like burning glass. This summer

Lisa had insisted he start wearing a hat, he was developing sun cancers on his cheeks, but he had left the hat in the car. A gull flew overhead, mewing harshly like an Outback crow.

Then White said, 'What's it got to do with us?'

'We thought you might be interested,' said Clements, taking over the bowling. 'We understand he came from Melbourne, the same as you.'

'There's about three million people come from Melbourne. We dunno most of 'em. What sorta shit are youse trying to lay on us?'

'How come you can run for union office with a criminal record? You've done time, right?'

'I been rehabilitated,' said White, and beside him a slow grin spread across The Dwarf's baby face. 'My probation officer got me a second chance.'

'Who's your probation officer?'

'He's dead,' said White, and the smile on The Dwarf's face was now fixed like a scar. 'The poor bugger just give up and died. I got word only a week ago. He come from Melbourne, too, one of the three million.'

The heat and White's insolence were getting to Malone; but he kept the lid on himself. 'We want you, we can always get you through the WLU, right?'

'Next month I'll be the secretary, sitting right there in the offices. Drop in. You won't be welcome, but drop in anyway.'

Malone got back into the car and Clements went round to get in on the other side. He paused and looked across the pale grey glare of the roof at The Dwarf. 'You running for office, too?'

The giant widened his grin. 'Nah, I'm just Snow's campaign manager. I'll help count the votes when they come in.'

'Is there gunna be any need for that? I thought bastards like you would have the votes already counted.'

As they drove away Clements looked as if he might snap

68

the steering wheel with his furious hands. 'Jesus, how are they let run loose?'

'You heard the man. Rehabilitation. It's bullshit, of course, but they're getting away with it. But I don't want us getting mixed up in union politics, we've got enough on our hands. What d'you think? You think they had anything to do with Scungy's murder?'

'I dunno. The Dwarf looks big enough to have carted Scungy into your place under one arm. But you notice his feet? Tiny, at least for his size. Wayne Murrow said the heel-print in the lawn in your side passage was that of a big shoe, he guessed it might've been a size eleven or twelve. It was hard to tell whether Snow White has big feet. He was wearing the sorta boots builders' labourers wear, they always look big.'

As so often in the past, Malone was grateful for his offsider's eye for detail. 'What else did you notice?'

'Those containers where they came out from. They were all marked with red triangles – that means it's dangerous cargo. I remember from the days when I was with Pillage. There are three classes, marked by numbers. Class One would be explosives, ammo, whisky –'

'*Whisky?*'

'Sure. It's been known to blow up. Maybe I'm over-suspicious, just because they're crims. But why would they be marking containers with yellow chalk, which was what they were doing, when the containers have already been unloaded?'

'Maybe they were marking them for the delivery trucks?'

'Unless they've changed the system, the tally clerks do that. Neither of those guys is a tally clerk. In the old days when I worked on Pillage, before containers were used, stuff used to disappear off the wharves like a magical act. Whisky was always a target because it was easy to get rid of once it was outside. A shonky pub owner would buy a case half-price and both him and the bloke who'd swiped it would be happy. Think of the profit, you pinch a container full of it. If the containers are full of explosives or ammo cargo, that's a heist I'd rather not think about.'

'If Scungy knew they were pinching that sort of stuff, he'd never have told me. He hated giving me any information, even about the drug racket – I had to lean on him. He wasn't a natural-born nark.'

'So what d'you think? They found out he was working for you and got rid of him?'

'Maybe. Probably. I'm just puzzled why they chose to do it with a needle in his bum. That doesn't look their style. They'd do him with a gun or an iron bar, they're the sort who like the look of blood.'

'If either of them did it, why use the same MO on the Kissen woman? You think he, Snow White or The Dwarf, got kinky and thinks he's discovered a new way of bumping off people? I seem to remember they kill each other off with curare in the Amazon jungle, but it'd be new to Sydney.'

They drove up through the city and over to Palmer Street. Only when they got there did Malone realize that Sally Kissen had lived within half a dozen blocks of Scungy Grime. Clement parked in a lane off the busy street, which carried a steady stream of fast-moving traffic towards the Cahill Expressway and the Harbour Bridge. Palmer Street had been named after the shipping merchant who had built up the surrounding area. Long after his death the street had become famous for its brothels and sly-grog shops, two sources of income the merchant had overlooked. The pace of the city and progress had now put paid to those businesses: the prostitutes now worked William Street, just up the road, but they saluted the flag of history by renting rooms in houses like Sally Kissen's.

The Crime Scene tapes had been removed from the front of the house, but a uniformed policeman stood in the meagre shade of the front verandah. 'Anyone inside?' Malone asked.

'Two girls,' said the policeman. 'They claim they're just boarders, but I've seen 'em up the road, on the game.'

Malone and Clements went through the narrow hallway and into the living room. Sally Kissen would have won no prizes from *House and Garden* as a decorator; the room seemed to have been furnished from stalls at the Annual Kitsch Fair. There was a purple-and-red-striped lounge suite; a brass-topped coffee table and two brass sidetables; a 1920s drinks cabinet that opened out to show a mirrored back and, Malone guessed, probably played a musical fanfare; and a Persian rug that looked as if it might have come from a Teheran rubbish dump. There were two paintings on the walls of female nudes, painted, it seemed, by a misogynistic artist. The final touch, which Malone couldn't bring himself to believe, was three bright orange plaster ducks flying up one wall to the high blue yonder of the peeling ceiling. Sally Kissen had had either wacky taste or a wacky sense of humour.

The two girls sitting in the living room, drinking coffee and munching cookies, went with the room. One had hair so red her head looked as if it were on fire; the other had bleached hers bone-white. They were in black tights and green shirts, open down to the waist and with the sleeves rolled down. They wore no make-up and they looked plain and pale. One had to look twice to see that both of them actually had good features, but the game and their habit had blurred the edges. The rolled-down sleeves told Malone they were probably junkies.

'Those bickies Iced Vo-Vos?' he said.

'Yeah.' The redhead nodded, her spiky hair shivering; it was like watching a flame quivering in a breeze. 'They was Sally's favourites. Waddia wanna know? We know nothing – we told the other guys that. You just come back to do the heavy on us.'

'Where were you the night before last?' Malone sat down in one of the purple and red chairs. He noticed that at least the room was clean; Sally Kissen had been a good housekeeper.

'Out,' said the blonde. Her hair was long, brushed back and hanging down her back. She had a better voice than the other girl, not as harsh and with the vowels more rounded. 'We were at a party, we didn't get home till six yesterday morning.'

'You've got witnesses who'll back you up?'

The girls looked at each other; then the blonde said, 'No, I don't suppose so. They were boys down from the country.'

'Clients?' said Clements. The blonde nodded and he went on, 'Was the party at some hotel?'

'Yes.' The blonde was the intelligent one and the red-head seemed content to let her do the talking. 'Look, we had nothing to do with this. It's upsetting enough to know Sally is dead. We don't even know why she died.'

Malone told her.

'You mean she was *murdered*?' The redhead sat with her mouth open, a biscuit crumb on her bottom lip.

'We're not saying you had anything to do with it – we're just trying to clear it up. What are your names?'

The redhead blinked, licked the crumb from her lip. 'I'm Tuesday Streep.'

'Ava Redgrave,' said the blonde.

'You ever been in movies? You look familiar.'

'Just art films.' The blonde smiled, a mistake, since she had a lower front tooth missing. But she had a sense of humour and Malone wondered what she thought of Sally Kissen's taste. 'I don't think they'd be your cup of tea.'

'No. I like Bugs Bunny.'

Clements went upstairs to look at the actual scene of the crime and Malone stayed with the girls, accepting an Iced Vo-Vo when Tuesday passed him the plate, but declining a cup of coffee. 'Did Mrs Kissen have any regular male visitors?'

'We dunno, honest.' Tuesday, satisfied that Malone was

not going to book them, was prepared to be more forth-coming. 'She never really liked to admit to us she was on the game. She was funny, in a way.'

'She was a snob, believe it or not,' said Ava. 'She said she'd never worked the streets, like we do.'

'Where do you come from?'

'From the country.' He should have picked up the slight bush drawl in her voice. She hesitated, then added, 'Wagga.'

'What about you, Tuesday?'

The redhead looked at Ava, then she said, 'Melbourne. But that's all I'm telling.'

'Both of you, do your parents know you're on the game?'

The two girls shook their heads, then Ava said, 'We're both over twenty-one.'

You look it, he thought. 'Where do you buy your junk?'

'What junk?'

'Come on,' said Malone wearily, nodding at the rolled-down sleeves. 'I've got enough on my plate without doing the Drug Unit's job. I'm trying to find a murderer. You don't want him coming back here, do you?'

'You put it like that –' Ava rubbed her arm; Malone wondered how many needle-marks were hidden there under the sleeves and on other parts of her body. 'We buy it from a guy up the Cross. But Sally didn't use it. She used to, but she gave it up, she said, a coupla years ago. She was on coke, though, but I don't know where she got it. Maybe the guy who killed her.' All at once she shivered, as if for the first time she realized the murderer might come back to this house. She looked at Tuesday. 'I think we better move out.'

'If you do,' said Malone, 'I'll want to know where I can find you. And I don't mean up on your beat in William Street. That's no address.'

'Why d'you have to bother us?' said Tuesday, a whine in her voice.

Malone shrugged. 'We didn't start this, love. The cove who stuck the needle in her did that.'

Then Clements came back downstairs. 'If there was anything up there, the Crime Scene guys would have picked it up. Unless the murderer cleaned the place out first. You girls dunno if Mrs Kissen kept a diary or anything, do you? An appointment book?'

'An appointment book?' Ava looked at him. 'What d'you think this is – the Quality Couch?' That was the city's top brothel, where clients could run an account and regulars were given bonus sex as a Christmas gift. 'I dunno if she kept a diary. She was kind of funny, like Tuesday said. Sometimes she'd talk with us, sort of reminisce. Other times she was like a brick wall. I don't think she was the sort to keep a diary.'

Then abruptly she stood up, an ungainly movement; she was taller than Malone had expected and she moved with that awkwardness he had seen in some tall women. She went out of the room and when she came back she was carrying a wall calendar.

'Sally used to make notes on this. I dunno if it'll help.'

It was a calendar about eighteen inches square with a separate fold-up page for each month. Each page was an illustration, the male equivalent of a *Penthouse* centrefold. Malone wondered that Sally Kissen, in her trade, had any time for men; or were these the sort of clients she dreamed about? Mr January, one hand placed strategically, smiled coyly at Malone. Below the oil-glistening beefcake, on the calendar itself, several dates were ringed and initialled. Sunday, the day before yesterday, was initialled A.H. and so was the previous Sunday. A.H., it seemed, liked to get the week's dirty water off his chest before starting a new week. Malone wondered if Mrs Kissen charged double-time for weekend work. There had been an attempt to form a prostitutes' union and he remembered now that Sally Kissen had been one of the spokeswomen for it He couldn't remember whether she had advocated penalty rates.

'You any idea who A.H. might be?'

Both girls looked at the calendar, seemingly oblivious of the male flesh exposed to them. 'Mostly, we were never here when she let her visitors in – she tried to keep 'em out of our way. It was her snobbery bit again. She didn't have much time for the way we have to work. She was one of the old-time pros, but they didn't have to work the streets the way we do – she always worked out of a house, she said. There's too much competition now. We've practically got to strip naked up there in William Street to attract customers. It's okay in this weather, but it's no fun in winter, standing around freezing your arse off.'

'You could buy a fur coat,' said Clements. 'Wear nothing under it and just flash it when the customers go by.'

'Who's got enough left over to buy a fur coat?'

After I've paid for my habit: Malone finished her remark in his mind. He wondered what had brought this girl to this neighbourhood and line of work, wondered what her parents, secure and comfortable in Wagga Wagga or out on a neighbouring property, thought of this end to their hopes. He shut his mind against the thought that any of his own children might some day let him and Lisa down. Which was stupid, he knew: the shut mind was worse than a shut door.

'Do you have a pimp?'

Tuesday looked blank; Ava looked offended. 'We don't like that word.'

'Righto, choose your own word. Bludger? Ponce?'

'Tuesday has a boyfriend. He looks after us, occasionally.'

'Just occasionally?'

'Yes.' The atmosphere was noticeably cooler. Why, Malone wondered not for the first time, were women so defensive of their men, even those who made slaves of them? But no amount of detective work would ever give him a satisfactory answer. Lisa had told him so, giving him no clues.

'What's his name and where does he live?'

'Why d'you wanna know that?' Tuesday demanded; her red hair seemed more fiery. 'Leave him outa this!'

Malone said mildly, 'I only thought he might like to move in here with you, just for safety's sake. *Your* safety.'

'We're moving out. We'll move in with Leroy, he's got room.' Ava looked at Tuesday, who blinked, then frowned, as if she did not like the idea.

'Leroy who?' said Clements. 'If he's got a record, we can easily check on him. There wouldn't be too many Leroys who are pimps.'

Tuesday flashed him a look of hatred; the temporary harmony was gone, it was *you* and *us* again. 'You really are shits, aint you?'

'I guess so,' said Clements, looking unoffended; he had heard it so many times before. 'But so's Leroy. Now where can we find him?'

Tuesday looked at Ava, who said, 'You better tell 'em, honey, otherwise they'll never get off our backs.'

Tuesday hesitated, then she gave Clements an address in Bondi, ten minutes' drive away. 'His name's Leroy Lugos. But don't tell him who gave you the address.'

Malone stood up. 'If any feller comes here asking for Mrs Kissen, don't let him in. Try and remember what he looks like, then phone us. Here's my card.'

'If he murdered Sally,' said Ava, 'why would he come back?'

'To do the same to you,' said Malone and picked up the last Iced Vo-Vo from the plate on the brass coffee table. 'Mind if I have this? They're my favourite bickie.'

'Shove it up your arse,' said Tuesday.

There was a crude retort to that, but Malone let it go. He alternated between anger and pity for girls like these two; he had decided there was nothing to be done for them. They supplied a commodity that had been in demand since Adam got the first erection. Most cops no longer took any notice of the soliciting laws and left the girls alone; the few who had hang-ups about commercial sex, the poofter-bashers, now got their work-out grabbing homosexuals in public toilets.

The two detectives drove out to Bondi Beach. Clements parked the car and they got out, turning their faces to the nor'easter that had suddenly sprung up and was coming in across the sea. They left their jackets in the car and walked across to the promenade. Malone had put on his hat, a grey-green pork-pie that, if elderly crims had walked by, or even his father, would have identified him as a plain-clothes man of the late 1940s; the Ds of those days had all worn pork-pie hats, like a uniform. But Malone had just been born then, didn't know what even a uniformed cop was.

Far out sea and sky seemed to merge; the horizon was just a faint pencil-mark. The surf was rising, shark-toothed waves rolling in. Though it was Tuesday, a supposed working-day and the annual summer holidays over, the long white beach was crowded. The recession had been creeping, like salt erosion, over the country since the middle of last year; lately, its bite had increased and thousands more had been thrown out of work. In the good times that had lasted for so long, the Bumper Years, as sentimental economists, a contradiction in terms, were now calling them, the beaches had been populated only by waiters, night-shift workers and the dole-bludgers who worked harder at polishing their surf-board technique than they did at looking for a job. Today, Malone guessed, more than half the beach's population would be on the dole, though not as bludgers. They lay on the hot sand being eaten into by melanoma and hopelessness. There were two generations of voters who had to learn that 'tighten your belt' was not something you did after a course of aerobics.

'The Lucky Country,' said Clements sourly. 'You

reckon any of them are thinking about the Gulf war?'

'Are you?' He had looked at the headlines this morning, but had already forgotten them. 'Let's go and talk to Lee-roy.'

The address they had been given was a coffee lounge and café across from the promenade, the Larissa. It was clean and attractive and cool inside; and popular, too, judging by the number of customers at the tables. Malone and Clements walked down to the rear of the long marble serving counter and told the girl who came to take their order that they would like to talk to the owner. She went back up the counter to the man on the cash register, who frowned, then came down to the two detectives.

'We're looking for Leroy Lugos,' said Malone.

'You police? Ah.' He was middle-aged, fleshily handsome; he might have been on his way to being a Greek god when young, but indulgence had got in the way. There was just a trace of accent in his thick voice, but otherwise he was all-Aussie: he was suspicious of police. Or maybe he had been suspicious of police back in Athens or Larissa or wherever. 'I aint seen him today. He could be over on the beach.'

'He could be,' Clements agreed. 'Would you like to close up the shop for ten minutes and come over to the beach and pick him out for us?'

'You wouldn't expect me to do that! Close up the place?'

'I think he would,' said Malone. 'He's a real bastard on hot days.'

The café owner looked at them; then he sighed and nodded. 'That's him in the back booth. The one in the blue T-shirt.'

'Thanks,' said Malone. 'Could we have two iced coffees down there?'

'On the house?'

'Why not? We're both corrupt.'

They moved down to the back booth, where Leroy Lugos sat with two youths both younger than he. Clements told them he and Inspector Malone would like to talk to Mr Lugos alone and, after a worried glance at Lugos, they got up and moved up to the front of the café. The two detectives slid into the booth opposite Lugos.

'What's this about?' It was a polite question, no belligerence.

'You're Leroy Lugos. Lee-roy – that your real name?' Clements had taken out his notebook.

'Leroy is an American name,' said Malone. 'You don't hear it much out here. Your mother or father American?'

'No, I chose it myself.' He was still polite, if strained.

'You didn't like the name your parents chose?' This was fencing stuff, but Malone was prepared to take his time.

'Ulysses? Would you like it?'

Malone grinned and shook his head; and Clements said, 'Did you choose Lugos, too? It wouldn't have been Lugopolous, would it? I saw it over the door when we came in.'

Lugos hesitated, then nodded. 'Okay. Ulysses Lugopolous. Who'd believe it and how far would I get with it, a wog moniker like that? Are you sympathetic to wogs?'

'All the time,' said Malone.

He wondered if Lugos really was Tuesday's boyfriend besides being her pimp; he seemed too intelligent, too particular. He was in his early twenties, good-looking, black hair expensively cut, dressed in a T-shirt and jeans that would have cost more than Malone's polyester suit. He had an amiable look to his thin, handsome face; but it was a mask, there was a sharpness behind the easy smile and the amused eyes. He would never be a Greek god, there was no money to be made on Mount Olympus.

'You know Mrs Kissen is dead?'

'Who's she?'

Malone patiently told him. 'You mean your girlfriend Tuesday didn't ring you to tell you what happened? You didn't see her last night and she told you then?'

Lugos sipped on a Coke, waiting while the two

79

detectives took their iced coffees from the girl who brought them. One hand went to the gold chain and cross round his neck; one wrist wore a thick gold bracelet and the other a gold-banded watch. Malone wondered if he ran not just Ava and Tuesday but a stable of girls.

'Yeah,' he said at last, 'she told me.'

'It doesn't upset you?'

'Why should it?' He was less polite now. 'I hardly knew her.'

'The same thing could happen to one of your girls.'

Before he spoke Clements had made a sucking noise through his drinking-straw, an angry gasp. Malone recognized the symptoms: the big man was ready to get rough with Lugos. Malone leaned back, glanced under the table: Lugos wore Reeboks with no socks. Malone was willing to bet that, when they stood up, Clements would tread on one of the Reeboks, accidentally of course, and Lugos would suffer a badly bruised instep or even a broken toe. Clements, who had played rugby when he was a youth, knew the use of a heavy boot in a ruck.

'What do you do for a living?' Malone asked.

'I'm unemployed. Isn't everyone?' He was becoming cheeky now. 'There's a recession on, but I don't suppose you cops notice the difference. You're never made redundant, right?'

'It's part of the perks,' said Malone coolly, while beside him he could feel Clements shifting like a water buffalo getting ready to charge. 'So you're on the dole?'

'No, I'm living on capital. I'm independent, I don't believe in the welfare state.'

'Does Tuesday contribute towards your independence?'

Lugos finished his Coke, pushed the glass away from him and sat back. Above his head was a poster inviting you to the Greek isles; they belonged to the past, which is becoming increasingly like everyone's idea of heaven. But Lugos didn't belong there, he belonged here in Sydney, in the present of the quick buck for sex and anything else that could be traded. Malone decided that he would check as soon as they got back to Homicide on whether Lugos had a record. Whether he had one or not, he was not an honest citizen, independent or otherwise.

'Look, what's the point of all this? Are you trying to pick me up for pimping? No way, mate. I'm just a friend of Tuesday's and that's all.'

'Were you a friend of Mrs Kissen's?' said Clements, voice thick with iced coffee and suppressed anger. 'You offer her protection or anything?'

Lugos succeeded in looking bored; he ran the hand with the gold manacle over his thick hair. 'Look, you're wasting your time. I know nothing and I got nothing to hide. Now excuse me, I gotta go.'

'Just another question or two,' said Malone. 'Do you supply Tuesday and Ava with heroin?'

Lugos looked at him with feigned amusement; but his acting wasn't quite good enough. 'You don't expect me to answer that, do you?'

'You just have.'

The feigned amusement turned to real anger; abruptly he said, 'Get stuffed!'

He slid out of the booth, but he was a little slow; Clements stood on his instep as he, too, got up. 'Geez, I'm sorry. My feet are always getting me into trouble.'

Lugos winced and his face darkened; he kept his temper, but only just. 'What's next? Your fist gunna slip into my face?'

'We're subtler than that,' said Malone. 'We'd like your home address.'

'You can always find me here. That's my uncle, the owner.'

'Some time, we might like to see you in private. If we had to arrest you, you wouldn't want us to do it in public, would you?'

'Arrest me? What for?' Lugos' voice cracked.

'Murder. How'd you like that one?' It was bluff, but that is not a legal offence.

'You're fucking crazy!' Then Lugos became aware that the crowded café was an interested audience. In the next booth were four rock musicians; they turned their dark glasses towards Lugos and the two detectives, like four fake blind men who'd heard coins rolling down the aisle. Lugos dropped his voice and gave an address, a block of flats at the southern end of the beach. 'I tell you, you're picking on me because I'm a wog, right? You're all the fucking same –'

'Try your luck with the Discrimination Board,' said Malone. 'Here's my card.'

Lugos snatched the card, turned abruptly and went limping up through the café and out into the bright glare of the street. Clements looked at the black stare of the four pairs of dark glasses.

'Who's your lead singer? A seeing-eye dog?'

He was in a mood to wreck the place. He followed Malone out of the café in time to see Lugos get into a bright red Porsche and screech away from the kerb.

'You think he might drive off a cliff?' said Clements hopefully.

CHAPTER THREE

I

The Keller flat was the upper half of a two-storeyed Edwardian house in Glebe. The area had once been called The Glebe: a year after the establishment of the colony of Sydney four hundred acres of harbourside land had been granted to a clergyman as part of his benefice. Now it was mostly populated by academics and students from the nearby university, a godless lot; long neglected and run-down, it had over the past twenty years become gentrified. Its narrow main street was lined with tiny art galleries, bookshops, health stores. and cafés where it was possible to order everything but a good old Aussie pie or sausage roll. The locals sat in the cafés and discussed the latest Almodovar or Bertolucci film, then donned dark glasses and turned up their coat collars and drove out to the suburbs to see fluff like *Pretty Woman*. It took courage, or to have been born there, to be a low-brow in Glebe.

The Kellers' street was pleasant and tree-lined. The house was decorated with ornate brickwork and iron lace; a jacaranda stood to one side, a green carport for Romy's Toyota. The front lawn was neatly trimmed and hydrangeas were a purple wave breaking against the base of the house.

'I look after the garden,' said Peter Keller. 'The owner thinks grass cuts itself. Knows nothing of Nature, doesn't care.'

'He teaches history at Sydney,' said Romy from the kitchen doorway.

'An associate professor of Australian history,' said

Keller. 'A joke. How much history has Australia had?'

'More than enough for me,' said Clements, wondering if the older man had a sense of humour but doubting it. 'I never got better than fifty per cent in exams in history.'

'I wanted to go to university to study history, but I never had the opportunity.' Keller's English was good but stilted; which was surprising, since he had told Clements he had first learned it from US Occupation troops in Germany after World War Two. He never used any of the slang, no matter how dated, that Clements had expected. 'I was very happy when Romy went to university. Even though it was here in Sydney.' He made it sound as if she had studied in Addis Ababa.

Clements, a generous man, had brought lobster and king prawns and Romy was preparing them and a salad while he and her father sat in the high-ceilinged living room and drank German pilsner. The walls were decorated with steel engravings of nineteenth-century villages and landscapes, with operatic clouds boiling up in the grey skies and giving the impression that if a gramophone needle were applied to the scratchings, a Wagnerian piece would boom out. The furniture was heavy and dark and seemed to be sprouting wooden grapes at every corner. There was no wall-to-wall carpet, but a huge thick rug was laid on polished floorboards, a rug decorated with a lush pastoral scene; Clements' heel rested in the ample navel of a dryad. The Kellers had brought all their furniture with them when they had emigrated to Australia ten years ago and it seemed that Romy had had no opportunity to add any decorative notes of her own. Unless she, too, was homesick for Bavaria.

'It was Romy's mother's idea we should come to Australia. She was Austrian, not German, from the Tyrol. She wanted sunshine all the time. She went once to Spain for a holiday and fell in love with sunshine. She read about Australia, sunshine all the time, so we came. She died two years after we got here. Heat stroke.' He said it without irony or bitterness. Clements didn't know how to respond, so sat silent. 'I wanted to go back to Germany, but Romy was at university, she insisted we stay. I was cursed with strong-willed women.'

'Aren't we all?' said Clements, who had managed to avoid them all his life but felt he had to say something.

Keller didn't smile: Clements could only imagine that Romy had inherited *her* sense of humour from her mother. 'Do you like women?'

'Yes.' Clements saw, through the kitchen doorway, that Romy had paused to listen to his answer. Then she smiled and went back to slicing a red pepper into the salad.

'What do you feel when you have to arrest a woman for a crime?'

Out of the corner of his eye Clements saw that Romy had paused again; he took his time before saying, 'I don't enjoy it. How did you feel?'

Keller, too, took his time. 'I once arrested a woman who killed her three children. I did not sleep for three nights.' He abruptly stood up. 'I think it is time to eat.'

The dining table was at the end of the big living room. Keller opened a bottle of German Riesling, which Clements found too sweet for his taste but at which he smacked his lips and nodded in approval. 'Romy tells me you are working together on two murders?'

'Father, do we have to talk shop at dinner?'

'Do you mind talking shop, Sergeant?'

'Not so long as we don't go into details,' said Clements, mouth full of lobster, memory full of dead humans. 'And call me Russ, I'm off-duty.'

'I grew up talking shop, as you call it. I was ten years old when the war, *our* war, ended. Too young to be in the Hitler Youth, thank God.' It came out as *Gott*, as if his tongue had slipped back all those years. His voice had a defensive note to it, but Clements wasn't sure if he had picked it correctly; Keller had his head bent over his plate.

'I ran messages for the Americans. I was born in Garmisch-Partenkirchen and we were in the American Occupation zone.'

He had told all this to Clements before; but those years were a blank in history's pages for the Australian. He had been born in the Dark Ages, the late 1940s, and nobody he knew, not even his parents in the country, ever seemed to talk about those years.

'I ran messages mostly for an MP, a military policeman. He came from Chicago, he had been a police sergeant before the war. He knew all the gangsters, Al Capone, all of them. I wanted to be a policeman from the day I met Sergeant Lemke. But I never met any gangsters.' He looked up and smiled, the first time he had smiled all evening. 'Just ordinary people.'

Clements wondered how ordinary the woman had been who had murdered her three children.

'Who do you think committed the murders you are investigating? Ordinary people or gangsters?'

Clements drank some of the too-fruity wine. 'I dunno. I don't think it was an ordinary person.'

'The lab has established it was alcuronium chloride,' said Romy. 'I was going to tell you officially tomorrow.'

'What's that?' said her father.

'An artificial derivative of curare.'

'Very clever. Or are you looking for an Amazonian Indian who has emigrated to Australia?' Keller smiled again. 'You see? I know where it comes from. They use a blowpipe to shoot darts –' He pursed his lips and blew out. 'I saw it in a movie. We learn so much about killing from movies and television. Sometimes I think film directors are frustrated murderers.'

'Perhaps it has to do with working with actors.' Romy also smiled, all at once looking like her father's daughter, a resemblance Clements had not noticed up till now.

'We had a poison murder once in Starnheim,' said Keller.

Clements looked enquiringly at Romy, who said, 'That was where I was born, where we lived. It's not far from München. Munich,' she translated for his benefit. 'It had about twenty thousand people in it when we left. It was famous for its brewery and that was about all. Oh, we had our share of zealous Nazis. My grandfather was one.' She appeared to have to concentrate all her attention on drawing the sweet meat out of a lobster claw.

'This is not the time to discuss such things.' Keller's voice was abrupt, harsh, quashing what was obviously a taboo subject; Clements wondered why Romy had raised it. Keller, after a moment's awkward silence, went on, the harshness only slowly dying out of his voice: 'Our poison murder baffled us for months. The man died of what the local doctor said was cerebral haemorrhage. In Starnheim we did not have coroner's doctors as smart as Romy.' He smiled at her, forgiving her for mentioning Nazis. 'Months afterwards, we dug up the body and found the man had died of strychnine poisoning. We suspected the wife all along, but the doctor did not support our case, he insisted the husband had died from cerebral haemorrhage. The wife left Starnheim and went to live in München. Then we found out that the doctor, the coroner's doctor, was visiting her every weekend. After that . . .' He raised his wine glass. 'I was just a uniformed policeman, but I solved that one. I became a detective for a while, an unofficial one.'

'What happened to the wife and the doctor?'

'The wife went to jail and the doctor, unfortunately, committed suicide. He was charged, but acquitted. But, of course, he confessed by committing suicide. It is very satisfying, to solve a crime. You must be pleased when that happens?'

'If the solution is the right one, yes,' said Clements, thinking of cases where he and Malone had settled for second best. 'Are you pleased, Romy, when you help us solve a case?'

She surprised him: 'I really don't care one way or the other. Are you ready for dessert?'

When dinner was finished Keller rose from the table, excused himself almost formally and went off to work, changing into his spotless white overalls before he left. 'I am on late shift tonight. Don't wait up for me, Romy.'

She went to the front door with him, kissed him, then came back into the living room. 'He's not happy here, he's homesick. Bavarians, more than most Germans, get that way.'

'Are you homesick?'

'No.' She began to clear the table, Clements helping her carry the dishes out to the kitchen. 'I'm like Mother, I love the sunshine.'

'But – ?' Clements could be clumsy in his relationships, but sometimes he read women better than the women themselves suspected. Twenty-three years of listening to lies, excuses and threats, the lot of a cop, does not necessarily turn an eardrum to rubber.

Romy looked at him curiously, as if with new interest; she was still getting to know him, attracted to him though still undecided why. 'You think there is something else? Yes, there is,' she added after a moment. 'I wouldn't go back to Germany because I'm not sure how Father would fit into the new Germany, now it's been reunified. He hates Communism, he thought Reagan was the real Pope. He was never a Nazi, because by the time he'd grown up there was no Nazi party. When he talks about my grandfather, which is rarely, he never condemns him. He says that both Hitler and my grandfather were right in what they believed.'

'But that's all over. Only the Jews remember it.'

'Isn't that enough?'

'You mean that makes me sound anti-Semitic? I'm not. But for Aussies my age and younger that war is, I dunno, about as remote as the Crimean War or the American Civil War. We've got splinter groups out here, like the

National Front, but it's hard to take 'em seriously, I mean as Nazis.'

'They are still there in Germany. And I'm afraid my father might join them if we went back there. He's rigid in his thinking, always has been.' She moved to him, put her arms round his neck. 'Leave the dishes. I washed my hair tonight. Twice.'

He held her to him, feeling the body conditioned by aerobics and swimming, a long way yet from dying. 'How old are you?'

'Thirty. In my prime, as they say. In my prime and with lots of stamina.'

'The girl I've been looking for.'

Later, after they had made love twice in her bed, each showing off the benefit of experience (for love-making is a matter of pride as well as affection, women now as cocksure as men), she sat naked on the side of the bed and looked over her shoulder at him. 'Are you serious, Russ?'

He didn't answer at once, looking at her as carefully as he might at a suspect. This room was hers, as the rest of the flat wasn't; even he, not a connoisseur of furnishings, had recognized that the flat belonged, in every way, to her father. This bedroom was light and airy, facing north, suggestive of sunshine even at night; the furniture was modern and expensive, a careerwoman's environment, on the walls framed prints of birds of paradise, of brilliant tropical flowers. There were books on two shelves: novels by women authors, Jolley, Atwood, Allende; non-fiction whose titles suggested social history, though there was none that hinted she had any interest in Germany; there were half a dozen medical reference books. On a desk by the window stood a small computer. He was suddenly aware that she was very much more at home in this room than she ever would be in his untidy pad in King's Cross, where the books, mostly paperbacks, were a mess that showed his undisciplined search for knowledge.

'About us?' Again a pause, then he said, 'Yes. Are you?'

'I don't know. I've been in love twice before, *really* in love, but both men let me down. Have you ever been really in love?'

Dozens of times; but you could never tell that to a woman, not one sitting naked on the side of her own bed, still feeling you inside her. 'Once or twice. Do I have to make some sort of committal right now?'

She smiled. 'Commitment. You're not in court.'

But he was in court: her scrutiny of him told him that. She saw a big man running a little to fat but with muscle still visible; he was not handsome but he had a frank open face that would never be a mask. He had thick wavy brown hair on a well-shaped head and, beneath the sheet, his sexual equipment was a delight to behold and to hold But all of that was surface, she knew little or nothing of the depths of him. She had read Galen, knew that that Greek medico and philosopher had claimed that the faculties of the soul varied according to the temperaments of the body; Russ seemed disgustingly healthy, but that didn't say that his soul, if he had one, was in the same condition. And she wanted a man with soul, she had lived too long with a man who didn't have one.

He reached across and took her hand. 'Romy, I'm a slow decider – at least, in things like this. I jump to a conclusion sometimes on a case, but that's different. Let's take a little more time, okay? I've been a bachelor a bloody long time.'

She ruffled his hair, then stood up. 'Take your time.' Then she stopped at the door, half-turned; it was unintentional, but the pose was one of the best a woman can make: half-profile, head turned over the shoulder, breast showing, curve of hip into thigh, reverse curve of calf. Clements, a connoisseur of naked women, though he would never have confessed it to anyone, shook on the verge of commitment. 'Are you *desperate* to solve these two murders?'

The question was so unexpected, so out of train, he wasn't sure at first that he had heard her correctly. 'Desperate? Why?'

'I shouldn't want to be married to a man who was married to his job. My mother was.'

Then she went out to the bathroom, leaving him desperate to find the solution to *her*. Which meant that he was still some way from commitment, his natural state.

2

Malone and Lisa sat by the pool in the last of the evening light, which was stained ochre by the smoke from the bushfires to the west and the south of the city. The children splashed in the pool with none of that noise that usually erupts when children and water meet; it was almost as if Scungy Grime was in the pool with them. Outside in the street a young constable from Randwick sat in an unmarked car, the sentry at the castle gate half-asleep from the day's heat. The neighbours seemed to have accepted the police presence as necessary. Lisa had told Malone that Mrs Bass, next door, had taken tea and scones out to the officer on morning shift. Law and order had to be sustained.

'When are they going to bury Mr Grime?' Lisa said.

Malone shrugged. 'They're trying to find his next of kin. He had a wife who left him ten years ago. Maybe she doesn't want to be found.'

'I've often wondered about criminals' wives, the ones who stand by them. Do they have criminal minds, too, or is it just a woman's foolishness?'

'Like yours, you mean?'

'Do you want to joke? Is that the answer to the way we feel?'

She looked at the pool, where the children frolicked like

dolphins where yesterday morning death had floated. She had been in the water and her one-piece white costume shone as it caught the last of the evening light; her blonde hair was wet and lay along her head like a dark gold cap. She was sitting very still, her knees drawn up and her arms outstretched so that her hands rested on her insteps. Even though she was in profile to him he could see the anguish in her face.

'Do you want me to ask for a transfer out of Homicide?'

She looked back at him, face expectant; then the expectancy died. 'You'd never do it. Do you really *enjoy* it, looking into murder?'

He thought about it; or pretended to. He had thought about it constantly for years, but had never talked with her about it. About individual murders, yes; but never the abstract subject. '*Enjoy* isn't the word. I don't enjoy taking in a murderer, because that means someone has had to die for there to be a murder. But yes, the work is *interesting*, more interesting than any other police work. But if you insist, I'll try for a transfer to Fraud or Traffic or, God help me, even Community Relations.'

'Don't put the onus on me. I'm not insisting on anything.'

It was going to be one of those husband-and-wife arguments that would go round in circles, the disagreements of people in love who fear, subconsciously, that their argument could lead to disaster; so they hold back, bickering rather than making points, getting nowhere but neither retreating, which is some sort of victory for both. It is called a happy marriage, which both knew it was.

Then Claire climbed out of the pool, wiped water from herself with her hands and came and sat on the end of the banana-chair where Malone lay. She, too, was in a one-piece costume, the woman in her beginning to bud; her blonde hair was slicked back like Lisa's and once again he marvelled at how, sometimes, she looked so much like her mother. He looked at both of them and his heart ached.

'How was the first day back at school?' he said.

'Oh, all anyone wanted to talk about was our murder.'

'What did that come under? Biology, social studies?' Then he saw that he had hurt her with his flippancy and he reached out and ran his hand over her wet head. 'Sorry.'

She stood up. 'It's not funny, Dad.'

'I know that. No more jokes, I promise.'

She picked up her towel and went into the house, slamming the screen door behind her. Lisa said, 'You asked for that. Did you notice she said *our* murder? She mentioned it when she came home this afternoon and I chipped her about it. She said the girls at school kept referring to it as *your* murder. Meaning the Malones' murder. We should have it registered as a proprietary venture.'

'Now *you're* joking.'

Her shoulders slumped; all at once, in the last of the yellow light, she looked older; and he was suddenly, irrationally, frightened. 'I never thought it would happen, but it's getting me down at last. Being a policeman's wife. A Homicide wife.'

3

'My wife never liked my profession,' said Jack Aldwych wryly. 'But so long's I never brought my work home, she said nothing about it.'

'Did you ever feel any guilt about what you were doing?' said Janis Eden.

'What's guilt?' Aldwych smiled at her while he lifted his glass. He knew nothing about the grape, but Jack Junior was a wine snob and he let the boy have his head. There was Christ knew how many thousands of dollars' worth of stock in the cellar and Jack Junior was buying all the time, taking advantage of the present wine glut. Aldwych had noted that Janis, too, was something of a wine snob. Shirl, his wife, had loved sherry: she had not been a snob about it, just drank too much of it. She had had her reasons, but he would never tell those to anyone, least of all to this smartly dressed smart-arse at his table.

'I remember my wife once said, she went to church a lot, that the Bible says, The wicked flee when nobody chases 'em, but the righteous are as bold as a lion. You ever notice the lion is an endangered species?'

'He's incorrigible,' Jack Junior told Janis, smiling affectionately at his father. 'Mum spent years trying to reform him, but she got nowhere.'

'She knew what I was when she married me.' He had felt guilt at times, but only for the pain his actions had caused Shirl. She had suspected he had ordered certain killings; she had said nothing about them, but he had recognized the signs. Those would be the days when she would suddenly have 'woman trouble' and retire to one of the spare bedrooms, to stay there till the murders had dropped out of the news. Shirl had been an intelligent woman who had used her intelligence to play dumb: ignorance, if not bliss, had at least been wearable.

The Aldwyches, father and son, lived in this big two-storeyed house in two acres of garden in Harbord, a small seaside suburb neither fashionable nor notorious. The house was made of timber, no protection at all against bullets, but no rival gang had ever attempted to shoot through the walls. It had twelve rooms, all of them expensively furnished by Shirl, who had felt no guilt at all about spending her husband's money, no matter how he had obtained it; Jack Junior, ever since his mother's death, had been trying to persuade his father to sell the house and move closer to the heart of the city. So far he had got nowhere with that suggestion.

They were eating in the large dining room, the three of them seated at one end of the long table, with Aldwych at the head between his son and Janis. The table could

94

have seated twenty-four with no crowding, no elbows in the ribs; but Shirl had never realized her ambition to have the sort of glittering dinner parties she saw in the old movies they ran on daytime television. She had kept none of her friends from her girlhood, they had all faded away as soon as they had realized who and what she had married; and she had never accepted any of Aldwych's friends into the house as her guests. It only occurred to Aldwych, after his wife's death, that one half of the table had never been used.

'Do you like the house?' he said.

'I love it!' Janis had already demanded that Jack Junior take her over every square foot of it. 'It's priceless, it's heritage stuff.'

'Jack wants me to sell it.'

'Oh don't!' The girl's ambition, Aldwych decided, was also priceless; she wanted not only Jack Junior but everything he might inherit. 'Some developer will knock it down and build flats.'

Jack Junior, smiling just as affectionately at Janis as he had at his father, said, 'Janis belongs to every heritage and environment group going. You name it, she belongs to it.'

'Yeah?' said Aldwych, unimpressed. He had never been plagued by do-gooders and he wasn't about to become vulnerable now. 'Why?'

She gave him a direct look. 'It's the best way of coming across bargains. I've seen four houses I want Jack to buy. He holds on to them till the market improves and then sells them at a nice profit.'

'The Greenies must love you,' said Aldwych, one eye on his son.

'They don't know the real Janis,' said Jack Junior.

Do you? Aldwych wondered; then decided that his son was perhaps smarter about women than he had thought. 'Why wouldn't you sell this house then, Janis?'

'Because I think you love it too much. You want to spend your declining years here, don't you?'

His declining years? He wondered how her direct approach affected the junkies she was supposed to rehabilitate.

Mrs Jessup, the cook-housekeeper, thin as a bread-stick and as salty, brought in the dessert. 'It's pineapple upside-down cake,' she explained to Janis. 'Six nights a week Mr Aldwych wants it. I make it in me sleep. You want whipped cream or runny?'

When she had gone back to the kitchen Jack Junior said, 'She is heritage stuff, too. She frowns on me because I like girls.'

'Not because you like girls,' said his father, throwing a little sand into the works: this girl at his table had to be shown she was not the only runner in the field, 'but you like too many of them.'

'Better girls than boys,' said Janis, looking at Aldwych out of the corner of her eye. 'Did you meet many gays in your profession, Mr Aldwych?'

'Only one. He used to kill people for me.'

'Okay, Dad, that's enough!' Jack Junior's voice was sharp.

Aldwych's smile was as evil as a snake's, one that had destroyed a thousand Edens. He winked at the one beside him. 'You notice how holier-than-thou all the businessmen are getting to be since the high-flyers have been sent to jail? Relax, Jack. Janis knows I'm only kidding.'

Jack Junior's face remained stiff for a moment; then it relaxed into his pleasant smile. 'I know, Dad. But maybe Janis doesn't.'

'I'm smarter than you think, Jack,' she said, and Aldwych, who knew at any waking moment exactly how his own face looked, saw a reflection of his own smile in hers.

Later, when Jack Junior was taking her home, she kissed Aldwych goodnight; though it was on his cheek, it was not a social kiss. She's a whore, he thought, one who'd ask for a blank cheque. He would have to have a strong word with Jack Junior.

Driving away from the house in his dark blue Daimler, Jack Junior said, 'You want to spend the night at the flat?'

His mother had welcomed his bringing home girls, *nice* girls, but she had never allowed them to stay the night. 'You sleep with a girl under my roof, she's got to be married to you,' she had laid down the law, and he had never argued with her. He had bought a flat in Double Bay, on the south side of the harbour, where girls were readily available, and his mother had furnished it for him. She could turn a blind eye, something she had been doing all her married life, just so long as she did not have to do it under her own roof.

'Why don't I? I don't think I could face my mother with all her piety –' Her mother had rediscovered religion after Janis' father had committed suicide; she flagellated herself for his sin. 'Not after a couple of hours with your father. Jack, he's so *honest*.'

He grinned. 'He wouldn't thank you for saying that.'

'Does he think you're honest?'

'I *am*. Everything I do in business is strictly above board.'

'Everybody must know where your money comes from. Or *came* from.' She found it hard to believe that criminals actually retired.

'Of course they do. But do you think they care, once I've washed it clean? If they tried to trace all the laundered money that's passed through banks in Australia in the last ten years, the banks would be even shakier than they are now. I see that every tax dollar that's due is paid, the companies give to charity, we pay over-award wages so there's never any trouble with the unions . . .'

She was silent for a while as they went down the expressway towards the Harbour Bridge. Beyond the high curve of the steel arch the tall buildings winked a thousand eyes, all of them cold and calculating. The city had no regal elegance, but it was not as brash and cheap as its detractors from other States claimed. She loved it, wanted to own it and, three months ago, had set about taking possession. Her investment banker sat beside her, laundered money all ready to be put back into the dirt again.

'Your dad's proud of you, isn't he?'

'I'm not sure. Mum was. She wanted me to be everything that Dad wasn't.'

'What would your mum say if she knew that you're exactly like him? Maybe not as ruthless, but exactly like him in other respects.'

He turned his head and smiled. 'Who's going to tell her?'

'What if someone tells *him*?'

'He'll kill me.'

CHAPTER FOUR

I

Leroy Lugos had no record; but Ulysses Lugopolous did. Not in Sydney, but in Melbourne, as Andy Graham found out within half an hour of being put on the trail by Malone. In past years co-operation between the police departments of the various States had been only a little above that between the old KGB and the CIA; the rivalry had been on a par with that between the police themselves and the crims and almost as bad as that between the State sporting bodies. But now, with crime on a national scale, raised to that level by business entrepreneurs who had taught the crims the virtues of vision and organization, old jealousies had been buried and co-operation was the motto. Especially when a police department had been fortunate enough to unload a crim into another State.

Andy Graham came into Malone's office with the computer print-out. The first thing Malone said was, 'Sit down, Andy.' He had to be anchored, otherwise he would be all over the small office like a Great Dane with fleas. Clements moved his chair to allow Graham to sit beside him. 'What have you got?'

'Ulysses Lugopolous –' Graham had trouble with the name. 'He was picked up in March eighty-eight, he was nineteen then, with a hundred grammes of coke in his possession. He got three years, but served only eighteen months, all of it in Pentridge.'

'Was he selling the coke?' Malone asked.

'He tried to sell some to an undercover cop.'

'They know where he got it? A hundred grammes is a

99

fair whack for a nineteen-year-old kid to be peddling. What would it have been worth?' He looked at Clements, the treasure-chest of trivia.

'Then? I'd be guessing. It didn't come into fashion out here till eighty-six, eighty-seven. But the street turnover now is seven hundred thousand bucks a kilo.'

Malone nodded to Graham, and the young detective went on, looking impatient at being interrupted: 'Well, okay, he's just served eighteen months, right? So where did he get the stuff? He worked as a storeman for a drug company!' He looked up in triumph; Malone waited for him to leap up on the desk and bark. 'He'd know all about drugs, about things like Alloferin!'

Malone and Clements nodded, digesting this with less excitement than Graham had expected; but they looked at each other with satisfaction. Malone was no philosopher, being too Irish for that, but he had come to believe that nothing in the world is unconnected to anything else. Skeins, most of them invisible, link men and events with more harmony than most of us are prepared to admit. He no longer believed that coincidence is a phenomenon, it was everyday, part of life; or, anyway, of a policeman's life. Clues are only the footmarks of coincidence.

'Andy, go back and talk to Melbourne again. Ask them what they have on Snow White –' He looked at his notebook. '*Dallas* White. And also on Gary Schultz, aka The Dwarf.'

Graham leapt up; five minutes in a chair was purgatory. 'Right!'

He galloped out of the office and across the big room to the computer desk. Malone looked after him, sighed. 'You think he helped his mother with his birth? Told her to get a move on?'

'I was once as enthusiastic as that,' said Clements. 'Once. I think it was a Thursday.'

'You get anything on Janis Eden?'

Clements looked at his notebook. 'She works on a freelance basis for the St Sebastian's Drug and Alcohol Clinic. She was a staff worker for three years, but three months ago she went casual. Very competent, had a rapport with the junkies she worked with. She's twenty-six and has a degree from New South Wales Uni. She's unmarried, was born in Wahroonga, still lives there with her mother and has never been in trouble.'

'Where'd you get all this? Though I shouldn't ask.'

'I used to date a girl in the Social Welfare Department. She's married now, has a coupla kids, but old loves never die, isn't that what they say?'

'I guess so. My first love was Loyola MacPhillamy, she was seven and I was eight, and Lisa reckons I still mention her in my sleep.'

'Loyola MacPhillamy – that's quite a mouthful in your sleep.'

'That's why Lisa believes it's an old romance. She says no grown man's subconscious could dream up a name like that.'

When Andy Graham came back he was nodding appreciatively. 'I got on to the computer first, then I rang Melbourne. It must be the recession down there. The Vics seem glad to talk to just anyone. Anyhoooo . . .' He flourished his notes, saw Malone looking at him warningly and at once sat down but leant forward, straining at the leash. 'Schultz has done time twice, robbery and assault, manslaughter – he broke a guy's neck. But he's been clean for the last three years. Charged once, but acquitted. Dallas – Snow? – White, he's been in three times, bank robbery, drug running, assaulting an officer. The guy I spoke to said he's a real bad bugger and we're welcome to him. I thanked him, naturally.' He looked about eighteen when he smiled, an innocent eighteen.

Malone said, 'They sound a nice pair. Did your Victorian mate say if they put the heat on White and Schultz to leave Melbourne?'

'No. He said things have been very quiet down there,

except for petty crime, house-breaking, car-stealing, stuff like that. He said it was the recession.'

'Things are worse down there than anywhere else,' said Clements with the satisfaction of a New South Welshman, one whose State level of crime was keeping up the employment level, at least amongst cops. 'You've heard the joke. What's the capital of Victoria? A dollar-fifty.'

It was an old joke: the Romans had cracked it about Carthage.

'Do you mind? I haven't finished.' Andy Graham could stiffen with indignation sitting still for once. 'There's more. Dallas White was in Pentridge the same time as Ulysses the Greek. The guy I spoke to had no idea whether they were in the same block, but they were in jail the same time, all right.'

Malone nodded to Clements. 'Russ, I think you and I had better go back and have another talk with Snow White and The Dwarf. Andy, get on to the Drug Unit and see if they have anything on those girls down at Mrs Kissen's. Check, too, if they have anything on Leroy.'

'Right. Anything else?' Andy Graham had his own addiction: he loved to work.

'Yes, get on to the dispensaries in all the Sydney hospitals, private as well as public. Check if they're missing any of their supply of a drug called Alloferin.' He wrote down the name and pushed the piece of paper across to Graham.

'*Every* one?'

'Even the maternity hospitals and the old folks' nursing homes.' Then he reached for the phone. 'Excuse me a moment, I'm calling Lisa, see if she's okay.'

'Give her my love,' said Clements, and Graham nodded in agreement, though inspectors' wives were out of his league. 'Ask her if she's heard of Loyola MacPhillamy lately.'

They went out of the office, leaving Malone to call home to make sure it was still secure. 'Everything's all right,' said Lisa, 'but it's sweet of you to call. No, I mean it, darling. I've only been sitting by the phone for two hours.'

If only Eve had used sarcasm on Satan instead of on Adam, we'd all still be in the Garden of Eden . . . 'I tried to get you before, but you were engaged.'

Nine times out of ten that one worked. He belonged to the school of men that believed a woman could not pass a phone without making a call. Lying is a sub-division of communication and the telephone has assisted in its development. The lie worked this time: Lisa admitted she might have been on the phone. 'Mother called. And *your* mother. And Mother Brendan called.' She stopped then; he recognized a pregnant pause when he heard one. Then she went on, 'You might explain that one.'

'I wasn't going to tell you – I didn't want to upset you. Keith Elgar said he'd keep an eye on the girls and Tom.' Elgar was the senior sergeant at Randwick police station. 'The station is right opposite the school and he said it'd be no trouble for a man to pop over there now and again. He said they'd do it as unobtrusively as possible.'

'Mother Brendan evidently doesn't think they've been unobtrusive. She's raising bloody hell.'

He hadn't wanted to tell her till this evening. 'Darl, it's going to get worse. Greg Random had me in half an hour ago. We're to have full protection. It's either that or you and the kids will be moved to a safe house and a couple of minders move in with me at home.'

'Jesus!' she said softly; she swore only at the extreme. 'We went through this before.' That had been two years ago, when his name had been on a police assassin's hit list. 'Not again?'

'I'm sorry, darl.' He could offer nothing more: it was a husband's credit card, always ready.

She was silent; then she sighed and he could see her gathering herself, at which there was no one better; she would never fall apart, not even if the world itself fell apart. God, on Judgement Day, had better have things in proper order.

'All right, let's have the protection squad or whatever it's called. I'll go up and collect the kids now, before Mother Brendan expels them. Do I have to feed the minders? I'll draw up a menu.'

Dutch sarcasm could be thick enough to fill the hole in any dyke; but he didn't say that. 'They're on their way now, I think.'

'Just a minute.' There was a long silence; then she came back on the line: 'They've just arrived. Two young sexy-looking cops who look as if they might prefer an older woman.'

'Send for Mother Brendan.' She laughed and he knew he had been forgiven. 'I love you.'

He hung up, sat for a long moment staring unseeingly at the glass wall of his office. He felt the anger starting up in him again that he had felt on Monday morning; he would kill anyone who destroyed his family. At that moment he felt criminal.

'Coming?' said Clements from the doorway and brought him back to sanity.

On their way over to Darling Harbour he told Clements of the police protection that Random had ordered. Clements said, 'The sensible thing to do.'

Malone looked at him sourly. 'That's bloody obvious. But it doesn't mean I have to like it. If Snow White is responsible for putting Scungy in our pool and for that warning I got over the phone, I think I'll drop him in the water. You can look after The Dwarf.'

'I thought you might suggest that.'

But White and Schultz were not at Darling Harbour on Number 9 wharf. 'They went over to Glebe Island,' a tally clerk told the two detectives. He was a bearded sparrow of a man who spoke at machine-gun speed; he had a calculator in his hand which he kept clicking, as if counting off his wordage. 'I dunno which wharf, I could find out. No problem, glad to help, all I gotta do is –'

They thanked him and drove away while he was still in mid-sentence. 'He seem nervous to you?' said Clements.

'I couldn't make up my mind whether he was scared of us or of Snow White and The Dwarf. But I'll bet he's already on the blower, telling 'em we're on our way.'

Glebe Island was five minutes' drive away; not strictly an island but a tiny isthmus. The western side of it was a bulk wheat terminal, towering grey silos looking like a bank of huge up-ended sewer pipes; a yellow mist hung in the still air as grain poured down chutes into the holds of a ship. The eastern side of the isthmus was a container terminal, a vast yard only intermittently cluttered with the stacked metal boxes; these terminals were always a fair chart of the economy and right now the chart held little cheer. Across the water was the century-old refinery of CSR, Colonial Sugar Refinery, founded and named in the days when nobody objected to the word 'colonial'; the smell of molasses thickened the already thick air and alcoholics, driving by, thought they were passing Rum Heaven. As Malone and Clements drove on to the long wharf the body of a man was being fished out of the water.

There was no sign of White or Schultz, but as the two detectives got out of the car they saw Roley Bremner standing alone in the shade of a big crane. He was staring at the small group of men, six or seven of them, laying down the sodden corpse and pulling a small tarpaulin over it. The hard balls of his face had turned pulpy; his freckles had darkened against his paleness, looked like saltpetre marks. Malone had to speak to him twice before he became aware of the two policemen.

'Eh? Jesus, it didn't take you long to get here! Who called you? You always this prompt when someone's been done in?'

'We're not here for *him* –' Malone nodded at the heap

under the tarpaulin. 'What d'you mean – someone's been done in?'

'It's bloody obvious, isn't it? I dunno what happened –' His voice was hoarse and soft, as if he were trying not to be overheard. It was a shock to Malone to realize that the tough, squat man was scared. 'That's Jimmy Maddux, he was the union man on this site, one of my sidekicks. Actually, he was the organizer for me in the elections coming up. He called me up about an hour ago, said could I get over here in a hurry, he had something he wanted to show me, said he didn't wanna spill it over the phone. I couldn't get over here till five minutes ago. Just in time to hear someone yell they could see him floating in the water between the wharf and that ship there, the *Southern Pacific*. He's dead,' he said, as if they might think Maddux was just sheltering from the sun beneath the tarpaulin.

Clements walked over to the group of men, showed his badge, then knelt down and lifted the corner of the tarpaulin. He touched the dead man's head, which rolled like that of a day-old infant, then he pulled the tarpaulin back over the corpse and stood up. 'I think you better move him back into the shade, but leave him there until the doc and some of our Crime Scene fellers arrive. Anyone called the local police yet?'

'Not yet,' said one of the men. 'Christ, we only just drug him outa the water.'

Clements went back to the car, made two phone calls, one to the local station, the other to Police Centre; then he came back to Malone and Bremner still standing in the shade of the big crane. He looked directly at Malone and said flatly, 'His neck's been broken.'

Malone said nothing, but Bremner sucked in his breath. 'How the hell did that happen? Blokes get killed on the wharves, but it's usually something falls on them or they get run over . . .' His voice trailed off.

Malone said, 'Roley, we came over here to have another word with Snow White and The Dwarf –'

Bremner looked up at him, frowning. 'Nah, nah.' He shook his head. He was wearing a blue terry-towelling hat whose limp brim did nothing to keep the sun off his face. 'They wouldn't be that obvious, no way.'

'You don't believe that, Roley. They're the sort who'd pick the obvious and then bluff it out.'

Bremner hesitated, then shrugged. 'Yeah, yeah, I guess so. But Christ, why do that to poor Jimmy? They might of had a go at me, I wouldn't of been surprised that happened, but Jimmy –? I better go and tell his missus. He's got a wife and four kids, all of 'em youngsters. He was only, I dunno, thirty-five, six, no more. I was grooming him to take over from me eventually, y'know?'

'Roley, before you go, can we have ten minutes? Is there anywhere around here we can get a cuppa?'

'There's the amenities room. But I think I oughta get out to see Molly Maddux –'

'Roley, you're not looking forward to that. I've been through it, I *know*. Let's have a cuppa first.'

Clements said, 'I'll have a look around out here, see if I can locate Snow White and his mate.'

Malone and Bremner walked across to the low building where the workers' amenities were housed. The big canteen room was almost full, but the two men found a table apart from the crowd and sat down. The talk in the room had been subdued when Malone and Bremner walked in, but as soon as Malone was identified as a cop a silence fell, as if everyone in the room had suddenly become deaf and dumb. Heads turned, eyes stared: when staring at a cop, Malone had noted, few people ever tried to be discreet. He was a public object.

'It's the meal break,' said Bremner. 'That's why there was practically no one out on the wharves when this must of happened.'

'Roley, this is off the record. D'you think White and The Dwarf could have done this to Jimmy Maddux? Why? What's the prize if they win the election from you?'

Bremner sipped his tea. 'I been trying to puzzle that one out. It don't matter as much as it used to, running the waterfront. Back in them days, the days of your dad and my early days, there was political power on the wharves. The Commos, they had clout then and they ran the Seamen's Union and they could tie up the whole country, right around, if they wanted to. But that's not on these days. There's something called micro-reform, whatever the hell that is. Blokes like me, no education, just experience, we got no clout in union affairs these days. Snow White and The Dwarf, they're even dumber than me when it comes to what's needed to get on in the unions today. I had a twenty-two-year-old kid down from Unions Hall the other day, he kept talking about learning curves and level playing fields and more interface with the bosses, his head was about ten feet above his bloody shoulders. In the end I threw him out. Snow White and The Dwarf, they'd of probably broke his neck.' Then he shook his head. 'Sorry. I shouldn't of said that.'

'Righto, let's say those two are not looking for political power. What about smuggling?'

Bremner raised a ginger eyebrow. The crowd was no longer paying attention to them; the room was now a buzz of talk, though there was no laughter or argument. These men were rough and tough, but death still touched them. A thousand deaths in Baghdad or Bangladesh was just news, but a mate's death was a tragedy.

'My dad told me what it was like in the old days,' said Malone. 'There was drug smuggling, not as much as today maybe, but it went on. Gold. Emeralds and diamonds, before we discovered our own diamonds. I'm not accusing you of anything, Roley, but how much drug smuggling comes in by ship these days?'

'You'd have to ask the Customs blokes that, or the Federal cops. Most of it's been coming in by air, they run mules, I think they call 'em, outa Singapore and Bangkok. But I heard some talk they been switching to ships lately, that way they bring in bigger shipments. You think Jimmy got on to something there?'

'Where's that ship – the *Southern Pacific*? – come from?'

'I dunno. Hey, Chicka, where's the *Southern Pacific* from?'

One of the men at the next table turned around. 'Auckland. Before that, Suva, I think.'

Bremner turned back to Malone. 'There you are. You better check with Customs, see if Jimmy called them, too.'

There is nothing a cop likes more than to be told how to do his job. 'Yeah, that might be an idea. Would Jimmy Maddux have a locker here?'

'Sure. Why?'

'Roley, he had his neck broken. Now it could've been an accident, but just in case it wasn't . . . I'd like to look through his locker, see if there's something there that might explain why he called you to get over here urgently. You'd like this cleared up, wouldn't you?'

Bremner looked down at his empty cup. 'I dunno, tell you the truth. This's kicked me in the gut. If they was going for me, I wouldn't mind – I wouldn't like it, sure, but I'd be able to handle it. I been through it before.'

'Murder?'

'A coupla times, about twenty, twenty-five years ago. But now . . . I dunno.' He looked up. 'I got a coupla years to retirement. I was gunna fight Snow White in the election, just for – well, decency's sake.' He was one of the old school, Malone recognized, just like Con Malone: any mention of the virtues was an embarrassment. 'But if it's gunna come to this – I'm a married man, with kids . . .'

Malone said, 'Roley, I don't know if White and Schultz had anything to do with this. Maybe it *was* an accident . . .' He shrugged. 'But Normie Grime's death wasn't an accident. So Sergeant Clements and I will be coming down to the waterfront again. And maybe again and again.' He stood up. 'Let's go and have a look at Jimmy Maddux's locker.'

The meal break was finishing as Malone and Bremner walked out of the big room; men who had stood up to leave their tables paused as the two men went by. They resent me, Malone thought: for the moment none of them sees Maddux's death as murder, so why am I here? The wharves were union territory; outsiders were not welcome, especially outsiders who thought they had authority. He wondered how many of these men would vote for Snow White on election day; how many, for decency's sake, would vote for Roley Bremner. He suddenly felt political, a dangerous state of mind for a policeman.

As they came out of the main room they met Clements, face streaked with sweat, his jacket over his arm, a small plastic bag in his hand. 'The locals have arrived, I let them take over. The Crime Scene fellers are on their way.' He held up the plastic bag. 'I got these off the body. A notebook, pretty pulpy from the water. Car-keys, a house-key, two small keys –'

'One of them looks like his locker key,' said Bremner.

'Any sign of our friends?' Men were filing past them, so Malone named no names.

'Nobody's seen them.' Clements was equally circumspect.

But when the three of them walked into the locker room, White and Schultz were there, The Dwarf sitting on a bench and White standing in front of an open locker. There was no one else in the room, but Malone had the feeling it was crowded; then he realized it was Bremner who was giving him that feeling. The shorter man had edged closer to Malone as if for protection, almost pushing the detective up against the lockers. It was a shock for Malone to realize just how terribly scared the tough little man was.

'We just heard the bad news about Jimmy Maddux.' White ignored the two detectives, spoke directly to Bremner as if the latter was alone. 'How'd it happen?'

'He had his neck broken,' said Malone and looked at

The Dwarf for a reaction. There was none: being slow-witted sometimes makes one a good actor.

'Tough titty,' said White. 'Did they call you guys in, for an accident?'

'No, we were looking for you. We went to Number 9 wharf, but they said you'd come over here. You just get here?'

'My car broke down. The heat stuffed up the fuel pipe, a vapour lock. I get elected next month, I think I'll see we get undercover parking for the workers. Come on, Gary, time we clocked on.'

'What ship are you working on?' said Malone.

'The *Southern Pacific*, right?' White looked at Schultz, who nodded and stood up, adding to Malone's impression that the room was crowded. Beside him, he felt Bremner tense. White went on, 'You wanna talk to us, you better come out there. I can't afford to bludge on my mates, let 'em do all the work. Not while I'm running for office, eh, Roley?'

'We'll see you in a few minutes,' said Malone and had to lean back hard against the lockers as Bremner stepped back to allow White and Schultz to go past him.

Malone looked at Clements, who said, 'This is when I enjoy being a mug copper.'

'You gunna pinch 'em?' Bremner looked suddenly hopeful.

'We'll do our best,' said Clements and avoided Malone's warning eye. The big man thought positively, sometimes too much so; he never manufactured evidence, but only because Malone had never given him a licence. He knew, too, that manufactured evidence, so often in court, showed its trademark. 'We'll vote for you.'

'Let's look at Jimmy's locker,' said Malone, before promises got out of hand.

It was the old intrusion into a stranger's life. Malone had been doing it for more years than he cared to count, but he felt the same distaste as he had felt the very first time. But Jimmy Maddux's locker held no secret: no fetish, no lie, no confession. It contained only the expected paraphernalia of a working man: a spare set of overalls, a couple of T-shirts, a pair of heavy work-boots, two copies of *Modern Motor*, a towel, soap, two packets of cigarettes. 'And this,' said Clements, holding up a diver's face mask.

'That wouldn't be Jimmy's,' said Bremner. 'He was dead scared of the water, he couldn't swim across this room if his life depended on it. We used to joke about it, if he fell in the harbour.' Then his face went stiff. 'He did that, didn't he? Fell in the harbour.'

Clements, a travelling supply store, took another plastic bag from his pocket and dropped the mask in it.

'Could he have found it out on the wharf?' Malone said.

Bremner shrugged. 'Maybe. I dunno why anyone would be diving around here, there's only muck on the bottom.'

'That ship, would Customs have cleared everything on it?'

'The *Southern Pacific*? Probably. I dunno for sure. They check the papers of the ship out in the stream, before it berths. Then when the containers are unloaded, they check the seals on the containers before they pass 'em. You wanna go and talk to 'em? They got an inspector's office here.'

As they came out of the locker room, Malone saw, in the distance, the Physical Evidence team just arriving. 'You'd better get over there, Russ. Tell the locals and the Crime Scene blokes we're treating it as murder till the GMO tells us otherwise. Give me the diving mask.'

Clements handed over the plastic bag. 'It's bloody hot out there. I heard one of the wharfies say it's just topped forty degrees.'

'If it has,' said Bremner, 'they'll be knocking off. Weather like this, it gets bloody unbearable down in the holds. And the ironwork gets too hot to handle. They'll knock off, it's in the award.'

'When's it get too hot for cops to work?' Clements asked

Malone, but went trudging off across the wide concrete apron towards the three police cars and the van parked at the foot of the big mobile crane.

'When *does* it get too hot for you?' said Bremner.

'When the politicians start breathing down our necks. Where is the Customs office?'

The Customs officer, Bill Dibble, was middle-aged, stout and balding, a dynamo run down; in his youth, he told Malone, he had been a cross between a bloodhound and a greyhound. 'But when you don't get support from Canberra, when the government, doesn't matter which one, doesn't give you the money to do the job . . . You know what I mean?'

'Stop bellyaching, Bill,' said Bremner. 'Tell the inspector what he wants to know. You got anything suspicious on the *Southern Pacific*?'

Dibble leaned back in his chair, gestured at the sheets on his desk. 'Those are copies of the manifest. Any of the stuff listed there could have prohibited stuff, drugs, gems, gold, hidden in it.' He pulled out a sheet, ran a sausage of a finger down it. 'Whitegoods – refrigerators, stuff like that. They don't try hiding it in those any more – it's old hat, they know we'd be on to it. Canned foodstuffs – that could be a possibility. We've found paddles of cannabis hidden in tins of chick-peas, ten to a tin. But that was on a ship from Tripoli, in Lebanon. Sure, there could be something hidden in the cargo. But we go on risk assessment, it's all that we can afford to do unless we get a definite tip-off. We look at the general profile – what country it's come from, who sent it, who it's going to. In this case, all the containers are for reputable firms, the Customs agents have sworn for them. The agents work with us, they don't want to lose their licences. And the ship's from Auckland, not a usual source for drugs. The Kiwis work pretty closely with us.'

'It was in Suva before Auckland,' said Malone.

'It didn't take on any cargo there, just discharged.'

'Has any of the cargo left the wharf?'

'No, the freight agents will have their trucks here first thing in the morning. It's all been released. I can get our fellers down here with the sniffer dogs if you think there's any drugs in the containers –'

'How long can you hold a cargo?'

Dibble spread his plump hands. 'As long as we like, if we suspect something. But you hold up cargo, the receivers suspect something and just don't turn up.'

Malone put the plastic bag containing the diving mask on Dibble's desk. 'Don't touch it – there may be prints on it. Jimmy Maddux had something important he wanted to tell Roley here. We found this mask in his locker. He did no diving, in fact Roley says he was dead scared of the water. Does that suggest anything to you? As I understand it, you Customs blokes are born suspicious. Be suspicious now.'

Dibble grinned at the insulting compliment, or complimentary insult, and stared at the diving mask. Then he nodded. 'Yeah, it does. We've never had it happen here, not so far, but there was a memo sent out about six months ago, a reprint of something the Drug Enforcement guys in Washington had sent us and the Federal police. The drug gangs, the Sicilians and the Colombians, they're packing the drugs, heroin and cocaine, into metal boxes. Then they send a diver down at the home port and he clamps the boxes to the hull of a ship with magnetic clamps. They stay there till the ship docks at the destination port. Then at night the receivers send down a diver, he releases the boxes . . .' He spread his hands again. 'There was a series on Channel Nine about three weeks ago –'

'I saw it,' said Bremner.

'That happened in Hamburg – the stuff was on a ship out of Karachi. It was fiction, but it was based on fact, dead true. We haven't come across the method here, not yet. But that's not to say it hasn't been tried and we just didn't catch 'em.'

'Could you get a diver to look at the hull of the *Southern Pacific*?'

'I guess so. I can't authorize it, it'll have to be okayed by head office. And the Federal cops will have to come into it, I mean if we pick up anything.'

'I'm not interested in the smuggling. All we're looking for is anything that'll lead us to whoever murdered Jimmy Maddux.' And Scungy Grime and, who knows, Sally Kissen. 'How soon can you get a diver?'

'I could get one over here in an hour. But first I'll have to check with our CET – the Contraband Enforcement Team. If there's a chance of something being there under-water, they wouldn't want to check it in daylight. That could tip off whoever's supposed to pick it up. No offence, Inspector, but drug-busting is our territory, not yours.'

The territorial imperative, the old barbed-wire boun-daries between bureaucracies: but Malone knew they had to be respected. Murder had no priority, not unless a bureaucrat was murdered.

'We'd rather do the job after dark,' said Dibble. 'Just in case, you know what I mean?'

'Call me as soon as you know something one way or the other,' said Malone and left his card with Dibble.

Outside, in the yellow glare that seemed like a soft physical blow against the eyes when one stepped into it, Malone said, 'Roley, could you find out for me if Normie Grime was working at the weekend? And Snow White and The Dwarf.'

Bremner seemed to go a shade paler, but he just nodded. A moment, then he said, eager to be gone, 'I gotta go now. I don't want Jimmy's missus to find out on the radio what's happened, not before I get to her. That'd be too much for her.'

'Where does she live? We probably will have to come and have a talk with her.'

'Jesus, is that necessary?'

'I'm afraid it is, Roley.'

Bremner squinted at him in the sun; then he nodded reluctantly. 'Yeah, I guess it is. Jimmy lives over in Balmain.' He gave Malone an address; the detective made a note of it. 'Will I drop a hint you'll be coming? Sorta prepare her?'

'Not at this stage, Roley. Don't mention murder to her yet. One shock at a time is enough.'

Bremner went off to his car and Malone, careful not to exert himself in the heat, walked across to the group congregated around the body of Jimmy Maddux. As he passed his and Clements' car he dropped the diving mask on the front seat; he had glimpsed White and Schultz coming away from the side of the *Southern Pacific* towards the police team. Behind them other wharfies were clattering down the loading ramp.

Clements and Romy Keller detached themselves from the police group as Malone approached. The GMO was wearing a large straw hat and a sun-dress with narrow shoulder-straps; she looked the coolest person in sight, adding even a touch of glamour that, Malone thought, was incongruous in the surroundings. The sole woman member of the PE team, flushed and sweaty in her blue shirt and woollen skirt, cap pushed forward over her eyes, looked envious of Romy.

'His neck was broken by a blow from the side,' said Romy. 'Possibly a karate chop.'

'No accident?' said Malone.

She shook her head; the wide brim of her hat rippled like a straw wave. 'I wouldn't say so. If he'd broken his neck in a fall, there'd be contusions to his head – there are none. It's a clean blow. Do you want me to treat it as murder?'

'I think so. The Glebe detectives will do the paperwork, but you let me know if you come up with something else. Call Russ. You've got his number?'

'I'm not sure,' said Romy and gave Clements a smile that doubled the meaning of what she had said.

Clements walked across with her to her car and Malone moved quickly to White and Schultz as he saw them turning to go. He manoeuvred himself in front of White, preferring not to be stepped on by The Dwarf.

'You leaving, Mr White?'

'Yeah, I decided it was too hot. It was over fifty, down there in the hold.'

'*You* decided?'

'Yeah, I'm the temporary union delegate. They just elected me, the guys.'

'That was pretty quick, wasn't it?'

'Us wharfies, we make up our minds real quick. We don't hem and haw like the rest of the country.'

Malone looked up at The Dwarf. 'Who nominated him? You?'

The giant nodded. 'I nominated him. I seconded him, too. Nobody argued.'

'What would you have done to them if they had? Never mind, forget I asked . . . Mr Schultz, do you know anything about karate?' The Dwarf looked at White; and Malone said, 'It's a form of martial arts, I understand you can kill people with one blow –'

'I fucking know what it is!' The Dwarf looked more annoyed that he should be thought ignorant of how to dispose of people than that Malone should be accusing him of something.

It was White who took up Malone's implied suggestion: 'What are you getting at, Malone?'

'Jimmy Maddux –' He looked back over his shoulder; the shrouded corpse was being loaded into an ambulance. 'The doc says he died from a blow on the neck. Your big mate once did time for breaking a man's neck.'

'It was only manslaughter.' The Dwarf looked pleased, as if he had done his victim a favour.

'Inspector –' White was all at once formal; even his

voice seemed to change. 'Are you saying Mr Schultz had something to do with the death of Mr Maddux?'

'I don't think I used those words. But a man dies of a broken neck and on hand is a feller who's done time for the same sort of offence. Wouldn't you be suspicious?'

'I'm not the suspicious type.'

Smart-arse crims are a bargain lot; but Malone guessed that White was more than just a smart-arse. 'Well, I am, I'm afraid.' He looked up at The Dwarf, dark and threatening against the sun. 'Keep that in mind, Mr Schultz.'

He left them on that, walked across to the unmarked car as Clements came back. 'Finished, Russ?'

Clements looked across the roof of the car at White and Schultz; they were within earshot, just. 'For the time being – I've picked up a coupla things to follow up.'

Malone looked back at White. 'You'll be staying around for the union election?'

'Sure, why not?' White had all the arrogance of a small-time despot; Malone could imagine how he would have run a prison yard. 'Things need cleaning up around here, wouldn't you say?'

As they got into the sweat-box of the car Malone said, 'Get their addresses from Roley Bremner. If they're running for election, their proper addresses should be on the union roll. I remember that from my dad's day.'

'Did Con ever run for anything?'

'Once, as union president. He got three votes, all his own.'

2

'Something is happening,' said Leslie Chung. 'It's in the air, Jack. You can smell it, like cheap joss-sticks.'

Jack Aldwych's gentle grin was more like a crumbling of his heavy face than a working of the muscles. 'You're not gunna believe me, Les, but I never smelled a joss-stick.

I don't have any time for anything outa Asia, except Chinese food.'

Once a month he met Chung for lunch here at this restaurant in Dixon Street, the main artery, if not the heart, of Chinatown. The small sub-district had a heart, but no outsiders, including Jack Aldwych, knew where it was located. Tourists were always welcome, and so were the businessmen who came down here from uptown for lunch and dinner; but the locals had their own Great Wall, invisible though it was, behind which were thoughts, schemes, loyalties that the rest of the city could only guess at. The Chinese population, the first, after the Aborigines, to suffer racism in Australia, were still the most cohesive of the country's immigrants. They might not have their ethnic soccer clubs, their mosques or their temples; they did have the glue of their ancestry holding them together. They dressed Western-style, their young people danced to Madonna's raunchy songs, but inscrutability was in their blood like an inoculation serum.

'You're too Australian, Jack. You're old enough now, you're retired, too – why don't you throw away your prejudices? Another fifty years, Jack, and Asia will rule the world.'

'I'll be dead and gone then. You mean you blokes from the Triads will run everything, beating even the Japs?'

Chung smiled easily; he always succeeded in looking as if he never took offence at anything. 'Jack, you've known me, what, twenty years? You've never been able to connect me with the Triads. They don't exist, they're a figment of imagination, like Fu Manchu and Charlie Chan.'

'Bullshit,' said Aldwych amiably.

He had been retired a year from what he had always referred to, with his gentle knife-blade of a grin, as 'my empire'. He had broken all contacts with his old associates, with Tony Lango, who ran the Calabrians, and Dennis Pelong, who ran anyone stupid enough to work for him, with Arnold Debbs and one or two other politicians who had come to him for help, with ex-Chief Superintendent Harry Danforth, who thought corruption was a fringe benefit any sensible cop was entitled to; Aldwych had broken contact with all of them except Leslie Chung. The Chinaman was his last link with the old way of life, a sentimental connection that he would never confess to Chung. Kings can exile themselves, which is preferable to being exiled by others, but they like to be reminded of the power they once exercised. Thrones are never second-hand furniture, not in the minds of those who once sat on them.

Leslie Chung was middle-aged, with thin black hair and a thin handsome face that, when he passed amongst strangers, was as impassive as a wax mask; Aldwych occasionally joked that Les worked at being the inscrutable Oriental. He always wore, even on this hot day, dark blue suits, impeccably cut by Cutlers, blue-striped Battistoni shirts, always a black silk-knit tie and black shoes that were made for him by Lobb in London. He had a wife and two daughters, both of whom were pupils at one of Sydney's most expensive schools; but none of his associates, including Aldwych, had ever met the family. He was a jewellery and gem importer and the legend was that the Chungs had entered that trade when an ancestor had been appointed gem-cutter to the last Ming emperor; ancestry is a conceit worn by everyone lucky enough to know his own parents, and it was Leslie Chung who, quietly as ever, had spread the legend. He was wealthy, his money made in mysterious ways, and he was totally without scruples. Aldwych would have loved him like a brother, if he had been capable of such stupidity and if Les had been white.

'I think you're well out of the game, Jack.' Chung picked delicately at his food with a fork; with chopsticks there was always the chance that food would fall on the Battistoni shirt. 'I think there's going to be war.'

Aldwych knew that he wasn't referring to what was happening in the Middle East. Real criminals recognize only their own wars, against their own kind or against the police; outside conflicts, world wars, were only remarked for the opportunities they offered to make money. Crims have a talent, unmatched by statesmen or generals, for getting to the heart of the matter. 'Who's gunna start it?'

'I'm not sure, but I think it might be Denny Pelong. Since you retired, he thinks Sydney is his turf. His problem is, he doesn't know who to declare war on. Someone's muscling in and he doesn't seem to have a clue who it is.'

He was beyond all this now; but kings, like commoners, can't resist gossip. 'You mean drugs?'

Chung nodded. 'Whoever it is, they're making life difficult for Denny.'

Aldwych grinned. 'Couldn't happen to a bigger bastard. What're they doing?'

'They, whoever they are, they're tipping off the Customs guys when a shipment is coming in. Haven't you noticed in the papers? There have been seven busts at the airport in the last couple of months. That's small stuff, I don't know why Denny uses that channel, but that's always been one of his troubles. He has big ideas, but a tiny mind. The bust that's hurt him, though, is one up north. The story hasn't reached the papers yet. The Customs Coastwatch patrol picked up one of his planes coming into a landing strip somewhere west of Darwin. Customs were tipped off by someone, probably the same crowd. Denny is out of his mind, you know what he's like. The stuff in the plane was worth eight million on the street. You like the Peking Duck?'

'It's not as crisp as usual. Let's go out to the kitchen later and scare the shit outa the chef, eh? What makes you think it's another mob that's doing the tipping-off? It could be just another bloody do-gooder, the world's full of 'em. Greenies, anti-smokers, welfare workers –'

'Get off your soap-box, Jack. You were always against

drugs. You're not feeling any sympathy for Pelong, are you? I'd be disappointed if you were.'

'You hate the bastard as much as I do, don't you?' Aldwych sat back against the red imitation leather. They were seated in a booth at the back of the restaurant, an empty booth with a chair up-ended on its table between them and the other booths; the restaurant manager respected the privacy of favoured clients, and no one was more favoured than these two diners. They owned the place, Chung in his wife's name, Aldwych through one of the companies managed by Jack Junior. 'No, I ain't feeling anything for him. I might go to his funeral, but only to laugh. Yeah, I'm anti-drugs, I hate the shit. But do-gooders get up my nose, they're trying to take over the fucking world . . . You don't watch out, they'll beat you Asians to it. Or is Asia full of do-gooders, too?'

'I don't think so. Not since Buddha's day.'

'What about Confucius, wasn't he a do-gooder?'

'Only when it suited him. He was no egalitarian, Jack, he'd never have voted Labor.'

Neither had Aldwych; all sensible crims vote conservative, or at least for conservatism. 'Well, if it isn't a do-gooder snitching on Denny Pelong, who is it?'

'That's the eight-million-dollar question. You want lychees for dessert?'

'Lychees and ginger ice-cream.' They ordered the same meal every time, but whoever played host, each taking it in turn, they always went through the ritual of asking the other what he wanted. They were two mandarins, but it was only Chung, the lesser of the two, who thought in those terms. 'What are you going to do, Les, if strife breaks out? Stay on the sidelines?'

'Neutrality is a wise man's investment.'

'Who said that? Confucius?'

'Leslie Chung. If it were you and Pelong fighting over the turf, it would be a different matter . . . Here's your

122

son, come to pick you up. You're fortunate, Jack. He's a credit to you.'

'To his mother, not to me.'

Aldwych never drove himself. Jack Junior or Larry Quick always acted as his chauffeur; that way there was never any harassment from over-zealous traffic cops; both chauffeurs drove sedately, with Aldwych, a nervous passenger, always keeping an eye on the speedometer. Both drivers, too, were always punctual, never keeping Aldwych waiting.

Jack Junior slid into the booth beside his father, shook hands with Chung. He was wearing a lightweight suit with an open-necked monogrammed shirt, but his face was streaked with sweat; he wiped it with a silk handkerchief, monogrammed, of course. 'You always look so cool, Leslie. How do you manage it?'

Chung winked. 'Mind over sweat glands. How's business?'

Jack Junior shook his head, made a face. 'Now would be the time to buy, everything's going at fire-sale prices. I'm looking around.'

'Keep your money where it is,' said his father. 'You spend too much money, you dunno where it is. Look at that banker feller over in Perth –' He named a man who had figured prominently in the news over the past six months. 'He was juggling fifteen, sixteen, balls in the air all at once. All of a sudden he finds two of 'em are his own. Stay liquid till we find out if the country's gunna go down the gurgler or not.'

Jack Junior looked around him. The restaurant was half-empty; six months ago one had had to book two weeks in advance to get a table. 'Look at this. Where's everybody eating these days? Are they bringing their lunches to the office in a brown paper bag? How's the gem and jewellery business?'

It sounded like any conversation at a dozen other tables where the uptown businessmen were congregated in misery; but it was just a veneer of words. Leslie Chung never discussed his real business with anyone but his peers, who were few; and Jack Junior was, of course, too legitimate, too straight. It was no worse than the hypocrisy practised at the other tables, except that in this booth Aldwych Senior sat and listened with amusement. Hypocrisy always amused him, though he had never practised it.

'You ready, Dad? I've got the car parked in a loading zone.'

Aldwych smiled indulgently at his law-abiding son, said to Chung, 'He's learned from me. Never antagonize the cops over small things, not even the parking police. Let me know how the war goes.'

'The Gulf war?' said Jack Junior.

'No, just a figure of speech,' said his father. 'Cancel the lychees, Les. Tell the chef he'd better smarten himself up on the Peking Duck, or else.'

Father and son walked out of the restaurant, two tall men who carried themselves well and with pride. The other diners looked up at them, some of the businessmen nodding to Jack Junior, with whom they had done business. All of them looked at Jack Senior, with whom they had done no business at all but for whom they had secret admiration, if no public respect. Larceny is like homosexuality, every man has a little of it in himself: most just don't let it out of the closet. One of the reasons Aldwych never went to the races was that he didn't like rubbing shoulders or shaking hands with people who would snub him once they left the course. A couple of other well-known crims had told him how it was, but they managed to grin and bear it.

There was no ticket on the Daimler, but a Grey Bomber was standing by the car, her notebook and pen ready. Jack Junior gave her a pleading smile. 'It was here for just a couple of minutes. I had to pick up my father. He has a heart condition.'

She was in her forties, plump, case-hardened against

men and their pleading smiles. 'If I give you a ticket, will he have a heart attack right there?'

Aldwych gave her his own smile, which had no pleading in it; he had never pleaded for anything, not even for his life when it had been threatened. 'My son is telling fibs. I'm as strong as an ox. He parked the car here because it was convenient and it's a helluva hot day.'

'I like an honest man,' said the Grey Bomber. 'Buzz off.'

As they drove away Jack Junior said, 'You have a way with women. Janis thinks you're honest, too.'

'I thought she'd be shrewder than that.'

Jack Junior looked sideways at him; then changed the subject: 'What war were you and Les talking about?'

'I told you, it was a figure of speech.'

'Don't con me, Dad. You and Les Chung don't meet for lunch to swap figures of speech.'

'Slow down.' Aldwych had one eye on the speedometer as they swept on to the approach to the Harbour Bridge. 'Les said that Denny Pelong is getting into some sorta strife over drugs. Someone is tipping off the Customs, and Pelong's getting shitty about it.'

'Wouldn't you?' Jack Junior took the Daimler into the inside lane to allow four surfies, boards strapped to the roof of their Toyota rust-bucket, to hurtle past, weaving in and out of the traffic like a video-game car. Then a motorcycle cop buzzed by in pursuit and Jack Junior heard his father grunt in approval. There were certain laws, not many but a few, that Aldwych thought should be policed rigorously. 'You're not involved, are you? You haven't come out of retirement and not told me?'

'I'm too old to make a comeback. Too shrewd, too. Anyhow, you know how I feel, dealing in shit. What gives you the idea I might be involved?'

'I don't know. Lateral thinking, I suppose.' Jack Junior had done a year at Stanford in California and business-school jargon still occasionally crept into his speech; most of the time his father didn't understand what he was saying, but he never queried it. After all, he had paid for Jack Junior's education. 'That cop coming to see you yesterday about – what was his name? – Grime. Scungy Grime?'

'That was force of habit, all coppers suffer from it. They'll probably be coming to see me till I topple into my grave.'

They drove in silence till they had crossed the Bridge, then Jack Junior said, 'Dad, why don't you make another trip? You're just sitting around almost as if you're waiting to topple into your grave.'

'Where would I go? This fucking war, who wants to get blown up by some terrorist?'

'Go on a plane from some neutral country. Garuca or Malaysia. Go to Europe. I remember the first time you went there with Mum, you said it was the first time you'd discovered history. Another thing you discovered was the balconies where all the dictators had shouted from. You said that Aussie politicians might do better if they went on to balconies instead of on television. You said all politicians look better from a distance.'

Aldwych smiled, glad, like all amateurs, that one of his jokes had survived. 'It's winter in Europe. I'm not going somewhere to have my balls froze off. Didn't someone write a book about that? *Ball-less in Gaza* or somewhere?'

'It was *Eyeless in Gaza*, I think, something like that.' Jack Junior, a lonely child, over-protected by his mother, had grown up an addicted reader. The library in the big house at Harbord was his and over the last few years he had introduced his father to the habit of reading. But Jack Senior, as with everything, took books in moderation. His own experiences would make a book, though he would come back from the dead to kill anyone who tried to write it.

Father looked sideways at son. 'Jack, are you trying to get rid of me? What's on your mind?'

Jack Junior drove carefully along the narrow main artery of Military Road. A hundred and twenty years ago, guns had been hauled along this road to Middle Head, guarding the entrance to the harbour, in anticipation of an invasion. Jack Junior had been shocked to read that the suspected invaders were the French, or, a double shock, the Americans; Jack Senior, never one to trust an ally, had just nodded and remarked that history was only the story of hypocrisy. 'Dad, if something is on, I mean about to start up, I don't want you involved. You're retired, stay retired.'

'I intend to. Go on.' Aldwych's voice was quiet, toneless.

Jack Junior recognized the signs. 'All right, forget it.'

'No, go on. Why do you wanna get rid of me?'

'Dad –' Jack Junior decided on confession. 'Someone rang me at the office this morning. I don't know who it was, it was just some guy. He said someone was talking to the wrong people and they thought it might be you. I asked who the wrong people were and he said you'd know.'

'They're barking up the wrong tree. I think I'd better have a word with them.'

'Who?'

'It's Denny Pelong, for sure. He wouldn't of phoned you himself, I don't think he knows how to dial a number –' He had never had any respect for Pelong's intelligence; the man had the cunning of a shithouse rat, but couldn't read a road map on the Nullabor Plain. 'I'll go and see him.'

'Dad, I don't think that's a good idea –'

'You worried for me?'

'Of course I am! Christ, you've gone all these years without getting hurt –'

'Keep your eyes on the road or we're both gunna get hurt . . . Oh, I been hurt all right. Your mother just never told you. Twice I got shot, when you were little, once I got a knife in me, another time a mug tried to carve me up with a razor . . . You don't look surprised?'

'Well, no. Mum always tried to protect me – for years I thought you were just an SP bookie. It wasn't legal, running a starting-price shop, but it wasn't – well, *criminal*. I was fifteen before I found out what you were really up to. *That* was a shock. Anything after that . . . No, I'm not surprised you've been knifed or shot, even if it was years ago. But why take the risk now?'

'Slow down.'

Jack Junior had accelerated as they went up the hill above The Spit, past the mortgages sweltering in the heat, above the yachts and cruisers flying For Sale pennants. Life was getting tough for the battlers, even the middle-class yuppies; but Aldwych had no sympathy for them. It was a dog-eat-dog world and he never failed to marvel that most mugs thought otherwise. He had never bothered with mortgages, had never indulged himself with a rich man's toys; he was as conservative fiscally as he was politically. His money was safe, wisely invested by Jack Junior.

He had never seen his son so concerned for him; it was kind of touching, enough to make any father feel proud. He just wondered why he harboured a nagging suspicion of Jack Junior's concern.

'Okay,' he said at last, 'I'll stay out of it. But if they phone you again . . .'

3

Malone sat in front of the computer, almost hitting the keys at random; almost, but not quite. The computer may, some day, solve all crimes without a cop's having to leave his desk; but a human finger, prompted by a human brain, will still have to press the first key. The old 'murder box', the stand-by of detectives for years, had gone. Clements had kept the 'murder box' for the team of Malone and himself, a battered, stuck-together shoebox into which had gone every small piece of evidence connected with the crime of the hour; the box had gone, was now in the police museum, and so had the feeling of closeness to a crime, a *touching* of the murderer, an identification of the case with Malone and Clements that, at least in their own minds, made it 'theirs'. Now everything went into the computer, was stored in the data bank, was available to anyone who had the entry code. But no computer has yet been built that can, of its own accord, duplicate the random thoughts of a man. A man, for the time being, is still safe in his own irrational thought processes.

He had punched in his entry code: 8747 – Scomal. Complex codes were not encouraged, as if the computer was telling cops that it thought they were simple-minded men. The central data bank for the whole of Australasia was here in Sydney: crims from Auckland, Perth, Port Moresby, Oodnadatta, even Canberra, met here in an identification parade that none of them was aware of. Malone's fingers did their idle work and a name came up to join the parade: Dallas George White. It was not an entirely irrational turn-up: his name was lodged as securely in Malone's mind as it was in the data bank. Other names followed: Gary Schultz, Normie Grime, Sally Kissen, Ulysses Lugopolous, Ava Redgrave, real name Jean Auburn, Tuesday Streep, real name Shirley Strunk, John Aldwych . . . Malone kept running the names, looking for some connection.

Half an hour ago there had been a conference in the office of Superintendent Greg Random, head of the Regional Crime Squad, over at Police Centre. It had not been a large gathering; Random did not contribute to the theory that minds multiplied produced a greater sum of intelligence. He was a senior officer now, but the habits of his days as the member of a two-man team still clung. He and Malone got on well.

'So what have we got? So far this week – and it's only

Tuesday – so far we've got three murders close in and another three on the outskirts. Those three don't concern us, Parramatta can look after them. But the Minister has been on to the Commissioner and the Commissioner's been on to the DC and he's been on to the A/C Crime, and *he's* been on to me. It seems that the Minister wants them all cleaned up before you knock off and go home tonight.'

'So far we don't have a definite link between any of them,' said Malone. 'It's just a gut feeling I have.'

Random wrinkled his long nose. 'I don't think the Minister would know what a gut feeling is, even though he's a farmer. Not good enough, Scobie. How many men have you got on this?'

Malone indicated himself, Clements, Graham and Truach. 'Just us four so far. There's help from the Randwick Ds on Scungy and the Glebe fellers are doing the leg-work on Maddux. The same GMO, Dr Keller, is on all the murders – she's teed up the forensic pathologist on the needle cases. Fingerprints have their fellers on Grime and Kissen, but so far they've found nothing. There were some prints on the wall beside Kissen's bed, but they could have been her customers – there were at least four different sets. None of them in the record. Right now they're checking the diving mask. The prints on our pool gate were mine.'

'You have any spare men?'

'I've got two fellers away in the bush, down at Albury on that hitch-hiker murder, and most of the others are working on pre-Christmas cases.'

'That's another point raised by our lord and master. There are twelve unsolved murders on our books. He says it doesn't make the government look very good.'

'Jesus Christ Himself couldn't make that government look good,' said Clements. 'They are the greatest bunch of –'

Malone chopped him off before politics caught alight.

'Five of the murders are of Vietnamese – I was working on one when I was employing Scungy. As far as we can see, none of them is related. Four of them occurred out in the west, but try to get anyone out there to talk . . . Out there around Cabramatta, Little Vietnam, it's the country of the blind. No one sees anything. A man gets shot right in front of them and they say they were looking the other way and saw and heard nothing. Let Gus the Great himself go out there and try to get something out of them.'

Random nodded sympathetically at the bitterness in Malone's voice. 'I know, Scobie. But the fact remains, our record isn't looking good at the moment. We had all that bad publicity last year, with the SWOS and the Tac Response guys getting over-eager . . . Even the crims are sending us sympathy notes.'

'Really?' said Andy Graham.

'Really,' said Random, straight-faced and patient. 'I think you'd better come up with something pretty quick, Scobie. I'll get the PR lot to put out a release that we have several leads, that we hope to have an arrest within a couple of days.'

'Which murderer are we supposed to be arresting?' said Clements. The mood in Random's office would have turned milk sour.

'Take your pick. How about being close to picking up Grime's killer? That might scare off whoever's trying to scare you, Scobie.'

'It might not, too, Greg. Let's say we've got a lead on Jimmy Maddux's killer. I'd like to put a bit of pressure on White and Schultz.'

But since his return to Homicide, since sitting down here at the computer, he had managed to put pressure on no one, least of all White and The Dwarf. The names on the screen did not connect. The data bank knew nothing of the fact that Leroy Lugos was the pimp for Ava and Tuesday; it said nothing about Scungy Grime ever having known Dallas White or Gary Schultz. The computer, he felt, would be right at home in Cabramatta, another territory where connections were never made.

Then the phone rang: it was Roley Bremner. 'Scobie, I got some information for you. Normie Grime was working night shift Sunday night on Number 8 wharf. Snow White and The Dwarf were working next door on Number 9. That help you any?'

Never discourage an informant, especially one on your side. 'I think it might, Roley. Did you see Mrs Maddux?'

'Yeah, she took it pretty crook. I didn't hang around. Her family's looking after her. I find out anything more about them bastards, I'll let you know.'

He hung up and Malone sat gazing at the phone. Then: 'Inspector?'

Malone looked up. Peter Keller stood in the doorway of the big room, immaculate in white overalls, like an engineer in a dust-free, germ-free laboratory; he carried a broom and a black plastic rubbish bag and behind him in the corridor was a commercial-sized vacuum cleaner. 'May I begin cleaning?'

'Is it that late?' Malone looked at his watch. 'Sure, go ahead.'

He stood up, arched his back, then slipped the cover over the computer. Everyone else in Homicide left it uncovered, but he always covered his typewriter at night and he automatically did the same with the computer.

Keller stood watching him. 'The computer, it helps your police work? We did not have them in Germany when I left, not in our area. The secret police had them, of course, but not us.'

'West Germany had secret police?'

'Of course. Doesn't every country? East Germany had its *Stasi*, thousands of them. Now Germany is one again, the *Stasi* are looking for jobs, but who will employ an ex-Communist secret policeman?' He smiled. 'Perhaps the CIA?'

Somehow Malone had not expected any humour from the rather dour-looking German. 'Maybe. Were you law and order cops expected to co-operate with the secret police?'

'In Germany, Inspector, all bureaucracies are expected to co-operate. It is in our nature. Of course, it didn't always happen. Not in my time. Less so now, I should imagine.' He looked at the covered-up computer. 'A wonderful invention.'

'Can you operate one?'

Keller had begun to empty the waste-baskets. 'No, Inspector, I am old-fashioned, out of date. Technology makes me feel I am an idiot . . . There were times when I would have given my pension for the information one could find in a machine like that. I was telling your colleague, Sergeant Clements, last night, I very much wanted to be a detective. But it never happened. I had the tenacity. That is what one needs as a detective – tenacity.'

Malone smiled. 'And luck.'

'Yes,' said Keller. 'And luck. But I never had that, either.'

He went on down the room, moving from desk to desk, criss-crossing from one to another in a pattern as methodical as a military marching routine; there was a Teutonic thoroughness to him that was almost a caricature, but Malone knew from experience that stereotypes were only moulds with the cracks in them papered over. He wondered sometimes in whose mind's eye he, too, was a stereotype. He certainly knew where the cracks were.

He picked up his jacket and was halfway out the door when the phone rang in his own room. He went back to it. 'Inspector Malone? It's Bill Dibble, from Customs. Head office has okayed the divers – they'll be at Glebe Island at nine-thirty this evening, when it's dark. I thought you'd like to know, in case you wanna be here.'

Malone sighed. He had been looking forward to a swim, a light supper and an early night. 'I'll be there.'

Malone lifted himself out of the pool, caught the towel that young Tom threw at him. 'Da-ad –'

When *Dad* was stretched into two syllables, it was always a sign that one of his kids was going to ask a favour. 'Righto, what is it this time?'

'Dad, the kids at school in my class, can I bring 'em home tomorrow afternoon? They'd like to talk to the cops who are protecting us.'

'How many kids?'

'Twenty-eight,' said Tom, innocent enough to quote a true figure, something he would learn not to do in years to come.

The picture of twenty-eight curious kids crowding into the Malone back yard was too much: Malone couldn't be angry, could only be amused. 'Tom, the Police Commissioner would be out here like a shot –'

'They'd like to talk to him, too –'

'Pull your head in, nerd,' said Maureen, hauling herself out of the water and sitting on the edge of the pool. 'There's no publicity, understand? I dunno why . . .'

Malone looked down at the young constable standing waist-deep in the pool. 'What do you think, Dick? You want to be interviewed by twenty-eight kids?'

'Fifty-three,' said Maureen. 'If Tom has his class, I wanna have mine.'

Constable Elmore, only two years out of high school, grinned. He was blond and good-looking, a hunk, as Claire had described him to her mother, who had agreed; but he was still a boy, still had a long way to go to prove himself as a cop. Lisa, and to a lesser extent Malone, had tried to make him part of the family while he was here on duty, but he was not entirely at ease with the situation. He preferred senior officers to show more rank than Malone was showing in a pair of swim-trunks.

'Kids frighten me, sir.'

'Garn,' said Maureen, who, in her short time, had frightened more than her fair share of adults. 'We're harmless.'

Then Lisa came to the back door. 'Time to eat. What's going on?'

'Tom and Maureen want to bring the school down tomorrow afternoon for a press conference. Seven hundred and thirty-three, I think, was the last figure I saw in the school report.'

'Sure, why not?' said Lisa. 'That's only seven hundred more than we had here yesterday.'

Malone looked down at Constable Elmore, who had started to grin but abruptly stopped when he saw the look on Malone's face. 'Put your head under water, Constable. This conversation isn't fit for the ears of an unmarried man.'

'It's gunna be a domestic,' Maureen informed the young officer.

Malone flicked her with his towel and she yelped. 'Inside!'

'So can I have the kids here tomorrow?' said Tom, not giving up.

'Your mother just said no.'

'I didn't hear her –'

'You're just too young to hear the nuances in a woman's voice,' said his mother.

'What's nu – what you just said?'

'Inside!'

The two children disappeared into the house. Lisa held open the screen door for Malone. She looked past him, at Constable Elmore lifting himself out of the pool and shaking the water from himself. 'Gorgeous, isn't he? You going out again tonight?'

'As a matter of fact –'

'Oh, don't apologize. Dick doesn't go off duty till twelve.'

'Dick?'

'Yes, lovely name, isn't it? Has sexual overtones, too.'
'I think I may turn into a wife-beater –'
'Great! That means you'll be staying home to do it?'
He kissed the top of her head. She was the constant in his life that he needed, someone to paper over the cracks.

CHAPTER FIVE

I

The waterfront at night always seemed unreal to Malone; the play of light and shadow made it another world. The darkness above compressed the scene; the cranes, the ship loomed larger. Sounds, against the silence beyond the wharf, were magnified; the occasional shout from a wharfie on the night shift sounded more urgent than the shouts Malone had heard during the day. He would not have been surprised if aliens from outer space had appeared at the ship's railing above him, asking if they needed to go through Immigration.

'The divers are working from under the wharf,' Dibble told him. 'They came round by launch and slipped in there, just paddling. The wharfies won't know they're there.'

'It must be pitch black down there.'

'It probably is, but they won't switch on their torches till they go below the surface. These guys are used to working in all sorts of conditions.'

He and Malone were standing in the shadow of a stack of containers, obscured from the teams unloading the holds of the *Southern Pacific*. Malone had checked that White and Schultz were not on this shift. Two senior Customs men were hidden amongst other stacks of containers and plainclothesmen from the Federal police were in a car parked up by the wharf gates. So far the police and Customs presence was undetected.

The heat was still oppressive and the night air seemed to have thickened; Malone's nostrils were stuffed with the mixture of salt air and the smell of molasses from across the narrow bay. He began to wish for an early end to the night.

'If they find nothing –'

Then Dibble's walkie-talkie crackled and he held it up to his ear. A voice, its excitement showing through its mechanical flatness, said, 'They've got something! They're bringing it up now!'

'Okay, here we go!' said Dibble and, considering his bulk, surprised Malone with the speed with which he took off; he still had some of the greyhound swiftness of his youth of which he had boasted. Malone, caught flat-footed, was some yards behind him by the time they reached the steps that led down to the launch moored out of sight of the ship. A few moments later the two senior Customs men tumbled down the steps and into the boat.

Dibble took the boat cautiously round the end of the wharf and crept it, engine ticking over quietly, in under the stern of the *Southern Pacific*, between the ship and the wharf. It slid in beside the divers' launch, where three men in diving suits crouched, while a fourth hung from its side in the water. The darkness was intense here, the divers in their black suits indistinguishable but for the gleam of water on the rubber.

'What've you got?' The senior Customs man was named Radelli; tall, thin and prematurely grey, he had the watchful eye of a well-trained guard dog. Malone, meeting him, had wondered if he did his own sniffing. 'That it?'

One of the divers flicked on a narrow-beam flashlight and held up a slim metal container, painted yellow and attached to two long magnets. 'We brought up only one – there are another five still down there. We've covered the whole of the hull below the waterline. There's nothing else. But this'd be enough.'

Radelli took the container. It had a screw-on top, like the lid of a Thermos flask; waterproof tape was wrapped round the join. He opened it, tipped it up and six plastic bags filled with white powder slid out. He pierced one of the bags with a penknife, tasted the powder and nodded. 'Cocaine.'

'Don't they know there's a recession on?' said Dibble. 'That's yuppie stuff. What're you gunna do, Luke?'

Radelli carefully rewound the binding tape, handed the container back to the head diver, who snapped off his flashlight. 'Put it back. We'll post a watch for the next twenty-four hours – the ship is due to go out on Thursday morning's tide. If they don't come for it before then, then we'll know they're on to us.' He looked up at the side of the ship towering above them like a steel wave about to break. 'Someone on board could have been keeping an eye on this end, knowing where the stuff was. Chances are one of the crew is part of the set-up.'

'We've been pretty invisible,' said the head diver.

'We'll try and stay that way. Back off over to the CSR wharf. You guys be prepared for twenty-four-hour stand-by.'

'Shit!' said the diver in the water.

'Not in your wet-suit,' said Radelli and for the first time all night smiled, a pale rip in his face.

Dibble eased the launch away from beneath the ship, took it back to the wharf steps. Once up on the wharf again he looked at Malone. 'You gunna join 'em in the stake-out?'

'You're welcome,' said Radelli, making it sound like a *get lost* dismissal.

'You're looking for smugglers, I'm looking for a murderer.' Malone felt let down. Against reason, he had hoped that Schultz would have bobbed up out of the water, ready to confess everything as soon as he was nabbed. He had suffered from the lack of enthusiasm that infects any professional who has to work in someone else's show; Radelli's indifference to his presence had only increased his own desire to get home as quickly as possible. 'You have first choice, since he's in your territory.' If Radelli caught the mild sarcasm, he didn't show it. 'If you grab anyone, let me know and I'll be in to see him. The Feds will hold him, I take it?'

Radelli and the other senior Customs man left; Dibble accompanied Malone across to his car parked behind the Customs office. 'Thanks for showing me that diving mask, putting me on to this. It'll look good when the report goes in.'

'I'm glad someone will look good.' Then Malone heard the sourness in his own voice. 'Sorry, Bill. I'm cranky from the heat, it's been a long hot day. And I'm not getting anywhere. I'm pretty sure I know who killed Jimmy Maddux, but why? Did Maddux find out about the stuff being stuck to the bottom of that ship?'

'Who do you suspect? Never mind, don't tell me, I don't wanna know. I got enough headaches, without that sorta information. Maybe Jimmy Maddux saw whoever it was swimming around at the stern of the ship? He could've made the mistake of letting the guy see him.'

'There's the matter of the diving mask being in Maddux's locker – how would he have got that off the swimmer?' Then he stopped, his lethargic mind suddenly slipping into another gear. 'Unless –'

'Unless what?'

'Unless Jimmy Maddux wasn't as afraid of the water as everyone thought? I wonder if he was the contact man for whoever is bringing the stuff in, but someone, someone from another mob, got to him first?'

2

'Who suggested you come here?' said Janis Eden.

'I – I just heard about it,' said Ava Redgrave. 'Everybody on the street knows about this place.'

Janis sat back in her chair, her head brushing against the wall behind her. This cubicle she called her office was designed for one-on-one counselling; another person in the so-called room would have made a truism of three is a crowd. The new State government spent more words than money on drug and alcohol rehabilitation; it believed in 'self-help' as a slogan, even though too many of the country's entrepreneurs had given a new meaning to the term. Janis, a true conservative, had voted for the new government, but she wished it had increased the budget enough to provide decent accommodation at least for herself. She did not care much for her fellow counsellors, most of whom were lefties and suffered from dedication.

'What's your problem?' But the rolled-down sleeves had already told her what the problem was.

'I – well, it's smack. Heroin.'

'What's your name?'

'Ava Redgrave.'

She had a good counsellor's talent for not showing reaction till it was needed; but mentally she rolled her eyeballs at the name. At least it was better than yesterday's visitor, Jesus Christ Smith. 'How long have you been on it?'

'Two years, almost.'

'What do you do, Ava?'

'I – I'm a receptionist.'

Janis sighed. 'Ava, if you and I are going to get anywhere, we'll have to at least show some of the truth. Otherwise you're wasting my time and yours.'

Ava was sitting straight up in her chair, knees together, hands folded in her lap. Janis wondered if she had been convent-educated, it was the way some schools still taught their girls to sit, as if keeping one's knees together locked in the libido. Ava looked down at her hands, then she seemed to relax, her shoulders drooping, her knees slipping apart. 'Okay, I'm on the street. It's the only way I've been able to pay for my habit.'

Another one, thought Janis: the market out there was unlimited. She sneezed; she hoped a summer cold wasn't coming on, and took a handkerchief from her pocket. She never brought a handbag with her to a counselling; no matter how much you trusted the client, you never put temptation in their way; it was a standard rule. Twice in her first month as a counsellor she had been relieved of her wallet.

'Do you work for yourself or for someone? I mean, a pimp?'

'I – I work for a guy. He gives me the stuff at cost price.'

No dealer, not even a pimp, was ever that generous. 'Do you want to give me his name?'

Ava frowned. 'Are you supposed to ask that?'

There were no definite rules on such a question, but most counsellors, as a matter of ethics, did not ask it. With Janis, ethics were like ticks: she kept her head free of them. 'No-o. But the dealers are as much a part of our problem as they are for you. If you want to tell me, I promise it will go no further.'

Ava hesitated, then said, 'His name's Leroy Lugos. Do you know him?'

She had come to know the names of most of the dealers here in the King's Cross area; but she had not heard of Leroy Lugos. 'Where does he get the stuff?'

'I don't know, I've never asked. But he's always got it.'

That meant he was not a part-time dealer, that he had a major source somewhere. 'Okay, let's forget him for the moment. Why do you want to give it up? The heroin, I mean. The determination is yours, we can only support you in it.'

Ava was silent. She looked up and about her, everywhere but at Janis. The tiny room was painted pale pink and held two medium-sized prints, both of them restful landscapes; there were no anti-drug posters, no strident threats or warnings to those who came into this room seeking help. It was doubtful if Ava saw her surroundings at all; she was looking for courage but found none. She looked back at Janis.

'I'm scared, really shit scared. The woman where I live, she was on the game, but not on the street like me, she was murdered on Sunday night. Some kinky client killed her with a needle.'

'An overdose?'

'No, it was some poison, one of the cops told me. It killed her almost immediately, he said. They warned us he might come back, do the same to me and my girlfriend. I – I just decided it – it wasn't worth risking being – *murdered*. It happens, y'know, I mean to us sometimes. The guys we pick up, most of the time we've never seen 'em before.'

'I know,' said Janis, sounding sympathetic, hiding her sudden concern. Had this woman, whoever she was, died the same way as the man Grime? The coincidence chilled her, but Ava would never know that the well-groomed girl opposite her was disturbed. Janis had learned to act, for the best counsellors are good actors, otherwise their audience would never sit still for them. Counsellors have problems of their own; the act is to hide them. 'Where do you come from originally?'

'The country. Wagga.'

'Your parents alive?'

'Yes. They don't know where I am, I think they've given up on me.'

'Do you want to go home?'

Ava looked down at her hands again. 'Yes, I think so. At least I'd be safe there.'

What from, the murderer's needle or your own? But Janis did not believe in being cruel to be kind; she had no conscience, but she wasn't malicious. 'The first thing is, we'll get you introduced into our programme. You'll see someone downstairs in the clinic, they'll probably advise methadone –'

'If – *when* I come again, will I see you or someone else? I – I feel I can trust you.'

'I work here at the Cross only two days a week. I do another day at St Sebastian's, with patients there who have your problem. If you come here and I'm not here, they can get me on my beeper and you can come over to the hospital and see me there, okay?' She stopped and looked hard at the girl. 'It's not going to be easy, Ava.'

'I – I know that. But I want to try –' She suddenly shut her eyes, looked as if she wanted to weep. Somewhere in another cubicle someone started to cry. But tears and self-pity were part of the atmosphere in this building.

Then the phone rang. Janis picked it up, recognized the voice at once. 'You're not supposed to ring me here . . .'

'I know that, for Crissake,' said Snow White. 'But I thought you'd wanna hear the bad news. We lost the stuff, the whole fucking lot. It's still there in place, but we got Buckley's chance of picking it up. They're watching it. I just thought you'd like to know, you're so fucking smart.'

'Thank you, Mr Black,' she said and hung up in his ear. Then she looked across at Ava, who was wiping her eyes. 'As I said, Ava, it's not going to be easy.'

3

That morning, Wednesday, Malone went over to Balmain to see Jimmy Maddux's widow. He didn't take Clements: two big cops crowding into her home would be amongst the last things a grieving woman would wish for. A young uniformed officer drove him in a marked car; Malone would have preferred an unmarked one, but he had no choice. Balmain, as he remembered it, had never been an area to welcome mug coppers.

The tiny suburb occupied a peninsula on the south side of the upper harbour. Its narrow streets seemed to meet each other accidentally. On top of the ridge were a few large houses, built by ships' masters and shipbuilders in the middle of the last century, most of them now occupied by academics and architects and one or two successful writers and artists. Down the slopes were the narrow houses of those who had given Balmain its character over the years: a motley mixture of immigrants, a village that saluted the flag of the Balmain Tigers, the local rugby league team, before it would think of singing the national anthem. Fair Australia advanced only when the Tigers won the premiership.

The Madduxes lived in one of the narrowest houses in one of the narrowest streets. Malone got out of the police car, saw the curtains flick back at windows like the sidelong glances of a dozen eyes, and said to the driver, 'Come back for me in twenty minutes. I don't want them throwing stones at you.'

The young cop grinned. 'It's okay, sir, they know me. I play for the Tigers' seconds. Reserve grade.'

'You mean they let cops play for the Tigers?'

'We get a dispensation, a sort of annulment for the weekend. It's like the Catholic Church – so long as we confess our sins on training nights, they pick us for the weekend games.'

He drove away and Malone shook his head at the improving intelligence amongst young cops and especially amongst the Tigers. He went in through the rickety wooden gate and in two strides had reached the peeling front door. Jimmy Maddux, it seemed, had not been a home handyman.

The door was opened by a young woman only a kilo or two ahead of a weight problem. She was not pretty, but there was a suggestion of liveliness about her round face that, before yesterday, might have made her attractive. Now her face was slack, her eyes red-rimmed, her hair uncombed. She had that blank look of shock that Malone had seen before on the faces of young women, those who had not expected to be made widows so early. Behind her, in the small narrow house, there was a subdued babble of voices. This, of course, was a village: he should have known that everyone would have rallied round the grieving Molly Maddux.

145

He introduced himself. 'I'm sorry to intrude, Mrs Maddux, but I have to ask a few questions –'

'Why?' Her voice was a flat whine.

The door was pulled wider and another young woman, slimmer, more in control of herself in every way, stood there, her arm going round Molly Maddux's shoulders. 'Look, come back some other time. For God's sake, she's just lost her husband! Where are your bloody feelings, for God's sake?'

He kept his tone as gentle as he could; in circumstances like these it was always the outsiders, the family comforters, who were aggressive, who got up his nose. 'I don't want to upset Mrs Maddux any more than she is. But her husband was murdered –'

'*Murdered?*' The round plump face seemed to flatten like dough flung against a wall.

'Didn't you know?'

'Roley Bremner said it was an accident –'

He had told Bremner not to mention the word *murder*, but since then the media had exposed the accident for what it truly was.

'No, love, it was murder.' The other young woman pressed Molly Maddux's shoulders. 'It was on the news last night and it's in the papers this morning. But we kept it from you . . .' She looked at Malone. 'I'm her sister. She's taking Jimmy's death hard enough as it is . . . We're keeping it from the kids, too. They're only seven and eight, the eldest, and the twins, they're three. The older ones'd understand murder is different.'

If they don't understand, the kids at school will tell them. He often wondered why people tried to protect children from tragic news; inevitably, eventually, they learned it from the wrong sources. 'Look, I know this is a bad time, but there's never a good time for this sort of thing –'

'You're not gunna go away, are you?' said the sister.

He sighed; the sun was hot on his back, baking him, but

it was not the real cause of his discomfort. 'No, I'm afraid not. Let's get it over with.'

The two sisters looked at each other, then Molly Maddux nodded and stepped back from the doorway into the narrow hall. 'Come into the bedroom, there's too many people out the back.'

'The family and neighbours,' her sister explained. 'I'll come in with you. I don't think she oughta be left alone with you. Nothing personal.'

Malone smiled, but said nothing. He followed the sisters into the front bedroom, a room bursting under the pressure of the double bed, the wardrobe and the dressing-table; a small cheap print of Hans Heysen's gumtrees hung above the bed, like a tiny window on a larger, uncluttered world. Malone himself had been born in a room like this, though the house in Erskineville, another working-class inner suburb, had been slightly larger than this. But the atmosphere was the same, a hundred years or more of battlers' hopes that had gone mouldy, never able to escape through the front door to realization. Malone himself had escaped, but Molly Maddux's fate was written in her dulled eyes. He wondered if the dreams had died only yesterday.

The sisters sat down on the chenille-covered bed and Malone leaned against the wardrobe. It was like conducting an interview, he thought, in a phone booth. 'Did your husband ever talk to you about enemies?'

'Enemies? Jimmy?' She shook her head. The whine had gone out of her voice, it was softer, almost a whisper: she had just suffered a second shock, one more devastating than the first. It could happen, Malone knew: most people are prepared, even if only subconsciously, for death; but not for murder. 'He got into fights occasionally – he had a pretty touchy temper. But enemies? No, no.'

'Did he talk to you about this election that's coming up? The union election?'

She was silent for a long moment; she seemed to be

having trouble putting her thoughts together. 'The union election? Yeah, once or twice, but he never said much about what went on at work. Not lately.'

'Not lately? Why was that?'

Molly Maddux hesitated, looked sideways at her sister, then up at Malone. 'We aint been getting on too well lately. We used to argue, have fights.'

The sister also looked up at Malone. 'Is this necessary? You don't have to pry, do you, I mean into personal stuff, do you?'

Malone slipped off his jacket; the room was stifling. He wanted to loosen his tie, but restrained himself. Not out of any dress code, but because he felt, somehow, that it would be an insulting comment on how some other people had to live, in these cramped, stuffy hot-boxes. 'Look – what's your name?'

'Sheryl. Sheryl Longman.'

'Sheryl, prying into other people's business doesn't make me jump up and down with joy. I hate it, if you want the truth. But yes, it *is* necessary. We have to find out who killed Jimmy – whoever it was, he isn't going to come forward and confess it.' He looked back at Molly Maddux. 'Why were you having fights, Molly? Did you or he have something on your minds, something that got you short-tempered with each other? You said Jimmy had a pretty touchy temper.'

She hesitated again, then drew a deep breath, pulled her thoughts together. 'We used to fight over money. He made good money, but somehow it all went. He liked to bet, on the horses and dogs, and he drank a lot. But –' She avoided her sister's eye this time. 'I wasn't any good with it, either. I mean, saving money. It just seemed to, I dunno, run away, you know . .' Her voice trailed off.

For the first time Malone saw the coloured photo in the cheap tin frame on the dressing-table: a solidly built, curly-haired man with his arms round two boys who wore beanies and scarves in black and gold, the Tigers' colours. 'Was Jimmy close to your children?'

She glanced at the photo. 'He thought the world of 'em, especially the two boys. That was another thing we fought over – he said if we went on spending money the way we were, the kids would never have a better life than us. He was always talking about a better life, but somehow, I dunno . . .' Her voice trailed off again.

'Molly –' This was the difficult bit: 'Molly, could I look through his papers? His bank book or building society book, if he had one. A notebook, if he kept one. That sort of thing.'

'For God's sake!'

'I *know*, Sheryl. Molly?'

She hesitated, then she got up, opened the door of the wardrobe as he stood aside, and took out an old-fashioned tin box. 'It's locked. He always carried the key with him on his key-ring.'

It was Sheryl who voiced Malone's query: 'You mean he kept a *locked* box? One you weren't supposed to look into? Jesus – *men*!' She looked up at Malone. 'Do you keep things from your wife, if you've got one?'

'Quite a lot,' he said. 'Only I don't keep them in a locker. Molly, did they give you back Jimmy's personal things when you identified the body?'

'She didn't identify him, his brother did,' said Sheryl. 'Yes, they give us Jimmy's things. I'll get them.'

She went out of the room. Molly Maddux sat back on the bed, stared up at Malone with a terrible, bruised look on her face. She was glistening with sweat, rivulets of it running down her temples out of her dark hair, but she seemed unaware of it. 'Why would anyone wanna murder him?'

'I don't know,' said Malone, not even daring to hope that the locked box in his hand might contain something that would open up another window on Jimmy Maddux.

Sheryl came back with the key-ring and Malone selected

149

one of the keys. He opened the box, tilted it on to the bed as both women leaned forward. The contents tumbled out: a birth certificate, an insurance policy, two packets of condoms, some letters held together by a rubber band, two silver medals, a gold pass for the Sydney Cricket Ground and the Football Stadium, and a bank pass-book.

'Could I see the letters?' said Molly.

But first Malone held up the silver medals. 'These Jimmy's?'

'Yeah, when he was at school up north, he come from a little place near Murwillumbah, he was the school swimming champion. He won those medals.'

'Molly – Roley Bremner told me it was a joke down on the wharves that Jimmy couldn't swim.'

She nodded. 'Yeah, Jimmy told me about it. He told them that. The truth was, he was scared of sharks. When he first come to Sydney, he went swimming in the harbour and was chased by a shark. He'd take the boys to the beach, but he'd never go in the harbour. Can I see those letters?'

Malone held on to the letters, instead held up the gold pass. 'How could Jimmy afford this? It costs six thousand dollars to join, plus something like two or three hundred a year. If you were always short of money, like you said . . .'

'I dunno, I just dunno. He took the boys once or twice to the stadium, but he told me someone had given him tickets. Can I see those letters?' Her voice now was sharp.

'I don't think you'd better, love,' said Sheryl quietly.

Molly looked at her sister, frowned, then suddenly her hand shot out and she snatched the bundle of letters from Malone. She tore at the rubber band, snapped it off and dropped the loose letters, a dozen or so of them, into her lap. Malone watched the two women; he began to feel sick, wanted to roll back everything he had started. Sheryl glanced at him, her eyes suddenly sharp with hatred, then she looked back at her sister.

Molly was reading a few lines of each page of the letters;

her hands were shaking and the pages fluttered as if in an unfelt current in the stifling, airless room. But of course there was a current: one between the sisters that Malone, standing so close to them, could feel.

'*Darling Jimmy* . . . Oh shit! Sheryl, how could you, you bitch? My own sister!'

'It was all over, Molly. Look at the dates – it was all over three years ago. It started when you and Jimmy were having that rough time, when I thought you were gunna break up – you told me so yourself, you said you were gunna leave him –'

'I was pregnant with the twins – and he was sleeping with you! I could kill you! And him – oh, I'm glad he's gone! I'm glad, glad!'

Malone stepped out into the narrow hallway, pulling the bedroom door closed behind him. The sisters had lowered their voices, evidently not wanting the rest of the family and the neighbours to know what was going on between them; Malone could hear the angry murmuring, but not make out what was being said. A small boy, about Tom's age and size, came to the end of the hallway and glared at Malone.

'Where's me mum? Who are you?' He was afraid of no one, a Tiger of the future.

'I'm a policeman. Your mum's in the bedroom – she asked me to step out here while she talks to your Aunty Sheryl. It's okay, go back where you came from. That's what your mum would want.'

'Are you gunna make trouble for Mum?'

I've already done that: the anger behind the closed door sounded fiercer. 'No. I'll be gone in a minute. Go back.'

The boy gave him another belligerent look, like that of a certain Tiger hero being sent from the field by a referee; then he spun round and was gone. Malone drew a deep breath, wanted to be gone from here as soon as possible.

He opened the pass-book, which was still in his hand. It had only four entries, the first three months ago. They were for varying amounts, but all in round figures: $2000, $1500, $1500, $2500, all in cash deposits. Jimmy Maddux, it seemed, had had another life locked away in the black metal box.

There was a sudden silence behind the closed door; then it was pulled open and Sheryl stood in the doorway for a moment. 'You bastard! I hope you realize what you've done!'

Then she pushed past him, hitting him in the ribs with her elbow, and disappeared into the back of the house; the voices out there were abruptly stilled. Malone stood in the hallway, wondering if he shouldn't just open the front door and walk out. Then he looked in at Molly, still sitting on the bed, her face red and tear-streaked, the letters now just a torn litter of scraps spread around her like mocking blossoms.

'I'm sorry, Molly. I should've taken the box away with me –'

She shook her head dumbly. Then she gave a great sigh, more like a giant sob; he had heard one or two people make that sound just before they died, an inarticulate last goodbye. She stared at him, as if not seeing him; then her eyes came into focus. She looked at the pass-book in his hand, said in a soft, matter-of-fact, resigned voice, 'More bad news?'

'I don't know. Did you know about this?'

She took it from him, looked at the entries, then looked back up at him, puzzlement wiping the blankness from her face. 'I've never seen *this*! Where'd he get all this money?'

'I don't know, Molly. Unless he won it on the horses or the dogs – ?'

'I'd of known. I know the bookie – he'd of told me –'

'Well, there's that, and the gold pass . . . When did he get that?'

'I dunno – I never knew he had it. But he took the boys to see the footy – I suppose he must of used that pass –'

That would have been at least four months ago, before

152

the football season had ended; could the gold pass have been a first payment? 'I'll leave everything else, but I'll have to take this pass-book and the gold pass with me, okay?'

She handed back the pass-book, taking one last look at it and shaking her head. 'Will I get it back? I guess the money belongs to me and the kids, right? He owes it to me,' she said bitterly, her grief for the moment forgotten.

She had the battler's practicality; money might slip through her hands, but she would keep grabbing for it. He couldn't blame her. 'You'll have it back as soon as I've traced where it came from.'

She looked down at the contents of the metal box still spread on the bed. She picked up the two packets of condoms. 'I wonder who he used these on? He always made me take the Pill after the boys were born. The twins were an accident – I forgot to take it and he was ropeable about that. Jesus, what a shit! I knew he was a bastard, but you expect that, don't you, I mean part of the time? We aint perfect, none of us, are we?' She began to scoop up the scraps of the letters. 'Take these with you, will you? Otherwise I'm likely to try and stick 'em together, so's I can read 'em again and make myself sick. Get rid of 'em somewhere, burn 'em.'

'Whose letters are they? Just Sheryl's to him? Nobody else's, like someone explaining about the money?'

'No, just Sheryl's.' He believed her; she was in no mood to protect the bastard who had been her husband. 'She was always the educated one, she went to business school. I worked in a factory, she worked in an office. Her letters are *typed*, you notice? Geez, even I know better than that! Typing love letters! Take 'em, don't read 'em, promise!'

Her anger was starting to bubble again. He pressed her shoulder, then took the scraps of paper and stuffed them into his pocket. 'I'll burn 'em, I promise.' He went out into the hallway, opened the front door; the heat outside attacked them both. 'I'm sorry, Molly.'

'I know.' She pushed a wet strand of hair back from her face, squinted in the glare. 'Life's a bugger, aint it? But you get used to it.'

She closed the door on him. He opened the rickety gate and, true to the nature of the moment, it fell off its hinges. He propped it up against the fence, stepped out into the street and looked up and down its narrow length for the police car. It was parked up at the corner. Malone walked up towards it, to the young constable sitting on a fender, signing autographs for three young boys. He straightened up as Malone approached, waved the boys away and grinned in embarrassment.

'Sorry, sir. They were after my autograph.'

'You're in the *seconds* and they ask for your autograph?'

'This is Tiger country, it's like that over here.' They got into the oven of the car. 'Did you play any sport when you were young, sir?'

'A bit of cricket.' He had played for the State, never for the *seconds*, but he couldn't remember ever being asked for his autograph. Life was indeed a bugger, as Molly Maddux had said.

4

Leroy Lugos pulled up the red Porsche outside Dennis Pelong's house in Sans Souci and sat for a moment looking out across the expanse of water where the George's River ran into Botany Bay. He couldn't understand why Denny lived out here in the boondocks, seven or eight Ks, maybe more, from the Cross, the heart of the nation; way out here, he was sure, cousins married cousins and other impediments to human intelligence occurred. If he had Denny's money, which he hoped to have some day, he would buy himself a penthouse right on the water at Point Piper or Double Bay, right there amongst the silvertail snobs, and he would shove it up their noses every day, metaphorically speaking, of course. He had too much sense to lay a finger on anyone, unless it was a woman.

The Pelong house was a near-mansion, dwarfing everything else in the suburban street; its security turned it into a near-fort. The high wall was topped with iron spikes and barbed wire; two Rottweilers growled at Leroy through the iron gates. He announced himself through the intercom and a thug, disguised as a gardener, appeared, opened the gates and led the dogs away.

'Go in the front door, sport.'

The front door was opened by one of the impediments to human intelligence. She was forty if she was a day, over the hill but unaware of it, a wog like himself but an Italian one.

'Lee-roy! What are you doing way out here in Sansuzy? Come in, come in! Denny, guess who's here? Denny, it's Lee-roy! He's come all the way out here from Sydney all by himself!'

She beamed at him and suddenly he realized that under the dyed beehive that passed for her hair, behind the thin pretty face with its three coats of paint plus varnish, Luisa Pelong was as shrewd as himself. He had met her only once before, at a nightclub in the Cross where Danny had thrown a party, and she had sat across from him hardly saying a word all night, playing the dumb blonde except that she wasn't blonde.

'Hello, Mrs Pelong. Your husband sent for me.'

'Mrs Pelong? Well, I do like that, definitely! It shows respect for older women, right? It's like that with you Greeks, aint it, same as with us Italians. I never found out what it's like with my hubby's people, 'cause I dunno where he come from. Oh, here he is! Where did you come from, sweetheart?'

'I been out by the fucking pool,' said Sweetheart. 'You know that.'

'Sweet,' said Luisa, touched his cheek and went away up a flight of marble stairs.

The house was all marble and chandeliers and enough gilt furniture to throw off a glare. 'The wife decorated it.' Denny Pelong had the voice of a growling Rottweiler. 'You like it?'

Leroy knew he had better like it or he would have his kneecaps broken. 'Love it! Is she a pro?' That was the wrong word: Pelong's expression told him so. 'I mean a profession decorator?'

'Nah, she just picked it up. You wanna sit out by the pool or come inna the study?'

The thought of Denny Pelong in a study was too intriguing to resist. 'Let's stay inside. It's so bloody hot outside –'

'I thought you wogs loved the heat. Okay, let's go in here.'

He led the way into the study. There was no marble in here; it was all panelled timber. There was a red leather suite, offset by a green leather wingbacked chair, a large antique desk, brass lamps, a huge globe of the world and a wall of shelves lined with books. Denny Pelong, in his white linen safari suit, fitted in like an expensively clad gorilla.

'The books are the wife's.'

Leroy glanced at them: Jackie Collins, Barbara Cartland, Judith Krantz and a leatherbound set of Mills & Boon. 'She a great reader?'

'All the time. Siddown. You wanna a drink?' He opened up the world; it was a bar. 'I only drink soft stuff till it's dark, okay?'

Leroy sat down, wondering if the heat had got to him on the way out here, even though he'd had the air-conditioning working in the Porsche. I dunno why I'm here, he thought, and in a minute I'm gunna start thinking I haven't arrived, I'm dreaming it all. This place is bloody unbelievable.

Pelong poured two bitter lemons, then sat down behind the desk. He was in his middle fifties, built like an old-fashioned front-row forward, all bulk and slow movement, with a broad flat face tinged with the dark complexion of his mother, a Torres Strait Islander whom he hadn't seen since he had run away from home when he was fourteen. His intelligence, Leroy thought, was second to anyone's you cared to name; but ruthlessness and a one-track mind had taken him to the top of Sydney's criminal heap. He was a murderer, only God and the Devil knew how many times; he had served time for only one killing, but he had been in jail at least another half a dozen times. He had two daughters, neither of whom, Leroy reckoned, had any chance of getting a husband, unless the poor bastard was suicidal.

'What did you wanna see me about, Mr Pelong?' He was not respectful, just clever.

Pelong nodded, pleased to be called Mister. 'You been having any trouble up the Cross?'

'No. Why?'

'Things are happening, Leroy. I lost a guy yesterday, a wharfie I had on me pay-roll – he kept an eye out what was coming in, gimme tip-offs if some other bastards were bringing in the stuff. He was gunna be a real help to us, he'd been running around like a blue-arsed fly in some election they got coming up. He was working to keep the present union bloke in office, some stupid honest jerk who wouldn't trouble us, 'cause he wouldn't know what was going on if we was up him. The opposition, they're the trouble. A Melbourne lot, real bastards.'

'So what happened?'

'They broke my guy's neck. Jimmy Maddux, that was his name.'

'He the guy that's in this morning's paper?'

'Yeah. He got on to me, told me he'd come across a shipment, it was stuck to the bottom of some ship with magnets or something. I seen 'em doing that in Europe and the States, it was on TV a coupla weeks ago.'

'I saw it.'

The ratings had been high for the show, augmented by the audience of the entire drug-dealing population of New South Wales. They had viewed it as an educational film.

'He said there was no chance of us hijacking it, so he was gunna tell his boss, the union bloke, and get him to let the police know. It would of made Jimmy look good with his boss and the boss look good with the cops. But the other mob got to Jimmy first. They broke his neck.'

He said it without horror or disgust, as if it were an everyday occurrence; Leroy felt his own neck go stiff. 'Who are the other mob?'

'I dunno for sure. Some Melbourne jerks, I've heard of some of 'em, Snow White and a coupla others, but someone's running 'em and I dunno who it is. You heard anything up around the Cross?'

'Nothing.'

'The cops been near you?'

Leroy hesitated a moment. 'You know I run some girls up around the Cross and on William Street, a sorta sideline?'

'Sure. That's your business, not mine. I done the same m'self years ago. They causing you any trouble?'

'No-o. But a coupla the girls, they lived with an old crow named Sally Kissen –'

'Sally? Shit, I knew her! A good sort when she was young. I read about her, she was done in Sunday night – You mean your girls are mixed up in that?'

'No, not exactly. But the cops have interviewed 'em and then they came and talked to me. A guy named Malone, an inspector, and a big jerk named Clements, a sergeant. They have nothing on me, but I think they're gunna be watching me.'

Pelong got up, went back to the globe and refilled his glass; he pulled down the northern hemisphere, closing the bar, not asking Leroy if he wanted a refill. 'That's gunna be awkward. We had a shipment come in from Bangkok, the weekend. It's all ready to go on the street.'

'I'm sorry, Mr Pelong. It's too much of a risk, they pick me up –'

'That's a risk you gunna have to take, aint it? You don't get paid what you do, Leroy, for sitting on your arse waiting for everything to be safe. You pick up the stuff this evening, the usual place, and you tell your customers it's available, only the price is going up. This fucking war business in the Gulf, it's gunna be a, what-they-call-it, a godsend. You tell 'em Iraq was a main place we got the stuff from, they aint gunna know no difference.'

'Do we get any smack from Iraq?' He wanted to giggle at the rhyming, but managed not to.

'I dunno. Fucking dates is probably all we import. But the hopheads you sell to, they aint gunna know no difference. So the price goes up and you start selling tonight, okay? I don't wanna hang on the stuff longer'n we got to, case these other bastards start muscling in. I think things are gunna get dirty.' He didn't look perturbed. He leaned on the globe, his huge hand obliterating most of the Middle East, though he didn't know it. He had no mind for geography, he knew only his own territory, which had no map. 'You carry a gun, Leroy?'

'Shit, no! I never went in for the stand-over stuff, Mr Pelong –'

'I aint talking stand-over, I'm talking protection. For y'self. I told you, it's gunna get dirty. These guys start muscling in, breaking more necks, you aint gunna be able to talk y'self outa trouble. You'll need a piece. Here.'

He went to the desk, opened one of the drawers; it contained half a dozen hand-guns. He took out a Colt .45 automatic, though Leroy wouldn't have known it from a howitzer, laid it on the desk and put two boxes of ammunition beside it.

'You better carry it with you alla time, in case. You know how to use it?'

It was politic to say yes: 'Sure.'

He picked up the gun, trying not to be too gingerly

159

about it. He was wearing a pale blue shirt with long sleeves and the cuffs turned back, just so; white cotton trousers, tight in the right places; and white shoes with no socks. He had thought he looked gorgeous, just right for a visit to the seaside boondocks, but it was not the right gear for an accessory like a gun. Pelong saw his problem.

'You carry a gun, you gotta wear loose things, otherwise it stands out like a horny cock. Here.' He handed Leroy a large manila envelope. 'You better start wearing a jacket or something, something with pockets in it. Or maybe a shoulder holster under your shirt.'

I don't believe this. He had been a criminal since he was twelve years old, but he had always dodged the violence; except against women, and you never needed a gun with them. 'You think they'll come looking for me?'

'I dunno, Leroy.' Pelong couldn't have sounded more indifferent. 'Just keep looking over your shoulder, that's all you gotta do.' He led the way out into the big entrance hall. 'Hey, Luisa, Leroy's going!'

Mrs Pelong appeared at the top of the marble stairs, came clack-clack-clacking down them in her high-heeled sandals. 'Come out again, Lee-roy, come for dinner and bring a girlfriend. You've got one, haven't you?'

'Dozens of 'em,' said her husband. 'You want a whore having dinner with us?'

'Why not?' The smile was a mile wide, every inch of it false and mocking. 'It won't be the first time. We have whores here all the time, Lee-roy, every time Sweetheart invites his business associates and their women.'

'Jokes all the fucking time,' said Sweetheart and turned on his heel and went back into the study without saying goodbye to Leroy.

Luisa Pelong opened the front door, looking Leroy up and down. She was in the mood for a man and this one looked all right. She had been upstairs having a secret drink, but only one; two drinks and she was a danger to herself and any man within clutching distance; her Mount of Venus turned volcanic. But this young stud, she decided reluctantly, was too close to home.

'Actually, my hubby is a real softie underneath, a real heart of gold. You musta noticed that?'

He looked at her: the smile was still there, but the dark eyes were mocking. He got the feeling she fancied him, in a cold-blooded sort of way. He had never been to bed with an older woman; he was fastidious, uncertain of the wrinkles you'd find under the pants of someone over thirty-five. 'Sure. Sure I did. He's a – a sorta father-figure.'

'You think so? Geez, I hadn't thought of that. You think he might make Father of the Year? Bye-bye, Lee-roy. Don't get killed or anything serious.'

She shut the door on him and he went down the steps and out the gates before the Rottweilers came out to do something serious to him. Once in his car he sat with the air-conditioning turned full on, not so much to blow the heat out of the car but to blow the disbelief out of himself. He was not naïve: he had always been on the fringes of danger and he knew the consequences. But he had never seen himself being actually engaged in a war, being given a gun and told to defend himself with it; that was for stupid bastards who joined the army. He was suddenly afraid, surprised at the trembling of his hands on the steering wheel. He looked at the manila envelope, at the shape roughly outlined in it, then he shoved it in the glove-box, started up the car and drove back out of the mirage to the real world.

He parked the car in a lane off William Street, debated whether he should take the gun with him, decided against it, locked the car and walked three blocks down to Palmer Street. The police watch on Sally Kissen's house had been removed. He let himself into the house with the key Tuesday had given him, shouted 'Tuesday? Ava? You home?' and walked in on the two girls in the living room.

Tuesday was all ready for the evening shift, dressed in gold fishnet stockings, black underwear and a gold basketballer's jacket with UCLA stamped on the back. Ava was in a blue cotton wrap and was drying her long blonde hair.

Tuesday got up and kissed Leroy. 'You want a beer or a cuppa coffee or something? I got heaps of time.'

'Nothing.' He sat down on the purple and red lounge. 'What's the matter with you, Ava? You not going out? You got the curse or something?'

'No.' She looked at him from under the white waterfall of her hair; then she threw it back and said bluntly, 'I'm finished, Leroy. I'm giving it up.'

'Giving what up?'

'The game. And the smack, too. I'm going home, I called my parents today and they said they'll have me back. I'm going home soon's I've done the programme.'

'What programme?'

'The drug rehabilitation bit. I met a nice girl this morning who's going to help me. She said it won't be easy, giving it up, but I knew that.'

'I don't believe this.' He shook his head, an act. 'You decide what you're gunna do, you don't even talk to me about it? What sorta shit is this?'

Tuesday was standing in the doorway that led to the kitchen, looking apprehensive. 'Leroy, honey, don't get angry with her –'

'Shut up!' He didn't look at her, just stared at Ava. 'You're outa your head if you think I'm gunna let you go just like that!'

She returned his stare, continuing to dry her hair with the slow rubbing of a towel. 'What'll you do, Leroy? Beat the shit out of me? You lay a finger on me again and I'll put this right through you.' She shifted slightly in her chair, produced a carving knife. 'I'm not kidding, Leroy.'

'She's been waiting for you,' Tuesday offered from the doorway. 'I been trying to talk to her –'

'Didn't I tell you, shut up!' He couldn't believe the way this day was turning out. He had read his horoscope in one of the Sunday papers and it had said today would be full of joyful surprises; it was full of surprises, all right, but none of them was fucking joyful. 'Ava, I'm not gunna let you walk out on me like this. Who you gunna go. to when you want the stuff?'

'You just don't get the point, do you, Leroy? I'm giving up on the stuff – or I'm going to try to. While I'm with you and Tuesday – no offence, honey – I'm never going to give it up. Just get it through your wog head, Leroy, you and I are finished. *Finished!*'

She had never dared to talk to him like this before; she had always been more independent than Tuesday, but she had always gone just so far and no further, had always known who, in the end, held the whip. Or rather, the smack. He looked at Tuesday, still standing in the kitchen doorway.

'You got any stupid ideas, too?'

'Honey, no! I *need* you, you know that –'

'Don't tell him that,' said Ava; she sounded weary, as if she knew it was fruitless to advise Tuesday. She was turning the carving knife over and over in her hand, as if whetting it on an invisible steel. 'He's got you, but you don't have to tell him.'

Leroy stood up. His head had suddenly started to ache, he wanted to be out of here before he blew up. 'I'm going now. You'll be back, Ava. When you can't do without the stuff, you'll be back.'

'Goodbye, Leroy.'

Tuesday said something to him, a sort of cry, but he didn't hear her, just turned his back and went out of the house. He went back up to his car, anger growing in him with every quick step. When he got into the car (would you believe, there was a parking ticket on the windscreen? Jesus, what a day!) he reached for the glove-box, took out the envelope, felt the gun through the thick paper. He was tempted to go back to the house in Palmer Street, let Ava have the first shot he would ever fire right between her eyes. Then he began to cool down, put the envelope back in the glove-box and sat back. The bitch was the least of his problems at the moment.

He drove out to Newtown, three or four kilometres from the Cross. He found a parking space in a side street, got out and locked the car. This was a tough area, a mix of street gangs, not all of whom lived around here. Some of them were skinheads, a species that frightened him: he was a wog, a dandified one, too, a natural-born target for their violence. He locked the car, hoped the windscreen wouldn't be smashed by the time he got back, or the paint-work scratched; then he walked quickly round the corner into King Street, the narrow main street, and into the cake shop. The window was empty of cakes, the display case also empty, and the owner was busy cleaning up. He looked up as Leroy opened the screen door and came in.

'You're always on time, Leroy.' He was middle-aged, running to fat, as if he ate too much of his own product; he wore a yellow T-shirt streaked with flour and a flour-dusted apron. He was as olive-skinned as Leroy, but the latter had never thought to ask him if he was a wog. Some-how the owner, for all his amused and friendly eyes, was not the sort who invited such questions. Leroy was secretly afraid of him, though he did not know why. 'Your order is all ready for you. A nice passionfruit pavlova.'

Leroy took the large cake-box, managed to share the joke: 'Bit heavy for a pavlova, isn't it?'

'Depends what base you use. Here, sign for it. You know how the boss likes to keep the books shipshape.'

Leroy signed the small book, thanked the owner and left. All the heroin that came in through the airport or wherever came to this shop, where the owner cut and packaged it. Leroy knew he was not the only dealer who came here to collect, but he had never met any of the others and he knew enough not to be too curious about them. Each dealer had a time and day to come and the instructions were also a threat: don't ever come any other time. Leroy had often wanted to look at some of the other signatures in the receipt book, but had resisted the temptation to ask the owner for the opportunity.

He went round the corner into the side street, was relieved to see there were no skinheads in sight. He opened the boot of the car, lifted the lid and was leaning in to put the cake-box on the floor when he felt the sharp prick in one buttock. He tried to turn his head, aware of someone behind him, but his neck was suddenly stiff, as if it had been broken. He felt his breath suddenly go, then something happened in his chest and he fell forward. Far off he heard the voice, he couldn't tell whether it was a man's or a woman's, say:

'Goodbye, Leroy.'

CHAPTER SIX

I

Malone was at home watching *Derrick*, on SBS, wondering why, on television, a German detective could, without ever changing expression, solve a crime in an hour, when the phone rang.

'Another one, Scobie. Newtown police have just found Leroy Lugos hanging out of the boot of his car, just off King Street. You want me to pick you up?'

'Where are you?'

'I'm at home, I been watching *Matlock* on video. That Andy Griffiths, he's a genius. I wish we were as good as him.'

Malone hung up, gave Lisa the bad news. 'Don't wait up for me.'

'Did you think I was going to?' But she would; or at least stay awake in bed.

'Dad –' Maureen and Tom were asleep in their rooms, but Claire, who had just finished her Year 9 homework, had come into the living room and slumped down on the lounge beside her mother. 'How long are those guys going to be guarding us?'

'Why? Are they getting on your nerves?'

'In a way.' She pushed back her blonde hair, a gesture that was an unconscious imitation of her mother. He loved all his kids equally, but if ever he lost Lisa, God forbid, she would live on in Claire. 'They're nice guys –'

'Especially Dick,' said Lisa with a sly smile.

'Yeah, he's *really* nice. But I can't bring any of my

166

friends home – Mum says no, not till everything's back to normal. When's that going to be?'

I wish I knew, love. 'Soon. By the end of the week at the latest, I hope.'

'Oh God, that's forever!' She threw herself against the back of the lounge, put her arm round her mother's shoulders. 'Why don't you divorce him, Mum?'

'I'd miss out on his pension. Have your shower and go to bed.' Lisa stood up and went out to the kitchen.

Malone kissed the top of Claire's head, said, 'It'll all be back to normal soon,' trying to sound convincing, and followed Lisa out to the kitchen.

She was standing at the sink, looking out at the back yard and the pool, the water a ghostly green from the lights in the side walls. 'I've looked out there a dozen times since Sunday. I still can't believe there was a dead man floating there. How close are you to solving it all?'

'It's getting worse.' He owed it to her to be candid. 'Tonight's murder, I think it might be connected to a couple of the others.'

'Who's doing it?' He had told her of the murders by the poisoned syringe.

'We haven't a clue.'

'Whoever's doing it, is he likely to try it on the kids?'

The thought horrified him. 'He'd never get to trial if we caught him. I'd kill him first.'

She didn't show any surprise at what he said; she said calmly, 'It would be a bit late, wouldn't it? I can never see what satisfaction people get out of an eye for an eye.'

He agreed with her. Cold-blooded revenge would never be in his nature; but hot-blooded anger might be something he could not control. 'It's not going to happen,' he said determinedly. 'Just don't think about it. No one's going to get near you or the kids.'

She turned from the window. 'Just don't let him get near you.'

He put his arms round her, held her tightly. Then Claire

came to the kitchen doorway, pulled up sharply. 'Sorry –'

Lisa kissed Malone on the lips, lightly, released herself from his arms and smiled wanly at their daughter. 'You don't have to be embarrassed when you catch your parents in a clinch. It's a natural thing.'

'I guess so.' Claire went to the fridge, poured herself some flavoured mineral water. 'But what if Dick or the other guy saw you?'

'I'd explain it was police procedure,' said Malone. 'For married cops.'

'Oh God, Dad. You and your jokes, you're as bad as Uncle Russ.'

Fifteen minutes later Uncle Russ knocked on the front door. By then Claire was in bed, but he kissed Lisa when she opened the door to him. 'It'll be just a token appearance by us. I'll see he's home by midnight.'

'Come to dinner tomorrow night. Bring your new girlfriend, this doctor.'

'That'd be nice. There's just one problem. We were gunna take her father out to dinner. She does it every year, on the anniversary of their arrival here. I dunno whether they think of it as Australia Day or Germany Day.'

'Bring him, too. I'll bake an anniversary cake, with candles. How many?'

'Ten, I think. You'll like Romy. I dunno about her old man – he's a bit stiff.'

'So's mine.' She kissed Malone as he passed her.

'Meaning me?'

'Who else? If Dick's out there, ask him if he'd like to come in and keep an old lady company.'

Once in the car, Clements' own, Malone said, 'If it's only going to be a token appearance, why me? Why couldn't you have gone on your own?'

'Because this time the media mob are there. Whoever gave it to Lee-roy phoned the TV newsrooms – the TV crews were there before the cops. Someone is trying to make mugs of us!' The big man's venom slurred his voice.

The narrow side street in Newtown was thronged with people, police cars, an ambulance and television vans. Clements was carrying no warning light, so he had to force the car through the crowd. He parked it beside one of the police cars and he and Malone got out and ducked under the Crime Scene tapes and crossed to the Porsche, its red paintwork garish under the glare of the lights trained on it. The boot lid was raised and the Physical Evidence team was already at work on the car. Beside it Leroy Lugos' body, in green plastic, lay on a stretcher. Joe Gaynor, a senior GMO, close to sixty and ready for retirement, stepped over the stretcher as he saw Malone and Clements approach.

'I suspect this may be another curare job, Scobie. All the symptoms. I can't find any evidence of any wounds, not even a bruise. I'm not going to strip him for the benefit of these bastards.' He waved a bony hand at the cameramen, who were just out of earshot but gave him sour grins, anyway, from behind their eye-pieces. Gaynor was a tall thin man, taller than Malone by several inches, with a narrow face in which all the lines, indeed all the features, seemed to run down to the long spade of his chin. He was one of the old school who believed there should be no publicity for the dead, especially the murdered dead. 'I'll let you know in the morning. If it is another curare job, I'll turn it over to Dr Keller, if her plate isn't too full.'

Malone thanked him, left Clements to talk to the PE team and went across to the local sergeant of detectives. 'What've you got, Irv?'

Irving Rubens was one of the few Jews in the Department, a solidly built, handsome man who, as a detective constable, had worked with Malone some years before. 'We got the call at the station about an hour ago, maybe less. When we got here, the TV mob was already here. It'll make great TV, a dead man hanging out the boot of a bright red Porsche. It'll be a change from the war pictures.'

'Don't be sour, Irv. Leave that to me, that's what I'm paid for. You get anything on who called the TV people?'

'It was a call to the stations' switchboards. None of the switch-girls could remember whether it was a man or woman's voice – the girl at Channel Fifteen said the voice sounded as if it was disguised. Maybe she watches too many detective series, who knows?'

'What about Lugos, the dead bloke?'

'A real dude – you knew him?' Malone nodded. 'He's never been seen around here before, not by us, anyway. We found a cardboard cake-box under the body. Would you believe, a passionfruit pavlova on top of a nice little bundle of heroin packets. Whoever did him in evidently didn't know what he was carrying.'

'How much heroin?'

'At a rough guess I'd say at least a hundred thousand bucks' worth, maybe more.'

'What have you done with it?'

'It's in my car, waiting for the Drug Unit fellers to come and claim it. In the meantime, we've been around the corner and pinched the owner of the cake shop. I haven't talked to him, he's down at the station with one of my men. You wanna see him? If you don't mind me asking, Scobie, what brought you out here tonight? You'd have had it all on your desk at Homicide tomorrow morning. You looking for work?'

'Instinct, Irv.' He then told Rubens about the murders of Grime and Sally Kissen. 'I'd already talked to this bloke –' He nodded at the shrouded body of Leroy Lugos being loaded into the ambulance; the cameras swooped like metal birds. 'Can you get rid of this mob? Close off the whole street, at least till we have the car taken away.'

There must have been a hundred or more in the crowd, mostly young people. None of them appeared shocked, just curious; some of them feigned boredom, the laid-back look that had replaced the smart-arse cracks of Malone's generation. Today there was an acceptance of death amongst the street gangs that was almost callous. He wondered if the same stoical attitude prevailed amongst the young about to die in the Gulf war. He doubted it.

'Who are these? Locals?'

'We've got the lot around here, Scobie. A lot of good, honest workers –'

'It was like that when I was born here. My mum and dad still live down the road, in Erskineville.'

Rubens looked surprised, as if, somehow, he had expected Malone to have come from some silvertail area. 'Yeah? How about that! Yeah, well, there's lots more than them around now. We've got gays, lesbians, junkies – we put out two thousand needles a month in our needle exchange programme – neo-Nazis, kinky perverts – you name it, we've got it. Including more crims to the square mile than anywhere else in the country. For some reason they all come back here as soon as they get out of jail, like this is some retraining centre for them to get back into whatever game they were in before they were sent away. I can put up with the crims. It's that lot there –'

He nodded to about a dozen youths standing in a tight group beside the ambulance. They wore a uniform of heavy boots, torn black jeans and black sleeveless T-shirts; their heads were shaved along the sides, with a flat spiky crop on top. One of the youths turned round as a television camera focused on him. On his black T-shirt was a white-lettered threat: Fuck a Wog With a Boot. He grinned fiendishly at the camera, then spun round. On his back was another threat: Fuck a Jew, Too.

'Some of 'em live around here, some of 'em come in from Christ knows where. They've caused the uniformed boys a lotta trouble, busting in the windows of some of the wog shops – the main street's full of 'em, Lebanese, Turkish, Greek, Thai – King Street's full of cheap eats. There's a Jewish jeweller, they've done him a coupla times, but so far we haven't been able to catch 'em.'

'They cause you any bother?'

'Because I'm a Jew? They know me, they know I'd circumcise 'em with a chain-saw if they tried anything.'

'Leroy was a wog. Maybe he was lucky they didn't get to him before he was stuck with the needle.'

'You sure that's the way he was killed?'

'No, but I'm willing to bet on it. Let's go and see the cake-shop owner. I'll get Russ.'

Newtown police station was only five minutes from the scene of the crime. It was a nondescript three-storeyed building next to the fire station; if ever terrorism comes to Australia, the authorities have, too often, conveniently located possible targets close together. Or perhaps, Malone thought, they had worked on the assumption that, if the police station was bombed, the fire brigade would not have far to come to put out the blaze. Though he doubted if the authorities would have been as far-sighted as that: the long view was not a national habit.

Malone and Clements followed Rubens up to the first floor, to the detectives' room. The cake-shop owner was in the interrogation room, a windowless cubicle designed to give first-time offenders an idea of what confinement meant.

The two Homicide men sat down in chairs against the wall while Rubens went outside with the young detective constable who had been minding the suspect. Malone introduced himself and Clements. 'You mind telling us a few things about yourself?'

'The name is Mitre, Sydney Mitre. I own the Matilda cake shop. I think that's all you need to know.' He was wearing lightly tinted glasses, taking any shine or glint from his eyes. He had thick loose lips, but Malone guessed he would not be loose-lipped when it came to questioning. But he had an air of resignation about him, something an experienced cop can smell, and that was promising. Yours is the next move, Inspector.'

Rubens came back, sat down on the chair on the opposite side of the small table from Mitre. The four men crowded the room and Mitre, as if suddenly feeling oppressed, shifted his chair back till it was against the wall behind him.

'Mr Mitre, did my constable tell you what they found in the back of your shop?'

'No, Sergeant.' Mitre, it seemed, was naturally polite.

'Four cake-boxes containing packets of heroin, with a street turnover, we reckon, of between four and five hundred thousand dollars. Plus the heroin we found in one of your cake-boxes in the boot of a Porsche around the corner from your shop. The car boot, incidentally, also contained the body of a young man named Leroy Lugos. I don't think things look too good for you, Mr Mitre.'

Mitre looked at Malone. 'I love Jewish humour. Do you think I should get my lawyer to join us?'

'I think it might be an idea,' said Malone. 'Suspicion of murder, dealing in heroin – I think you'll need your solicitor and a couple of QCs at least.'

Mitre held up a plump hand pale with flour. The flour that streaked his T-shirt and apron and arms somehow made him look less heavy than he was, as if parts of him were ectoplasmic. He ran his hand through his hair, turning it greyer. 'Hold it, gentlemen. No murder talk, I know nothing about that. I want to call my lawyer.'

'Sergeant Clements will call him for you.'

'I think I'm entitled to make my own call –'

'Normally, yes.' Malone avoided Rubens' eye. 'But the public lines are out tonight and we can't let you use the police private lines.'

'You're harassing me –'

'Yes, I think I might be. But what witnesses have you got?' He didn't look at Clements or Rubens, but he knew their faces would be blank. 'Give him your lawyer's name, Mr Mitre, and then you and I will have a little chat while we're waiting for him to come. Okay?'

Mitre hesitated, then he gave Clements a name and a number. Clements went out, closing the door, and Mitre leaned his chair back against the wall. 'How did the deceased – is that what we call him? – die?'

'We're not sure yet. We think he died from curare poisoning. A curare synthetic called Alloferin. You've heard of it?'

The tinted glasses had tilted slightly, catching the light. 'Yes. I was a chemist before I became a pastrycook.'

'That's quite an admission – in the circumstances.'

'Do you think I'd have admitted it if I'd given the deceased the syringe?'

'How do you know a syringe was used?'

'How else would you administer it?' He shook his head and a thin film of flour rose from it. 'Don't let's waste our time on the murder, Inspector. I had nothing to do with it.'

'Okay,' said Rubens, coming in a little strongly; he looked as if he felt *his* prisoner was being taken away from him. 'Let's forget the murder. Let's talk about the heroin.'

'Ah no, Sergeant. Not till my lawyer arrives.' He looked up as Clements came back into the room. 'He on his way?'

'You're out of luck,' said Clements. 'That was his home number, was it? All I got was his answering machine. I left a message, said it was urgent.'

'You're lying, Sergeant.'

Clements moved round to the corner of the table, stood over Mitre. 'The last time a prisoner said that to me, I accidentally fell on him. Make another remark like that and I'll squash you like one of your own eclairs.'

Mitre was not intimidated. 'I know you won't do that, Sergeant, not after all the bad publicity the police have had over the past year. You're bluffing and I don't blame you – it's always a good ploy. Incidentally, I don't make eclairs. I can, but I don't run a patisserie. My selling point is that the Matilda is a good, old-fashioned, dinky-di Aussie cake shop. Lamingtons, raspberry-jam-and-cream sponges, pavlovas, even rock cakes. No foreign muck, is my motto. The funny part is, the wogs love them.'

'Heroin is foreign muck,' said Rubens.

The plump face was suddenly still, the glasses turned downwards, catching no light. 'I'll wait for my lawyer. May I have a cup of tea? Milk, no sugar.'

'Would you care for a couple of lamingtons with it?' said Malone.

Mitre smiled, but said nothing. The three policemen left him alone and went out to the main room. 'What d'you reckon?' said Rubens. 'You think he had anything to do with killing that guy?'

Malone shook his head. 'He's too smart to have someone bumped off so close to home. Let's look him up, see if he has any record.'

The computer showed no mention of Sydney Mitre. 'I'll try the Pharmacy Board in the morning,' said Clements. 'Why would a chemist give it up to become a pastrycook? There's more money in a chemist's shop than selling lamingtons and custard tarts.'

'Maybe he wasn't a pharmacist,' said Malone. 'Maybe he was an industrial chemist, something like that. Let's wait for his lawyer, see who turns up.'

'The name he gave me was Evans,' said Clements.

And that was who turned up: Caradoc Evans. The Welsh have never made as much impression in Australia as other emigrants from the British Isles; it may be that their devotion to rugby and choral singing, not nationwide sports Down Under, has not fitted them for success. Caradoc Evans, however, was a criminal lawyer, a field where putting the boot in and hymnal eloquence are assets, and he was a definite success. Malone wondered how an honest pastrycook could afford him.

'Well, what are they accusing you of, boy?' Evans still had a Welsh lilt and he played the part, as if he had arrived only yesterday from the Rhondda. He was in his fifties, bald, short and stocky, a pensioned-off scrum-half who would grab the balls of any heavier opponent who tried to dump him. He knew how to play dirty, but disguised it with light charm. 'Perhaps you'd like to fill me in, Inspector?'

Malone did so. 'I think Sergeant Rubens has him dead-set on the heroin charges. I'd like to talk to him about the murder. I'm sorry you had to be dragged out in the middle of the night. We suggested not calling you till the morning, but your client wouldn't hear of it.'

'I came as soon as I got home and heard the message. I've been to a preview of *Godfather Three*. Very disturbing, makes you thankful we live in a law-abiding country like ours.'

'Wales or New South Wales?'

Evans winked, a Welsh wink full of suspicion masquerading as bonhomie; they had been using it on the English since the days of Owen Glendower. It did not work with Malone, another Celt. 'We're on the same side, Inspector, aren't we? That of law and order. May I consult with my client?'

Malone looked at Rubens, who nodded.

The detectives left Mitre and his lawyer alone in the interrogation room. Ten minutes later the door opened and Evans beckoned them in. 'My client has decided to come clean, as the saying is. He denies any connection with the murder, but he admits you may have found some illegal substance amongst his pastries. He will plead guilty, as a contribution to law and order.'

'I'd like to ask him a few questions,' said Rubens.

'Ah no, no. You won't be answering any questions, will you, boy?'

'No,' said the middle-aged boy. 'No questions.'

'We might be able to offer you a deal,' said Rubens. 'You tell us who brings in the heroin and we'll see what we can do with the Crown Prosecutor.'

'My client tells me he has no idea who sent the heroin to his shop. It just turned up instead of an order for self-raising flour. A mistake, obviously. The regrettable part is that my client took advantage of someone else's mistake – temptation is a terrible thing. He decided, as the saying is, to get into the act.'

'And Leroy Lugos turning up to collect a cake-box full of the stuff?'

'Purely fortuitous.'

'It wasn't very fortuitous for Leroy,' said Malone. 'A poisoned needle in your bum isn't everyone's idea of a lucky dip.'

Clements, so far, had been silent. In rugby terms he now came in from far out on the wing: 'Mr Evans, don't you represent Denny Pelong?'

It had been a wild pass and Evans, caught on the wrong foot, had taken it; now he looked as if he wished he could pass it on. 'You know, Sergeant, I can't discuss other clients.'

'Sorry I mentioned it,' said Clements. 'Do you know Denny Pelong, Mr Mitre?'

The tinted glasses caught the light as Mitre raised his head; they were opaque, he looked utterly blind. 'Pelong? It's a peculiar name. No, I don't think I know him. What does he do?'

'Just about everything criminal,' said Clements.

'I think we should prepare the statement you want and my client will sign it.' The lilt had gone from Evans' voice; we're deadly serious now, boy. 'Then we can all go home.'

'Not quite,' said Malone. 'He'll be held till we put him before a magistrate in the morning. There may be another charge by then.'

'What charge?'

'An accessory before the fact of murder.'

2

When Caradoc Evans rang Denny Pelong at 11.30 that night with the news of Leroy Lugos' murder and the heroin

177

bust, Pelong went outside and, fully clothed, flung himself into his swimming pool, where he beat the water in a fury. His wife, in a shortie nightgown, her face glistening with night cream, came downstairs when she heard the commotion and out to the side of the pool.

'You're disturbing the neighbours, sweetheart. You know how they hate all-night swimming out here in the suburbs.' She came from Redfern, where the neighbours don't have to worry too much about swimming pools and what time of day they are swum in.

Pelong told her to get fucked.

'The neighbours don't like that, either, sweetheart. Not out in the back yard.' She started to walk back into the house, then paused. 'You want me to get the dogs to jump in with you?'

Then she went into the house, smiling like a cat that had just scratched the eyes out of a Rottweiler.

3

Malone left it to Rubens to appear in court the next morning with Mitre. 'Hold him as long as you can without bail.'

'Give the magistrate some Old Testament stuff,' said Clements.

'What's that?' said Rubens.

'Doctored evidence. You Jews invented it, didn't you?'

Rubens looked at Malone. 'Is he anti-Semitic?'

'He's just anti-religious. You should hear what he has to say about us Catholics. He's a lapsed born-again Christian, they're the worst. Christ gave him away.'

Rubens grinned. 'Did they ever tell you at your Catholic school that old fable about the Apostles being in that locked room and Christ turning up from the dead to say there was no God?'

'Not at school, they didn't. But I picked up an old drunk priest one night and he told me about it. He told me to give it the deaf ear. He said, "We're all doubters at some time, son, and it doesn't do to encourage ourselves." It's good advice that I've stuck with. Don't let's doubt that we'll nail Mr Mitre.'

First thing next morning Clements got in touch with the State Pharmacy Board. No, they had nothing on a Sydney Mitre, but if the police wished, they would get in touch with the boards in other States. The police wished. Half an hour later the Pharmacy Board rang back.

'South Australia,' said the woman from the Board, no more than a pleasing voice, 'they deregistered a pharmacist three years ago for supplying restricted drugs without a prescription. His name wasn't Mitre, however, not his surname. His name was Sydney Mitre Pelong. P-E-L-O –'

'I know how to spell it,' said Clements.

'Peculiar name, isn't it? You've heard it before?'

'Once or twice.' Clements thanked the pleasant voice, hung up and looked across at Malone. 'Waddia know! Our friend Syd Mitre is a relative of Denny Pelong.'

Malone pondered a while. 'Do you think Syd and Denny would have had Leroy done in?'

'No,' said Clements without hesitation.

Malone nodded. 'Neither do I. Why would they kill off one of their own dealers, just around the corner from their supply point? Give Irv Rubens a ring, tell him Syd's real name but tell him to hold off on Denny Pelong for a while. Irv can handle the heroin bust, I don't want us to get into that. But keep Denny Pelong out of it till we've gone a bit more into Leroy's murder. Have you heard from Doc Gaynor?'

'He's handed the body on to Romy. It's another curare job, she's established that, so she's covering the three murders.'

'Four. You're forgetting Jimmy Maddux. Have you seen this morning's papers? A plague of murders, one of them called it. Some of these fellers should be writing advertising copy.'

'It's a change from writing war headlines. Or reading them. Do we set up a Crime Room out at Newtown? Send a coupla our guys out there?'

'Send Andy Graham, he's got enough energy for half a dozen of us, he can drive them crazy instead of us.' Malone was sitting in front of the computer, tapping information into what he still thought of as the murder box. 'See this? I got on to the Sydney Cricket Ground, got them to check who paid for Jimmy Maddux's gold pass. Coolibah Investments Services, a private company.'

'It doesn't sound like Jimmy Maddux's own company.'

'No. I'm having it searched, we'll find out who runs it.' He turned from the computer. 'In the meantime, you can go out to Bondi, talk to Leroy's uncle and then have a look at his flat and talk to the neighbours.'

'What are you gunna do?'

'I'm going down to see Ava and Tuesday. I've just had a thought. What if Scungy Grime had been a client of Sally Kissen? Or of the girls? Maybe these curare murders all came out of the one location.'

'What about Jimmy Maddux?'

'Possibly unconnected.'

Clements was sceptical. 'I don't buy that and I don't think you do.'

'Why do you throw a bucket of cold water over me just when I think I'm inspired?'

He took his own car, the Commodore, down to Palmer Street, parked it on the pavement, something he growled at if anyone did it in Randwick, and knocked on the door of the Kissen house. It was opened cautiously by Ava, who peered at him suspiciously against the bright morning light. Then she recognized him and slipped off the door-chain.

'You can't be too careful. What's it about this time? Leroy?'

'You heard about it?'

'I saw it last night on TV. They ran it with the late-night

180

war news. I thought it was Tel Aviv or Baghdad or somewhere at first, all those ghouls hanging around.'

She led him into the small living room, where Tuesday
sat on the purple and red lounge, her knees drawn up
under her chin. She was in a cheap imitation-silk green
robe, her bright red hair awry, like a small fire caught in
a willy-willy, and last night's make-up was a tear-molten
mask. Ava was pale, her face a little gaunt, but she was
holding herself together. She offered Malone coffee and
Iced Vo-Vos, evidently the brothel's standard morning
snack.

'I didn't tell Tuesday what had happened to Leroy, not
till this morning. She was working last night.'

'You weren't?'

'No. I'm off the game, as of yesterday. If it interests
you, I'm off the junk, too. Or trying to be.'

'Good luck.' Malone munched on one of the cookies.
'Tuesday, did Leroy ever say anything to you about being
threatened by anyone?'

Tuesday wiped her eyes with a tissue. She seemed careless of how she looked; Malone was not a customer. 'Leroy
would never tell me nothing like that.'

'Leroy was a big-head,' said Ava. She was in shorts
and a shirt, again with long sleeves, and her long white-
blonde hair was tied in a pony-tail. She was wearing no
make-up and she gave the impression that she was trying
to scrub herself clean of her past life. Malone guessed,
however, that she had a long way to go, a lot more
scrubbing to do. 'He would never let you know he had
any competition.'

'You oughtn't to speak ill of the dead.' Tuesday mur-
mured the words as if she were reading them from a
tombstone.

'I know you loved him, honey, but let's face it – he was
a shit.'

'Did he run any other girls besides you two?'

'No!' Tuesday flared; the robe slipped open, she was

181

naked underneath, but sex was dead in this house, at least for the time being.

'Honey –' Ava shook her head chidingly; she was mothering Tuesday. 'He had half a dozen girls besides us. You just never wanted to know . . .' She looked at Malone. 'I dunno if ever anyone threatened him, but it was possible.'

'He had a gun in the glove-box of his car when they found him. Did he ever show it to you, tell you what he intended doing with it?'

'He never owned a gun in his life!' Tuesday was vehement, sitting bolt upright on the lounge. Malone had seen other women like this, the ones who would never bury the men they had loved. 'He was too smart for that! He hated guns!'

Malone put down his coffee cup, changed tack 'Did Sally Kissen ever have a man come here named Normie Grime? A little middle-aged feller, very neat, not much bigger than a jockey. He lived down the road, in the 'Loo. That's him, when he was much younger.' He passed over the photo he had taken from Grime's flat, of Grime and his parents.

The two girls looked at the photo, then at each other. Then Ava said, 'Yeah, I think that's him. He used to come here. Not regularly, maybe once a month. I bumped into him once or twice when I was going out or coming in. He never said much, but he was friendly, sort of. We never knew his name, though. That was one of the rules Sally had in the house – no names. It was one of the rules from what she used to call her "better times". In those days she used to have big-money clients. Politicians, businessmen, one or two of the big gangsters.'

Malone fired a wild shot: 'She ever mention Denny Pelong? You've heard of him?'

'Sure. You work around the Cross, you hear all the names like that. But Sally never mentioned him.'

'Did Leroy?' Malone looked at Tuesday.

'I told you, Leroy never told me nothing. I didn't wanna know.' She looked resentfully at Ava as she made the admission.

Malone changed tack slightly again: 'So those initials on that calendar you showed me, they could have meant nothing?'

'I dunno. They could've been true initials, but no names.'

'When did you last see this little feller, Normie Grime?'

Ava looked at him shrewdly. 'Wait a minute – why are you asking about him? Did he have something to do with Leroy?'

'I don't know. He died the same way as Leroy, a poisoned needle in his bum.'

Tuesday retched; for a moment Malone thought she was going to throw up. Then she found her voice: 'You mean both of 'em, Leroy and this feller you're talking about, they died the same way as Sally?'

Malone nodded. 'Whoever killed them all used to come to this house. This place is the only connecting link.'

'Jesus!' Ava clasped her hands together; the knuckles showed white. 'You better get out of here, Tuesday, find somewhere else.'

'What about you?' said Malone.

'I'm going home to Wagga, soon's I get a referral from my counsellor. She said she'd help me.'

'What's her name? Your counsellor?'

'Janis Eden. You know her?'

'I've met her, but I don't know her. Did she know Leroy was your supplier?'

'Yes, I told her. Why?'

'In her job, she's probably heard of all the dealers. She just might know something you and Tuesday don't.' He stood up. 'Well, good luck. Both of you. Find somewhere else to live, Tuesday, but ring me and let me know where. I'm not going to harass you –' as he saw the look on her face. 'I just want you to stay alive, love, that's all.'

Ava followed him to the front door. 'You married, Inspector?'

'Yes. Why?'

'I wouldn't have minded going to bed with you. Just social, not professionally.'

'Thanks for the compliment, Ava. But I'm happy with the bed at home.'

'Lucky you. You'd be surprised, the number of guys who aren't. Half our clients are married guys.'

'How's business, now the recession's on?'

'There's more bargaining. I'm glad I'm giving it up. It's getting that way, it's like selling it at K-Mart.'

4

Malone went back to Homicide, got there just as Clements arrived back from Bondi. 'How'd you go?'

'His uncle didn't seem particularly upset – I got the feeling he thought Leroy's death was good riddance. He said he'd tell the family down in Victoria, they can come up and claim the body.'

'You think Uncle is involved?'

'In the drugs? Not a chance. Uncle wants to keep his nose clean . . . I got him to take me along to Leroy's flat. He lived well. The flat's right on the end of the beach, beaut view of the bare tits at the southern end. Everything that opens and shuts in it – he must've spent a fortune on electronic equipment. Hi-fi, video . . . Uncle was chewing his teeth with envy.'

'You find anything?'

'Nothing with names in it. Only this –' He handed Malone a folder.

Malone opened it. He scanned the list of names in the portfolio statement, the single sheet the folder contained. 'I've never heard of any of these companies. No blue-chip stuff.'

'Look at the names. Near East Land and Exploration. Cook Islands Catering – that's a good 'un. Macao International Bonding. They're all off-shore, they all sound as shonky as a two-dollar watch. His money was being laundered. It's not a big portfolio – what is it, three hundred and eighty thousand all up? – but it's not bad for a twenty-two-year-old. He was on his way.'

Malone looked at the name on the bottom of the folder. 'How about that! Coolibah Investments Services. A good Aussie name, nothing off-shore there. No address, just a box number. Where's Phil?'

Phil Truach came in, shaking his head at having his name yelled aloud twice. 'I've been having a leak, if that's all right? I can remember once, you could take your time about it, just standing there staring at the wall, listening to the gentle pissing sound –'

'We'll have to watch him, I think he's a pervert,' Malone told Clements. 'Phil, what have you dug up on Coolibah Investments?'

'Nothing so far –'

'Phil, get to it, even if your bladder's bursting. Tell your contact in Companies Registration that if he doesn't come up with it in ten minutes, you'll be down to arrest him for obstruction of justice.'

'You're kidding. When was a public servant last arrested for not doing his job? I think it was about eighteen thirty-four –'

He went off with his usual sour patience, as if he had long ago worked out that life, not just police work, was no more than an accumulation of small items, that, come the end of the world, everything would be reduced to small pieces again.

Then Irving Rubens phoned. 'Scobie? We got the beak to hold Mitre without bail for another forty-eight hours. If we don't come up with something by then, he'll let him go on bail of a hundred grand.'

'Well, I guess we're lucky to hold him for that long. Anything else?'

'Yeah, Fingerprints have just sent us a report on the gun we found in the Porsche – it should be on your fax. One set of prints belonged to Lugos. There's another set, which they checked with their records. They belong to – guess who?'

'Don't tell me. Denny Pelong? Have you been out to see him?'

'I went out there before I got the Fingerprints report. He wasn't home. His wife – she's a real bimbo, but a shrewd one – she said he was out playing golf, she didn't know where. What golf club would let him on its course? I play golf. I think I'll take up bowls or something if they're gunna let shit like Pelong on to a course. I wonder what his handicap is? Anyhow, I got the Rockdale station to let me have one of their boys keep an eye on the Pelong place, let me know when he comes home with his golf bag. Jesus! I wonder what Greg Norman would think?'

'Irv –' Malone was not a golfer; if Saddam Hussein and Denny Pelong played a two-stroke or a two-ball or whatever it was called at the Royal and Ancient, it would not worry him. Some day he would have to tell Rubens about the West Indian fast bowler who had got life for murdering his wife, though, thankfully, not with a cricket bat. 'Irv, I sympathize with you. But Russ and I are going out to Sans Souci. I think I'd like a few words with Mrs Pelong while we're waiting for Denny. I'll let you know what happens.'

'Okay, I'll wait to hear from you.'

Malone recognized the sudden change, the tone of voice of a cop being pushed into the background by someone of senior rank. It couldn't be helped, it was the way of the world. Ten, even five years ago, he had sounded exactly like that himself. You climbed the ladder of promotion: even if you had the best of intentions, the rung beneath your foot was always the neck of some other poor bastard.

He consoled himself with the thought that Irv Rubens would occasionally tread on other cops' necks.

Malone and Clements were on their way out of the room when Truach came back, smiling as if he had just been permitted the pleasure of a long urination. 'Coolibah Investments Services. A subsidiary of Thursday Island Holdings. Which is owned outright by Dennis and Luisa Pelong. That make you feel better?'

Clements drove himself and Malone out to Sans Souci in an unmarked police car. The heat had eased a little and a cooling nor'-easter came in across the waters of Botany Bay. Far out, on the southern headland of the bay, Malone could see the oil refinery, now listed secretly as a possible terrorist target. In the past couple of weeks, since the Gulf war had turned serious, Special Branch had been working round the clock, day and night, trying to trace terrorists who, as far as Australia was concerned, had no track record. Maybe homicide was not such a tough job after all.

The young constable from the Rockdale station was parked at the end of the street, looking bored and sleepy; but he came awake and scrambled out of the car when Malone introduced himself and Clements. 'Pelong's just come home, sir. He drives a white Rolls-Royce, it's parked there in the driveway. Watch out for the dogs, sir, they'll eat you alive.'

Most of the houses in the street were modest; Pelong's was easily the largest, built across two wide lots. It belonged to the Conspicuous Anonymity style of architecture favoured by celebrities and gangsters: no expense spared, then the whole lot surrounded by a high stone wall. The two Rottweilers bared their teeth through the bars of the iron gates. Then the gardener appeared, carrying a pair of shears in one hand and a gun in the hip pocket of his overalls. Malone showed him his badge.

'I don't need to show you this, do I, Fred? What's with

the gun? You going to shoot bugs off the roses? Where've you been?'

'G'day, Mr Malone, howyagoing?' Fred Cargo was in his fifties, weatherbeaten and as tough as a jarrah stump, a stand-over man since his kindergarten days; he was an old-fashioned crim, the sort who gave no quarter to cops and expected none in return. It was a form of honesty. 'I been up at Bathurst, doing a coupla years.'

'What's it like up there now?'

'Ah, bloody crowded. This business of stiffer sentences, it aint gunna work, you oughta tell the government. Jail aint what it used to be, fulla small shit. You announce yourself to the house over the intercom?'

'Just like at Government House. Only they don't have Rottweilers there.'

'They oughta, a whole bloody pack of 'em. All those bloody Arabs on the loose.'

'You expecting the Muslim Brotherhood to attack Mr Pelong?'

'The – Muslim Brotherhood? What are they, like Arab Masons?'

'Sort of,' said Malone, the very occasional staunch Catholic.

The front door was opened by Mrs Pelong, in shorts and a halter top. Her dark hair hung loose and she wore only lipstick; she looked wan and haggard: a wife, Malone thought, worried for her loved one. Then he saw the bruise under her jaw and the one on her upper arm and he changed his mind.

'The police – second time today! What'll the neighbours think? My hubby's out by the pool. He loves a dip after a round of golf. Do you two gentlemen play golf?'

'No,' said the gentlemen.

Malone's eyes were busy at the corners as they were led through the house; Lisa always wanted to know about the houses he visited, especially those of successful crims. He wouldn't know how to describe this one: everything looked cheaply expensive, or expensively cheap, like the furniture one saw on late-night TV commercials. 'You like it?' said Luisa Pelong, missing nothing, not even the discreet sidelong glances.

'Very nice. Mr Pelong's choice?'

'No, mine. My hubby has no taste for decorating.'

She seemed oblivious of how her hubby had decorated her with bruises; or perhaps she didn't care. She led them out on to a patio beyond which was a pool at least twice as large as the Malone pool at Randwick. Dennis Pelong, in swim-trunks, sat at a table under a large umbrella. Malone and Clements took off their jackets, accepted the offer of light beers from Luisa, who went back into the house to get them, and sat down. Pelong said nothing till his wife had disappeared, then he glared at Malone from under the black hedge of his brows.

'So what's this all about? The wife tells me she had a visit from another copper this morning.'

Fred, the armed gardener, had come round from the front of the house and was busy amidst a splendid display of roses along the back fence. He now wore a large straw hat under which his ears were cocked like microphones to pick up the voices coming across the still pool of water.

'I think you may be having a lot of visits from us, Mr Pelong.' Malone had had nothing to do with Pelong up till now, so there was no first-name rapport. He indicated himself and Clements: 'We're here because we're investigating the murder of Leroy Lugos.'

'I dunno nothing about that.'

'Scungy Grime? He was murdered, too.'

'Nup.'

'Jimmy Maddux?'

'Nup.'

That had been too pat: he hadn't asked who Maddux was, an obscure wharfie with no criminal record. Luisa came back with four beers in long glasses on a silver tray, handed each of the men a glass, took the fourth herself

189

and sat down next to her husband. She put on dark glasses against the glare; Clements took a pair from his shirt pocket and put them on. Malone and Pelong remained squinting at each other, though Malone did tilt his hat forward over his eyes.

Malone sipped his beer, nodded approvingly. Then: 'You didn't ask me who Jimmy Maddux was.'

'I don't wanna know.' Pelong's beer remained untouched in front of him. He was not a pleasant sight, a broad mix of muscle and fat mossed with damp black hair, his stomach bulging like a soft boulder over the electric-green trunks he wore. His face had all the sensitivity of a bull's, but he had never led a life in which sensitivity counted for much.

'You didn't ask me anything about Scungy Grime, either. But I guess you knew *him*?'

'Yeah, I knew him. He worked for Jack Aldwych one time, dint he? A sneaky little shit.'

Malone looked at Luisa. Her shapely legs were crossed, in that pose of women who know they have good legs and can manipulate them provocatively. There was no expression on the thin pretty face under the dark glasses, but a little colour had come back into her cheeks, as if she were beginning to enjoy herself.

'Don't take no notice of my hubby's language. I tried to make a silk purse out of an old jockstrap, but I didn't have any luck, did I, sweetheart? He talks like that to the neighbours, too – when he talks to 'em at all.'

Pelong picked up his beer and buried his face in it. Malone said, 'Did any of those men I named ever come here, Mrs Pelong?'

Pelong's face abruptly appeared above his glass; the black eyes squinted even more as he glanced at his wife. She ignored him, smiled at Malone. 'You know better'n that, Inspector. What sorta wife contradicts her hubby?'

'An honest one?' asked Clements.

'You a married man, Sergeant?' Clements shook his

head and she smiled again. 'You got a lot to learn, hasn't he, sweetheart? No, Inspector, I never heard of any Leroy Lugos or Scungy Grime or Jimmy Maddux.'

'You remembered all their names.'

'I got a phonographic memory – I hear something once, I remember it. I do all my hubby's book-keeping in my head, nothing's ever written down, is it, sweetheart?' She was mocking all three men; yet Malone found he couldn't dislike her. She would never wear her bruises with pride, but they would always be only skin-deep, just below the surface and never on her psyche.

'What about Joey Trang, a Vietnamese?'

'Oh yeah, we knew him. He was our gardener, before we took on Fred.'

Malone looked back at Pelong, who appeared to have relaxed again. 'Did you sack Joey, or promote him?'

'I had nothing to do with him. He worked for the wife.'

'What did he do for you, Mrs Pelong?'

'He just gardened, nothing else. I fired him because he was no good. He could only grow rice – you don't get much scope for rice-growing in Sansuzy. Put him amongst the roses, he was always pricking himself.' She smiled again: take that, or leave it.

'You know he was murdered?'

'Yeah, we read about it.' She was answering all the questions now; Pelong sat quiet and expressionless. 'There's been a lotta murders lately, hasn't there? You must be busy.'

'Busy enough.' Malone finished his beer, put down his glass on the wrought-iron table. 'You have anything you want to ask, Sergeant?'

It was an act between them: swap the bowling. 'Just one thing –' said Clements, taking off his dark glasses, squinting like the other two men. 'We've got a man in custody, says his name is Syd Mitre. Actually, we know his name is Sydney Mitre Pelong. He a relation? He deals in drugs. We understand you do that occasionally. Nothing in the books, of course.' He grinned at Luisa Pelong.

'You got anything on me about dealing in drugs?' said Pelong. 'You're pissing inna the wind.'

Clements ignored that, looked at Luisa. 'You said you'd never heard of Leroy Lugos. You were inside the house when Inspector Malone mentioned him.'

'That's probably why I've never heard of him.' Her smile was brazenly defiant: catch us if you can.

'What about this other Mr Pelong? Syd?'

'I've never heard of him, either. But then I dunno any of my hubby's family. He says he don't have any, isn't that right, sweetheart?'

'I'm a fucking orphan,' said Pelong, and a crack of a grin flickered for a moment in the rock of his face. 'An only child.'

'Syd has heard of you,' lied Malone, taking up the bowling again. 'He told us to give you his regards, Mrs Pelong. A really good sort was how he described you. He didn't have much to say for you, Mr Pelong, not as a husband.'

The squinting eyes closed just a trifle; but it was enough. 'How me and the wife get along is none of your business.'

'I didn't say it was. It's how you and Syd Mitre get along that's our business. He's being held without bail on a charge of being in possession.'

'Possession of what?' said Luisa.

As if you didn't know. 'Heroin. We're also holding him on suspicion of murder.'

'Syd?' Pelong's growl squeaked a little.

Luisa's eyebrow went up above her dark glasses in resigned exasperation. 'You've goofed again, sweetheart. You'll never learn.'

Men are bad-tempered with unintelligent wives; intelligent women just shrug resignedly at their dumb husbands; it is the difference between the species. Luisa had made her bed, wanting someone who would supply it with silk sheets; Denny had been her choice, the worst mistake of her life. She had all the creature comforts she had craved, but got the wrong creature. One foot paused above the menopause, she felt the urge for someone younger, less of a brute. She had been attracted to Leroy, but she had her standards: you didn't sleep with the help. Not with a hubby like Denny to burst in on you.

Pelong felt the near-impossible, the anger at himself of the egotist. He jammed the dark glasses by his hand into the patterned ironwork of the table-top; the glass of one eye-piece broke. He shouted across the pool, his voice carrying on the still water, 'Fred! Get rid of these visitors before the fucking neighbours complain!'

'Stay there, Fred,' said Luisa quietly, her voice carrying just as effectively. 'I'll attend to this . . . Yes, Inspector, we know Syd. We were always afraid he'd turn out to be the black sheep of the family.'

Malone had never seen any sin in admiring the enemy: that way you never underestimated him. Or her. 'What is he? A brother? Cousin?'

'A cousin,' said Pelong, struggling hard to contain himself; his stomach was fluttering, as if he might be having labour pains. He had indeed goofed, as Luisa, the bitch, had told him in front of these cops; but he was not going to sit here and act fucking dumb. 'We give him some dough to start his pastrycook shop. What are you grinning at?'

'Your joke, sweetheart.'

'What fucking joke?'

'Never mind,' said Luisa. 'Inspector, we dunno anything about what Syd does outside his cake shop. My hubby isn't his cousin's keeper. Have you finished your questions?'

'Not quite, Mrs Pelong. You own a company called Coolibah Investments Services, part of a company called Thursday Island Holdings. Coolibah paid for a gold pass membership, six thousand dollars' worth, for Jimmy Maddux at the Sydney Cricket Ground and the Football Stadium. Why was that? In case you didn't read it, Jimmy Maddux was murdered the day before yesterday. His neck was broken. He worked on the wharves over at Glebe Island.'

There was a swift change in the bowling: Clements came on at the other end: 'Leroy Lugos was murdered, too. He had a portfolio file marked Coolibah Investments Services.'

The Pelongs looked at each other, then Luisa said, 'I don't think we wanna say anything more. Not without our lawyer.'

'That's Caradoc Evans, right? Nice guy, for a Welshman. We're surprised he's not already here. He must've rung you last night to tell you about Syd's troubles.'

Malone came in again: 'I think you've got trouble, too, Mr Pelong. We found a Colt Forty-five in the glove-box of Leroy's car. Besides his, it had your prints on it, too.'

Luisa turned her head, held it stiffly, as if she could not believe what she had just heard. Pelong glanced at her almost sheepishly, addressed himself to her rather than to the two detectives: 'I give it to him to protect himself! Jesus, he was scared shitless –'

'Don't say any more, not till we see Mr Evans.' She stood up, tucked in her halter top, showing the outline of her bra-less breasts. She liked attention, even from busybody cops; it was another way of showing contempt for Denny. 'Say goodbye, sweetheart.'

Pelong said nothing, but Malone said, 'Not goodbye. We're putting a twenty-four-hour police surveillance on your house, don't attempt to leave till you're ready to talk to us, with or without Mr Evans. If you try to leave, we'll haul you in and hold you at Police Centre. You'd better be ready to talk to us by ten o'clock tomorrow morning. Thanks for the beer.'

Luisa led the two detectives through the house to the front door. 'Nice house,' said Clements. He was no judge; the waiting room at Central railway station was *nice* compared with the dump he lived in. 'All in your name?'

'How'd you guess?' These two cops were all right, she

wondered where they had been all her married life. Christ knew, there had been enough other cops in that life. She opened the door, told the snarling Rottweilers on the doormat to get lost and they went meekly away. Once again Malone had to admire her. She looked at him. 'Denny had nothing to do with those murders, Leroy and Jimmy Maddux.'

'Let him tell us all about it tomorrow morning, Mrs Pelong.'

She closed the front door on them, stood leaning with her back to it. She wondered what life would be like in Europe, where most of their laundered money was banked. But she knew she could never take Denny there to live, not amongst the snobs of Switzerland, where, she had been told by Caradoc Evans, they looked down upon everyone else from their mountain-tops. She couldn't imagine the bankers of Zurich taking to being called the fucking neighbours. Not for the first time, she began to wonder how she could get rid of Sweetheart.

CHAPTER SEVEN

I

'There's no two ways about it,' said Snow White, watching a lone yacht hurrying home across Botany Bay. 'We gotta do Denny Pelong.'

'Do him?' She knew what he meant, but something, a thrill of fear (like the first injection of heroin?), made her want to hear him state it explicitly.

'Kill him.'

When Janis had come down into St Sebastian's underground car park three-quarters of an hour earlier, The Dwarf had been waiting for her, towering over her small Capri as if it were a Dodgem car in a fairground. 'Snow wants you to meet him out at La Perouse. He'll be waiting for you.'

It was she who had suggested La Perouse as their first meeting place. It was half an hour's drive from the centre of the city, the last several kilometres open enough for one to see if one was being followed. On this steaming hot day she wished he had suggested somewhere closer. She had just finished a counselling session with an addict who had been violent and she had had to call on two of the hospital wardsmen to restrain him. She had been looking forward to meeting Jack Junior at his apartment and having a swim with him in the condominium's pool. She could not suggest that Snow White join them there.

'All right, Gary. You coming with me?' She was relieved when he said no; she wasn't sure he would fit into the Capri. 'Thanks for the message.'

'A pleasure.' He gave her an almost sweet smile, then

he went out of the car park, walking light-footed on his small feet, almost mincing, though she doubted that anyone would use that word in describing him, at least not in front of him. He always treated her with the utmost respect, never swearing in front of her as Snow White did, and she trusted him more than she did White. But only up to a point: she had no experience of how far one could trust a murderous thug and that was what The Dwarf was.

She picked up her car-phone to dial Jack, but waited as a Toyota van drew in beside her and two of the hospital cleaners got out. She said hello to them, though she didn't know their names, and then when they had gone she called Jack. 'I'll be late. I have to see Mr Black –' He had warned her that no real names were to be used over the phone and nothing was ever to be put to paper. He was teaching her business principles; or lack of them. 'No, I don't know what it's about. I'll be at your place as soon as I can.'

'We'll have a swim, then we're taking Dad to dinner. Chinese.'

That would be the third time this week they had been with his father; Jack Junior was getting to be as bad as a previous boyfriend, who had always wanted to bring his mother. Or had Jack Senior begun to suspect something?

'Lovely. I'll wear my jade.' Which she would do some day soon: jade, emeralds, rubies, diamonds. Normally she was as level-headed as a calculator, but occasionally she went giddy at the thought of being rich.

She drove south out of the city, towards La Perouse on the northern arm of Botany Bay. The sun beat in at her from the west, scorching the side of her face, but occasionally it disappeared behind clouds scurrying up from the south. Out here the terrain was sandy and small one-storeyed houses sat behind sparse brown lawns. In the main this was battlers' territory, where no one dreamed of jade or diamonds but every week bought lottery tickets, where to survive without debt was some sort of riches. She gave none of the locals a thought as she drove past the houses; sympathy was not one of her weaknesses. Beyond a ridge to the east was Long Bay Gaol, but she was glad she could not see it; she did not like to be reminded of the rewards of unsuccessful crime. She kept her eyes on the road ahead, except for the occasional glance in her driving-mirror, though she could think of no reason why anyone should be following *her*. If Snow White was not at the meeting place, then she would know *he* had been followed.

He was there, sitting in his 1960 green 3.8 Jaguar, his toy. It was beautifully preserved and he had told her, not boastfully but matter-of-factly, how he had broken the arm of a kid he had caught trying to steal the hub-caps. She parked the white Capri a hundred yards up the slight rise behind the Jaguar, got out and walked down and slid in beside White. To any casual observer it would have looked like an assignation, a thought that made her smile. She was fastidious about her men and Dallas White would have been one of the last she would have picked as a lover.

'G'day. You're late.' If he had any charm at all he didn't waste it on women.

'I had some trouble at the hospital. With a junkie.'

'Jesus, they're a pain.' It didn't seem to occur to him that he was talking of a customer who, multiplied by thousands, was going to make them rich. It was like a fast-food franchiser complaining because *his* customers were ruining the environment by throwing away their styrofoam containers.

Then he told her what they would have to do with Denny Pelong. After he had said 'Kill him', she sat staring out across the blue waters of the bay as the wind, increasing from the south now, began to chop the blue into white chips. The temperature had dropped suddenly and the white clouds had turned grey, kangarooing up from the south. A crowd of tourists was hurrying back across the narrow causeway from the tiny island off the point; elderly Americans from one of the cruise ships that came into Sydney at this time of year. Some had come ahead of the others and were congregated round a grey-bearded Aborigine who stood in front of a small arsenal of boomerangs, assuring the tourists that these were better weapons than Scud missiles, that if they missed their target they returned to sender and could be used again – 'President Bush has personally ordered a dozen, just in case.' The Aborigine and the Americans smiled at each other, both of them appreciating the sales talk, and money and boomerangs passed from hand to hand. Then the tourists got into two coaches and were driven away and the elderly Aborigine packed up the remainder of his stock, put it in the boot of a new Ford Fairlane and drove off. He had missed The Dreamtime, but the present was paying off.

'Do we have to go that far?' Janis said at last. 'Get rid of him?'

He had waited impatiently for her to say something, beating a gnarled hand on the steering wheel. 'Look, you better get your priorities right. You wanna make money, a lotta money, or you wanna pussyfoot around, being squeamish? I don't mean you gotta kill him personally, we'll do that for you. We already got rid of one guy for you –'

'Maddux, you mean? I didn't ask for that.'

'Who said you did? Look, Janis, you gotta understand – we act on initiative, we don't hang around for policy meetings. We aint some political committee, meeting to find some reason why something *shouldn't* be done. We hadda get rid of Maddux and quick. He was gunna tell someone he'd found that shipment of ours on the bottom of that ship at Glebe Island. I dunno who he was gunna tell. Maybe his union mate Roley Bremner? Customs? I dunno. He might even of been working for Denny Pelong. But he hadda be shut up and Gary did it. The cops think he did it, but they can't prove nothing.'

'Who *did* tell Customs about the shipment? That was a pretty substantial loss. I can't take too many like that.'

'I think it might of been that fucking Malone, the cop from Homicide. He's a real pain in the arse. We give him one warning, when we dropped that little prick Grime in his pool, when we found out Scungy had been grassing for him. Scungy was on to us, you too.'

She felt a sudden stab of unease. 'Me? How?'

'He followed me and Gary one time when we met you. We tried to catch him that night, but he got away from us. We was gunna do him, but that same night someone got to him with the needle. By the time we caught up with him, he was dead. We found him in the entrance to the flats where he lived. So we put him in the car and took him out and dumped him in Malone's pool. We thought it a bit of a joke at the time, but now I dunno.' He looked more surprised than perturbed, as if doubting his own actions was not usual with him.

'We still don't know who killed him.'

'There was another one last night, a young guy named Lugos, he worked for Denny Pelong. Same method, needle in the bum.'

'There was a third. A prostitute down in Palmer Street. She knew Lugos, his name was Leroy Lugos. He ran some girls around the Cross. I'm counselling one of them. She was in to see me at lunchtime, she told me about Leroy.'

White turned away, looked out across the bay. Far over, as he knew, was where Denny Pelong lived. Nearer, running out from the southern point, was the long wharf of the Kurnell oil refinery; a tanker was moored there now, discharging oil. He had learned from talk on the waterfront that security had been tightened there since the start of the Gulf war. He had no interest in any wars but his own, he couldn't care less what the fucking Arabs did so long as they stayed off his turf.

'It's gunna rain. I washed the car this morning, I don't like getting it muddied . . . I think there's a third party in this game, but I dunno what they're up to. Do they think they're gunna scare the shit outa us and get a piece of the action, either from us or Denny Pelong? Pig's arse, they are.'

She wondered if Jack Junior conducted his business meetings in these terms. She had just read a book in which Wall Street types, straight out of Yale and Harvard, had been as foul-mouthed as the street types she dealt with at the drug clinic. Had her father been as vulgar as this at his stockbroking meetings? Only after his suicide had she realized she had never really known her father. He had been jovial and affectionate towards her and her brother, but he had loved the good life, the constant liquor, the lunches and dinner parties, the Mercedes and the yacht, and when the good life had been taken away from him, all the joviality and affection were suddenly gone and he was a weak and bitter man. Her mother, who had loved the good life just as much, had caved in after the suicide and gone back to the religion of her childhood, had given up laughter and taken to mealy-mouthed piety, swapping Zampatti for sackcloth and blaming herself for her husband's suicide. Janis sometimes wondered where the steel in herself came from.

'What about the Vietnamese, Trang, whatever-his-name-was?'

'We done him. We found out he was dealing for both us and Pelong. We couldn't let that go. That's conflict of interest. They oughta send guys to jail for that, but they don't, not the white-collar crims.' Like all crims, he didn't like the law being manipulated for those who were not, strictly, professionals. He looked sideways at her, grinned. 'You got a conflict of interest, you know that? You sell the shit to the junkies, then try to tell 'em how to get off the stuff.'

'You think I ought to go to jail?'

'You'll never go to jail, love. You're too fucking smart. You know, I been working for you, what, three months? You come up with cash for the stuff, no worries – but where d'you get it from? Someone's backing you. Who is it?'

'Dallas, you don't need to know that.' She had no doubt that he would find out eventually, but for the moment it was her own secret. Jack Junior had warned her that if ever it became known that he was the source of her funds, he would drop out. She had been surprised how respectable he had wanted to remain, while greed gnawed at him like cancer. That, she gathered, was his mother still exerting her influence from the grave.

'If we get rid of Denny Pelong, I think our cut of the take has to go up. It's me and Gary who're taking all the risks.'

'Who do you think is taking all the risks in the Gulf war? It's not the generals. But that's the way things are, Dallas. The guys who supply the money and the brains, they stay away from the shooting.' She had a woman's contempt for war as a means of resolution.

He grinned again. 'You think of yourself as some sorta general?'

'If you like, yes. And I'll decide how the take is going to be cut up.' She was a little surprised at her own bravado. But even as a child she had always been prepared to take on challenges: abseiling with her brother, water-skiing with her father. She had no physical fear and she was not going to be intimidated by this thug she had recruited. 'You'll get your fair share, but don't you tell me how much it's going to be.'

The grin remained frozen on his rugged face: it pointed the thin line between a smile and a snarl. 'Don't get fucking smart with me, love.'

She turned her head away, looked up towards the small crenellated tower at the top of a rise in the park across from them. It had been built some time before 1920 as a watch tower against smuggling; it amused her that two smugglers, herself and White, should now be sitting metaphorically within its shadow discussing the business of smuggling. Two young Aborigines in jeans and black T-shirts stood looking down at the Jaguar, their expressions impossible to read at this distance. The area around here was still, officially, an Aboriginal reserve; here, two hundred years ago, the Aborigines had looked down on the first European settlers as they had sailed into the bay. The first to step ashore had been the British; two days later two French ships, under Jean, Comte de La Perouse, had anchored off the small beach round the point. Anglo-French relations, for once, had been amicable, whether because they were at the other end of the world from their usual squabbles or because they wanted to impress the local savages with their civility, Janis didn't know. The Aborigines then might have looked down on the newcomers with the same expressionless stare as the two young men up by the tower. Whatever it was, it would not have been civil; civility does not come easily to people about to be conquered. Janis knew her country's history; had she not been so selfish, she might have been patriotic. She looked back at Snow White, who was only patriotic at sporting fixtures and then only if he had got good odds on Australia's winning.

'I think you should understand one thing, Dallas. I am not frightened of you, so don't threaten me. If anything happens to me, the financial backing goes out the window, understand? You need me more than I need you. It's just like the war, Dallas. Good generals and the money behind them are hard to find, but soldiers, grunts, I think they call them, are a penny a dozen, especially in a recession.'

He stared at her, then the grin thawed and he nodded his head in admiration. 'Jesus, you're something! You make Mrs Thatcher sound like Mother Theresa.'

'Well, just keep that in mind. Okay, if you have to get rid of Mr Pelong, then do it.' She was surprised, but not much, at the matter-of-fact callousness of her instruction. But she had been callous to begin with, getting into this venture. She knew the percentage of those buying heroin who would die from an overdose: the collateral damage, as the military spokesmen would call it. It was all in a cause. Maybe not a *good* cause, but hypocrisy was not one of her faults. 'If you have to, then you have to.'

'What about this other guy, the one with the needle?'

'Get rid of him, too, if you find him.' She had one moment of squeamishness; she could not bring herself to say the word *kill*. Which *was* hypocritical, though she would not admit it.

'Okay, I'll be in touch.' He leaned across and opened her door. 'That's a nice perfume.'

That surprised her almost as much as anything else he had said. 'It's Arpège. Do you have a girlfriend?'

'A couple. Maybe I'll buy each of 'em a gallon of that. Here comes the fucking rain. I'm gunna get the car wet.'

She ran back up to her own car as the first drops began to splatter on the still-warm roadway. She was struggling to put up the top of the Capri when the two young Aborigines appeared, one on either side of the car, and took over from her. When they had the top secured, they stood back, both smiling, and one of them gave a mock bow.

She hesitated, feeling the rain becoming heavier, then she said, 'Can I give you a lift somewhere?'

'Nah.' Both of them were good-looking boys, with a touch of white in them, the ultimate conquering. 'We'd ruin your reputation.'

As she drove away they were still smiling: no, *laughing* at her. All at once, for no reason at all, she hated them. A mile further on, driving now through pelting rain, it occurred to her that the blacks were only part of her problem. Her father had left her with a burdensome legacy. She trusted no man, not even Jack Junior.

She would have felt her lack of trust vindicated had she seen one of the young Aborigines take a notebook from the pocket of his jeans and add the number of the Capri to that of the Jaguar 3.8.

'Do you like Australian wines?' said Lisa.

'Some of them,' said Peter Keller. The Germans, thought Lisa with Dutch prejudice, had never been noted for their diplomacy. 'This one, yes, very much. It is from South Australia, the Barossa Valley? Where the Germans are settled? I wanted to go there, to feel at home, but my wife wanted to be on the beaches of Sydney. So did Romy.' He made an attempt at being a man martyred to the whims of his women. It didn't go down well with Lisa, who knew, as all women do, who are the martyrs in any marriage.

The rain had stopped and the evening was mildly cool, though still humid. The Malones, the Kellers and Clements were dining out in the small patio between the house and the pool. Malone had lit some burners to repel any mosquitoes, and a gentle breeze, all that was left of this afternoon's southerly buster, rustled through the jacaranda in the Cayburns' back yard. The police guard had been removed this afternoon and Lisa felt that peace had once again settled on her house. The only jarring note, in her present mood, was Peter Keller. She felt guilty about her antipathy to him, wondering if it had something to do with her Dutchness.

'The war's going well,' said Clements, not helping things: Lisa had been thinking about another war on another continent, one fought before she was born.

'It's unreal,' said Romy. 'I watch all those smart bombs homing in on their targets and it's not like watching a war at all, it's more like some kids' video game.'

'That's what our Tom said,' said Lisa. 'I had to veto him watching the news.'

'I'm looking for the one they home in on Saddam,' said Malone, though he could not get excited about the war. Perhaps it was the Irish in him. Never having invaded anywhere themselves, they have never understood the value of imperial wars.

'When the war is over, he should be caught,' said Keller, skilfully boning his blue trout. 'We should hang him. Or better still, chop off his head.' He removed the fish's head with a clean cut.

'I don't know that Australia would agree to that.' Lisa was prepared to disagree. 'We don't believe in the death penalty.'

'You sure?' Malone smiled at her. He could sense her dislike of Peter Keller and he knew she would be regretting having suggested the dinner. 'Call for volunteers to hang Saddam and you'd be trampled to death in the rush.'

'We don't have the death penalty in Germany.' Romy, Clements noted, spoke as if she were still German, still in Germany.

'A pity, too,' said her father. 'An eye for an eye . . . The Old Testament had so many good things in it. Today, even judges have bleeding hearts. A woman is raped and the man who did it gets – what? – three or four years, with time off for good behaviour. What about his behaviour while raping the woman? They should castrate him.' He began to chew on the trout, nodding in appreciation. 'Beautiful fish, Mrs Malone.'

'Call me Lisa,' she said, suddenly determining to be less disagreeable. 'A rape case would be different with a woman judge.'

'How many women judges hear rape cases?' said Romy. 'How many women judges sit in criminal courts in this State?'

'One, maybe two,' said Clements.

'We need a dozen at least. Hard-hearted ones,' said Romy, but then she smiled.

Lisa had been hoping they would get through the evening without any shop-talk, but she should have known better. Politicians talked politics, cricketers talked cricket: why should a forensic medicine specialist, two policemen and an ex-policeman be different? She gave in: 'Have you traced where this killer might be getting his curare substitute, what's-it-called?'

'Alloferin,' said Romy. 'No, there's not much hope of that. Hospitals don't have to keep a tight record of it. It's not like some other drugs, morphine for instance, where the stock has to be signed for as each shift comes on. We don't stand much chance of catching him that way, not unless he's caught in the act of stealing it.'

'Luck,' said Keller. 'Every policeman needs it, yes, Scobie?'

The discussion went on, till Lisa grew bored with it and changed the subject to that of music. To her surprise, Peter Keller seemed to welcome the change, plunging into an enthusiastic monologue on the bicentenary of Mozart's death, asking if she had seen the recent screening of *Don Giovanni* on television. 'Every year Romy and her mother and I would go to Salzburg . . .'

'You like music, too?' Lisa asked Romy.

'Love it. I'm trying to educate Russ that there's music beyond Elton John and INXS.'

'Ach!' Keller threw back his head in mock disgust. 'What music do you like, Scobie?'

'Glenn Miller.' Malone grinned down the table at Lisa. 'Russ and I often dance together when things are slow at Homicide.'

'He always wants to lead,' said Clements.

Keller stared at them both, then he laughed, though awkwardly. 'I always take things so seriously. Music, everything.'

'We'll change that,' said Clements. 'Another ten years here and you'll be like the rest of us. We never take anything seriously.'

'Except sport,' said Lisa, still only half an Aussie.

Then Malone, who had learned a few graces from Lisa, raised his glass and toasted the tenth anniversary of the Kellers' coming to Australia. Claire, who had finished her homework, came out to say goodnight; Maureen and Tom were already in bed. Keller beamed at Claire and raised his glass to her.

'To you, Fräulein, and your beauty.'

For a moment Claire was flustered, toasts to beauty were not common amongst the natives; but she recovered quickly, borrowed some of her mother's poise. 'Thank you, Mr Keller. I think my mother and Romy are beautiful, don't you?'

My diplomat, thought Malone with pride.

'Oh, indeed, indeed.' Keller raised his glass again; he was all at once the life of the party. 'To all the beautiful women here tonight.'

Malone and Clements raised their glasses. Lisa smiled at Romy. 'Aint it wonderful? Civilized at last. Should we call in all the other women in the street? It'll never happen again.'

By the time the evening was finished Keller had had a little too much to drink, but he was jovial rather than awkward or argumentative. He became almost the archetypal Bavarian; Lisa waited for him to forget Mozart and start singing beer-hall songs. At the front door he kissed her hand, not with a mock flourish but as if that were his everyday farewell to women. Lisa responded graciously, then gave her cheek to Clements' kiss. 'Next time, kiss my hand, Russ. Teach him how, Peter.'

They were all at the front door when the phone rang. Malone cursed, knowing only bad news came at this time of night, and went back down the hall to take the call. Romy and her father stepped out on to the front porch, but Clements remained in the doorway.

'Damn,' said Lisa, instinct telling her that she was going to be left alone to clear up the dinner things.

Malone came back up the hall. 'That was Phil Truach. Denny Pelong has just been shot, down in Dixon Street.'

Aldwych sat back, pushed away the plate of lychees and ginger ice-cream. 'No, I'd better not. I'm getting too old to eat so much just before I go to bed.'

'I'll have them,' said Jack Junior, who had already had one serving of dessert.

'Watch it,' said Janis. 'You're going to finish up looking like one of those Japanese wrestlers. How do men like that make love?'

'Squashily,' said Jack Junior.

Aldwych had been watching the interplay between the two of them, the glances, the smiles that were as intimate as notes passed between them. Happily married for forty-five years, he had not had much experience of young women, not today's young women. Jack Junior had brought home a few, but they had been uncomfortable with Aldwych, his reputation frightening them into acting like novice nuns. But this one, this Janis who seemed to have Jack Junior on a string, was altogether different. She amused him, but he wouldn't trust her out of his sight. He had always had a suspicious nature and, now he was retired, he had more time to indulge it.

Leslie Chung was in the next booth with his wife, a small, very attractive Chinese woman loaded with enough gold and diamonds to have saved a couple of shaky corporations from bankruptcy. Aldwych had never understood a woman's, and less so a man's, need to wear jewellery, and he had never bought Shirl anything other than an engagement and a wedding ring; he had been shocked, after her death, to find she had bought herself a boxful of rings, bracelets and necklaces. He wondered now if Les Chung had a couple of minders out in Dixon Street to make sure that Mrs Chung was not mugged.

He turned round as Chung, leaning over the barrier between the two booths, touched him on the shoulder. 'Jack, you see who's just come in?'

Aldwych looked towards the door of the restaurant where the manager, face like an Oriental sun, was greeting Denny Pelong and his wife. He led them to a booth, ignoring or oblivious to the disapproval of his two bosses at the rear of the restaurant. He was the sort of restaurateur who believed that in bad times any customer was welcome who could pay the bill. Especially one who was known to throw tips around with an abandon that was heretical to the other diners and usually spoiled their last course.

'Who's that?' said Janis.

'Denny Pelong.' He turned back to her, smiled. 'He likes to think he's my successor.'

'Is he?'

'I wouldn't know. I told you, I'm retired. I got no more interest in who runs things any more. Does the chairman of BHP keep shoving his nose in after he's retired?'

Janis looked at Jack Junior. 'What do you know about him?'

He swallowed a lychee, gave her a look that his father, who might have caught birds on the wing if he'd been so disposed, didn't miss. 'Pelong? Nothing. I told you, Dad and I never discuss that side of his life.'

'Of course,' she said, accepting the warning. She had never seen Pelong before and she felt a curious excitement at at last observing the enemy, the man whose death penalty she had okayed. She shifted slightly in her seat to get a better view of him. 'Who's the woman with him?'

'That's his wife, Luisa.' Aldwych was watching Janis rather than the Pelongs. 'She's the brains in the family.'

'She looks like a bimbo, that dress and hair-do.'

'You're a snob.' But he smiled when he said it.

'Of course. Is she a criminal, too?' Then she looked at him and managed a blush, false but polite. 'I'm sorry, that was rude of me.'

'Why? We established the other day, when we first met, that I'm a crim. Or an ex-crim. We both know what we are, Janis.' He gave her his old crim's grin, evil and chal-

210

lenging; she felt a sudden chill, recognizing another enemy. Then he looked at Jack Junior. 'What's the matter, Jack? You choking on a lychee?'

In the next booth Fay Chung, glittering gold seemingly at every joint, said, 'What's the fuss?'

'I wish you wouldn't wear so much jewellery,' said her husband.

'You're a jewellery importer, what do you expect me to wear? Rubber bands?'

Les Chung sighed; he loved his wife dearly, even though she was expensive. He came from Shanghai, she from Canton: they both knew the value of a dollar. He had brought her here tonight at her insistence; normally they dined at more expensive restaurants in the eastern suburbs, where they lived. But tonight, she had said, she felt *Chinese* and she had named the place where she wanted to dine. It had turned out to be her husband's part-owned restaurant.

'A man named Denny Pelong has just come in with his wife.'

She swivelled round; she was always curious, never inscrutable. Then she looked back at him. 'The gangster? And there's one in the next booth?' She lowered her voice; she had been introduced to Jack Aldwych for the first time this evening. 'How do you *know* people like that?'

For almost twenty years he had kept her ignorant of the dark side of his business; but now he looked at her and he knew that she *knew*. 'Mr Pelong used to buy jewellery for his wife.'

'And him?' She nodded at the next booth, her voice still low.

He sighed again. 'Jack is my partner in this restaurant.' *And the gambling club upstairs, the real money-maker.*

'Oh, my God!' She was a Christian Chinese. 'And all this time we've been going to expensive restaurants and we could have been coming here for *nothing*?'

He wondered why her thrift didn't extend to other

things besides eating out. But he loved her and so forgave her. It was easier: his father and his grandfather and, twelve hundred years before them, a T'ang philosopher, had told him a woman's patience could always outlast a man's.

Up at the front of the restaurant the Pelongs, neither of them burdened with philosophical thoughts, sat in the morose silence of warring couples. Luisa was even more loaded down with jewellery than Fay Chung; her hands glittered like tiny chandeliers and the gold necklace she wore could have hobbled a buffalo. The jewellery was the reason for their quarrel; he had insisted that she wear it, all of it. 'What the fuck you think I bought it for you for?' he had shouted. 'I'm fucking depressed.'

'You wanna wear it then?' she had shouted in reply; the neighbours, she knew, would have had their windows and ears wide open to this latest battle in the Pelong house. 'You buy me jewellery because *you're* depressed?'

'No, because I wanna see you wearing it. It bucks me up, makes me feel good – I see all the rocks on you and it tells me what I can afford – I can afford as much fucking jewellery for my wife as any rajah –'

'Rajah? Where we gunna eat then? Some bloody curry palace?'

It was she who had nominated where they would eat; she told him she felt like Chinese tonight, though she meant food, not character or personality. So here they were in this Chinese restaurant in Chinatown, with the rest of the diners, it seemed, made up of Japanese tourists, come all the way from Yokohama or Kobe or wherever to eat Chinese food in an Australian restaurant. In the quirky way that memory works, it reminded her of an old faded cartoon her father had once shown her, of a Turk taking an Australian bath, sitting in an antiquated tub naked but for his fez. She smiled at the thought and Pelong looked at her suspiciously.

'You're up to something.'

212

'No, I'm not, honest, sweetheart.' She laid a hand on his arm; the glare from her rings and bracelet made her squint a little. She was not stupidly vulgar; she knew she shouldn't be wearing this much jewellery to a place like this. Rocks like hers should be worn to State dinners at Parliament House, but she couldn't see her and Sweetheart being invited there; this new government didn't invite criminals to dinner, not even white-collar ones. But if wearing the rocks pleased Denny, okay. He'd had a bad week and things might get worse. 'What's the matter?'

He had turned round and was staring down towards the rear of the restaurant. He turned back. 'Fucking Jack Aldwych is down the back there. And fucking Les Chung.'

Four Japanese in the next booth, ears tuned to pick up the local idiom, nodded to each other. Australia was just what they had been told it would be, a robust country.

Luisa looked down towards the back booths, saw Jack Aldwych gazing at her. She raised her hand and gave him a forty-carat wave. He smiled at her in return and said something to the auburn-haired girl beside him.

What Aldwych said was, 'You have to admire her, putting up with someone like her husband.'

'In my job,' said Janis, 'I'm continually amazed at the men some women choose. As a sex, we're masochists.'

'Not you,' said Aldwych. 'Is she a masochist, Jack?'

'Are you talking sex or just in general?'

Aldwych was suddenly uncomfortable. He was an old man, he had never gone in for kinky sex with Shirl, and you certainly never talked about it in front of a girl young enough to be your granddaughter. Not even one as brass-bound as this one next to him. 'Finish your lychees, Jack. It's time we were going.'

In the next booth Fay Chung said, 'Les, how does a man like Pelong stay out of jail?' Meaning: how do you, if you know him so well, also stay out of jail? It is a little-known historical fact that wives invented the micro-chip: they can squeeze a dozen questions into one. 'He must have a record as long as your arm.'

'Not *my* arm. He and I have no association whatever.' Which was not strictly true. There *had* been an association at one time, but it had been temporary, during another gang war, and it had not been an easy one. Pelong had an abiding hatred of all Asiatics and Chung had an equally durable contempt for intelligences as far below his own as Pelong's. 'He eats here occasionally, pays without complaint and tips too much. The waiters love him.'

'Has anyone ever tried to kill him?'

'What makes you ask that?'

'I don't know. I'm just in the mood for those sort of questions.'

'Drink up your tea. It's time we were going.'

The Aldwych party and the Chungs left at the same time. As they passed the Pelong booth both Aldwych and Chung, without losing stride, said goodnight to the Pelongs. The three women, Janis, Luisa and Fay, looked at each other with that swift appraisal that has put women on a par with Indian scouts and security cameras; they missed nothing of importance in each other, taking in the abundance or absence (in Janis' case) of jewellery, the cut and expense of dress and, most important, the intelligence in each other's eye. Out in the street the Aldwyches and the Chungs parted.

Aldwych paused as he recognized an old acquaintance. 'G'day, Fred. What're you doing down here amongst the Chinks?'

'Howyagoing, Jack,' said Fred Cargo. 'I'm working for Denny Pelong. I'm his sorta Jack-of-all-sorts.'

'His minder?'

'Yeah, sorta. I'm retired, but. Like you, Jack. I don't wanna go back inside.'

'You shouldn't be working for Denny, then.'

'It's his missus I'm really working for. Nice lady. Who else is gunna give a fifty-eight-year-old ex-con a job?'

'Still, watch out for Denny. Take care, Fred.'

He moved on, not having bothered to introduce Jack Junior and Janis, who had lingered nearby waiting for him. He had used Fred Cargo once or twice as a stand-over man, but he was now part of the past.

Jack Junior was about to follow his father when he saw that Janis had not moved, was looking around.

'What's the matter?'

The Dixon Street mall was crowded. The nearby Entertainment Centre had just spilled ten thousand people into the streets; Billy Joel had sent them home flushed and excited and singing snatches of his songs. Janis was looking for Snow White and The Dwarf, but she didn't feel Jack Junior had to know that. She had discovered that he was a worrier, something his father certainly wasn't. At dinner she had all at once begun to wish that Jack Senior was her partner.

'You notice something? A crowd like this and nobody notices anything.'

'*You* noticed something,' he said.

'What?'

'That nobody notices anything.'

She smiled at him, but more to herself. Oh Jack, Jack, how long am I going to be stuck with you? He was her means to an end, but she did not want him with her till the end.

Half an hour later, inside the restaurant, Denny Pelong abruptly announced he had had enough and wanted to go home. 'Whatever you say, sweetheart,' said Luisa. 'You go and tell Fred to collect the car while I go to the little girls' room. You got your credit card?'

'Course I got it –' Then he checked his pockets. 'No, I musta left me fucking wallet at home.'

'I'll pay, sweetheart. You go and tell Fred.'

Denny Pelong stepped out of the restaurant. The crowd had thinned a little, but the mall was still lively with people, most of them youngsters in groups, still thrilled by the Joel concert, too wide awake to go home. There was no sign of Fred Cargo. Pelong suddenly had a moment of inexplicable panic, something he had never experienced before.

He was looking up the mall, half-aware of raucous music approaching him from behind, when the hitman did the job. He was a young man, dressed like most of the concert crowd in jeans and summer shirt, and he carried a portable stereo, a 'ghetto-blaster'. Strapped to it was a pistol fitted with a silencer. The stereo was blasting out a Billy Joel hit as it was pushed up against Pelong's back. He went down, with two .22 bullets in him, to the tune of 'You're Only Human'.

4

'I don't fucking know,' he said in the moment before he lapsed into unconsciousness; if he were to die, it was a remark unlikely to go down in any list of famous last words. He had been asked by a police officer, on the scene within two minutes of the shooting, if he knew who had shot him. He did not give his denial out of any criminal code of honour; he would have squealed with all the power in his punctured lungs if he had recognized his assailant; his only code was to repay any wrong done to him in any way he could.

It was Fred Cargo who had gone into the restaurant to give Luisa the news. She went pale, but she took it better than he had expected. 'Where the hell were you, Fred?'

'I went for a leak, Mrs Pelong –'

Malone and Clements arrived ten minutes later, Clements bringing his own car, with blue light flashing on the roof, down the mall to join the police cars and the ambulance which had just arrived. They had left Romy and Peter Keller with Lisa, Malone telling her to ring for a cab to take them home. The mall was crowded again, but the throng was held back by the police cars and, now, by the media vans and cars nosing into the scene. The blue and red lights of the police cars were oddly out of place in the Chinatown colour scheme of orange-red and yellow, like spots of paint dropped on the wrong canvas.

The PE team was already at work, the Crime Scene tapes strung out, but Phil Truach was the only Homicide man present.

'Nobody saw anything, Scobie –'

'Where the bloody hell was the surveillance? There was supposed to be a bloke on Pelong's tail round the clock.'

'He went for a leak –'

'You just said Fred Cargo went for a leak, too. Thank Christ it's not a cold night – the whole of bloody Chinatown would have gone for a leak.' Malone's anger had been building up all during the quick trip in from Randwick. Not at the fact of Pelong's being shot but at the growing multiplication of events that would mean more headlines. If this kept up, the Gulf war was in danger of being relegated to the Deaths Notices page. 'Where's Mrs Pelong?'

'She's over there by the ambulance. He's in pretty bad shape. They're taking him to St Sebastian's.'

'Anyone in the restaurant?'

'No, I got the manager to clear out the place. Upstairs, too. Did you know they've got a gambling club up there?'

Malone looked at Clements. 'Did you know that?'

'I can't believe it,' said Clements.

The three Homicide men exchanged looks that said nothing; illegal gambling had nothing to do with them. The bureaucracy of crime prevention saved many headaches. Then Truach said, 'Most of those in the restaurant were Japanese. This isn't gunna do much for tourism.'

'It hasn't done much for Pelong,' said Clements, watching Pelong, festooned with drips, being loaded into the ambulance. 'You want me to talk to the wife, Scobie?'

'Let her go for the moment. We'll talk to her at the hospital. Let's see what we can dig up here.'

Ten minutes later they had dug up nothing. 'I believe Fred Cargo when he says he went for a leak,' said Clements.

'Maybe he did,' said Malone. 'Maybe someone paid him to go and splash his boot. It wouldn't be the first time it's been done.'

With the departure of the ambulance, the crowd began to disperse, going back into the restaurants that were still open or going home. The police at work were never as interesting as a corpse or someone close to being a corpse. Billy Joel had provided better entertainment.

Malone and Clements left for the hospital, with Truach to follow as soon as the PE team had done their work. As they drove up to the hospital in Darlinghurst, Clements said, 'At least this wasn't a needle-in-the-bum job, so it wasn't the same guy who did Lee-roy.'

'Not unless he's changed his MO.'

St Sebastian's was the biggest hospital in the inner city, halfway between the sleaze of King's Cross and the brittle gaiety of the Oxford Street homosexual community. Its public and private sections stretched along an entire block; it catered for the poorest and the wealthiest, all within a kidney stone's throw of each other. It was run by nuns dedicated to St Sebastian the martyr, whose name was usually invoked against the plague, possibly the one disease not to be found in the neighbourhood. Tradition had it that he had been a beautiful youth who had spurned the advances of the Emperor Diocletian, a career decision that enhanced his sainthood in the eyes of the nuns and made him a fool in the eyes of the community further up the road. Even saints can't please everyone.

Denny Pelong was in the operating theatre in the private section, where, Malone and Clements were told, the doctors were fighting to save his life. The two detectives found Luisa Pelong in a small, otherwise unoccupied waiting room. A television set was turned on in one corner of the room and on the wall nearby was a garish colour print of Sebastian decorated with Diocletian's arrows, a picture of doubtful comfort to anyone waiting in the room for news of a dying relative. Luisa was leaning back in a chair, staring with uninterested eyes at a late-night movie. The first thing Malone noticed was not the jewellery but that this afternoon's bruise on her jaw was hidden by cleverly applied make-up.

'Mrs Pelong?'

She started, as if she had been woken from a doze, then looked up at the two men as if puzzled as to why they should be disturbing her. Then she frowned. 'Oh Christ, you don't wanna talk to me now, do you?'

'Better now than tomorrow.' Malone pulled up a chair opposite her, his back to the television set; Clements sat down on a couch at an angle to both of them, St Sebastian poised above him to shed a shower of arrows on him. 'We don't like things to go cold on us. Do you know who did it?'

She shook her head. There was a cup of tea on the small table beside her chair and she picked it up and began to sip it. Behind Malone Mary Astor told Humphrey Bogart, *'Oh, I'm so tired, so tired of lying and making up lies.'* Luisa looked at Clements. 'Turn that off, would you?'

Clements got up and switched off the television. *'The Maltese Falcon*, I've seen it a dozen times, I reckon. The more I see it, the more I wonder how Sam Spade was taken in by that woman.'

Luisa gave him a look that should have sent him down to Emergency. 'Is that supposed to mean something?'

He smiled, sank back on the couch. 'We're on your side, Mrs Pelong. Right, Inspector?'

'All the way. But I hope you don't mind me mentioning it, Mrs Pelong, you don't look too shocked. Upset, maybe, but not *shocked*.'

'Mr Malone, you know who Denny is, you know what

his life's been. I'm upset, why the hell wouldn't I be? But no, I aint shocked. This aint the first time I've sat in a room like this, waiting for him to come out alive. You marry a guy like Denny and you marry the consequences. I read that somewhere, only I think they said it better.'

'You said it well enough. I understand you were still in the restaurant when it happened?'

'I'd stayed to pay the bill and go to the loo.' She was about to drink again from her cup, but now she put it back in the saucer. 'Are you trying to say something, Mr Malone?'

'Not at present, Mrs Pelong.' He gave her a moment to make of that whatever she liked; but she did not take the bait. 'Did you see anyone in the restaurant you or your husband knew?'

She didn't hesitate: 'Yeah, there was Jack Aldwych and Les Chung, they was in two booths right at the back. Not together, I don't think.'

'Did you speak to them? Or your husband?'

'No, we just said goodnight to 'em when they left. That was about, I dunno, about half an hour before –' She looked down at her cup, still half-full, then put it back on the side table. 'Before what happened to Denny.'

Over the years Malone had become accustomed to dealing with women in circumstances like these; but there was no one way of doing it, no two women were the same. Pure grief from a widow was both the simplest and the hardest to deal with. Molly Maddux's anger at her husband's duplicity had somehow made it easier for him to cope with her. Now he was feeling his way, cautiously, with Luisa Pelong, who might yet be a widow. He could not get her reaction into focus, it was as if she were showing her feelings through an almost closed door, giving him glimpses that ranged from numbed worry through almost to indifference.

'Do you think they had anything to do with the shooting of your husband?'

'I wouldn't know.' She tightened her lips, as if locking her mouth shut.

He recognized the signs: he was going to get no more from her tonight. 'Righto, if that's the way you want it, Mrs Pelong.'

That unlocked the mouth again: 'Want what?'

'Do you want us to find out who tried to kill Denny, or don't you?'

She stared at him, then she nodded. 'If you can, yes. But I'm not gunna help. I don't wanna be next.'

'Why would anyone want to kill you?'

'Why would anyone wanna –' But then, unexpectedly, she laughed softly, shook her head at her question and looked at him from under her brows. 'That's dumb, aint it? Someone has been wanting to kill him ever since I first met him.'

He stood up, nodding to Clements, who also rose to his feet. 'We'll have to talk to you again, Mrs Pelong.'

'You or someone else?'

'Will it make any difference?'

'My hubby used to say, never talk to the monkeys, always talk to the organ-grinder.'

'That's original,' said Malone, straight-faced.

'Don't kid me, Inspector. Denny's never had an original thought in his life.' She began to take off her jewellery, put it in her handbag.

'We're going to put a police guard on your husband, just as a precaution.'

'Have you asked permission?' A middle-aged nun, dressed in an old-fashioned habit, all in white and pale grey, stood like a large gull in the doorway.

The territorial imperative again: it was never so defiantly upheld as in a hospital. 'Not yet, Sister. But I think it'd be a good idea, don't you?'

'Who are you?' The brogue was as thick as a Connemara mist.

'Inspector Malone.'

Her features didn't relax, but he knew he had scored better than a McTavish or a Leibowitz would have. 'Mother Catherine will have to approve it. But I'll tell her you recommended it.' Then she looked at Luisa. 'Your husband is still in the theatre. One of the doctors would like to talk to you.'

'How is he?' asked Malone.

'Not well, Inspector. If you're thinking of waiting to question him, put it out of your mind.'

'We'll come back tomorrow. Will you be here, Mrs Pelong?'

'Where else?'

The door of her was still more than half-closed to him. She stood up, gathering herself together; she was undiminished by the removal of her jewellery. She followed the nun down the wide silent corridor. This private section was more like a hotel, there were no emergency cases being rushed to operating theatres, no blood on the walls or floors. A uniformed police guard sitting outside the door of one of these expensive rooms was going to stand out like a gargoyle.

Luisa, halfway down the corridor, looked back over her shoulder; she was defiant, of the two detectives, of whatever she might have to face. Malone waited for her to swing her hips at them, but she didn't, and he was glad of that. She had a sort of cheap dignity about her, which was all she could afford; diamonds and bank accounts in Switzerland, of which he knew nothing, do nothing for real dignity, which is natural wealth. He had to admire her, even though she irritated him.

When they got down into the hospital foyer Truach was just coming in the front door. 'I came up with nothing more, Scobie. He was shot by the Invisible Man. How is he, still alive?'

'He's still on the table.'

'What about his wife?'

'I dunno. She could have had Pelong set up. I don't

think they're too happy together – he bashes her around, I think. She said she stayed behind to go to the loo and to pay the bill. Why would the wife pay the bill? Mine never pays for me.'

'I checked with the young cop from Central who was first there. He said Pelong had nothing on him. No wallet, no credit cards, nothing. She *could*'ve been paying the bill. Fred Cargo told me Jack Aldwych and Les Chung were in there tonight. She mention them?'

'Yeah. We'll talk to them. Russ and I'll go over to see Aldwych, you go out and talk to Les Chung.'

'*Now?*' Truach looked at his watch. 'It's midnight.'

Malone looked at his own watch. 'You're five minutes slow. What're you waiting for?'

Truach gave his twisted grin. 'You're a hard man, boss. I think I'll report you to the union. Where does Les Chung live?'

'Ask Russ. He's got Elvis Presley's last seven addresses.'

Clements produced a thick notebook, flipped through it, gave Truach an address in Rose Bay. 'There's no minder, no guard dogs. Just go straight up and press the doorbell. Les Chung is respectable, at least to the neighbours.'

As they went out they passed a plaster cast of St Sebastian pierced from all angles by metal arrows. To Malone it seemed that in the saint's agonized stare one eye was askew, as if he were saying: *All this for a halo*? Join the club, thought Malone: police work was much the same.

'You notice he had an arrow in his bum?' said Clements.

CHAPTER EIGHT

I

Going home in the Daimler Aldwych had said, 'They're showing *The Maltese Falcon* tonight. I watch it every time they run it.'

'I've never seen it,' said Janis, who was not a late-night-movie fan. After ten o'clock, if she was not otherwise engaged, she read, usually books about men or women who had succeeded, or sometimes failed, in the power game. 'I've heard of it. What's it about?'

'A conniving woman,' said Aldwych, sitting in the back seat, but watching that Jack Junior didn't try any cowboy act in the late-night traffic.

He's getting at me again, was Janis' instant reaction. But the thought didn't frighten her. If she was going to play in the big league in the future, then she had to learn to deal with a big-league player from the past. It was another challenge. 'Does she win out in the end?'

'No.'

'It must be an old-fashioned movie, then. Have you seen it, Jack?'

Jack Junior looked sideways at her. 'A couple of times. Dad likes to see himself in the Humphrey Bogart part.'

'Keep the speed down . . . No, I see *you* in that part. I prefer Sydney Greenstreet. He's the leader of the villains.' He smiled at Janis as she half turned and looked at him. 'Stay and watch it with us.'

'She has to get home, Dad. It's late.'

'No, no, I'll stay. Do you have a spare bed in that big house?'

'There are half a dozen that have never been slept in.' Jack Junior's tone suggested that he would prefer that the beds remained unslept in.

From the back seat Aldwych was once again aware of the undercurrent between the two younger people. He was not an expert in analysing affairs; he looked on advice-to-the-lovelorn columnists as criminal as himself. He could plan the robbing of a bank, a betting scam, the deployment of a string of brothels; but he was a novice in the field of romance. He could barely remember his and Shirl's courtship; their marriage had been comfortable rather than passionate. Something was going on between Jack Junior and this girl and he couldn't, for the life of him or of Jack, put his finger on what it was. Shirl had been simple, if not simple-minded; the women of today were too complex and ambitious for their own good. He would have to have a word with Jack, though for the moment he didn't know what the word would be.

They watched the film on the television set in the living room. It was a big room, with a twelve-foot ceiling and rich burgundy silk drapes. The furniture was a mixture of styles; Shirl Aldwych had had an eclectic eye, only spoiled in her last years by cataracts that had resulted in one or two aberrations such as the Spanish bishop's chair that stood in one corner. Aldwych occasionally sat in it, adding to the aberration. Still, Janis remarked, whatever the mixture of styles, the room smelled of money, laundered so long ago that it could almost be classed as old money.

The movie entertained Aldwych as much as ever. When Sydney Greenstreet, huge, urbane, walked out of his last scene with the words, 'Well, sir, the shortest farewells are the best,' he clapped, as he always did. In the semi-darkness of the big room Janis looked at him, but he just smiled at her and returned his gaze to the screen.

When Mary Astor finally sank down in the elevator, staring with enigmatic dark eyes at Humphrey Bogart through the grille of the elevator doors, he looked again at Janis. She had already turned to face him.

'She was too clever,' she said. 'That was her trouble.'

'You think a woman can be too clever?'

'A man, too. All the financial pirates we've had in the last few years, they were all men. All too clever and all flat on their faces now. No women, though.'

'Do you mean women are cleverer than men? That if they don't get too clever, like Brigid O'Shaughnessy in that fillum, they don't get caught? Do you think she's right, Jack?'

'I never criticize women in general,' said Jack Junior. 'Not in front of a woman.'

'You remind me of the big man in the movie,' said Janis, ignoring Jack Junior, still looking at his father. 'The Sydney – Greenstreet? – character.'

It was the ultimate compliment; but he recognized it for the flattery that it was. 'No, Gutman, that's the character's name, he's smoother than I ever could be. Education, you need it to be smooth. Jack's educated, aren't you, Jack?'

'But not smooth, I hope.'

Aldwych looked back at Janis, gave her his old man's smile; if he lived long enough, if Jack Junior produced children, it might even turn into a fair facsimile of a benevolent grandfather's smile. 'You're smooth, Janis.'

It was not a compliment; and she knew it. But from anyone else she would have accepted it as praise.

Then outside the dogs began to bark. Father and son looked curiously at each other, both abruptly alert; then Jack Junior rose and went out of the room. In the hall he called, 'It's all right, Blackie, I'll see to it.'

'We usually don't get visitors this time of night,' Aldwych told Janis. 'It used to happen in the old days, but not any more.'

She had a moment of panic. Had something gone wrong with Dallas White and Gary Schultz and they had traced her here? Then there were voices in the hall and Jack Junior came back with the policeman Malone and another big man who was obviously also a cop. Aldwych didn't rise from his high-backed leather chair, but, she noticed, he did not look resentful of this middle-of-the-night intrusion by police. It occurred to her that he might welcome any sort of disruption to his retirement, any reminder of the bad old days.

'You remember Miss Eden, Inspector? Hello, Russ. The dogs didn't bite you? I'd better have their teeth seen to. It's all that canned food you see on TV.'

'Bull terriers,' said Malone. 'They're a change from Rottweilers. I had a brush with a couple of them this afternoon out at Denny Pelong's.'

'How is Denny? I saw him tonight, but we just nodded hello.'

'He's not too well, Jack. Just after you left that restaurant tonight, someone put two bullets into Pelong's back. We've been to the hospital and he's still in surgery. They don't know if he's going to make it.'

Janis somehow turned her face into a mask. God, had Dallas White tried to kill Pelong right there outside the restaurant where she had been dining? Had he been trying somehow to implicate her?

'Are you expecting me to be upset? Forget it, Scobie. I couldn't care less what happens to Denny Pelong.' Aldwych looked at Janis out of the corner of his eye. 'Are you shocked to hear me say that, Janis?'

'Not at all. You forget, I'm a social worker. We're case-hardened.'

As soon as she said it she knew it was a mistake. It was a flippant remark, even if true of herself. But it switched the attention of the two police officers to herself, something she didn't want. She had been too clever.

'Do you know Denny Pelong, Miss Eden?' said Malone.

'No. Should I?'

'Not necessarily. But he is one of the biggest, if not *the*

227

biggest, drug dealer in the State. I thought one of your junkies might have mentioned him.'

She had made another mistake. But before she could remedy it, Jack Junior interrupted: 'Inspector, would you and Sergeant Clements like a drink? A cup of tea or coffee?'

'Tea, thanks,' said Malone, and Clements nodded.

'Janis –' Jack Junior turned to her without rising from his chair. 'Would you mind? The kitchen's out there to the right.'

There was a sudden tension that spread out like a radiation to touch the other three men; then Janis smiled, or at least bared her teeth like the bitch bull terrier out in the garden. Aldwych recognized it; but Jack Junior had already turned away to speak to Malone and Clements, playing host. Janis went out to the kitchen, walking stiff-legged, looking, against all the odds, prudish and spinsterish. The latter, of course, is now an obsolete word, or anyway condition; but Jack Junior had just set their relationship back a hundred years. She was seething and could have boiled the water for the tea on her chest. He would pay, oh my God, how he would pay!

Jack Junior, not oblivious of what he had done but intent on safety, said, 'Inspector, my father is retired, you know that. I'm a respectable businessman and Dad is proud that I am. Why, now, would he want to get himself involved in the shooting of someone like this Pelong?'

'Mr Aldwych, I didn't suggest anything like that . . . I don't think, Jack, that you hired a hitman to get rid of Pelong –'

'Thank you, Scobie,' said Aldwych with rough urbanity, in his Sydney Greenstreet role.

'I think you'd be too smart to be there just before it happened. But why were you, Les Chung and Denny Pelong all there in the restaurant tonight?'

'Coincidence. The sorta thing that buggers up evidence in a court.'

'Not always. Anyhow, you ran this town once –' Aldwych didn't deny that: he *had* run it and Christ help anyone who tried to dispute it. There had been no urbanity in him in those days. 'You must have a hint of what's going on, even today. Something *is* going on, Jack. Russ and I are building up enough murders to fill a morgue. I was hoping you could help us out.'

Aldwych took his time; then he said, 'Les Chung and me were discussing it the other day. Someone is trying to muscle in on Denny. I dunno who. And according to Les Chung, Denny dunno, either. That's all I can tell you, Scobie.'

'What are they trying to muscle in on? Drugs, girls, gambling?'

'Drugs, I think. What am I saying? I'm giving information to a copper.' He smiled at Jack Junior. 'Your mother would love me for it, if she knew.'

'Jack –' Malone was speaking to Aldwych, but he was watching the son. The younger man was as alert as one of the bull terriers outside might have been. 'Have you ever heard of an ex-con from Melbourne named Dallas White? Snow White. He has an offsider, a huge bastard called The Dwarf. His name's Gary Schultz.'

Aldwych shook his head. 'Sorry, Scobie. They're new to me. I never had anything to do with the Melbourne mob. They were a vicious lot,' he said piously, Sydney Greenstreet now playing the Pope.

'Oh, indeed,' said Malone, equally pious.

All four Sydneians sat a moment in silence, looking down their noses at the Melburnian low-life. Down south the high-life of Melbourne had an equal contempt for the citizens of Sydney, high or low. It was what Federal politicians, when away from home, called the spirit of nationalism.

'I shouldn't say this in front of Dad,' said Jack Junior, 'but if these crims are killing each other off, shouldn't that please you?'

'My loving son,' said Aldwych, but he was smiling, unoffended by his son's public spirit.

'We'd gladly sit back,' said Malone, 'except that the media and all the law-and-order do-gooders keep beating their drums.'

Janis came to the door. 'Jack darling, I can't find a tray.'

Jack Junior hesitated, not wanting to lose his grasp on this interview. But Janis stood stock-still in the doorway, firm as a wife. He got to his feet and followed her out to the kitchen, closing the door there behind him. At once she attacked him:

'Don't you ever do that again! I am not your bloody tea-lady!'

'Janis, I had to get you out of there. You were ready to start baiting them – you're baiting Dad, too –'

'He's baiting me – haven't you noticed?'

Jack Junior had found a silver tray, was putting cups and saucers on it. 'Make the tea strong, that's how Dad likes it.'

'Don't tell me what to do! He'll get it as it comes!' Then she simmered down, took the tray from him. 'Are there any biscuits or cake or anything? What are they talking about in there?'

Jack Junior found a tin of biscuits. 'They mentioned a couple of guys from Melbourne, a guy named White and his mate, someone called The Dwarf. What's the matter?'

'What? Nothing.' She had kept from him, at his demand, the names of anyone with whom she was involved in the drug smuggling. He had agreed to supply the finance, but, in the early stages, he had said, he wanted to know no more than was necessary. It was contrary to his usual business practice, but what he was doing was contrary to anything he had ever done in his life before. His mother's ashes were spinning in the wind.

He put his hand on her arm, his grip hurting her. '*Come on!* Do you know these guys?'

The electric kettle was boiling. She jerked her arm

away, turned and poured the boiling water into the china teapot; for a mad moment she had the urge to pour the water over him. She hated men who hurt her physically: Jack Senior would be interested to know she was *not* a masochist.

'You said you didn't want to know any names –'

'I want to know now! Come on. Are they working for you?'

She put the teapot on the tray, added a milk-jug and sugar-pot. She had noticed the quality of the china; Jack's mother had spent his father's money well. When she made her own money she would not spend any time in a kitchen, but she had remarked that this kitchen was the sort that would give the average housewife, which she was not, a culinary orgasm.

'Yes.' She picked up the tray, paused and looked at him, taking delight in the fact that she knew she was going to shock him: 'They are the ones who tried to kill this Denny Pelong.'

'Jesus Christ!'

'Open the door,' she said calmly.

He stared at her, seeing for the first time the icy calmness of which she was capable. All at once he was frightened of her; he had none of the gangster's gorilla courage that had enabled his father to survive so long. He opened the door, following her out of the kitchen, his mind quickening again, wondering already how he was going to get rid of her and get out of this venture that looked as if it might turn into an unholy bloody mess. He knew that if he had his father's character, the simplest solution would be to kill her; or have the killing done for him. But he also knew that he could never go that far. He was his mother's son as well as his father's. He had inherited his father's greed for power, but his weakness would always be his mother's morality, there in his genes like another disease.

In the living room the tea was poured and handed

around with the biscuits. 'Iced Vo-Vos?' said Malone. 'I haven't had 'em in years.'

'My favourite,' said Aldwych. 'Them and Monte Carlos. My wife always had old-fashioned tastes.'

Just like Sally Kissen, the whore, thought Malone. He wondered if Arnotts, the biscuit manufacturers, had ever thought of calling on them to appear in their commercials.

'If Denny Pelong falls off the perch,' said Aldwych, chewing on an Iced Vo-Vo, 'I wonder who'll take over?'

'Maybe the Triads.' Clements had been quiet up till now; but he had seen that Malone's mouth was full of biscuit. 'Or the Vietnamese. Nice cuppa, Miss Eden.'

'Thank you. The Asians, they're a problem?' She hadn't even considered them, despite the killing several weeks ago of Trang, the Vietnamese.

'They're going to be,' said Malone, swallowing the biscuit. 'Do your clients ever talk about them?'

She shook her head, the light glinting on the auburn shine of it. She's a looker, Malone thought; and a lady, though he had learned from experience that not all ladies were to be trusted. She held her cup delicately, little finger raised; she had the knack of biting into a biscuit without leaving crumbs around the corner of her mouth. Something told him she would wield a knife with the same delicacy, whether on a plate or at someone's throat.

'No,' she said, 'my clients never mention the Asians. Are they the ones who are doing these needle killings? It sounds sort of Oriental.'

'What makes you say that?'

'Well, Occidental killings –'

'That's a good one,' said Aldwych. 'Occidental killings.'

She gave him a smile that chilled the tea in his cup. 'Okay, Western killings. They are cruder, aren't they?'

'Would you say they are, Jack?' Malone looked at Aldwych, the expert.

'Killing is killing, Scobie,' said Aldwych, still the Pope. 'It's still a crime. Except like now, in the war.'

'I didn't know that,' said Malone, finishing his tea.

Aldwych smiled. 'I like you, Scobie. It's a pity you and me were never on the same side. We could of run this town.'

'I thought you did it pretty well on your own, Jack.' He got to his feet. 'I'm sorry to've kept you up so late. But Russ and I had to clear up that you had nothing to do with the shooting of Pelong. You can sleep easy now.'

'I always have.' Aldwych stood up.

'Do the bull terriers bite on the way out?'

'Never my friends, Scobie. Come back and see me when *you're* retired.'

Jack Junior showed Malone and Clements out, past the fangs of the bull terriers who, if they knew that the police officers were now friends of their master, preferred the tear-'em-apart enmity of the good old days. Once in the car Malone said, 'We're going to see that Eden woman again. She keeps turning up too regularly.'

Inside the house, when Jack Junior came back to join him and Janis in the living room, Aldwych, playing himself this time, said, 'All right, what are you two up to? And don't try any bloody lies with me!'

2

Malone was sitting at the computer, putting yesterday's and last night's events into the system. He had run back the data, but it read like nothing more than a shredded crossword puzzle. There was a thread, but it kept breaking off; and there was one element in the puzzle that eluded him. Who was the needle killer and why?

Then the phone rang in his office. He got up slowly, tired and stiff; he felt as he had occasionally felt years ago, after bowling twenty-five overs on a stinking hot day. He had had only four hours' sleep and that mostly broken by a mind that had tossed and turned more than his body.

He went into his office, half-expecting that the call would be the news that Denny Pelong had died during the night. The morning newspapers had carried stories on last night's shooting, but there had been no editorial comment, no remarks on the spreading of 'the plague of murders'. Saddam Hussein was the target for today, both for bombs and editorial opinion.

The caller was Inspector Joe Nagler, from Special Branch. 'Scobie? I bumped into Irv Rubens last night.'

Nagler was another of the few Jews in the Department. Malone wondered if the meeting last night had been accidental or whether, because of the Gulf war, Sydney Jews were gathering to form committees. Whatever they were doing, he had other things on his mind. 'Yeah?'

'He told me about those murders you've got on your plate and that you think they have something to do with a drug war. That right?'

'I don't know, Joe. I've got a dozen loose strings and I can't tie 'em together.'

'I know how you feel. I've got enough loose strings to make a shark net, only the bloody sharks would probably still slip through. Anyhow, are you interested in a character named Dallas White? I think they call him Snow White.'

Malone sat up. 'Very much. Go on.'

'Well, I don't know whether you know it, but we've been handling security at certain points with the Feds, I mean because of this Gulf business. We've had fellers out at Kurnell, at the oil refinery, and I've had a coupla guys hanging out at La Perouse.'

'La Perouse? You expecting the Abos to go to town for Saddam?'

'They've got more nous than that. No, we've just been keeping an eye out in case someone gets ideas about lobbing mortars or firing a missile –'

'Joe, come *on*.'

Even over the phone Nagler's patience was apparent.

'Scobie, you're more intelligent than that. Just because we've never had terrorism out here doesn't say there aren't people here capable of it. I don't know why I bother with you guys in Homicide – you live in your own little world of little murders –'

'Righto, Joe, I apologize.'

'Okay, then. Anyhow, we've had these guys on lookout at La Perouse, out on the point overlooking Bare Island. Yesterday afternoon there was a green Jaguar, an old model, parked there. Dallas White was in it on his own for almost half an hour, then a girl drove up in a red Capri and joined him. No kissing or any hanky-panky when they met –'

'Was she Jewish?'

'Pull your head in. They nattered together for twenty minutes or so, then they drove away independently. One of my fellers, an Abo, incidentally, took the numbers of both cars. I've checked this morning – the Jaguar belongs to Dallas White.'

'And the Capri?'

'That's registered to a Janis Eden.'

'Joe, I love you!'

'Watch it, sport, I'm a married man.'

Malone hung up as Clements came in, looking as if he, too, could have done with more sleep. He slumped down in Malone's spare chair, spread his heavy legs; never unrumpled at the best of times, he looked now as if he had slept last night in his clothes in the street. His thick-browed, heavy-jawed face had the slackness of a boxer who had stayed in the ring one punch too long.

'Pelong's still alive. I'm going out now to talk to Mitre, see if he can give us a lead. He goes up before the beak again this morning. You want him held?'

'Get the Police Prosecutor to put it to the beak that we don't want Mr Mitre to be the next victim. Mitre himself might decide that it's safer for him to stay in custody. Talk him into it.'

'I'm buggered.' Clements heaved himself out of his chair. 'Did Phil Truach get anything out of Les Chung last night?'

'Nothing. But he got an earful from *Mrs* Chung about getting them out of bed in the middle of the night.'

'She would've still got more sleep than I did. What're you gunna do now?'

'I'm going to talk to our girl Janis. Joe Nagler's just been on to me with some info. Janis is a friend of Snow White's.'

Clements opened his eyes wide, as if forcing himself awake. 'Well, well. It's a small world, aint it?'

3

Janis, too, had had a sleepless night. It had had nothing to do with the fact that she had been in a strange bed; she was not wanton nor a travelling saleswoman, but she had been in beds other than her own and never felt strange and restless. True, Jack had not come to her bedroom, but if he had, she would have kicked him out. She was still angry with him for his treatment of her last night. But he was the lesser of her troubles: Jack Senior was her big worry.

'What are you two up to?' he had said. 'And don't try any bloody lies with me!'

She had seen at once the change in him. All attempted urbanity had gone, he had reverted to type, he was the old gang boss, the emperor. She had looked to Jack Junior to answer, but he was blank-faced. 'I don't know what you're talking about, Dad.'

Aldwych had stared at his son; then he had switched his gaze to Janis. 'Okay then, what are *you* up to?'

She decided to take him on head-on: 'If I'm up to anything, as you call it, I don't think it's any of your business, Mr Aldwych.'

'It is, if it concerns him.' He nodded at his son. His old man's face had not suddenly become young again, but it had hardened, as if muscles under the slack jaws and loose cheeks had regained their strength. 'Don't get too clever, girl, or you could end up out in the bush somewhere.'

'Dad!'

'Shut up, Jack. I'm trying to save your hide. Now which of you is gunna tell me what's going on?'

It was Jack who told him: 'Dad, we've got a scheme going . . .'

Aldwych, without rising from his chair, if not urbane then at least composed, had generated a chilling anger as Jack had outlined the scheme. He had not exploded; the very low temperature of his anger was more frightening. For the first time Janis realized how Aldwych had risen to the top, that he was a cold-blooded killer who, even if he did not do the killing himself, would order it without compunction. She was suddenly and for the first time in her life terribly afraid.

'Jack, I never touched shit – you know that. I hate the fucking stuff.' He was talking to Jack Junior as if Janis was not in the room. 'It was a promise I made to your mother – the only time we ever talked seriously about what I did. I hated it, anyway. I still do. Why the hell did you have to get into it? Christ, don't we have enough money? Haven't you got enough to occupy you, running the companies? What the hell do you *want*?'

Jack Junior looked down at his hands, as if he hoped to find an answer there that would satisfy his father; but his hands were empty. Both the father and the girl next to him recognized the weakness in him, Aldwych with sorrow, Janis with contempt.

Janis said, 'He wants power. The same as I do. I want money, too. This was all my idea and Jack came in because he loves me.'

She wasn't sure why she was defending Jack. She wasn't even sure he loved her, he'd certainly never told her so.

But to mention love was always a good ploy, it softened the heart. If Jack Senior had a heart, something she was beginning to doubt. Though that thought didn't diminish him in her eyes. Her own heart did no more than pump blood.

Aldwych turned his head, looked at her as if he had forgotten she was there. At first she thought he was going to ignore her, turn away again, then he said, 'You got him into this?

She hesitated, still afraid, then nodded. 'Yes.'

'How many helpers have you got?'

'Just two.'

'Who are they?'

'What are you going to do with them if I tell you?'

He ignored that. 'Just tell me!'

For a moment she thought of defying him; but she could see the ruthlessness in him now. She had never had to face anyone like him before, a dictator who brooked no opposition. 'Two men on the wharves, Dallas White and Gary Schultz. Dallas White is running for union secretary and we're financing him. We'll run the wharves when he gets in, we'll be able to bring in our stuff more easily.'

'Bullshit.' Aldwych looked back at Jack Junior. 'Do you know these blokes? You didn't bat an eyelid when Malone mentioned them.'

'I didn't know about them till Janis gave me their names out in the kitchen, when we were getting the tea. That's the first I knew who they were. I knew she had some helpers, but I'd told her I didn't want to know. All I was doing was supplying the finance. Just like a bank.'

Aldwych permitted himself a thin grin. 'You're no different than a lotta the so-called legitimate banks. Some of them didn't wanna know, either.' It had been one of the pleasures of his retirement to see how some of the big-name banks had been suckered by some of the entrepreneurs. He had felt almost pious: at least his robbing of banks had been straightforward, a hold-up or a break-in.

'Well, anyway, your little scheme is over. Finished.'

Jack Junior and Janis exchanged glances then she said, 'It's not as easy as that, Mr Aldwych. We're committed.'

'Committed to what?'

'We've got a shipment of cocaine coming in – the ship it's on is already in port. We've paid half, we have to pay the other half on delivery.'

'Forget it.'

Janis suddenly generated her own anger, her fear of him for the moment pushed aside. 'It's not as easy as that! It's too big – it'll be worth at least five million on the street – we're not going to give that up!'

Aldwych had been defied before by women, by brothel madams such as Tilly Devine and Kate Leigh, the two toughest women Sydney had ever known; but this girl was different, she was challenging him without any of the back-up those other women had had. He studied her, wondering just how much hold she had over Jack Junior. 'Who's the shipment consigned to?'

'It's a shelf company, Dad. One that's got nothing to do with our legitimate ones.'

'Where's it coming from?'

'From Antofagasta, in Chile. It's come down there from La Paz in Bolivia.'

'Why cocaine? Heroin's the big seller.'

'That's next,' said Janis.

'Next?' Aldwych raised an eyebrow. Despite his distrust and dislike of this girl, she intrigued him. He had never worked with women at an executive level in his gang days; there had been only one executive, himself. 'How did you get into this?'

'I went to Los Angeles . . .'

That had been nine months ago, when her ambition to be rich had started to stir, before she had even begun to think of *power*. She had applied for a study grant and a benevolent government, eager to promote its image of helping women, had given her one. She had gone to Los

Angeles, made a perfunctory study of the drug problem there and the efforts to combat it, and spent most of her time making contacts in the trade itself. Then she had met the man from Cali in Colombia. She had had to spend a weekend with him in Las Vegas because, as he had told her, he was a ladies' man and all the women in Cali, even the ugly ones, missed him when he was out of town. He was insufferable, but he was part of the cartel and she had suffered him with a smile and the appropriate praise for his sexual prowess. She had perfected the co-ordination of closing her mind and opening her legs at the same time. He was United States- and Europe-oriented and she had had to explain to him where Australia was and that the natives were civilized enough to want to buy drugs; in the end he had seen the possibilities of the market and agreed to supply her once she had established the credit he demanded. He was a ladies' man but not in business.

'How did you make the first payment?' Aldwych said.

'By draft to an account in Panama.'

'What about the final payment?'

'That's to be made here, we don't know who to. We lost a shipment earlier this week, but they haven't come near us for payment on that, since we didn't collect the stuff. They may or they may not. The arrangement is that we pay only when the stuff is actually handed over, but we don't know just how tough these people are.'

'From what I've read,' said Aldwych, who never missed a crime story in the newspapers or on television. Do bishops give up reading the Bible when they retire? 'they don't give anything away for nothing. How's the stuff coming in?'

'It's packed between the plastic sheets in solar panels.'

Aldwych shook his head. 'Jesus, even I know you wouldn't import solar panels from Bolivia. Their only bloody industry is growing the coca bush for cocaine and herding those animals that spit at you, what d'you call 'em, llamas? Solar panels! From *Bolivia*!' He shook his head again. 'The Customs people here aren't bloody dills. But you're both bloody amateurs.'

'I suppose even you were an amateur once.' Janis was getting over her fear of him; and it hurt her to be told she was not a professional. 'You made mistakes.'

'Sure, who doesn't? But I was never an amateur, not like you two.' He turned away from her. 'If you didn't wanna know, Jack, does anyone know you're in this?'

Jack Junior looked at Janis, who said, 'Nobody knows.'

'Okay, Jack, then you're out of it. As of right now. If you can't protect your arse, then I'll have to do it for you.'

'Where does that leave me?' Janis was angry again. 'Where do I get the money for the final payment?'

'That's your problem.'

'No, Dad, it isn't her problem.' Jack Junior was tentative in his defiance, but he was not entirely without courage; he was also not without honour, an ironic distortion of the code that his father had once lived by: 'Not hers alone, anyway. I got into this mess with her –'

'You admit it's a mess?'

'Okay, yes, I admit it. But I can't leave Janis holding the bag. I'll see she gets the final payment to pass on.' He turned to her. 'Then I'm out of it. If you want to go on, you go on on your own.'

'I can do it,' she said doggedly, hating them both.

'You really think a woman can run a big racket in this country?' said Aldwych. 'And run the blokes who run a union? This is a man's country, haven't you woken up to that?'

'There are two women State Premiers.'

'Put in there because no blokes wanted the jobs. One State stinks of corruption and the other is so broke it should have Mother Theresa running it. Take the money from this shipment, Janis, and run.' He looked at his son. 'What's the cut?'

'Sixty per cent to us –'

'Not us,' said Aldwych. 'You.'

'Okay, sixty per cent to me, forty per cent to Janis.'

'All right, Janis, take your two million, less your expenses –'

'We split those,' she said. 'White and Schultz have to get their cut. They're asking for more –'

'You see? You've already got trouble. You pay that. Banks never pay the expenses and Jack was just your bank. Don't argue, girl. Just consider yourself lucky I'm retired. Otherwise I'd feed you to the bull terriers.'

'Dad!'

'Shut up, Jack.' He rose from his chair. He had all of what looked like Sydney Greenstreet's dignity; but, it might have surprised him to know, it was his own. Even Janis, hating him, recognized it. 'I won't be getting up early in the morning. You be gone, Janis, before I come down for breakfast – I don't talk to anyone at the breakfast table. And don't ever come to this house again. Goodnight.'

He went out and she stared at the empty doorway in a mixture of fury and amazement. He had wiped her as if she were no more than a chalk-mark on a blackboard. He had shown her what it was to be a real boss, an emperor. It added to her fury to know that she would never have the power he had.

'Come to bed,' said Jack Junior.

'We're not sleeping together!' She turned her anger on him.

'I wasn't suggesting it.' His mother's ghost still ran the morals in this house. All at once he wanted to be rid of Janis, he had seen the danger in her. He felt grateful to the Old Man, he would tell him so when this was all over. 'Come on, I'll show you to your room.'

That had been last night and this morning they had left the house in Harbord at seven o'clock. Jack Junior had driven her home to Wahroonga, dropping her at the front gate in the quiet, tree-lined street where the smell of respectability was as pervasive as that of the flowers and shrubs in the well-kept gardens. If cocaine were sniffed here it would be done with the little finger raised and it would not be referred to as a snort. Snorting was what was done when referring to socialist politicians.

'Stay away from White and Schultz,' said Jack. 'When the stuff is on the wharves, they'll let you know, I guess. But don't meet with them. When the contact calls for the money, I'll bring it to you.'

'In cash.'

'I'll get it today. Look after yourself.' He drove away, thinking of the line in last night's movie that his father always clapped: *The shortest farewells are the best.*

Janis had gone into the house, not the large one where she had been raised but the much smaller one bought after her father's death, and her mother, mouth withered with new-found piety, had shaken her head at her loose-living daughter but said nothing. Janis had showered, changed and come to work by train, travelling for the last time, she hoped, with the hoi-polloi. After this weekend, even though the dream of being an empress looked as if it had run on to the rocks, she would be rich enough to be at least a duchess.

She had left the Capri in the St Sebastian's car park when Jack had picked her up last night. She did not go to the clinic in Darlinghurst Road, but came straight to the hospital. She had just finished with her second client, a sixteen-year-old boy who had been on heroin for two years, was skeleton-thin, hollow-eyed and already halfway to the grave, when her beeper buzzed. She went to a phone, rang the clinic.

It was one of the other counsellors. 'Janis, there's been an Inspector Malone here looking for you. He's on his way over to the hospital now. I thought you'd like to know.'

The youthful addict shuffled past her, looked at her with dying eyes, went across the lobby and out into the street, where he disappeared, like smoke blown away, in the eye-shattering glare of the morning.

4

As Malone came out of the clinic he met Ava. At first, blinking in the glare, he almost missed her. The heat and the humidity compressed one; it was as if the city were wrapped in smothering plastic. The weather report had said this morning that if this heat continued for another month this summer would be the hottest ever recorded. This year looked as if it might be one of records: weather, unemployment, bankruptcies, murders. Enough to make you feel good just to be dead.

'Hello, Inspector.'

She was modestly dressed, a long-sleeved white shirt and a loose blue skirt; she wore dark glasses against the blinding sun and her hair was pulled back in a chignon. She looked respectable enough, Malone thought, to be mistaken for a counsellor. Though he was on his way to interview a counsellor who, he had begun to suspect, might not be respectable at all.

'Miss Eden's not here,' he told her. 'I'm going along to see her at St Sebastian's. You want to come?'

Ava hesitated, then she followed him across to the marked police car at the kerb. 'It'll look as if I'm being picked up again.'

'I'm your defence witness.' He introduced her to the young constable at the wheel. 'This is Miss Redgrave, a social worker.'

'G'day, Ava.' The young officer's grin tore every muscle in his face. 'How's business these days?'

'Hello, Darren.' She smiled at Malone. 'Darren's picked me up half a dozen times. Always very nice about it.'

When they entered the hospital Malone took Ava into a corner of the lobby. People were coming and going,

patients' visitors loaded with fruit and flowers and magazines, looking forward to meeting other visitors across the
patients' beds. Nobody took any notice of the tall detective
and the attractive young woman standing beneath another
of the hospital's over-coloured prints, this one of the Virgin Mary. Malone sometimes wondered if the Holy Family
ever shuddered at what passed for their likenesses.

'Ava, what do you know about Miss Eden?'

She took off the sunglasses, gave him a suspicious look.
'Has she done something wrong?'

'Not as far as I know. But she's close to a couple of
cases I'm on. Does she appear to you to know much about
the drug scene in this town?'

'She'd know everything, wouldn't she?'

'Not necessarily. She'd know the general workings, but
she wouldn't have to know who controls the importing of
the stuff. Leroy knew, didn't he?'

'I think so. Well, he *said* he did, but he was a real crap
artist.'

'Did he ever mention Denny Pelong?'

She shook her head. 'Not that I remember. But we'd
heard the name. You work around the Cross, you hear
names like his every day.'

'You ever hear of a Dallas White? Snow White?'

'No.'

'He has a mate, Gary Schultz. About the size of a house,
they call him The Dwarf.'

'Oh, *him*. Sure. He was a client of mine a coupla times.
You're right, he's huge. I was glad he never wanted to be
on top.' Above them Malone was sure the Virgin Mary
rolled her eyes. 'He knew I was on heroin, he used to ask
me questions where I got it.'

'He wanted some for himself?'

'No, he seemed more interested in – in the marketing
of it.'

It was difficult to imagine The Dwarf studying marketing. 'Maybe. When did you last see him?'

'I don't know, about a week or ten days ago, I think. I don't keep a business diary, you know. We were leaving the house and we bumped into Sally and that feller you mentioned, the one who died the same way as Sally and Leroy. Grime?'

'Did The Dwarf make any comment? I mean about Grime?'

'No. They just nodded to each other. It's often like that, guys seem not to want to recognize each other. As if paying for it is some sort of reflection on their macho image.'

Malone looked at her. 'Ava, how did you ever get into this game? No, don't tell me. Go home to – where is it? Wagga? – go home as soon as you can. It's getting dangerous around here and I don't want to get a call one night and find you with a broken neck or a poisoned needle in that attractive butt of yours. Go home today.'

She returned his gaze. 'Do you go through life holding girls' hands?'

'I'd like to, but the wife won't allow it. Take care, Ava. I'll tell Miss Eden you're waiting to see her.'

He found Janis Eden in a small cubicle, the walls bare of everything, even colour prints of St Sebastian or the Holy Family. There were two chairs, a table and that was all. It reminded Malone more of a police interrogation room than a place for counselling. He told Janis that Ava was waiting to see her, then he sat down opposite her.

'You're not surprised to see me?'

'They called me from the clinic, said you were looking for me. What's it about, Inspector?'

'Mostly you.' He decided to be direct. 'How much do you know about the drug scene, Miss Eden? Not around here at the Cross, the dealing in the streets. I mean the big picture.'

'What makes you think I know anything?'

'Because yesterday afternoon, out at La Perouse, you met with a man named Dallas White, who has a list of convictions as long as his arm and who we suspect of being up to his thick neck in drug smuggling.'

'You're mistaken, Inspector, I don't know any Mr White –'

'Janis, don't let's beat about the bush. I should imagine when you're counselling anyone in here, you demand the truth from them or you'd get nowhere. It's the same with us police. So let's cut out the bull. Your car and White's – yours, I believe, is a Capri and his is a Jaguar – you were observed and the cars' numbers taken and checked.'

'Were you following me?' That was a slip, and she cursed herself for it.

'Blame it on Saddam Hussein.' She frowned in puzzlement and he explained: 'With the Gulf war, they're afraid of terrorist attacks on the oil refinery at Kurnell. You two sit in a car at La Perouse, just across the bay from the oil refinery, and you're bound to attract attention. You could have been lovers, but I don't think Snow White is your type. Now why did you meet him?'

She was trapped; and she was not prepared for it. She had never expected the police to be attacking her so soon. She was not the least bit interested in the war in the Middle East; that was something between politically ambitious men, a fight over oil. But now she wondered if Saddam Hussein had, like herself, miscalculated. She had not thought of herself being in a war, at least not against the police; the analogy had not occurred to her. But of course she *was* in a war, against Denny Pelong, against the police, against even Jack Aldwych. He had declared it against her last night. It was a shock to her intelligence to realize how unintelligent she had been. Too clever, but not clever enough.

'Well, yes, I did meet Mr White.' Her mind was in high gear, almost out of control, as she sought some plausible reason why she should have been out at La Perouse yesterday afternoon. Her demeanour, however, was cool, relaxed, none of her tension showing.

'Why?'

'I don't think I have to tell you that, do I? The Consorting Act no longer applies, does it? You can meet with known criminals now, can't you, and not be charged? From what I've been reading, some of your police officers have been doing a lot of that.'

'Sure, and we've sacked them. You have some idea of the law?'

'In this job you have to.'

'You can meet with the Devil himself, if you want to, and we can't touch you. But it wouldn't look good if ever we hauled you in.'

'Are you thinking of hauling me in?' She was playing for time, trying to find some defences.

'That depends what we come up with on Dallas White. You sure you don't want to tell me why you met him?'

She hesitated, unsure that she should go any further. Weren't there minefields in a war? Then she said, 'He wanted to sell me information.'

'What about?'

'About drug distribution. He'd somehow got the idea that here at the clinic we were interested in that.'

'And you're not?'

'Not in the sense of wanting to find the dealers. That's the police's job, isn't it?'

'Then why would he come to you? Janis, this clinic of yours wouldn't have enough spare cash to buy a street map, let alone any real information. Especially from someone like White. There are some dumb cops, Janis, but most of us are reasonably smart. We have to be, otherwise the crims would run rings around us and do-gooders like you would be lying in the streets with your throats cut. Though, actually, I think Mr White and his mate, Gary Schultz – have you met him, too? – they go in for breaking necks. You might like to tell Mr White I said that, next time you meet him. He can sue me for defamation.' He stood up. 'You're lying, Miss Eden, but you'll keep.'

'If you repeat that outside, *I* might sue you.'

'Do that. It'd be nice to have everything out in the open. Did you know Denny Pelong is in the private section next door?'

'Yes, I'd heard.' She had gone out of her way to make enquiries. She was still waiting to hear from White, to hear his excuse for botching the killing.

'Denny's in the drug racket. If he survives, you might like to buy some information from him. He won't come cheap, but these days, in a recession, you never know.'

The cracks were cheap, pulp stuff, but they were more sensible and less dangerous than slapping her face, which he was tempted to do. She got under his skin as not even Luisa Pelong had done; there was a cold arrogance to her that put him and, he guessed, most men down as creatures far less worthy, in her eyes, than herself.

He left her, giving her rope to play with. She would not run away, nor attempt to disappear; he was sure she was not the type. Her arrogance, and whatever else drove her, would keep her on the scene.

When Malone left, Janis continued to sit in her tiny room, staring at the blank wall opposite. She had been challenged, something that usually stimulated her; but now she felt drained, even afraid. But she was more afraid of failure of the dream than of the consequences; that was the worst of it. She had tasted cream, but already it was turning to sour cheese. She wondered if Dallas White would consider killing a policeman.

Then her beeper startled her.

For a moment she thought of ignoring its call. It would be from the clinic to say another junkie was looking for her. To hell with the junkies. In her role as counsellor they might be her bread and butter; in her role as drug supplier, they would provide riches. If she survived . . .

She went along to the ward desk. Two ward sisters, one of them a nun, were there and a clerical assistant; all three of them gave her a smile and the clerk handed her the phone. 'It's for you, Janis.'

'From the clinic?'

But it wasn't the clinic, it was Dallas White. 'Who done it?'

'Who done it?' He was joking, of course. She saw the clerk and the two ward sisters look at her curiously; she turned her back on them, saw Ava Redgrave sitting on a chair just along the corridor. 'What are you talking about?'

'Denny Pelong, of course, who'd you think? I heard it on the radio. I tried to get you at the clinic, but you weren't there. Is he dead yet?'

'I don't know.' And she certainly wasn't going to turn and ask the ward sisters what they knew of Denny Pelong's condition.

'You can't talk now, that what you mean? Well, find out what you can, he's there in your hospital. If he snuffs it, it looks like someone else has done the job for us.'

She couldn't help the question: 'You mean you weren't there?'

'Christ, no. You do a job like that, you never do it in a public place.'

She hung up in his ear, her hand remaining on the phone. The minefield was proving denser than she had expected.

'Bad news?' said the clerk. She was grey-haired, plump and motherly, always ready with sympathy as well as the account.

'I don't know.' Janis recovered, dug up a smile from somewhere. 'You never know what to believe in this job, do you?'

Then she gestured to Ava to follow her back to the counselling room. It would be ironic, she thought, if she persuaded this girl to give up her habit and go back to where she came from.

Malone walked through to the private section. Here were the five-hundred-dollar-a-day rooms, cheap compared with what one had to pay in some other countries but still thought exorbitant by most of the voters. It was a national tenet that medical care shouldn't cost more than car repairs.

He went up to the floor where the intensive-care unit was located. The ward sister, not a nun, young, smart and with an obvious distaste for looking after gunned-down criminals, was not welcoming. 'Why did we have to be landed with Mr Pelong? Why couldn't they have shoved him in the public section?'

'Don't worry. If you save his life, he'll probably give the hospital half a million.'

'Dirty money.'

'Run it through the sterilizer. Can he talk?'

'Are you kidding? We've got tubes in every hole he's got, including the two bullet holes.'

'You're a real angel of mercy, aren't you?'

'No.' Then she smiled, relaxing as she realized that he was not the hard-nosed cop she had been expecting. 'We're not even sure he's going to pull through, Inspector. Even if he does he is going to be a paraplegic for the rest of his life. One of the bullets hit his spine before lodging in one of his lungs.'

'Is there a police officer still guarding him?'

'Yes. We don't like that, either. We've got some distinguished people in that ward. How do you think they're going to feel when they wake up and see a uniformed copper sitting opposite their bed?'

'Probably wonder why their sins took so long to catch up with them. Would you send my uniformed copper out here for a moment?'

The officer came out, a slim, good-looking young man obviously set like a jelly from sitting so still and silent in the small ward. It took him a moment to relax. 'Sorry, Inspector. It's a bit like being in a morgue in there. I'm afraid to cough, even.'

'Being in a morgue is easier. Has Pelong had any visitors?'

'Just his wife, sir. She's still here somewhere, I gather.'

'Nobody else?'

'We've got a guy downstairs, he's vetting anyone comes in asking for Pelong. But nobody's come up here except staff, cleaners and that . . . Sir, are you really expecting someone to come in here and finish off Pelong?'

The ward sister was standing a few yards away, pretending to be busy with a chart-board. Malone glanced at her, then looked back at the young constable and lowered his voice. 'I don't know. Someone might try it.'

'Shit! What am I supposed to do, then? Do I use my gun? It goes off in there, the other three guys are likely to die of shock.'

It was just the sort of dilemma to make a cop's day. 'Show your gun if you have to, but don't use it. If someone attempts to get at him, don't get too close to him –' A thought had just hit him hard: 'It might be someone trying to finish off Pelong with a poisoned needle.'

'You mean those curare killings I've been reading about? Geez, to think that last week I was complaining because I was on booze-bus duty!'

Malone patted him on the shoulder. 'Take it easy. You'll survive.'

'I hope so.' He looked at his watch. 'Another hour, then I'm safe for four hours. Maybe he'll die in the meantime.'

'A nice thought.'

The young officer went back into the ward and Malone turned and walked towards the ward sister. 'He looked worried,' she said.

'He's like you, careful of the hospital's reputation.'

'Did I hear him say something about using his gun in the ward?'

'No.' His gaze was direct. 'Where can I find Mrs Pelong?'

'If your officer uses his gun in that ward, I'll personally cut him open with a scalpel. Is that understood?'

'Don't deny it, you *are* an angel of mercy.'

'Balls,' she said, who had none. 'But don't quote me to the Mother Superior. Mrs Pelong is in the waiting room at the end of the corridor. A bit rough, but she's too nice for him.'

'Do you pass opinions on all the patients and visitors you have in here?' But he said it with a smile.

She smiled, too. 'All the time. Why should doctors be the only ones with an opinion?'

He went down to the waiting room. Luisa Pelong was wearing no jewellery today other than a small diamond brooch pinned to the navy-blue dress she wore. The bee-hive hair-do had been flattened and was worn close to her head, held in place by a blue velvet band. Everything about her looked discreet, as it should on a near-widow. She was watching an umpteenth repeat of *Barnaby Jones* on the television set in the corner when Malone walked into the room.

'Oh, Inspector.' She got up, turned down the television and sat down again. She looked and sounded more amicable than she had last night. 'They let you see my hubby?'

'No. Have you spoken to him?'

'Just for a few minutes. He hardly recognized me. He's gunna be in a wheelchair for the rest of his life, you know that? Tough, eh?'

'Tough for both of you, I should imagine.'

'That's what I meant.' Then she added, 'For our two girls, too.'

'Who shot him, Luisa? Did he say?'

'I asked him that and he told me to get – well, you know what he's like. I think he honestly don't know.'

'We've ruled out Jack Aldwych and Les Chung. We've

253

got one or two other leads, but they're pretty vague. What were your relations like with your husband?'

'My relations? You mean my mum and dad?' She was good at playing dumb, it was expected of her. The diamond brooch winked, but she couldn't be blamed for that.

Malone grinned. 'Come on, Luisa, you know I don't mean them. How did you get on with Denny? Things weren't too happy between you, were they?'

'Where'd you get that idea?'

'You were taking the mickey out of him all yesterday afternoon. There's that bruise under your jaw . . .'

Of its own accord her hand touched her jaw. She said nothing for a moment, staring at the television set as if she were hoping Barnaby Jones would step out of it and offer her some of his homespun advice. 'Okay,' she said at last, 'Denny and me, we fight like Kilkenny cats most of the time.'

Kilkenny cats: that was an Irish expression his mother used. He wondered where Luisa, an Italian, had picked it up. But he guessed she had picked up a lot of things: expressions, defences, lurks, anything that would enable her to survive, especially with Denny Pelong, her hubby, who was more dangerous and brutal than any Kilkenny cat would ever be.

'I have to ask you this, Luisa, just as an elimination. Did you have someone try to kill your husband?'

'No.' Her gaze was as direct as his own had been with the ward sister. He knew all at once that she was lying.

'Will you run his business if he's not capable of it?'

'He's just gunna be in a wheelchair. He's not gunna have his head in a sling.'

He couldn't help it: he leaned back in his chair and for the first time in twenty-four hours he laughed, more than just smiled. 'You're one of a kind, Luisa. I don't think Denny deserves you.'

'Neither do I. But that's just between you and me.' She looked up at him as he stood up. For the first time, standing above her, he noticed the odd grey hair showing in her parting. 'Is that all you want?'

'If I stayed here till they send Denny home, you wouldn't tell me any more, would you?'

'No.'

'I think we both know the truth, don't we?'

'I dunno. Living with Denny, you don't get to know much about the truth.'

'But you've learned to live with it?'

'Oh sure. It's got its compensations.' She would sit down tonight, before they brought Denny home, and add up just what she and the girls were worth. Denny, as far as she was concerned, was already on the breadline, her breadline. 'We could of been living in a caravan park out in the western suburbs and him still beating the shit outa me. Excuse the language.'

'You know we're going to keep a police guard on him till he's discharged from hospital? If anyone comes in here and tries a second time to kill Denny, our men are under instructions to do what they can to stop it. I just thought I'd mention it.'

'You mean they might start shooting in here? Won't that be bad publicity for you cops?'

'I don't think Denny'll care, do you? Not if we save his life. That'd look good on the Hinch programme, wouldn't it? Denny justifying police shooting. Good luck, Luisa. Stay out of the line of fire.'

He went out and along to the lifts, pressed the button and waited. When the lift doors opened he stepped in and stood beside Peter Keller.

'Hello, Peter! You work here?'

Keller was in his usual immaculate overalls, but without his cleaner's gear; he could have been mistaken for one of the more trendy doctors. 'The company I work for, they sometimes call us in here. They have the contract for the Police Department and some of the hospitals. You are here visiting that man Pelong?'

'How did you know?'

'You mentioned him last night when we were leaving, remember? Everybody in the hospital knows he is here. How is he?'

The lift reached the ground floor, the doors opened. 'He'll probably make it.' They both stepped out. 'You get home okay last night?'

'Oh yes. Thank you for dinner. It was a most enjoyable evening. I took the liberty of telephoning your wife to tell her so. You are a lucky man, Scobie, having a wife who approves of what you do.'

'Not all the time, she doesn't.'

He left Keller and went out to the police car waiting for him in one of the spots reserved for doctors. The concrete driveway had the reflective glare of snow; he passed cars that reflected heat as if they were about to explode. He would have to start wearing dark glasses, a habit he had always avoided. He was squinting too much, not seeing things clearly.

CHAPTER NINE

I

'I think Mrs Pelong got a hitman to work on Denny,' he said. 'But I don't know that we can prove it, take her to court on it.'

'Do we want to?' said Clements.

They were sitting in Malone's office eating pizza and drinking coffee, his only culinary achievement, that Clements had made. Tired of instant coffee in paper cups he had, just before Christmas, brought in a percolator and cups and saucers. Three or four times a day the Homicide room stirred to the aroma of fresh coffee. But only when crims and other outsiders were not in the room.

The two detectives exchanged glances, then Malone said, 'Should you have said that?'

'I don't believe I should have. But you know how things slip out.' Clements took another mouthful of pizza, wiped a string of cheese from his chin. 'If we arrest her, is that gunna make Pelong happy? Who's gunna look after him in his wheelchair? It'll save a lot of taxpayers' money if we let him be her jailer. Or vice versa.'

'She could try to kill him again.'

'Okay, then's when we try to nail her. Scobie, let's be practical. We've already got more than enough on our plate. If Pelong dies, who cares? Do you? Does the man in the street, whoever the hell he is, does he care? Pelong's scum. I'm just sorry whoever shot him didn't do the job properly. You feel the same way, if you're honest.'

'Righto, so it's between you and me. Will you sleep easy?'

'Like a baby. So will you. More coffee?'

'Ta.' Malone held out his cup. 'How did you get on with Mr Mitre?'

'He's suddenly got scared. Lee-roy getting the needle in his bum, then Pelong getting those bullets in him last night. He's willing to make a deal, start singing in exchange for a lighter sentence, maybe a bond, something like that.'

'Is he likely to give us anything on Mrs Pelong?'

'I dunno. So far he hasn't mentioned her. Irv Rubens and a guy from the Drug Unit are gunna talk to him. It's not our turf, but Irv will keep us informed.'

'Righto, that's one side of the paddock. The other side, I think, is Janis Eden and Snow White and The Dwarf.'

'Not Jack Aldwych?'

'I don't think so. I don't know about Jack Junior. Maybe he's no more involved than just getting into bed with Janis.'

'I don't think I'd fancy that. She's one of those women who smile at you while you're going cock-eyed with effort. Her idea of foreplay would be to spray dry ice on your balls.'

'You get around, don't you? Anyhow, I think they're the ones to watch.'

'Okay, that's two teams. But who's the solo player, the guy with the curare needle? If it is a guy. It could even be a woman, despite what Romy said about semen being found in Sally Kissen's whatsis. Those two hookers, Ava and Tuesday, they knew all the victims.'

Malone took a sip of coffee before he said, 'Russ, did you know Peter Keller was a cleaner at St Sebastian's?'

Clements was stirring sugar into his coffee, but now he paused, the spoon still in his cup. 'What are you getting at?'

'Last night at dinner, when we were talking about where the killer could pick up Alloferin and Romy mentioned it would be comparatively easy for anyone familiar with hospital routine to get hold of some, he said nothing about him working at St Sebastian's. He had a comment on everything else we talked about last night, but I can't remember him saying anything about working in a hospital. Has Romy ever said anything to you about him working there?'

'No-o. I can't think of any reason why it should've come up. She's told me he's interested in her work at the morgue. She has a computer at home that's connected to the morgue's system – I think it covers the whole Division of Forensic Medicine in the Department of Health. He occasionally helps her prepare her reports, using the computer –'

'He *what*?'

'He – what's the matter?'

Malone put down his cup, spilling coffee into the saucer as his hand jerked. 'He told me he hadn't a clue how to work a computer. He said something about technology making him feel an idiot. He was talking to me about ours, that one out there –' He nodded towards the big outer room. 'He could've tapped into it, got what information he wanted –'

'He'd of had to have an access code.'

'Russ, we're all careless with that. We scribble 'em on a piece of paper, they're on the print-outs. Do you shred your print-outs, every one of 'em? No, of course you don't. None of us do unless I give a direct order. I think we might do a little work on Keller. Get on to Criminal Intelligence, ask them to have Interpol check on him. He was on the force in – I forget the name of the place. You know it?'

Clements nodded. 'Starnheim, a town near Munich.' He looked worried. 'This isn't gunna be easy, mate. Romy's not gunna like it.'

'I'm sorry about that. But this isn't like it is with the Pelongs. We can't let this one run its course. I may be dead wrong about Keller, but I'd just like to know I am for sure. Maybe we'll turn up nothing on him. But I think I'm getting desperate, Russ.'

Clements got slowly to his feet. 'He's just not my idea of a serial killer. He wouldn't fit the profile . . .'

'Bugger the profile.' He was still in many ways an old-fashioned cop; instinct still counted as much as science. He knew it was often the wrong approach, but then science itself had just as often been turned and spun on instinct.

Clements shrugged. 'Okay. But I hope we come up with nothing. Then Romy won't have to know we suspected her dad. For the first time in my life, I think I'm serious.'

'About her? Good on you. Let's hope my hunch doesn't bugger it up for you.'

Clements went out of the room and Malone, no longer hungry, began to gather up the scraps of their lunch. He felt no excitement about his suspicion of Peter Keller; his feeling was more of concern for Clements. He dumped the lunch scraps in his waste-basket (who would collect them this evening? Keller?), was on his way out to the toilets for his postprandial leak when his phone rang.

It was Radelli, the senior Customs investigation officer. 'Inspector Malone? G'day.' He sounded slightly more amiable than he had two nights ago. 'You got any further with that murder over at Glebe Island?'

'Not much.'

'Well, you might like to know we think we're on to another bust. I don't know, but it might lead to something on your case, it could be the same crowd involved. We got a tip from the DEA in Washington, they have a man in La Paz in Bolivia. We know the ship – it's just docked. We're putting some undercover men on the wharf to keep tabs on it. The ship's at Number 8, Darling Harbour.'

'What's your plan?'

'We've gone through all the manifests, come up with the consignments that look suspicious. We'll get the sniffer dogs on to them.'

'There's just one problem. Our two chief suspects in that murder both work on the wharves –'

'I know that – you told me. They'll probably cotton on

to us, but we have to take that risk. If the stuff was packed in a car, we could take the car away on the pretext of steam-cleaning it for plant health reasons. But the ship's come out of Antofagasta in Chile and the cargo is a pretty mixed bag. But no cars.'

'Righto, I'll check where my two suspects are working. I'll let you know. Where can I get you?' Radelli gave him a number. 'I'll be back to you.'

He hung up, then called the Wharf Labourers Union. Roley Bremner came on the line, sounding short-tempered and aggressive, as if he was expecting the call to be from some media reporter, the bane of union secretaries: 'Yeah, what is it? Oh, it's you, Scobie!' His tone softened, something he seemed to recognize: 'Geez, mates with a copper! That'll lose me votes if ever it gets out. What's on your mind, mate?'

'First, have you seen Jimmy Maddux's wife again? How's she getting on?'

'Yeah, I seen her this morning. So-so. She had a good word to say for you, but. Evidently you treated her pretty kind. Thanks, mate. She told me about Jimmy. What a bastard! And I never knew. Just goes to show . . .' Then his voice dropped almost to a whisper: 'Still, he didn't need to be done in like that. I hope you gunna tell me you're about to pinch the bugger who did it, are you?'

'Afraid not, Roley, not yet. But we're close. Can you tell me where Snow White and The Dwarf are working right now?'

'Sure, just a minute.' He was gone for half a minute; then: 'They're both rostered on Number 8, Darling Harbour. Snow White bundied on there this morning. The Dwarf comes on this arvo for the three-till-ten shift. They're working on a ship called the *Golden Horn*, in from somewhere in South America, I dunno where, but I can find out. You on to something?'

'No. Roley. Just keeping tabs on them. How's the election campaign coming along?'

'They tell me I'm holding me own. I dunno. Maybe, maybe not. You could do me a favour and lock up the competition. Like this bloke Saddam. He's got the right idea. Maybe if I get elected, I'll be a dictator.'

'It's fashionable. Good luck, Roley.'

He hung up, called back Radelli, told him where White and Schultz were working. 'It's their mob, all right, that's expecting the shipment. They'll spot your undercover men, if they're strangers.'

'Bugger! Okay, we won't put them in. That makes it bloody difficult.'

Malone suddenly had an idea: 'Luke –' Radelli had thawed enough to be called by his first name. 'I think my mate at the WLU might be able to help. Let me try my luck.'

He hung up, once more called Roley Bremner: 'Roley, how could you get Snow White off the wharves for, say, an hour, maybe an hour and a half?'

'What's going on, mate?'

'I can't tell you right now, Roley, but I want him out of the way for at least an hour. *Now.* Can you manage it?'

'Geez, I dunno. Let me have a think. I'll be back to you.'

Malone hung up, sat back in his chair and gazed at the phone. How did the world work before the telephone was invented? Sometimes it was to be cursed for its interruptions, for the bad news it brought; its drawback was that it couldn't be shot, as messengers were in simpler, more pragmatic days. Still, on balance, the telephone and its offspring, the fax, had probably contributed to progress. It had, at least, speeded up conspiracy.

His bladder was bursting by the time Roley Bremner rang back. 'I just been on to one of me mates out at Port Botany. He's the delegate there and he's working for me in the election. He's gunna do me a favour. He's calling a stop-work meeting for an hour – it goes from one-thirty to knock-off time for the shift, at two-thirty. I'm going out there to address the meeting. I'll see Snow White gets the message it's on. He'll be over at Port Botany soon's he hears about it. He's not gunna let me address a meeting without him being there, not so close to the election.'

'That's a lucky coincidence, isn't it, the stop-work meeting being on right when we need it?'

Bremner made a noise somewhere between a scoff and a cough. 'Mate, you asked for it, you got it. I haven't a clue what the stop-work is about, but me mate said no worries, he'll pull the blokes off at one-thirty. You better hurry.'

'That's rough on the stevedoring company, isn't it?'

'Tough titty. You work on the wharves, mate, you never worry about the bosses. You ask your dad.'

'I wouldn't be game. Thanks, Roley.'

He hung up, glad that he had managed to escape the us-and-them mentality, the workers and the bosses, that his father had tried to drum into him from the moment he had left school. He called Radelli: 'If you move quickly, my suspect, a bloke named Dallas White, will be off the wharf between one-thirty and two-thirty. He'll be out at Port Botany at a stop-work meeting.'

'Jesus, what's this one about?' Radelli, despite the fact that he was a Customs man, or perhaps because of it, had the usual prejudices about the WLU. 'They're always bloody going out.'

'Micro-economic reform.' That was the government's present catch-cry, though the voters at large, dead to jargon, hadn't a clue what it meant. 'I'm kidding, Luke. Just grab the opportunity and get your men and your dogs down to Darling Harbour. How will you explain yourselves to the other wharfies?'

'We'll tell 'em it's a routine search. They take those in their stride, so long as we don't bother *them*. Most of them are dead set against drug smuggling, anyway. They've got kids just like the rest of us.'

'I guess so,' said the wharfie's kid.

He hung up the phone, made it to the toilet just in time, gave himself up to the shivering ecstasy of relieving a full bladder. Then he went back to his office and spent the next hour on paperwork, unwillingly becoming a bureaucrat. Clements came in, said the Bureau of Criminal Intelligence had already contacted Interpol regarding Peter Keller, and went out again without offering any comment. Malone looked up from his papers and gazed after him. He had never seen the big man so stiff and withdrawn. Crumbs, he thought, what have I started? Lisa, if he told her, would nail him to the wall of their bedroom, would argue the merits of love and happiness against crime and punishment. She would always choose her friends' good against the public good.

At four o'clock Radelli rang. 'We've found it. It's cocaine, all right, packed in between the plastic sheets in a consignment of solar panels. The plastic sheets, they're opaque, so you can't see the coke, they're like giant sachets. Very ingenious, except who would import solar panels from Bolivia? It's amazing how stupid some clever people can be. You want to be there when we make the bust?'

'What's the drill?'

'We're going to let 'em collect the cases – the panels are packed in wooden cases. We'll keep 'em under surveillance, watch where they take the stuff and then we'll nab them when they open it up.'

'I'll send one of my sergeants from here, he knows White and Schultz. The Feds will make the arrest, I take it? . . . Righto, my bloke will just be an observer. His name's Russ Clements.' It would keep Clements occupied, instead of his sitting around worrying about Romy Keller and her father.

He hung up, went out into the main room and sat down in the empty chair opposite Clements. The latter had just made fresh coffee, but he did not offer any to Malone.

'You still cranky on me for what I'm doing about Keller?'

Clements bit his lip, an old habit when he was disturbed. 'I'm not shitty on *you*. It's just the bloody – well, I dunno, the way things just suddenly go arse-over-tip. Everything's been sweet between me and Romy. It's been a bugger of a summer for most people – the recession, the war, the farmers going broke. But for me it's been great. And now . . . What if we turn up something on her dad that means we've *got* to bring him in? You think she's gunna hold my hand and kiss me and tell me she understands? No way is it gunna be like that.'

'Look, I'm not saying any Hail Marys for me to be right about this. If Interpol reports nothing on him, then –'

'Then what?'

Reluctantly he said, 'Then we'll keep an eye on him but not make a big thing of it. We'll keep it just between you and me and not put it on the computer, just the way we did with some things in the old murder box. In the meantime, to take your mind off him, I want you to go down to the Customs office on Number 8, Darling Harbour –' He outlined what Radelli had told him and what the arrangements were. 'It may be a twenty-four-hour job, so get Phil Truach to stand by to take over from you.'

Clements wasn't looking at him, was staring at his big feet stuck out in front of him. 'Do you think Romy suspects anything about her father?'

'Russ, how would I know? You don't want to sound her out, do you?'

'Christ, no!'

'Righto, then. We play it between you and me till we have something definite on him.'

'What if Interpol clears him? Are we gunna let it go at that?'

Again there was the reluctance: 'Not necessarily.'

Romy Keller stood back from the cadaver of the six-year-old girl who had been murdered this afternoon by the child's father. This was the sort of post-mortem that increased her urge to break away from forensic medicine; she could remain relatively objective about the adult victims of murder, but child homicide turned her to anger that sometimes blinded her. She felt that way now, dizzy with emotion that made her stop working, made her unable to touch the bruised and battered body of the child.

'Take over,' she said abruptly to her assistant, taking off her rubber apron.

He was young, this was his first year at the morgue; working on cadavers day after day had proved more traumatic than he had expected. His bony olive-complexioned face had begun to take on the sallow look of the corpses he worked on. 'Romy, I don't know that I can –'

'Do it!' she said and left him, feeling disgust at her unprofessional conduct but unable to deny the urge to get out of the Murder Room before she cracked.

She went down through the long main room, avoiding the eyes of those working there, afraid that one of them might make the comment that would spring the tension in her, and went upstairs to her office. She sat down in the chair behind her desk, closed her eyes and wished all at once for sleep.

It had been a long hard day. She had been called in here at seven this morning and it seemed that bodies had been coming into the morgue in a continuous stream from that hour onwards. It had been one of those days when death, it seemed, had decided to catch up with life. There had been murder victims, including the six-year-old girl; accident victims; men and women who had died of heart or asthma attacks in public places: the waiting line had at one time suggested that there could have been a major disaster in the city. She had worked mechanically but with her usual competence till the body of the little girl had been brought in. Then she had collapsed, inwardly if not outwardly.

She opened her eyes, made herself face the truth. The core of her collapse had nothing to do with the overload of work; it had to do with the phone call she had made at lunchtime. She had called Clean Sweep, the contractors her father worked for, to ask where she might find him to tell him she would be late home for supper.

'Is he at the Police Centre?'

'No, Dr Keller. He's at St Sebastian's Hospital today. He's been working there three days a week for the past month.'

'Oh. Thank you. I'll call him there.'

But she hadn't called him. She had hung up, standing by the phone in the canteen, deaf to the hum of conversation of the other staff as they tucked into their lunch with relish undiminished by their morning's work. She was beginning to feel tired even then in the middle of the day, but she was not so tired that she did not at once catch the import of what the woman at Clean Sweep had told her. Her father had had access for a month to a supply of alcuronium chloride, Alloferin.

'Oh Father!' She had leaned her head against the wall beside the phone, oblivious for the moment of the sudden stares of those seated at the tables near her.

A young woman, an assistant pathologist, got up and came to her. 'Are you all right, Romy?'

Romy straightened up. 'Yes, I'm all right, Ginny.' She hated too much attention; she had experienced enough of that ten years ago in Starnheim. 'I felt a little dizzy – I've been on my feet too long –'

'Take it easy,' said Ginny, a pretty girl who always looked half-asleep even when wide awake. 'Where are the corpses going to go, anyway? They're in no hurry.'

Romy dug up a smile. 'I sometimes forget that. Thanks, Ginny. No, I'll be okay. I'll do as you say, take it easy.'

But she had not been able to take it easy. All the disgrace, the whispers behind the hand, the effect on her mother, all of it had come flooding back. All afternoon she had worked with the knife on the cadavers, wishing she could work with it on herself to cut out those memories.

She looked up now as Bob Gimbel, the Director, appeared in the doorway of her office. 'You okay, Romy? They tell me you looked a bit off. Something upset you?'

She wished she could tell him; but she couldn't. 'I think I'm just overtired, Bob.'

'Overworked, you mean? Who isn't here?' But he still sounded sympathetic. He was in his mid-forties, always neat and starched, one of those of the last generation to clean their shoes every day, a stickler for protocol, method and routine. Yet, as Romy knew from her first days here at the morgue, he was capable of sympathy and understanding. He knew that all pain didn't end in death.

'You think you'd better go home? We don't want you slicing off more than is necessary. Can young Wayne handle what's left in the Murder Room?'

'There's that child, the homicide case. I'd better go back and finish off –'

'No, I'll do it. Go home, Romy. You look like death warmed up, if you'll forgive the expression.'

So she went home, glad of the release but afraid of what she had to face. She let herself into the flat, stood just inside the front door and called out, as if she had stepped into someone else's place, 'Are you home?' He wasn't, nor had she expected him to be. She had spoken out of fear.

She stood irresolute for almost a minute, not moving. She was about to step over a cliff; she knew nothing of the abyss beyond. She had dealt in the results of murder for three years now; a dozen times at least she had faced a murderer across a courtroom when she had been called to give evidence. Now she was afraid, was certain, that, once again, she would have to face the murderer she lived with.

At last she forced herself to move. She went to her father's bedroom, did something she had not done since her mother's death, entered it without his permission. She went through the drawers of the big dressing-table that he had brought, along with all their other furniture, from Germany. In the bottom drawer, underneath three neatly folded sweaters, she found what she had hoped she would not find.

She took out the small cardboard box with the St Sebastian's label on it. Inside it were the syringe and two ampoules; the label on the box said there should have been five. She knew, with sickening certainty, that the missing three had been used on Grime, Kissen and Lugos.

She was sitting in the living room in the dying light of the evening when her father at last came home. He was much later than usual, but she would not ask him why. She heard him come in the front door of the flat, call out a greeting in German as he always did, then come along the hallway. He passed the door to the living room, going towards his bedroom; then she heard him stop. He came back, stood in the doorway.

'Romy? Is there something wrong?'

'Yes.'

'What?'

She held up the small box, then threw it across the room. It landed at his feet, but he didn't bend to pick it up. He looked down at it, then at her.

'You have been in my room, going through my things?'

'Yes.'

They were speaking in German, as they usually did when alone. But this evening she wished they were speaking English, or indeed any language but her own. German was the language of her memories, those that had come back like a metastasis, overwhelming her.

He had been standing stiffly, almost as if he were on

some sort of parade. But now he seemed to lose control of his legs; he leaned against the door jamb. For a moment she was tempted to rise and hurry to him; as she would have done only this morning. But she kept herself rigidly in her seat; it was he who had taught her control, or anyway bequeathed it to her. He drew a deep breath, then moved to his favourite chair and sat down, put both hands on the arms of it.

'You killed those people?' She was surprised at the steadiness of her voice.

He said nothing, but after a long moment he nodded.

'Why? Was it the same as that other time? An eye for an eye?'

Again he took his time about replying; then: 'No, it was not that. Would you understand better if that were the reason?'

'I don't understand anything at all at the moment. Why?'

And then slowly, deliberately, as if he were swearing out a police statement, he told her why.

3

That evening Malone and Lisa had gone to dinner at the home of new acquaintances, Will and Olive Rockne. They lived in Coogee, the small seaside suburb down the hill from Randwick, in a large blue-brick house built during World War I. Will Rockne was a local solicitor and he and Olive had a girl who went to Holy Spirit convent, which was where the Malones had met them last Parents' Day.

Malone had welcomed the going-out; anything to get his mind off the day. He had managed an hour's nap between coming home and going out; he had the sort of constitution that could be restored by the shortest of sleeps. His mother and father came out from Erskineville to baby-sit ('Baby-sit?' said Maureen. 'That's insulting!'). Malone also rang the Randwick station and asked if a patrol car could cruise by every so often during the evening. 'Just in case,' he said.

Wal Dukes had said, 'No worries, Scobie. I don't think too much more can happen. Our luck's gotta change.'

'Sure,' said Malone and wondered if Clements thought that way.

The evening was a pleasant diversion; Olive Rockne was a good experimental cook and she served Thai food. There was another couple at the dinner, the Sackvilles, the husband an accountant. Police work was mentioned only once. Malone wondered if Lisa had rung Olive and asked that the subject of Scungy Grime in the Malones' pool not be raised; but he didn't query her on it. He had had enough of interrogation for the week; he didn't want to add to it by interrogating his wife on her good intentions. He was content to listen to Will Rockne, an armchair statesman, talk about the Gulf war.

'Forget the peaceniks –' Will Rockne was an *almost* man: almost handsome, almost charming, almost sincere. Malone could not put his finger on what Rockne lacked. In the end, because he wanted to enjoy the evening, he decided to settle for the admission that we all lacked something. 'What's amazing is the way the country's got behind the government in this war. What do you think, Scobie?'

What Malone lacked was a full barrel of tact; once again the deficiency let him down: 'Well, what amazes me is the latent belligerence in the ordinary voter. Just before the Falklands war, Mrs Thatcher would have been lucky if Denis had voted for her. Then she declares war on Argentina and suddenly she's the greatest Englishwoman since Boadicea. The middle of last year George Bush was a wimp, then he goes into the Gulf and all of a sudden he's the greatest President since George Washington.'

'So you think we are all, at heart, warlike?' Stephen Sackville had said virtually nothing all evening, but his wife Emily was a lady of opinion. She was Lisa's age, but looked older: big, blonde and robust, she reminded Malone of the figureheads he had seen on old sailing ships. She would have reduced the Roaring Forties to a whimper as she forced her way into them.

'Maybe.' Malone had seen Lisa's warning glance; he scraped the bottom of the barrel for some tact. 'I wouldn't want to generalize.'

'If that is the case,' said Sackville, perhaps deciding that *his* spouse wasn't tactful, 'would that account for the criminal class?'

The criminal class. Malone had heard that phrase only once, at a seminar of criminologists he had attended as an observer; he had come away from it with the usual practitioner's amusement at the theorists. 'There's a sub-class of criminals, the regulars. Yes, I guess they've declared war on the rest of us, but I don't know they've ever said it out loud, like some sort of battle-cry. Some of 'em may have, but they're mostly kids. I don't think the really hardened crims think they're at war with us.' He wondered how Jack Aldwych would handle the conversation if he were at this table. 'But ninety-five per cent of crimes are committed by people who are not habituals.'

'But they're aggressive. Their latent belligerence, I think you called it, it's coming out?'

Malone realized all at once that Sackville was all latent belligerence; perhaps as a result of dominance by his belligerent wife. He backed off, smiling at Olive Rockne, his hostess. 'If I get started, I'm going to let this good food get cold . . .'

Olive Rockne recognized the tactful retreat. She was small and attractive, but Malone, a late developer as a judge of women, had decided she was just a little too *feminine*; she was frilly, even her hair; if she held any opinions, they were ones her husband, overloaded with them, had given her to hold. But she was not unintelligent and she saw that Malone did not want to get into any long discussion about crime and the law.

'Does he bring his work home, Lisa?' she asked.

'Never,' lied Lisa and that turned the conversation.

Going home she said, 'You were really tactful tonight. You're learning.'

He wondered how he could tactfully tell her of his suspicions of Peter Keller and what they might do to Clements' romance with Romy. He dropped her off at the house, then took his parents home to Erskineville, his father riding beside him, sitting tensed as if riding shotgun, and his mother sitting squarely in the middle of the back seat like the late Queen Mary. Brigid was Irish, but, to the disgust of Con, admired the English, especially their ladies. Malone had never had the heart to tell his mother that Queen Mary was actually German.

'You've got three wonderful kids,' said his mother from her throne. Long ago she had been a pretty girl, but she had never had the money or the vanity to save her looks. But Malone had noticed that a trace of youthfulness had crept back into her face as she had found a new life for herself in her grandchildren. 'You shouldn't go dumping dead men in your swimming pool.'

'He didn't,' said Con. 'Someone else done that. You get to see Roley Bremner?'

'Who's Roley Bremner?' said Brigid.

'I'm talking to him,' said Con, nodding at his son. 'Did you?'

'Yes. He was helpful.'

'I read about them other murders.'

'Do we have to talk about them?' said Brigid. She had a stern respect for the proprieties; talk of murder was outside them.

'It's his job, for Crissakes –'

'Watch your language. You don't wanna talk about them, do you, Scobie?'

'The kids wanted to talk about 'em,' said Con appreciatively. 'That Maureen. She'll make a great detective.'

'A detective for a granddaughter,' said Brigid, frigid at the prospect.

'Almost as bad as one for a son,' said Malone.

'I'm getting used to the idea,' said Con.

Malone dropped them outside the narrow terrace house in the narrow street. He patted them both on the shoulder; kisses between them would have been an embarrassment. Love was there, but it was silent.

'Thanks for looking after the kids.'

'You keep them away from any murders,' said his mother.

When Malone reached home Lisa was in bed but still awake. With her usual prescience, which is a female trait that only the best career ambassadors and successful con men achieve, she said, 'You've got something on your mind. It's been there all evening, you've looked guilty.'

He put on his pyjama trousers, slid under the sheet beside her and told her of his suspicions of Peter Keller. She was shocked, but her first remark was, 'And what's that going to do to Russ and Romy?'

'I thought you'd say that. I don't know what it's going to do to them. All I can hope is that they're both professional about it.'

'*Professional?* God, what a word! They're in love with each other, you're going to jail her father for three horrible murders, and all you can say is you hope they'll be *professional* about it.' She sat up, switched on her bedside lamp. She was nude, the way she slept during the hot summer months, but she might as well have been wearing armour. If he so much as raised a hand to touch her breast she would break his wrist. She was a born match-maker, a breed that never gives up, even when, sometimes, the intended matched pair have fled in different directions. She had been trying to match Clements with a woman for the past ten years, so far without success. She had had nothing to do with the matching of Romy with him, but she had recognized its possibilities. 'You can't do it. If her

274

father is the – the killer, let Romy discover it for herself. But keep Russ out of it. Let him comfort her – she'll need it.'

'How do I let Romy discover it for herself? Ring her up, anonymously, tell her to have her father checked through Interpol? I'm going to have to go through with it my way. I've got no option.'

She lay back, leaving the light on. 'How does Russ feel?'

'Like you.'

She reached up and switched off the light. He turned his head on the pillow and, as his eyes became accustomed again to the darkness, he saw her profile against the pale light of the window. He put his hand on her breast, but she didn't stir, just continued to lie on her back gazing at the ceiling.

'I'm lucky,' he said.

'Yes, you are. So am I.' She turned her face towards him. 'Can't you give them some luck, too?'

4

When Peter Keller had finished telling Romy what he had done and why, he waited for her to say something. But she said nothing; her judgement was plain in her face. He got up from where he had sat down opposite her, picked up the Alloferin box and went out of the living room and along to his bedroom. A minute or so later she heard him go into the bathroom; then she heard him showering. He was in the bathroom his usual amount of time, ten minutes; nothing, it seemed, could break him from habit. Then she heard him come out of the bathroom and go back to his bedroom. Ten minutes later, fully dressed, wet hair slicked back, he appeared again in the living-room doorway.

'I'm going out,' he announced and waited for her to comment.

But she had nothing to say. She was numb, not angry, not afraid, not even shocked: in her heart she had known it would happen again, that he had the capacity to kill without compunction. In the dim light of the unlit room she could not distinguish his expression; his face was just a pale oval above his dark suit. He remained motionless for almost half a minute, then he sighed, turned and a moment later she heard him going out the front door.

When he had gone she got up and went out to the kitchen and made herself some coffee. Then she went into the bathroom, stripped off and showered and washed her hair, cleansing herself of the day's work. But when she got out of the shower she still felt unclean.

She went to bed and for the first time in her life she locked her bedroom door. The phone rang once, but she did not get up to answer it. At midnight she heard her father come in, but there was no knock on her door, no whispered calling of her name.

In the morning he was gone. So were two suitcases and most of his clothes. Only then did she allow the tears to break.

CHAPTER TEN

I

When Malone walked into his office Clements was already there, a fax sheet in his hand. Without comment he handed it to Malone, who took it and glanced at it, then handed it back. 'So?'

'It's up to you,' said Clements, laying the Interpol report on Malone's desk. 'I'd appreciate it if you didn't ask me to be part of it. You want some coffee?'

He went out to get the coffee and Malone sat down and reached for the fax sheet. He wished he could tear it up, drop it in the waste-basket, there to be collected by Peter Keller, the innocent. Except that, unfortunately, Keller was not innocent.

Working without official authority from his superiors in Starnheim, often in his own time, he had pursued a woman and a doctor who were suspected of murdering the woman's husband. The two suspects had finally been brought to trial, mainly due to Keller's efforts. That fact had been admitted in the court, but he had not been commended for his efforts; Malone guessed that it was because he had flouted authority, a German sin. The woman had been convicted, but the doctor had been acquitted. A month later the doctor had apparently committed suicide. But it was known, though the evidence was only circumstantial, that Peter Keller had murdered him. There had been no official enquiry, but Keller had been quietly discharged from the police force. Two weeks later the Kellers had sold up their home and left Germany.

'An eye for an eye, a tooth for a tooth.' Malone looked

up as Clements came back with the coffee. 'He was sounding off about that the night before last. You think that's why he did it?'

'What other reason?' Clements slumped down. He was utterly exhausted, he felt boneless; he knew that if his skull was opened up (by Romy?), the post-mortem would reveal that his brain was severely bruised. 'I rang Romy last night. I dunno what I was gunna say to her. She didn't answer. Which was just as well, maybe. If I'd known last night what's in that report and I'd rung her and she didn't answer, it'd have scared the shit outa me.'

'He's not going to touch her, put that out of your mind.' Malone tasted his coffee; as usual, it couldn't be better. It was as good as Lisa's, which was the highest praise he could offer. 'We've got to bring him in, Russ, at least for questioning. I'll see you're not around when it happens. Is Phil Truach still on surveillance with the Customs and the Feds?'

'He was relieved by Terry Stratton – he should be reporting in here at noon. Nothing has happened so far down on the wharf, the container hasn't been collected. Customs have put a bug in it, so's they can follow it when it's picked up.'

'What's happening with Janis Eden?'

'The Drug Unit's got a team tailing her. Andy Graham is with them.' Clements finished his coffee and stood up. 'I think I better show some guts. I'm going over to see Romy –'

'There's no need,' said Malone.

Clements turned round, said, 'Oh Christ,' and went out to meet Romy as she came into the big room. He took her hand, but didn't kiss her; there was no one else in the room, but it was not embarrassment that stopped him. One look had told him he was greeting a stranger. He led her back to Malone's office.

Malone rose. 'Hello, Romy. I was going to call you. Get her some coffee, Russ.'

278

'Sure.' But Clements remained stationary for a moment, staring at Romy as if waiting for some sign of recognition from her. But there was none, so he went out of the office, stopped, as if he was unsure what he was supposed to be doing, then moved towards the percolator.

Malone looked after him, then at Romy. 'It's a guess, but you know why I was going to call you?'

She nodded. Her hair, usually worn loose, was drawn back, accentuating the strained, almost haggard set of her face. Malone had seen it countless times, as if women found their hair, their supposed crowning glory, a nuisance in times of stress. 'Russ knows, of course?'

'Yes. But I'm the one who found out about your father. Where is he?'

'I don't know.' She saw him raise an eyebrow. 'That's the truth, Scobie.'

'How long have you known he might be a suspect?'

Her nervous hands opened, then shut her handbag. 'I suppose, at the back of my mind, I've known since the other night, when he started to talk again about an eye for an eye. But I didn't want to think about it. Then last night –'

Clements came back with another cup of coffee. She took it from him, for the first time showed some of the old intimacy with him. 'Thanks, Russ. This isn't easy for either of us, is it?'

Then the phone rang. Malone excused himself, took the call; it was from Terry Stratton, one of his junior officers. 'Boss, the container's just been picked up – the truck's on its way. Guess who's just started following it in a green Jaguar?'

'Dumb,' said Malone to himself; there were lairs who could never resist showing off their cars or their women. Then he said to Stratton, 'Has Snow White got Schultz with him?'

'The two of them are in the car. The Federals think there should be an arrest within the hour.' Stratton was a precise young man whose reports, with their formal phrases and qualifying clauses, sometimes made the computer, programmed for jargon and bad grammar, break into hiccups. 'I'll keep you posted on the hour. Stand by.'

'Is it okay if I sit?' But Stratton had already rung off. Malone hung up, leaned back in his chair. He felt a lightening of the load that had been weighing him down, even though arrests were still to be made. He said gently to Romy, 'So you don't know where your father is?'

'No.' Romy sipped her coffee; it seemed to give her strength. Or perhaps it was that the two men's sympathy and understanding was more than she had expected. 'He had left the flat before I got up this morning. He took all his clothes with him, two suitcases full.'

Malone looked at Clements. 'Get on to Mascot, have Immigration stop him if he tries to leave the country.' Clements, for the first time that morning, moved quickly. Malone looked back at Romy. He held up the Interpol report. 'We know what happened in Germany before you left to come out here. Did he ever confess to you or your mother that he killed that doctor in Starnheim?'

'Never to me. I don't know whether he did to Mother. The subject was taboo.' She was speaking freely now, almost with relief at being able to tell someone her long-held secret. 'Once I tried to raise it with her, after we'd been out here two or three years, but she just cut me off. But there were small things that gave him away. He would talk about the case, the woman poisoning her husband, he would tell other people about it in front of Mother and me. And he was always talking about the leniency of the law. He had contempt for it.'

'An eye for an eye – he really believed in that?'

'Absolutely.'

'But why kill Grime and Sally Kissen and Leroy Lugos? Lugos, yes, if your father had a thing about people dealing drugs. But Grime and Sally Kissen? She was just a prostitute –' Then he stopped.

She looked at him as carefully as if she were dissecting him; she had read his mind. 'Yes, I've thought of that. If the DNA profile from the semen we found in her . . . Will I have to give evidence?'

'That'll depend on the Crown Prosecutor. We'll try and keep you out of it. Get them to call the pathologist.' Then Clements came back. 'Well?'

'Immigration will check for him on all international flights. The airport police are gunna watch for him on the interstate flights, but we may be too late there. He could already be in Melbourne or Perth or wherever.'

'He will go home to Germany,' said Romy. 'I *know*.'

'Well, we'll get him,' said Malone. 'I'm afraid this time he won't be able to complain about the leniency of the law.'

'That wasn't why he killed those people,' said Romy.

2

Janis Eden was at home when Dallas White called her. Her mother had asked her to go shopping with her – 'We never do anything together these days' – but Janis had pleaded that she had to stay home in expectation of a call from the clinic. As she watched her mother go down the path to the front gate, trailing her small shopping trolley behind her, she had experienced a rare moment of pity for the woman she had never learned to love. But the moment was short-lived, did not have time to weaken her: it was interrupted by White's phone call.

'I'm calling from a pub opposite the wharf. The stuff's just been picked up, it's on its way. Gary and me'll take care of it at the warehouse. We'll see you tonight –'

'I don't think you'd better,' she said. 'I had a visit from Inspector Malone yesterday. They know you and I met the day before yesterday out at La Perouse.'

'Shit! Are they keeping tabs on us?' White was silent

for a while. She could hear the hum of voices and the clinking of glasses in the background. There was a radio near the pub's phone and she could hear a flat nasal voice, common to race callers, giving tips for tomorrow's races. Then White said, 'I dunno, maybe we better let the shipment lay still for a while, leave it there in the warehouse. It'll be safe.'

'We can't afford to do that, not if they call and demand the money. It's cash on delivery, they said. We can't afford to make a payment like that and then wait around for weeks, maybe months, before we can sell the stuff. My banker isn't that generous.'

'Maybe you should go to one of the big banks, they used to be generous. They lent millions to some of the shonkiest jerks you wouldn't wanna know.' She could imagine him grinning at his remark. Real criminals were, in a way, snobs. He was silent again for a moment, then he growled, 'Okay, we'll take the risk. I've got an idea . . .'

'What?'

'I'll find one of Denny Pelong's stooges, I know one. He's dumb, wouldn't know his arse from his elbow. But he's greedy. Give him a chance to earn something on the side that Pelong don't know about and he'll fall arse-over-tip to get to it. I'll give him the word where the stuff is, tell him I don't have the cash to pay for it now it's landed here. He'll fall for it.'

'Where will he get the money? Not from Pelong. He's still in intensive care in St Sebastian's.'

'The stooge is never gunna get his hands on the stuff, so he won't have to cough up any cash. All we want is for someone to go into the warehouse, so's we can see if he's gunna be nabbed. If the cops don't swoop, then Gary and me'll go in and take care of the stooge and we'll grab the stuff.'

'It sounds too simple.'

'That's what life is, love. Simple. That's something the too-fucking-smart never learn.'

'Meaning me?' she said and hung up on his ear.

Ten minutes later she got the second call she had been waiting on. She had had two previous calls, both from overseas: this was a local call. She thought she recognized the voice and she wondered when he had landed in Sydney.

'Ramon?'

'No names, please. You have the money?'

'I can have it as soon as you want it.'

'Then get it. I shall meet you at noon at the Larissa Café at Bondi. Do you know it?'

'No, but I'll find it.'

'Bring the money in one-hundred-dollar notes. I shall see you at noon. Sit in the very last booth at the back.'

He hung up. She was not sure that he was the man she had dealt with in Las Vegas, but she hoped he was; if there was a hitch, she did not want to be dealing with some go-between. She was already beginning to exalt herself.

She rang Jack Junior at his office. Then she went out of the house, got into the rented Toyota and drove from Wahroonga into the city. Deciding that the red Capri was too conspicuous, she had locked it in the garage and gone into Chatswood and hired the grey Toyota. If she was being too-fucking-smart, she did not worry about it. Several times she looked in her driving-mirror to see if she was being followed. Once she thought a particular car, a pale blue Commodore, seemed to spend too much time behind her; but at St Leonards it turned off the main highway. She was too smart to recognize the simple routine tailing method of cars succeeding one another as the tail. She would have learned something if she watched crime series on television, but she watched only documentaries and current affairs on the ABC and SBS, as intelligent people like herself did.

She drove into the basement of the building in William Street where Jack had his offices. This was a building owned by one of the largest insurance companies in the country; its tenants would have lent added respectability to the Vatican. Landfall Holdings, the Aldwych holding company, had the aura of a top legal firm, one that would take briefs only from clients with irrefutable proof of their innocence or enough funds to buy the firm's own innocence. The girl at the reception desk introduced herself as Minerva, though Janis thought she looked a little too slick, too Friday-nightish in her mini-skirt and tight top, to be the goddess of thought and intelligence.

'Mr Aldwych is expecting you, Miss Eden. It's a pleasure to meet you at last, after talking to you on the phone.' She was looking Janis up and down with an eye that missed nothing.

Jack rose as soon as Janis entered his big office. He waited till Minerva had closed the door, then he gestured for Janis to sit down. He did not approach to kiss her, which piqued her. She did not want to be kissed, but she wanted the right of refusal. 'This is the last payment, Janis. You'll have to finance yourself from now on. You should be able to, if this shipment goes okay.'

'You'll get your share within a month.'

He shook his head. He was dressed like a banker was supposed to dress; he fitted perfectly into this large panelled office. The panelling might be fake; but then, she thought, so is he. She hated him, a feeling that made her feel good.

'All I want is repayment of this.' He gestured at the large briefcase, a Gucci, naturally, on his desk.

'So it's really goodbye? Your father's orders?'

'Don't be nasty, Janis. If you were his daughter, you'd be doing exactly what I'm doing. Paying heed.'

Reluctantly she agreed; she remembered the ruthlessness in the old man's face. 'Perhaps. Do we kiss goodbye?' She *would* kiss him, make it as cold as a witch's.

'I don't think so. There'll be time for that when you return the case and the money.' He was surprised at how easily he was shedding himself of her. He was not given to fantasy, so he did not see himself, despite his father's casting of the role, as Sam Spade getting rid of Brigid O'Shaughnessy. He had learned his lesson: never become a partner to a power-hungry woman. Be content just to be rich; there were worse burdens. 'Take care. Especially of your partners, White and what's-the-other-one's-name?'

She picked up the case; she was surprised how heavy paper money could be. 'I'll have to give them the money in this. I didn't bring a case with me.'

'Buy me another one when you're paying me back. You'll be able to afford it. Maybe a Louis Vuitton?'

She left him, smiling at Minerva on the way out, aware of the latter's stare at her legs and bottom, and went down to the basement. She took the Toyota out into William Street and headed east towards Bondi. She did not notice the pale blue Commodore in the traffic behind her, because this time she did not bother to look in her driving-mirror. When she took her eyes off the road it was only to glance at the briefcase on the seat beside her. She could smell the money inside it, as one can smell sex though it is hidden.

She found the Larissa Café without any trouble. She beat four surfies in a beat-up panel-van to the last parking space at the kerb. She gave them two fingers to their cheerful insults, then, leaning slightly against the weight of the briefcase, she walked across to the Larissa. She went down to the back of the café, which was filling up for lunch, and pulled up when she saw that the last booth was occupied. The boy and the girl holding hands, both of them as scruffy as stray dogs, were not the sort of messengers sent to pick up a quarter of a million dollars in cash.

'You'll have to wait,' said a waitress behind Janis. 'It shouldn't be long.'

Janis thanked her, walked the last few steps to the back booth and stood above the two young lovers. They looked up at her resentfully, as if she had interrupted them in bed.

'Yeah?' The boy wore dark glasses, like at least half of the occupants of the café. Janis thought the place might be a refuge for rock musicians; the walls were decorated mostly with travel posters, but photographs of rock stars, all in dark glasses, peered out from between the posters, like a gallery of the sightless. The café's sound system was playing a Midnight Oil tape; the lead singer was exhorting the diners to save the world, but the diners couldn't have been more indifferent. If the worst came to the worst, they would grill their hamburgers under the hole in the ozone. 'You want something?'

'If I gave you fifty dollars, would you give up this booth?'

'Why d'you want it?'

'Sentimental reasons.'

'Make it a hundred,' said the girl. 'We're sentimental, too.'

'Fifty,' said Janis, recognizing a sister under the black T-shirt and the jagged haircut.

'We're in love,' said the girl.

'So am I,' said Janis. 'Fifty.'

'We'll take it,' said the boy, stood up and held out his hand. 'C'mon, love. We can go somewhere else. Don't let's stand in the way of middle-aged love.'

'Up yours,' said Janis, gave them the money and they left.

She sat down, putting the briefcase between herself and the booth's wall. She looked at her watch: two minutes to noon. Then the man sat down opposite her.

'On time, Miss Eden,' said Peter Keller.

3

Romy had left, to go to work. 'It's better that I do, that I keep myself occupied.'

'It's not gunna take your mind off what he's done, working on corpses,' said Clements.

She smiled wanly. 'Russ, *anything* will be better than just sitting around waiting for you to call me. You will call as soon as –'

'Yes,' said Malone. 'We'll call you.'

When Clements came back from escorting Romy out to her car, he said, 'She's taking it better than I thought.'

'She hasn't had to face the worst bit yet. Wait till we bring him in and then the media gets to work on the story. One good thing is she isn't laying any blame on you and me for what we have to do. The other good thing is that *she* came to us. I think she'll be glad to have you hold her hand.'

'Sure.' But Clements still looked like a man who, in a familiar situation, had suddenly found himself on the wrong side of the border.

He went out to his desk to monitor the calls coming in from Terry Stratton, with the Customs squad and the Federal police tailing the contraband container, and from Andy Graham, with the Drug Unit team tailing Janis Eden. Malone reached for the paperwork in his In basket, for crime prevention, like any other business, has to be papered and carboned or what would be the reason for Administration?

At eleven-thirty Clements came to the doorway. 'Terry's just called in. The container's in one of those mini-warehouses, you know, the caged-in spaces you rent, out at Artarmon. There's nothing in the cage but the container. There's no sign so far of Snow White and The Dwarf. They've dropped out of sight.'

'What about Janis?'

'Andy says she's just pulled into the basement of a building in William Street. He's checking who the tenants are. She's dumped her red Capri somewhere, she's in a grey Toyota.'

'She's up to something. Righto, tell Andy to stay with her.'

At five past twelve Clements was back in the doorway. 'Christ, you're not gunna believe this! Andy's just phoned in again. Janis is sitting in the Larissa, that place where we met Lee-roy. And guess who's with her?'

'Russ –'

'Keller! Peter Keller. Andy says it took him a minute or two to recognize him as one of our cleaners –'

Malone was on his feet, grabbing for his hat and jacket. Two minutes later he and Clements were speeding up Oxford Street in an unmarked car, blue light flashing on the roof and siren wailing. They went through three red lights on their way to Bondi, twice narrowly missing cars whose drivers both thought they had right of way over any speeding police car.

'Bloody women drivers!'

'They were both men,' said Malone, grinning to relieve the tension that had gripped him as the cars had loomed up. He was not, and never would be, a comfortable passenger.

As they came down the hill towards the blue blaze of the bay Clements turned off the siren but kept the blue light on the roof. He jerked the car to a stop in a No Parking zone and he and Malone jumped out, the heat hitting them at once like a blast of resistance. Andy Graham was waiting for them with two Drug Unit plainclothes officers.

'They're still in there, both of 'em,' said Graham. 'They're right at the back, in the back booth.'

'Righto, radio the locals for back-up.'

'You want the Tac Response guys?'

'Not yet. I'm hoping Keller will listen to common sense.'

'What's he doing in there, anyway?'

'He's the curare killer –' Andy Graham's face opened up with shock, but Malone turned away from him to the two Drug Unit men. 'Sergeant Clements and I are going inside. Once we're down the back of the café, you come in and clear the front section. Get everyone out.'

'Will he use a gun?' asked one of the officers.

'I don't know. I don't think so. That hasn't been his style up till now.' Then it struck him that the Interpol report had said nothing about the way Keller had killed the Starnheim doctor.

He led Clements into the café. Every table and booth was full with the lunchtime crowd, virtually all of them young. The long room was loud with voices, the clatter of dishes and the raucous music from the sound system. The owner, seated at the cash register just inside the front door, recognized the two detectives as soon as they entered. He frowned and stood up, but Malone shook his head at him and he and Clements walked steadily without hurrying down to the back of the café.

Peter Keller, briefcase in hand, was just about to rise from the back booth, was half turned to face the front door. Then he recognized Malone and Clements. He dropped back into the booth, fumbled in his jacket pocket and produced a syringe. He dropped the briefcase on the seat beside him, reached across the narrow table and grabbed Janis' wrist with his free hand.

'Don't, Peter,' said Malone, keeping his voice as calm as he could. He had left his hat in the car, but he was wearing his jacket to hide his gun. Several of the diners, however, had recognized that the place had just been invaded by two cops. 'You've killed enough people.'

'I'll kill Miss Eden, too, if you try to stop me leaving here.' Keller's voice, too, was calm.

Malone didn't take his eyes off Keller, but he was aware of Clements quietly but firmly ushering the diners, one or two of them resentful, out of the nearby booths and up towards the front of the café, where, babbling and grumbling, the rest of the luncheon crowd were being shepherded out into the street by the two Drug Unit officers.

The door to the kitchen, only feet from the back booth, swung open and a waitress appeared, laden with plates. Clements stepped quickly behind Malone, pushed the girl back into the kitchen – 'Stay there. We're police' – and closed the swing door. Then he stood with his back to it, looking at Keller and Janis Eden. Malone glanced at him, but couldn't read the expression on the big man's face: it could have been anger or sadness or a mixture of both.

Then Janis said, voice tight but controlled, 'Do something, Inspector. Don't let him kill me!'

Keller was still holding her wrist, the needle of the syringe held only an inch from the flesh. 'If they let you come with me, you won't die.'

Malone had calculated the chances of jumping Keller before the latter could use the needle: they were nil. He was only four or five feet from Keller, but the older man was backed up against the wall of the booth, the table acting as a barricade. 'Do you have a gun, Peter?'

'No. This needle is all I need. If I stick it in Miss Eden, she will stop breathing in seconds and she will be absolutely dead in a few minutes.'

'How many times can you use it? Once, twice, maybe three times? You kill Miss Eden, maybe Sergeant Clements and me, but what then? There are three police officers, all armed, up there at the front of this place and more out the back.' There was no one but the cooks and the waitresses out the back, but Keller, an ex-cop, would expect the back exit to be guarded. 'You'll be shot before you get to the front door, Peter.'

In the haste to clear the café someone had forgotten to turn off the sound system. Another rock group was belting and yelping a number that Malone, an antiquarian when it came to pop music, had never heard of. An occasional phrase or two came through from the screamed lyric *Dead in bed . . . You bled . . . I bled . . .* Lunchtime music, he thought; and wondered why Keller had chosen this rendezvous.

'No.' said Keller. Then suddenly he shouted, 'Turn off that terrible music!'

Up at the front one of the Drug Unit men found the system, switched it off. The café was abruptly quiet. From behind Clements came the rattle of dishes, an incongruous sound even though it came from a kitchen. Was someone out there actually going ahead with the washing-up?

'No,' said Keller, voice quiet and calm again. 'You're too gentle a man, Inspector. I've observed you. You won't let me kill Miss Eden, not so that you can effect an arrest. You value a life, Inspector, even someone's like Miss Eden.'

'Do you think I value your life, Janis?' Malone kept his eyes on Keller, didn't glance at Janis. Talk, keep talking: that was the advice in situations like this.

Janis dragged her stare away from the needle to look at him. 'I hope so. Let him go. I'll go with him if he promises not to kill me.'

'Will you promise that, Peter?'

'How can I?' Keller's voice was still under control, but his face had now begun to sweat. The café was not warm; above the kitchen door an air-conditioner hummed. Janis shivered, but not with cold. 'All I can promise is that I *shall* kill her if you try to stop me leaving.'

'Where will you go? Back to Germany? Or to Bolivia and your friends there?'

'How do you know about them?' It was a slip: Keller shook his head in annoyance. But then he shrugged, as if conducting a debate with himself. What did it matter what the police knew?

'Romy told us,' said Malone; and saw the immediate hurt in the older man's face. 'Germans living in Bolivia. One of them the son of an old Nazi, a man who was a friend of your father's. Your father helped him escape from Germany right after the war, right? You've been in touch with the family ever since you came to Australia.

Romy knew that, but she never knew the family was in the drug trade. Neither did we, Peter. Are they?'

'You have no proof,' said Keller.

'Oh, we'll come up with proof eventually. Did you know who you were dealing with, Janis?' He didn't look at her, still kept watching Keller.

'No.' She was holding herself rigid, her gaze still fixed on the needle an inch from her flesh. Then she looked up, realizing she, too, had made a slip. 'I don't know what you're talking about!'

Malone ignored her. 'Romy told us why you killed Mr Grime and Mr Lugos, Peter. You thought they had learned who you were, what you were involved in. But why did you kill Sally Kissen? Just because she was a prostitute? Did you find it demeaning that you had to visit her every once in a while, that you had to pay for sex? . . . Sorry!' The needle had quivered above Janis' arm. 'All right, Peter, I'm not trying to cut your balls off in front of a woman. But why kill Sally Kissen?'

The sweat was glistening on Keller's face now. 'The woman had no respect –'

'You wanted respect from a whore?'

Keller ignored that, though the needle quivered again. 'She used to call me Adolf. The night I killed her she laughed – she said *Heil Hitler* while I was . . .' Adolf Hitler: A.H. on the kitchen calendar. 'She was high on cocaine. No man likes being laughed at, especially by a whore.'

'How did Scungy Grime know you were in the drug trade? He was working for me, you know.'

'I knew that. I don't know how he found out about me, but he was waiting for me one night when I came out of Mrs Kissen's place. He said he had a proposition to put to me.' Keller seemed intent now on confession; his gaze kept moving from Malone to Clements and back again. Except that he still had hold of her wrist and had the needle poised above her arm, he could have been oblivious

of Janis. 'I put him off. I told him I'd meet him the following evening. That was when I killed him, outside his front
door in the flats where he lived. I was as surprised as you
must have been when his body was found in your swimming pool. You were surprised, yes?'

'I was surprised, all right. So were my kids.'

'I'd never have done that, tried to frighten anyone's
children.'

*You have a child of your own, a grown woman, and you
don't appear to have given her much consideration.* 'What
about Leroy Lugos?'

'He had seen me once at Mrs Kissen's, when I was
leaving. I knew you had interrogated him – I tapped into
your computer. There was nothing about me in the data,
but I couldn't be sure Mr Lugos hadn't mentioned me to
you. So I killed him, to see if you would come looking for
me. You didn't.'

It was all so cold-blooded, a police report. 'But we have
now, Peter. How long did you think you could get away
with this?'

'Who knows? There are men in this city, Inspector, who
have been dealing in drugs for years and they are still free.
And look at the white-collar criminals who are still not in
jail. I used to have respect, great respect, for the law,
Inspector. But not any more. Romy has probably told you
what happened to me in Germany –'

'She just confirmed what we already knew. We checked
on you through Interpol.'

'Ah yes.' Keller nodded at the efficiency of the law
enforcement agencies. He raised himself in the booth and
looked up to the front of the café as he heard the sound
of approaching sirens. Malone turned his head and saw
the three police cars pull up out in the street, their sirens
gurgling away into silence. More theatrics, he thought:
why couldn't the buggers arrive without the fanfare? Then
he looked back at Keller as the latter sank down again on
his seat and went on as if undisturbed by the commotion

outside: 'I grew tired of being a poor man, Inspector. No money, no authority, nothing. If they had let me stay in Germany I should have been a chief superintendent by now. I have – had –' For a moment his voice faltered. 'I had a daughter who earned more than I did, who had authority, who had respect. You gave her respect, didn't you, Sergeant?'

'I gave her more than that,' said Clements quietly.

'Love?' Keller considered that, then shrugged. Then he went on, nodding at the briefcase on the seat beside him. 'I had no intention of cheating on my friends in Bolivia. They were going to pay me a nice commission on what I collected for them. It was going to be what they call an ongoing thing. But not now, that won't be possible any more. So I am taking this money and I'm going to disappear and start again somewhere. It happens, doesn't it? My friends in Bolivia had to do it and they succeeded. Now will you let me and Miss Eden walk out of here? Her car is across the road.'

Janis looked up at Malone. 'Let us go – *please!*'

'No,' said Malone and took out his gun. He reached for a chair up-ended on a table against the wall behind him, set it on the floor and sat down. Clements moved away from the kitchen door and sat with his haunches on the edge of the table, folding his arms. It all looked very casual to those officers still at the front of the café. A face appeared at the tiny round window in the kitchen door, but Clements glowered at it and it disappeared.

'No,' said Malone. 'We are going to stay here, Peter, till you either kill Miss Eden and then I shoot you, or you come to your senses and give yourself up.'

'No!' Janis' scream was little more than a whimper, caught in her throat. 'No, you can't let him do that!'

Malone looked over his shoulder at Clements. 'I think it might be an idea, Russ, if you went and called Romy. Ask her to come here –'

'*Nein!*' It was a guttural animal cry.

Malone looked back at Keller. 'When we bring Romy here, Peter, we don't want the two of you speaking in German. We want to understand everything that is said between you –'

'Nothing will be said between us!' Then Keller raised the hand that held the needle, ran the back of it over his glistening forehead. Then he lowered the needle again towards Janis' arm. 'No, don't bring her. She despises me, just as her mother did.'

'I don't think so,' said Clements, still quiet. 'I talked to her, Peter. She'll try to help you –'

'How? Don't be foolish, Russell. She can't help me. No one can but myself. And Miss Eden.' He looked at her, not menacingly but almost as if he were her father. 'We're birds of a feather, Miss Eden. Both despicable . . . You really would shoot me, Inspector?'

'You kill Miss Eden, Peter, and yes, I'll shoot you.' Malone raised his gun, hoping he would not have to squeeze the trigger. He had never had to shoot a man in such a cold-blooded way; he would hear the shot forever. He saw the look in Keller's eyes, saw that the man had read his intention and was truly surprised.

Keller all at once said something in German, perhaps a prayer, but only he and God would know, then he let go of Janis' wrist, pulled back his cuff and jammed the needle into his own arm. He looked at Malone, said something else in German, then he said in English, calmly and finally, 'It does not take long –'

4

Before the ambulance arrived to take away Keller's body, Clements said, 'Get Andy to give you a lift back to Homicide, Scobie. I'm going out to the morgue. I don't think there should be the risk that the bag will come in, they'll open it up and it's her father.'

'Stay with her, Russ. Stay with her till you fee she's okay to be left alone.'

'Thanks, mate.' Clements had never looked unhappier. When Keller had died, slumping forward on to the booth table, the big man had let out a slubbering sigh, as if he were about to weep. It had not been pity for the dead man; it had been pity for the daughter who would have to be told what had happened. And he had known it would have to be he who would tell her. 'I'll call you, let you know how she's taking it. I'm not gunna take any statement from her. Someone else can do that, okay?'

'Sure. I'll do it.'

Then Clements left and ten minutes later the ambulance arrived. In the meantime Malone had transferred his attention to Janis.

When Keller had fallen on his face across the table from her, she had reared back, hitting her head against the wall of the booth. At once Clements had pulled her out of the booth and half carried her up to another and sat her down. Malone had taken the briefcase from the seat beside Keller and opened it; the combination lock was set at zero, so he had no trouble in doing so. As he had expected, the briefcase was full of money, hundred-dollar notes. The case had looked to be an expensive Gucci one, till he had examined it further and recognized it as a not-very-good imitation, probably made in Hong Kong or Taiwan.

He took it up to Janis, sat down opposite her, while Andy Graham and the local police came down to take care of Keller's body. Malone looked at the closed briefcase lying on the table between himself and Janis.

'I haven't counted it, Janis, but there's a lot of money in there.'

One could almost see her collecting herself, like a woman who had dropped her belongings. She was still pale and her wrist was red where Keller had been grasping it; it seemed that her auburn hair was suddenly vivid, as if her paleness highlighted it. 'It's not mine. That man was carrying it when he sat down opposite me.'

Malone had to hide his admiration; she could lie like a military spokesman in wartime. 'You're trying to tell me he was a stranger to you?'

'I've never seen him in my life before.'

'He was a cleaner at St Sebastian's. He knew you. Who gave you the money?'

'I told you, it was that man's – Peter?'

'Peter Keller. The man you were giving that money to for the cocaine that's waiting for you –' Just in time he stopped himself from saying *out at Artarmon*. He was losing his patience with her, the tension of the minutes with Keller was having an after-effect. He glanced up at the two Drug Unit men who had come down to join him and Janis and now stood in the aisle. 'Do you want to take her away and question her? I think she's going to be difficult.'

'Sure, Inspector.' They were both young men, relaxed and relieved; it was a good clean bust, the dirty work had been done by Homicide. When they walked through the crowd outside with this good-looking suspect, the credit would be theirs. Though they would not expect any applause: half the crowd in this place were probably drug-users of some sort. Public appreciation of the police was to be avoided: it was like an Arab having a good word for a Jew, or vice versa. 'We'll take the money, okay? A Gucci, eh?'

'It's a fake,' said Malone.

Janis glanced at the briefcase, then frowned; but it was no more than a faint line in her otherwise smooth brow. What a cheapskate Jack was! She should have known. And if all had gone well, she would have given him the Vuitton case he had asked for . . . 'I repeat, that case isn't mine. If you knew me, you'd know that. If I can't afford the real thing, I don't settle for an imitation. That case was brought in here by that man who just killed himself.

Who would have killed me if you had let him.' She looked at Malone. 'And you would have, wouldn't you?'

'Then I would have killed him.' Malone was tired of her now. 'You wouldn't have died in vain, as they say.'

'You shit!'

'Maybe. We all have a bit of it in us, Janis.' Then, all at once worn out, he gestured for the Drug Unit men to take her away.

He sat for a few moments in the booth, then looked up as Andy Graham, for once not bouncing up and down, stood over him. 'You okay, boss?'

He nodded, then stood up, trying to get some ease of movement into his iron skeleton. 'You do the report on Keller, Andy. I'll give you the details. I'll wait for you outside.'

As he walked towards the front door of the café, the proprietor, who looked as if he had aged twenty years in twenty minutes, stopped him. 'Hey, who's gunna pay?'

'Pay what?'

'All the spoiled food? The people, they not gunna eat what they left on the tables when you ordered 'em outa here.'

'No worries, Mr Lugopolous. Hang a big sign out the front, saying the Needle Murderer Committed Suicide Here. You'll have to put on extra staff to handle the crowd.'

He walked out into the bright glare, stared across at the sea, brilliant as a blue sun, then up at the empty, careless sky. He really would have to buy some sunglasses, darken the summer.

CHAPTER ELEVEN

I

The Drug Unit officers held Janis for twenty-four hours, but in the end they had to release her. The sergeant in charge phoned Malone, who had come into Homicide on Saturday morning. 'We could get nothing against her, Scobie, nothing that would stand up in court. She's a clever bitch. She's gone free.'

'Her prints weren't on the briefcase?'

'Sure they were, but they prove nothing. She said Keller asked her to hold the case for him while he got into the booth.'

Malone smiled to himself. 'She's a beaut, isn't she?'

'I've never come up against a better liar. There were some other prints on the case, but those could be anybody's.'

Jack Junior's? But Jack Junior, with all his mono-grammed gear, surely wouldn't have anything to do with a Gucci imitation? 'Righto, Des, I guess she's beaten us for the time being. You kept the money?'

'Sure. That seemed to upset her. But what could she do?'

Clements came in late in the morning, looking like a long-distance runner who had found himself in the wrong race: the finishing line was miles further on than he had expected. 'I've just spent the worst bloody night in my whole life.'

'How's Romy taking it?'

'Badly. Not so much her dad's death and the way he died, but what he'd done. She carries more than her fair share of blame, that girl. I tried to talk her out of it, but . . .' He sat down. Coffee was bubbling in the percolator outside Malone's office, but he was dead to the enticing smell of it. 'She's gunna resign from the Forensic Division.'

'What's she going to do?'

'Christ knows. She doesn't. She's talking of going to Adelaide or Perth, finishing her obstetrics and going into practice.'

'Talk her out of that. She's done enough running away, she did that with her father, getting out of Germany. Resigning from Forensic isn't a bad idea – she doesn't want to be surrounded by more murder victims. You never know, we might get a copy-cat murder, another needle-in-the-bum job. Work on her, Russ.' He steadied himself, almost as if he were going to make the commitment himself: 'Propose to her.'

Clements bit his lip, said nothing for a moment, then rose from his chair. 'Yeah, I'll think about it. You never know . . .'

He went out to his desk. Malone got up, followed him out and crossed to the computer. He sat down in front of it, fed in his access code and ran the last week through the screen. The roll-call of names came up: some dead, one crippled for life, some of them still free and walking around. It was a scoreboard he had seen scores of times. A drawn game, they would call it in cricket.

He went home at lunchtime, collected Tom and took him into the Cricket Ground, where Australia and England were locked in the third day of a Test. They sat in seats on the apron below the Brewongle Stand, both wearing wide-brimmed hats, both smothered in sunblock cream, both wearing dark glasses. The heat, if anything, had increased during the week. The natives sat around them, frying themselves alive in the climate they claimed was the best in the world. Every second mouth was devouring a meat pie and chips; beer flowed like a brewery that had burst its vats. Great day, mate, they told each other, and watched the melanoma grow like a crop of dark daisies.

'Dad, I wish I'd been able to watch you play,' said Tom suddenly.

Malone had heard there was an old newsreel film of him in action. Ray Robinson, the great cricket writer, had once said that he had a smoother action than Lindwall's, than which there was no higher praise. He had thought once or twice of trying to get a copy of the film; but he knew in his heart that he never would. There was nothing sadder than looking back at what you once were.

'I'll tell you something better. You grow up and I'll watch you play.' And hoped he would live to see the day.

Then he heard someone say, 'There's Jack Aldwych, the crim.'

He turned his head and looked up at the private boxes, all of them stuffed with guests, all but the Aldwych box. There, Jack Aldwych sat with Jack Junior; it was odd, Malone thought, but they looked lonely. Then Aldwych looked down, caught sight of him and recognized him despite the wide-brimmed hat and the dark glasses. He smiled, gave a small wave, then gestured for Malone to come up to the box. Malone smiled in return, then shook his head.

'Who's that, Dad? D'you know him?'

'Just to nod to, that's all.'

'I think he wants us to go up and sit there. Why don't you, Dad?'

'I'll explain to you some other time.'

'Is it because you're a cop?' Malone saw several heads turn, noses come up sniffing the non-existent breeze. 'Geez, you miss out on a lot, don't you? It'd be great up there in that box.'

'Turn around and watch the cricket, or I'll rip your bloody arm off.' An old Aunty Jack television comedy had been revived just before Christmas. Tom had laughed

301

himself sick at it and for a week had been threatening his sisters with the series' catch-cry, *I'll rip your bloody arm off!*

He grinned now at his father and gently thumped him on the upper arm. Malone wanted to put his arm round him, hug the breath out of him; but real Aussie fathers didn't do that in public. Crumbs, thought Malone, don't let me get to be like Con. And stroked the back of his son's neck.

He and Tom went home at the end of the day, burnt and tired and happy. There were no calls waiting for him from Homicide. Saturday night the family sat in front of the television set and watched a rented video of ancient Laurel and Hardy shorts. Antics that had broken up an older generation had the same effect on Malone and Lisa and the children; laughter ran through the generations like common blood. After the children had gone to bed, Malone lay on the couch in the living room and Lisa came and sat on the floor beside him.

'Is it all over?' she said.

'Some of it. There won't be any more bodies in our pool.'

'What are we going to do about Russ and Romy?'

'*We* are going to do nothing.'

She thought about that for a while, then nodded. 'No, I suppose not. It's such a shame, though. She's just what he needs.'

'Is he what she needs? Let 'em work it out themselves.'

Sunday morning all the family went to Mass together. Then they came home and spent the day by the pool. Malone swam up and down in it, his only exercise for over a week, lazing through the water unpolluted by a murdered corpse. Lisa, Claire and Maureen read the Sunday papers. The two girls went through their usual sport of measuring the exposed teeth of the midget, non-luminous celebrities and habitual freeloaders at charity events on the social pages; there had been one week when the girls claimed to have measured enough enamelled inanity to have tiled a bathroom wall. Lisa told him over lunch that there was a two-page spread on the rising crime rate and there was an interview with Police Minister Gus Dircks in which he thought he was defending the police force but gave an entirely opposite effect. She also reported that the Gulf war was hotting up with increased bombing and that twenty-two experts had given their opinions on the probable outcome. The business pages were all doom and gloom: the recession was going to be much worse than all the economists and politicians had predicted. Malone didn't look at the papers at all, not even at the reports on yesterday's cricket.

Monday morning he was in his office when Luke Radelli rang him from Customs headquarters. 'No go, Scobie. We kept surveillance on the warehouse up at Artarmon all weekend, but we didn't catch the fish we wanted. Some nong turned up Saturday afternoon with a key to the place and went in and opened up the case. We grabbed him, but he was a moron, some stooge they'd sent in. You ever hear of that trick they try in India or somewhere, they send out a goat to bait the tiger?'

'I've heard of it,' said Malone. 'I tried it myself, once.'

'Well, they tried it on us and we fell for it. This guy we picked up, he's not worth charging. The point is, we didn't get the guys we wanted. We've confiscated the cocaine and we'll destroy it. But I'm afraid it's like taking a bucket of water from the ocean, there'll be more and more of it coming in. It and heroin and the other crap.'

'If the recession gets any deeper, maybe no one will have any money to buy it.'

'Some hope. I see you got your needle killer, though. Congratulations.'

'Thanks, Luke.'

He hung up, sat a while, then called Roley Bremner. 'How's the election going, Roley?'

'I think I'm gunna get back in, mate. Snow White and

The Dwarf all of a sudden have gone missing. They were rostered for work Sat'day and yesterday, but they didn't show. I see you got your name in the papers. You must be pleased.'

Not really. Life, as Molly Maddux had said, was a bugger. But it could be worse. He could be out of work or lying somewhere in a trench waiting to be bombed. Or Keller could still be on the loose, needle primed.

'Yes,' he said, 'I guess you could say that.'

Kirribilli
October 1990 – April 1991